THE LAST ROUNDUP

STAR TREK®
THE LAST ROUNDUP

Christie Golden

Based upon Star Trek®
created by Gene Roddenberry

POCKET BOOKS
New York   London   Toronto   Sydney   Singapore

This book is a work of fiction. Names, characters, places and incidents are products of the author's imagination or are used fictitiously. Any resemblance to actual events or locales or persons, living or dead, is entirely coincidental.

POCKET BOOKS, a division of Simon & Schuster, Inc.
1230 Avenue of the Americas, New York, NY 10020

Copyright © 2002 by Paramount Pictures. All Rights Reserved.

Originally published in hardcover in 2002 by Pocket Books

STAR TREK is a Registered Trademark of
Paramount Pictures.

This book is published by Pocket Books, a division of
Simon & Schuster, Inc., under exclusive license from
Paramount Pictures.

All rights reserved, including the right to reproduce
this book or portions thereof in any form whatsoever.
For information address Pocket Books, 1230 Avenue
of the Americas, New York, NY 10020

ISBN: 0-7434-4910-X

First Pocket Books paperback printing June 2003

10 9 8 7 6 5 4 3 2 1

POCKET and colophon are registered trademarks of Simon & Schuster, Inc.

For information regarding special discounts for bulk purchases,
please contact Simon & Schuster Special Sales at 1-800-456-6798
or business@simonandschuster.com

Printed in the U.S.A.

This book is dedicated
to Three Wise Men:

Robert Amerman
Mark Anthony
and
Michael Georges

Thanks, guys.

STAR TREK®

THE LAST ROUNDUP

Prologue

Lights flickered on inside the last of the mighty sky-ships. Smoothly, the oval vessel rose into the air, caught the sunlight on its shiny, metallic surface, and then disappeared. The stoic façade of the abandoned people finally shattered. A cry of pain and agony swelled up, a cry that their proud natures would never have permitted them to utter while their so-called masters were present to scorn their torment.

Takarik heard the cry of his people, and his heart ached for them. He let them wail and scream, sounds that he had never before heard any of them make. They were left alone on this place now, with no way to ever return to their homeland.

No way that they had yet thought of, at least.

When at last the deep, mourning sobs had subsided into soft sighs and shuddering whispers, he spoke.

"What a glorious day is now dawning for our people!" Takarik cried, lifting his arms as if to embrace the world upon which they had been stranded. His people stared at him as if he had gone mad. He smiled, and his eyes twinkled. He meant every word.

"Those who believed themselves to be our betters think they have rid themselves of us. After so many years of doing their hard labor, they no longer found us necessary, so they placed us here. And in so doing, they did us a very great favor."

"Takarik!" called an angry voice. "We have been removed from all we know! We have been callously disposed of, as if we were nothing more than their waste matter!"

"What you say is true, Minkar," Takarik acknowledged. "But we are not they. We do not have to regard what has happened in the same light as they do. What they have done, I tell you truly, is freed us. The land is rich with fruit and game. We have a small amount of technology that will enable us to build shelters and communicate and find and prepare food. We have our hearts yet, and our keen minds. And we also have this!"

He gestured to a youth standing behind him, holding what seemed to be an innocuous box. It was scratched and dented, but within it . . . ah, within . . . Takarik had deliberately hidden it in this shabby box, tucked it away casually with clothes and supplies as if it had no more worth than those ordinary things. It had escaped discovery during a cursory search by a guard who obviously thought handling such tainted things was beneath him.

With a ceremonial flourish, Takarik lifted the lid and withdrew the precious contents. He held it aloft proudly, and heard some murmurs. The gem was as large as his head, and even though it had not been faceted as so many precious stones were, it caught and seemed to hold the very sun. It was almost completely transparent save for its amber tinting like liquid sunlight, and without flaw as far as Takarik could determine.

"That we were able to bring this safely from our homeworld to here, without our captors ever discovering it, tells me that we have a great destiny in this place," Takarik continued. "Many of you have glimpsed this as you labored for those who deemed themselves superior. But many more of you have never seen it. Oh, you have heard the tales; so have our captors, but as far as they know, they are children's stories.

"We do not yet know its true value, for we have never been permitted to reveal its existence to others, but its beauty alone inspires us. We took heart in our labors, knowing that it shone for us alone. Our captors never even knew it was there. This gem, this precious jewel, has made the bitter journey with us to symbolize hope."

Carefully, he replaced the stone in its deceptively nondescript box.

"This place will become our new home, but we will never forget our true heritage. We will thrive here, in a place where we will finally have the opportunity to govern ourselves. We will live in the shelters we build, and eat what we have harvested. We will devote our culture to knowledge and development. We will always remember the Great Stone and its beauty, and know that the gods gave it to us alone. And one day, we will take what is rightfully ours, earned by our labor, our blood, our sweat."

He looked at their eager, upturned faces. Such hope was another expression he had never seen on visages that were more accustomed to not revealing their emotions at all, lest they suffer for it.

"It will not be in my lifetime. Nor in hers," he said, pointing to an infant in her mother's arms. "Nor in her child's. But one day, I promise, it will happen.

"I swear to you by the beauty of the Great Stone— one day, we will go home."

Chapter One

It was a dead world.

It had never supported life of its own. The planet known in Federation records as Polluxara IV had no intelligent life that might interfere with the Prime Directive. It sported not so much as a microbe, but within its lifeless, rocky exterior had once flowed a rich vein of what was then one of the most precious substances in the universe—dilithium.

It was this deposit that had led Earth, almost a hundred and fifty years ago, to establish a colony in order to mine the mineral. But now, once again, Polluxara IV was lifeless, save for the twenty-seven souls that stood safely encased in environmental suits on its still-radioactive exterior.

Captain James Tiberius Kirk, once Admiral Kirk, and earlier and since captain of the *U.S.S. Enterprise,* was one of the twenty-seven. The others were much younger and, at this moment, were quieter than he had ever heard them.

Kirk wasn't surprised. Standing at the site of a great tragedy had that effect.

Towering above them were the ruins of what had once been a colony of vital importance to a pre-Federation Earth. There remained only sharp shards of metal and other materials, warped, melted, twisted, and pulverized. The bodies were long gone, of course. What the Earth forces could come and retrieve to honor with a hero's burial had been so gathered, decades past. But there hadn't been enough remains to bury of most of them; hadn't been enough to find.

Kirk didn't speak immediately after they materialized. He let the cadets look around and absorb what they saw for themselves. The wide-eyed solemnity he saw in their faces—a mixture of species that would have stunned those who had died here a century ago—made him nod slightly in approval. Good kids, all of them. He'd been right to call in a few favors on this.

Time for the pop quiz.

"Cadet Singh," Kirk said sharply. Indira Singh's head whipped around.

"Sir!" she answered, snapping to attention despite the mute testimony to death that lay all around her.

"Tell me about Commander Lowe, if you please."

Light glimmered on her protective faceplate, but not so much that Kirk couldn't see her lick her lips nervously. "Commander Sabra Lowe led the mining colony here in the middle part of the twenty-second century. It was a state-of-the-art colony that turned out swift production of a very pure form of dilithium, almost ninety-two percent pure."

"How many other active dilithium mining colonies were there at that time?" Out of the corner of his eye, he saw Cadet Skalli Jksili raise her long, slender arm, but he ignored her.

"Only seven. Polluxara IV turned out—" Singh hesitated, and her dark eyes widened as she frantically sought the answer. "Four point oh seven two times the amount of the others." She breathed easier.

"Very good. You've just made an excellent start on your final."

A chorus of protest rose as the students realized that Kirk was apparently springing at least part of the final exam of his course, "Command Decisions and Their Consequences," on them here, now, unannounced. The sounds were oddly comforting to Kirk, standing here among the ruins. It was a sound that reminded him that life had to go on, no matter how many colonies—

"I did tell you to do your research," Kirk reminded them mildly, raising a hand to still them. They quieted at once. "Now. Cadet Brown. Tell me what happened here a few years later." He could see Cadet Skalli shaking her head in disgust.

Cadet Christopher Brown stood at attention, trying not to smile. Kirk had given him an easier question.

"Commander Lowe received advance warning of an attack. The scout reported that the Romulans, then a relatively unknown species, were approaching."

"And their goal was to completely destroy the colony, in order to strike fear into the heart of Earth forces."

"Negative, sir!" Brown's smile widened as he caught

Kirk's trick question. "Their goal was to take over the colony in order to harvest the dilithium."

"Which was to be used how?"

"To develop warp drive and create more ships to bring to bear against Earth forces in the war. Sir!"

"Very good. You too have a head start on the final, Mr. Brown. Cadet T'Pran, pick up the narrative from this point."

Cadet Skalli was now actually stomping in impatience. Kirk had once tried to curb these physical displays of her irritation, but it was impossible. It was simply a part of what she was—a Huanni.

T'Pran, a coolly beautiful young Vulcan female whose calm demeanor was the antithesis of Skalli's, predictably showed no emotion as she obeyed Kirk's request.

"There was insufficient time for Earth to send defense vessels. The colony had no weapons other than approximately two hundred handheld phase guns, fourteen primitive torpedoes, sixteen assorted pieces of mining equipment, and four thousand, eight hundred and twenty-seven detonation devices."

Not for the first time, Kirk marveled at how Vulcans used the word *approximately*.

"Very good. Cadet Lasskas, continue."

The translator turned Lasskas's hissing dialect into intelligible Federation standard, though it played a bit with sentence structure.

"Commander Lowe choice had none. Selected she to colony destroy, detonation devices all deployed at time same. Not Romulan hands fall into, precious dilithium, at time of war when vulnerable Earth. Died eight and forty and one hundred males and females by order of Commander Lowe."

"Most of that is correct, but there's something very wrong with that answer. Do you know what it is?"

Lasskas's sharp-toothed muzzle opened and his thick, green, forked tongue fluttered. Since the rest of his face was unable to move, that long tongue was the only indicator of his emotions. He clearly had no idea what Kirk was getting at.

"Anybody know what was incorrect about Cadet Lasskas's answer?" He could all but see their sharp minds turning as they tried to find the factual flaw in Lasskas's statement. They were all being too literal. Not even Skalli's hand was up this time. Her pale purple face was screwed up in frustration.

Kirk didn't enlighten them at once. He began to walk around the area, carefully.

"We're in a place of death, cadets. Even safely in our environment suits, we can feel it, can sense it. This is sacred ground. A place where lives were sacrificed in order to preserve noble ideals. One day, any of you might be looking at a similar scenario. I want you to take a moment and put yourself in Commander Lowe's position. Imagine yourself as commander of a colony of over a hundred people—people who looked to you to keep them safe . . . their families safe. Most of them hadn't signed on for this out of a desire for adventure or even any particular sense of loyalty. There was good money to be had for hard work on this planet."

They were quiet now, attentive. For the first time

since he started this class at the beginning of the semester, Kirk felt that he was finally managing to get through to them. Hitherto, he had thought them too starry-eyed to really listen. It had taken this—a risky visit to a devastated world that still leaked radiation from its death throes—to do it, but he thought he had succeeded. If they understood this one message, it wouldn't matter to him what they had scored the rest of the semester.

"And then you hear from one of your scouts, who is attacked and killed shortly after he sends the message, that Romulans are on the way," Kirk continued, his voice ringing in this silent place. "Romulans. You've never even seen them, only heard vague rumors about these faceless beings hitting outposts hard, then vanishing. And now, they're coming. For you."

A few of them shifted uneasily. Others gazed at him raptly. Chief among these was Skalli. Kirk quickly looked elsewhere. Skalli never needed much encouragement.

"They're coming for you," he repeated, "and your home planet can't do a damn thing to protect you. You're too far away. You know what they want, and you know their tactics. They've never left anyone alive before." He paused in midstride and whirled back, catching their eyes with his own hazel ones.

"But they've never wanted anything from an outpost before. They might take you prisoner. They might agree to let you go. You just don't know. Now do you see why Cadet Lasskas's answer wasn't correct?"

They stared at him blankly. Skalli was obviously

frustrated that she couldn't grasp what her instructor was getting at, and the rest seemed uneasy as well.

Kirk sighed. Maybe they were just too young. Maybe at their age, he wouldn't have been able to comprehend this either. After all, wasn't he the one who secretly reprogrammed the simulation computer in order to become the only Academy student able to wring victory from the *Kobayashi Maru* simulation?

"Cadet Lasskas's answer was factually correct. But you've got to take into consideration more than just facts if you're to be a good officer in Starfleet. You've got to consider things like hunches, intuitions, gut feelings . . . and knowing that you always have a choice." He glanced over at Lasskas, who was hanging his reptilian head. "You said Commander Lowe didn't have a choice. From our perspective, a hundred-odd years in the future, that statement seems obvious."

He spread his hands. "*Of course* she had to destroy the colony, and sacrifice every one of those one hundred and forty-eight men and women, didn't she? We *all* know that's what she had to do, don't we?" he said, exaggerating the words. "She couldn't risk having that much dilithium fall into Romulan hands at that crucial juncture. Just push a button. An easy decision. It's in all the textbooks, so it must have been obvious, an easy choice. It has as much relevance to us now as the fall of Lamaria, or the losses at Normandy in 1944, back on Earth. Which is to say, not very much."

Again, he surveyed them, standing tall and imposing. He had come to realize, somewhat ruefully, that to many of these youngsters he was a living legend. If he could

11

drum this lesson into their heads, he wouldn't mind the pedestal.

"But they *should* have meaning, damn it. Every single man who died on the beaches at Normandy had a life that was as dear, as precious to him as life is to any of you. Every single Lamarian who fell defending their home from a vicious onslaught once laughed, and cried, and loved."

He raised his arms and indicated their surroundings. "This particular site is unique. Because there's no atmosphere, it's going to be preserved this way forever. There's no grass here to soften this battlefield, no grave markers to bleach and fade in the sun. We'll always be able to stand here and look at what was willingly done for the good of others as if it happened yesterday. Just because these people died over a century past doesn't mean we should let their sacrifice count for nothing."

He softened his voice. "There is a quote from an ancient book on my world that says, 'Greater love hath no man than this, that a man lay down his life for his friends.' I disagree. It's noble to die for a friend, for someone you love and value. But how much nobler— and harder—is it to die for a stranger? Commander Sabra Lowe died for people she had never met. And she *made that choice freely.* Now that, cadets, is a command decision. And this is its consequence—both the ruins of Polluxara IV and the fact that you and I are able to stand here today, alive, free, and members of a Federation that values freedom and justice."

To his deep satisfaction, Kirk saw the flickering of understanding pass across some of the painfully youthful faces. He heard a slight thump and turned in the direction of the sound. Not surprisingly, tears were flowing down Skalli's purple face. She had forgotten she was wearing the environmental suit and had bumped her hand on the faceplate in an effort to wipe the river away.

The Huanni had only recently joined the Federation. Kirk had never seen such an emotional race before. It in no way compromised their intelligence or skills, which were considerable, but they were as open in their emotions as the Vulcans were closed—which was saying a lot. Skalli, the very first of her species to be accepted at Starfleet Academy, had come a long way in the single semester Kirk had known her. By Huanni standards, she was coldly logical. He had tried to be understanding of the outbursts while at the same time helping her learn how to control herself. She had confided in him that she wanted to be an ambassador one day. Kirk thought this highly unlikely.

To help her focus, he addressed her. "Cadet Skalli," he said. "We will take a moment to think of those who have died here so that we might live. Please, recite their names, slowly and solemnly." He knew that she, like all her species, had an eidetic memory, and this would be no challenge for her. But she would see it as an honor.

She looked up at him, and in her enormous eyes shone pride and a very intense form of hero worship. Kirk managed not to cringe. She composed herself, and with tears still streaming down her face began to list the names of the colonists.

"Commander Sabra Lowe. First Officer Jason Riley.

Second Officer Ramon Sanchez. Chief Engineer Jonathan Bedonie. . . ."

It took a long time, to recite a hundred and forty-eight names. When Kirk caught one of his students fidgeting, he glared at him until he stopped. They stood at attention, until finally, Skalli stated the last name.

Kirk waited a moment longer. At last he said, "We have twenty minutes before we return to the ship. I suggest you take the time to wander the colony and get to know it for yourself. Be mindful that though the residual radiation from the explosion is low it is still present, and that you are not under any circumstances to remove so much as a glove. Also be aware there are many opportunities for a careless cadet to slip and break a leg. I'd advise against it."

There were slight, wary chuckles at this. *It figures,* thought Kirk. *They finally start seeing me as a human being on the last day of class.* While it was obvious that the students were thrilled to be able to attend his class, he knew that they were more interested in seeing him than in what he was saying. But talking about major command decisions of the past few centuries—including a few historical ones he himself had made—had only served to remind him that all he was doing was talking. He was horribly bored, itching to get out and do something, which was one reason he had called in a few favors to authorize this field trip to a place that was still largely off-limits. Command decisions weren't textbook cases, they were real, and bloody, and bitter. And heaven knew he'd had more than his share.

"There will be an essay as part of the final exam. It

is free-form, and all I want from you is your impressions of Polluxara IV and what happened here. It will be due in my hands when we return to Earth orbit. The students who correctly answered my questions will receive extra credit. Those of you who didn't have that opportunity will just have to make sure your essays are even better."

"Captain, that's not fair!" one of them piped up.

Kirk merely smiled. "It doesn't have to be. I'm the instructor, and you're the students. You'll find that a lot in this universe isn't fair, but it has to be dealt with nonetheless. That, too, is part of being a Starfleet officer. Dismissed."

There were always those who loved writing essays in any class, and these students were abuzz with excitement as they hastened off to explore. And, of course, there were always those who loathed essays, and Kirk overheard the predictable grumbling from this segment as they departed with much less enthusiasm.

Kirk wasn't overly concerned. Most of them were outstanding students, and would pass even if they failed the final. He welcomed the solitude, for he, too, wanted a chance to roam this place and soak up the atmosphere.

"Captain Kirk?" The voice was bubbly, feminine, and quivering.

Kirk closed his eyes, gathering strength. He forced a pleasant expression on his face.

"What is it, Cadet?"

It was of course Skalli. She was nearly as tall as he was, though far more slender of build than most humanoids. Her large ears were perforce flattened against her head by the suit's headpiece and gave her a particularly mournful look. Her mercurial features set in an expression of sorrow completed the impression, and her large eyes still brimmed with tears, although Kirk was pleased to see that at least she wasn't actually crying now.

"Permission to speak freely?"

"Go ahead."

"Captain . . . do you. . . ." Skalli swallowed hard. "Do you think they were afraid? Commander Lowe and the others?"

"You heard the message they sent back to Starfleet before Lowe destroyed the colony. What do you think?"

Skalli tilted her head. "She did not sound afraid."

Kirk raised an eyebrow, silently encouraging Skalli to continue voicing her thoughts. "So . . . I suppose she wasn't."

"You still have much to learn about humans, Skalli. I can't know personally, of course, but I'm certain she was indeed afraid." He looked around. "To take that responsibility—to end your own life and that of so many others . . . you can't do it without wondering, without second guessing yourself." He looked back at her kindly. "Without being afraid."

"But her voice was so calm. . . ."

"One thing you'll need to learn if you want to be an ambassador, Skalli, is that you don't have to surrender to your emotions all the time."

She looked at him with a mixture of awe and disbelief. "So I have heard . . . but, Captain, I must confess, that seems impossible to me!"

"It certainly doesn't seem to come easily to your people," Kirk agreed. "But it can be learned."

He nodded in Cadet T'Pran's direction. She was standing on a jagged outcropping of metal, her hands clasped in front of her, her head bowed in meditation. "Vulcans used to be highly emotional, until they decided to embrace logic instead. Now they still have emotions, but they know how to control them."

Skalli laughed brightly, shifting from compassionate sorrow to mirth in an instant. "That, too, seems impossible!"

Some of the students frowned, clearly thinking Skalli—and by association Kirk—must be being disrespectful of the solemnity he had just encouraged them to experience. After laughing, Skalli continued to talk.

Kirk didn't dislike Skalli, but she was certainly a trial. *So was Spock, at first,* he reminded himself. *And look what happened there.*

But he was too old to take so young a creature through something as important as disciplining her emotions. It was just as well that this semester was over and he wouldn't be seeing the youngster on a regular basis. He didn't have the patience to—

"What?" he asked, hoping he had misunderstood Skalli's chatter.

"My personal advisor," she said brightly. "There was such a long waiting list for you! But because I'm the first Huanni to attend the Academy, they made a special exception for me and moved me right to the top of the line. Wasn't that kind! So now I'll get to meet with you every day, no matter *what* classes I'm taking!"

To his keen embarrassment, she threw her arms around him and hugged him tightly, then hugged herself and whirled around a few times.

"Imagine what they'll think back on Huan . . . little Skalli, who has the great, famous Captain James T. Kirk as her advisor!" She stopped and gazed at him with shining eyes. "It's going to be wonderful!"

"Wonderful," Kirk echoed, and wondered how the hell he was going to get out of this one.

Chapter Two

The transport vessel was small. Too small for Kirk's comfort, anyway. It might have had a crew of eight, a mess hall and even a room for recreational activities and exercise, but it was not sufficiently large for him to feel truly away from his charges. Alone in his cramped quarters, still imagining he could hear laughter outside his door, Kirk tapped the computer.

The image of a beautiful Native American woman appeared on the screen. She was approximately Kirk's age. Silver threads wound through her long, braided hair, echoing the twist of real silver necklaces about her elegant throat. Her dark brown eyes sparkled as she recognized her old friend, and her broad face lit up with a smile.

"Hello, Jim. You know, somehow I figured I'd hear from you any day now," Admiral Laura Standing Crane said, chuckling.

"How long have you known?" Kirk said dryly.

"A few days." She raised a raven eyebrow. "I was the one who authorized it."

Kirk leaned back in his chair and rubbed his hazel eyes. "Laura, Laura," he sighed, "what did I ever do to you?"

"Oh, come now, Jim, Skalli's a good kid. And you know how important it is to make new Federation members feel welcome at all levels in Starfleet—from the Academy on up. Who better than the great Captain James T. Kirk to help her learn how to get along with humans?"

Kirk winced slightly. "I think if I hear 'the great Captain James T. Kirk' one more time, I'm going to get myself surgically altered again and go hide out on Vulcan."

That made Standing Crane laugh openly. "You may have passed for a Romulan, but the Vulcans would spot you in a moment. Skalli requested that she be the one to tell you. I'm only sorry I wasn't there to see the expression on your face." She grew more serious. "How did the field trip go? No difficulties, I hope? It's my neck on the line, you know."

"No problems at all. It was sobering," Kirk said, "which was exactly what I wanted. Not even freshman cadets can stand on Polluxara IV and not think a bit. Thanks for authorizing it."

She nodded. "Of course. You know you've got a waiting list a kilometer long for next semester's class. Now that they know they're going to a quote-unquote off-limits area there'll be no stopping the flood of applications. What are you going to do with your summer?"

Kirk frowned. "Hadn't thought about it. Don't suppose that there's anything going on at Starfleet

Command that a living legend could help with?"

"Jim, take a little time and rest on your laurels. God knows you've earned a break after the Camp Khitomer negotiations. How about exploring those caves on Paggaru Two? I hear they're a real challenge."

"I don't want to rest on my laurels, I want to *do* something. Something other than standing at a podium reciting history to dewy-eyed kids who are only there because of who I am, not what I know."

Standing Crane leaned forward and regarded him with sympathy. "Jim, we've been friends for over thirty years. I know you're chafing, but there's really nothing here for you now. Unless you really *want* to help Spock negotiate with the Klingons."

Kirk laughed a little and held up both hands in a "back off" gesture. "While I respect Chancellor Azetbur greatly, I think I have had enough of the Klingons to last me for the rest of my life. At least tell me what you can about what's going on. I can pretend I'm not rotting away in obscurity on a transport ship crammed with twenty-six cadets, racing along at a heart-stopping warp two."

Standing Crane laughed again. "I suppose I have a few moments to humor an old friend. Actually, you might be interested in this, since Skalli's now your pet project."

Kirk rolled his eyes.

"The inhabitants of Falor, a planet in a solar system right next door to Huan's system, are now petitioning to join the Federation. We've just played host to a very large delegation of Falorians and it has been a time, I'll tell you."

"Anything like the Huanni?"

"Hmm, yes and no. They were clearly once members of the same species. Similar in appearance, but much stockier, less ethereal." Kirk knew what she meant. Skalli evoked images of a dryad from ancient Earth mythology. Huanni were humanoid in appearance, with long ears like a horse's and pale purple skin and hair. Skalli was tall and thin, her bones almost as delicate and light as an avian's. It seemed as though one good gust of wind would blow her away.

"How about the emotions?"

"They're much more controlled than the Huanni, thank goodness," Standing Crane replied. "But they have an insatiable curiosity and don't quite understand certain etiquettes. They're into everything, like children. They pelted us with more questions than a normal five-year-old would."

Suddenly Skalli seemed to Kirk to be significantly less annoying.

"They've asked to see every single starbase, visit every single member planet, tour as many starships as are available—frankly, Jim, we're getting overwhelmed! The Federation likes to be accessible to potential members, but this is just getting ridiculous. We found one of them in the kitchens before last night's farewell banquet. He had almost gotten stuck inside a cabinet and was meticulously examining—and sampling!—every single spice we had. One doesn't like to laugh at a respected member of an honored entourage, but honestly it pushed our limits!"

"I hope he didn't get into the Sakerlian spice. A

mouthful of that stuff would have caused a diplomatic incident."

"Too true," Standing Crane said. She sighed. "Oh, Jim, it is good to see you. It's been too long."

"So, maybe I purchase the lovely lady a drink at Gaston's when I return," Kirk said.

"Maybe the lovely lady will take you up on that when she can spare a moment," Standing Crane replied.

"Maybe that," Kirk said ruefully, "will be a while."

"More's the pity. Enjoy the rest of the trip . . . if you can," Standing Crane said. "Good-bye, Jim. And you be nice to Skalli!"

She was still smiling when her image disappeared, to be replaced with a blue screen sporting the official circular insignia of Starfleet Command.

Kirk leaned back in his chair and stretched. He eyed what he had brought for entertainment: old copies of fine books he'd read several times, a tattered deck of cards over which he, McCoy, and Scotty—the only other members of his old senior staff who enjoyed gambling—had spent many an hour.

But he was not about to ask these cadets, to him barely out of diapers, to join him in a game of poker, or even fizzbin. And he was heartily sick of solitaire.

There was a sound on the computer indicating that he had a message and Kirk smiled. Perhaps Laura had found that "moment." He thumbed the control and said, "Changed your mind about that drink?"

The words stuck in his throat. Onscreen was not the friendly, attractive face of Laura Standing Crane but the stern, haughty visage of Chancellor Azetbur of the

Klingon High Council. She cocked her head, clearly puzzled at his comment.

"Captain?"

Recovering immediately, Kirk smiled his easy smile and waved a hand dismissively. "Forgive me, Chancellor, I was expecting someone else. How are the negotiations coming?"

"Very well indeed," she replied. "Your friend Spock has a gift for bringing together at a table many who might otherwise prefer a fight. The others involved are also welcome contributors toward the peace we all seek."

"I'm delighted to hear it, but after serving with them so long, I confess I expected no less. Now, Chancellor, what can I do for you?"

"It is not what you can do for me, Captain Kirk." Her voice was as icy as he remembered it, even though they both knew now that he was no enemy to the Klingons, indeed one of their best friends by virtue of his salvaging of the peace negotiations. "It is what I am planning on doing for you."

"I'm . . . not sure I understand, Chancellor."

"You saved many lives a few months ago," she continued. "You perhaps saved my entire race."

He laughed slightly. "Come now, Chancellor. You give me too much credit."

"Indeed, I do not think so." Her eyes flashed briefly and Kirk wondered, as he so often did when dealing with Klingons, if he had inadvertently given offense. "I wish to repay you for what you have done. I owe you an honor debt, and Klingons always repay honor debts. I am invoking the *DIS jaj je.*"

Although Klingon had been in the computer's translation banks for several decades now, every now and then a phrase would be uttered that had the computer scurrying to catch up with the translation. This was such a moment, and Kirk and Azetbur stared at one another for an uncomfortably long few seconds before the computer offered the words, "The Year and the Day" as the proper translation.

Kirk was still baffled. He had no doubt that the translation was technically accurate as far as it went, but he remained unenlightened as to what it really *meant.*

Azetbur was regarding him expectantly. Her eyes were bright and her color was high. Clearly what she had just said meant a great deal to her.

With a silent prayer to whatever god controlled effective and harmonious communication, Kirk said, "Chancellor, I thank you, but this is not necessary. What I did, I did freely. There is no honor debt between us."

The god who controlled effective and harmonious communication clearly had the day off, because Azetbur tensed. "We wrongfully put you in prison, you and your chief medical officer. We expected you to die, James Kirk, and would have been glad of it. Despite this ultimately unjust treatment at our hands, you risked your life to save mine and those of numberless Klingons, those alive and those generations yet to be born."

The last thing Kirk wanted—well, the last thing other than to not have Skalli as his pet project—was to be in any way, shape or form further entangled with Klingons.

"I have no wish to offend you, Chancellor, but as far as I am concerned, all debts are paid. There's no need for. . . ." For the briefest of moments Kirk debated trying to twist his tongue around the guttural, consonant-laden language, then opted for the Federation standard words instead. "For 'The Year and the Day.'"

For a long, very bad moment Kirk worried that Azetbur would try to leap for his throat through the screen. Then, oddly, she smiled, showing sharp teeth, and settled in her chair. She looked like a cat who'd just cornered a particularly tasty-looking mouse, and he worried about *that*, too.

"As you wish, Captain Kirk. As far as you are concerned, then, there shall be no The Year and the Day. You will at least permit me to thank you again?"

"Chancellor, I was honored to be of service in so high a cause," he said, and meant every word. He hoped his sincerity would come through.

Apparently it did. She nodded, and seemed satisfied. "Then I wish you good day, Captain."

"And you, Chancellor."

Their eyes locked, then her image blipped out. Kirk blew out a breath. The Chancellor of the Klingon High Council wanted him to accept an honor debt. Well, that was something you didn't see every day. He congratulated himself for getting off so easily.

His door chimed. "Come in," he called, rubbing his eyes.

There was a slight hiss and Skalli stood in the doorway. "It's nineteen hundred hours and five minutes," she said. "We're all waiting for you, and we're hungry!"

Kirk regarded her for a moment, then rose. "Far be it from me to keep a roomful of hungry cadets waiting," he said. "After you."

Azetbur stared at the dark screen after the image of Kirk had disappeared, playing a little game with herself. She wanted to see how long it would take before her right hand, Brigadier Kerla, exploded in fury.

"Arrogant human *pahtk!*" Kerla spat. Azetbur permitted herself a slight smile.

"It took you three entire seconds," she said calmly. "I am pleased to see you are learning restraint. It will serve us well in our interaction with humans."

"He spurned the *DIS jaj je!*" raged Kerla, stamping about the small room, ignoring Azetbur's gibe. "That pompous, self-centered—"

"Patience, my old friend," Azetbur soothed. "He is only a human, after all. He does not know our customs. He could not possibly understand the honor I offered him." She rose. "Besides, he did not spurn it."

"With all due respect, Chancellor," said Kerla, "I was by your side the entire time. I heard what he—"

"He may have meant to *decline* the offer of the honor debt," replied Azetbur, choosing her words very carefully. "But one cannot decline such a thing. It will happen, whether he wills it or no. I have sworn the oath of *DIS jaj je*. I will honor it. No one can forswear me!"

Her voice rang clearly, and with an effort she brought her own bubbling rage under control. She knew that

Kirk was a good person. He had overcome his own prejudices to save people he had very good cause to regard as enemies. It was a misunderstanding, not an insult. She would not permit Kerla to view it as such, nor would she.

"But if you try to enact it, he will surely notice," said Kerla. "Notice, and protest."

Azetbur shook her head slowly. "He will not know of it. I will keep my word, and he will think he has . . . disentangled himself from us. Brigadier, I want you to contact the *K'Rator*. I have a mission for her captain."

Chapter Three

Commander Uhura contorted her beautiful dark face into a snarl and spat forth a string of harsh-sounding words. Fiercely, she brandished her *bat'leth*, then leaped forward. Blood-red robes trimmed in black fur swirled around her.

> *"Son of a black-hearted dog,*
> *My body is not thine,*
> *My heart is not thine,*
> *But my blade—yes, ah, yes,*
> *This I offer to thee,*
> *I offer to thy heart!"*

A mere meter away, Karglak offered his own guttural challenge, which climaxed with an earsplitting screech. He was clad in black and silver armor, and sprang forward to meet his adversary.

> *"In this conflict shall I scream my battle cry,*
> *Death is but another foe to defeat.*

*It is you who shall board the Barge of the Dead
In dishonor so great
That none shall remember your name!"*

Their *bat'leths* clashed, then clashed again. Uhura's muscles quivered under the strain and she knew a flash of fear. Good thing she kept in decent shape—

Grunting, they sprang apart. Thrice they circled, and then leapt at one another. This time Uhura felt the wind rush past her face as she narrowly avoided the curving blade. She uttered a single word with all the strength she possessed: *"Qapla'!"* and charged him.

Karglak fell beneath her, his own weapon knocked from his hands to skitter to a halt three meters away. Uhura straddled his waist. She was sweating profusely and breathing heavily. Under the hot lights, she could see the bare skin of her own arms gleaming with moisture.

Quick as a thought, she brought the *bat'leth* down and pressed it against his throat. For a long moment, they stared into one another's eyes.

Slowly, she eased back and removed the deadly blade. He was faster, and before she knew it she was caught up in his arms, his sharp-tooth mouth pressed down on hers, and they were locked in an embrace as violent as their battle had been.

A sudden silence and utter blackness descended.

"Hey, watch the teeth," Uhura grumbled, clambering off the most famous opera singer ever to have graced the planet Qo'noS. She dabbed at her lip gently, wincing. Her finger came away red.

Karglak leapt to his feet, gallantly extending a hand to help her up. She took it. "I regret any pain I may have caused you," he said. "But that was marvelous! Marvelous! I was so caught up in the drama I was . . . how do you put it . . . carried away."

She smiled at him. At least he'd agreed to start using a mouthwash during their up-close-and-personal duets. "It's all right, Karglak. I'll take it as a compliment."

"As you should," purred Lamork, the director of the specially written operetta. "Karglak is notorious for discourtesy to his leading ladies."

"An exaggeration," Karglak scoffed. "They are—what is your word—prima donnas. Anyone of an artistic temperament would have difficulty performing with such arrogant females. You, dear lady, are a professional." He put his hand on his heart, and executed a bow.

The operetta would be performed in conjunction with a medley of songs that represented the finest of Earth's musical traditions: ancient Peruvian and Aboriginal melodies, "Greensleeves," some Gershwin tunes, two arias from *Madame Butterfly,* "Ole Man River," "Bring Him Home," China's famous "Moon and Sun Song," among others, and of course the famous "First Contact, First Touch" from the opera *Songs from Space and Time,* widely regarded as Earth's finest musical piece since humans first made contact with other species.

Despite the bruises, scrapes, and occasional cuts Uhura was forced to endure as part of this historic extravaganza, she had to confess she was enjoying herself hugely. Music had always been a great love. When but a young woman she had been forced to choose between two promising careers: opera performer or Starfleet Officer. She had chosen the latter and never regretted it, but was delighted that her voice was now considered as valuable a tool in the peace negotiations as her diplomatic skills.

She had been surprised to learn how much Klingons loved opera, and what a long, rich history it had on their homeworld. Uhura couldn't help but smile as she remembered stumbling through rudimentary Klingon a few months ago, when the *Enterprise* was attempting to rescue its imprisoned captain. She had thought the language unmusical and unpleasant. Certainly it had challenged a human throat and tongue. But the more she heard it, the more intriguing it sounded to her, and when, at Captain Spock's gentle suggestion, she had finally listened to Klingon opera, she had been captivated. What power it had! What grand, sweeping stories it told!

When she approached Spock with the concept of a "musical exchange," an evening of Klingon opera and human song, he had seemed surprised. It had taken her a week or two, but she finally realized that it had been Spock's idea all along. He had only let Uhura think it had been her idea.

She, however, had been the one doing all the work: compiling the pieces and going over them with Qo'noS's most famous opera singer, Karglak. She had anticipated a difficult time, but to her delight and surprise Karglak was as eager as she to learn about new musical styles. They had each agreed to learn each other's languages, if possible, to honor the other's culture. He had taken smoothly to English and Italian, and she had to admit that despite his fearsome exterior, part of her melted—just a little—when he gazed into her eyes and sang "Some Enchanted Evening."

The mesmerizing effect he had on her ended after the performance, thank goodness. Positive cultural exchange was one thing, but the interspecies romance made so famous by *Songs from Space and Time* notwithstanding, she had no desire to exchange anything more intimate.

She mopped her soaking brow and gulped water with lemon while Lamork gave them notes. "Commander, you are doing a fine job with the range of the piece, but I would ask you to reexamine your Klingon. The 'r' comes from the back of the throat, not from the tip of the tongue. And the glottal stops are—"

Uhura sighed. "Lamork, I've no desire to permanently ruin my voice for one evening's performance. If I can approximate the sound well enough to be understood, what's the problem?"

Lamork frowned terribly. "You show disrespect for the composer's vision, *that* is the problem."

She kept her gaze locked with his, refusing to rise to the bait. "And Karglak hardly sounds French when he's performing as Emile de Becque, but you haven't heard me complaining."

"Commander," came a calm, cool voice from the back of the room. "Director Lamork. Please. We have no wish to start a new war on the eve of peace."

The voice, of course, belonged to Captain Spock. He

was out of uniform and gliding down the aisle to meet them in flowing blue, silver, and gold robes, the traditional garb of his people. "This was meant to bring two races together with a love of music, not divide them by the finer details."

Lamork turned his fearsome glower upon Spock, but did not respond to the Vulcan's chiding. Instead, he changed the subject. "I dare not hope," he said, sarcasm creeping into his voice, "that you are here just to be uplifted by the music."

"You assume incorrectly if you think that Vulcans have no appreciation for music and art, Lamork. Simply because we control our emotions does not mean we cannot appreciate beauty. Rest assured that on the night of the performance, it is unlikely that you will have a more attentive listener than myself. However, you are correct—I did come here to speak with Commander Uhura. Commander, if you please?"

Taking her lemon water with her and nodding to her fellow performer, Uhura stepped off the stage and followed Spock up a ways toward the end of the hall.

"How are the rehearsals progressing?" Spock wanted to know.

"Very well, actually," Uhura said. "Karglak is surprisingly easy to work with, though Lamork's a hell of a taskmaster."

"Any sign of conflict? Resentment?"

"Not really. Except over things like accents and hitting the notes right." She smiled, wincing a little as she did so as a brief stab reminded her of her cut lip. "It looks like artists remain artists, no matter what the culture. I don't think there's anything going on here except old-fashioned theater politics."

Spock frowned, noticing her wince and the swelling on her lip. "You are injured," he said.

"Oh, that," Uhura said, laughing a little. "Seems our Karglak got a little carried away during our duet."

"I would be mindful, Commander. It is my understanding that biting, especially around the mouth and face, is part of a Klingon mating ritual."

She stared at him, her jaw dropping slightly. He raised an eyebrow. Slowly, Uhura turned to look back at the stage. Karglak was watching them and as she looked at him, he smiled and waved a little.

"Uh oh," she said.

"No, no, no," said McCoy, his voice rising despite the delicacy of the situation. "Remember the heart is *there,* not there. That's the—" He glanced up at his Klingon counterpart. "That's the liver, right?"

Doctor Q'ulagh frowned terribly, and McCoy got the feeling that he, too, was running out of patience with the dissection. McCoy couldn't blame him. It had taken a lot of discussion—all right, call a spade a spade, *begging*—in order to convince the Klingon government to donate a cadaver in the first place. And now McCoy was watching some of the Federation's finest give damn good impressions of medieval barbers as they hacked at the corpse.

"It is not the liver," Q'ulagh responded, his teeth clenched and his eyes flashing. "It is the first of the two . . ." And the translator shut down, not even trying to translate the long flow of seeming gibberish that ensued. McCoy recognized it and nodded. The two whatziz were extraneous organs not found in any other humanoid species. He recalled what he knew to make sure he had his ducks in a row.

"These . . . uh . . . highly specialized organs secrete anti-inflammatory fluids and natural painkillers when the skin is damaged," he said. "It keeps a warrior on his feet longer. It is part of what makes a Klingon such a fearsome enemy in battle."

He threw that last part in on a whim. It was sincere enough, but this whole honor code thing was starting to wear a bit thin. However, when Q'ulagh visibly calmed and even nodded his head in admiration at McCoy's statement, the elderly Southern doctor recalled a statement his mama had made many years past: *You catch more flies with honey than vinegar, son.*

To his relief, his team of Starfleet doctors, some of them heads of medical schools, followed his lead. The Klingon doctors accepted the compliment and the tension in the room eased.

Dr. Malcolm Simpson, one of the finest surgeons to ever grace Starfleet, continued the dissection. One by one, the mysterious Klingon organs were removed and themselves dissected. The Klingons didn't understand it, but they didn't have to. Their chancellor, Azetbur, had told them to participate whole-heartedly in this special meeting of minds, so that an incident like the death of her father, Gorkon, would never again happen.

To this day, McCoy had dreams about that dreadful, tragic night. In his nightmares he again straddled the dying chancellor, who looked up at him with imploring eyes. McCoy read in their depths Gorkon's fierce desire to live, not so much for himself as for his people. Gorkon knew if this assassination attempt was successful, the tentative alliance the Federation and the Klingon Empire had formed would shatter like glass dropped on a stone floor. As it damn near had.

He vividly recalled the strange purple-magenta color of Klingon blood on his hands, searching frantically for the heart, doing everything he would normally do to save a dying human, and knowing that he was failing utterly with this Klingon.

I tried to save him, McCoy remembered crying aloud at his trial, a Klingon kangaroo court if there ever was one. *I was desperate to save him.*

Well, now he'd know how. And so would all these surgeons, who would teach their own students Klingon anatomy. There need never be another death on account of ignorance, not anymore. And the Klingons were learning the same things. There had been those who muttered that giving Klingons lessons in human anatomy was akin to providing them more efficient ways to butcher, but McCoy had shut up that line of talk quickly. They were becoming allies now, Klingons and humans, as unlikely as that seemed, and understanding one another physically was part of learning to understand one another culturally.

The dead Klingon was now empty of his organs. His belly and chest gaped open. The face was gone, peeled back early on in the autopsy in order to better access the brain. McCoy never liked being overlong with the dead; his job was to save the living. Seeing this corpse, which Q'ulagh had assured him had once been a proud warrior, McCoy felt sorrow brush him.

"Rest in peace," he murmured under his breath. Straightening, he cleared his throat. "Let's take a short break before we begin dissecting the human corpse."

"If you have no further need of the body, we will transport it into space. It is but an empty shell now," Q'ulagh said.

"Of course," McCoy said, although he was a bit taken aback by the Klingon's lack of desire for anything resembling a proper burial. Q'ulagh pulled out his communicator, uttered a few rough-sounding words, and the corpse and its attendant organs dematerialized.

As they were heading out the door, McCoy caught a whisper: "There went a good Klingon." Stifled laughter greeted the comment.

Fortunately, the Klingons were already gone. It was also fortunate that had they even heard the muttered words they would have taken them at face value. McCoy, however, knew what they were intended to mean. He whirled and grabbed Dr. Phillip Kingston by his bloody scrubs, taking the much younger man by surprise.

"Isn't it funny," said McCoy softly, "how old phrases just don't want to die? 'The only good Indian is a dead Indian' could maybe be forgiven when uttered by a prejudiced, frightened white soldier a few hundred years ago. But I can't believe I'm hearing it from the lips of a Starfleet officer."

Blue eyes blazing, McCoy turned Kingston loose

with a grunt of disgust. "You slip up one more time, and you're off this team."

The blond man's lip curled. "You can't do that," he said.

"The hell I can't. This was my project from the beginning. You're here because you're a top-notch surgeon. But I'm beginning to think you're not such a great human being."

He turned and stalked off, following the rest to the break area.

Damn, damn. You think you've come so far, learned so much as a species, and then something like this happens.

As the late, greatly lamented Chancellor Gorkon said at that ill-fated dinner aboard the *Enterprise* not so long ago, "I can see we still have a long way to go."

Chapter Four

The San Francisco skyline was beautiful at night, and Kirk stood for a while simply gazing at it.

He was completely, utterly, and thoroughly bored.

He had returned to Earth two days ago and had bid an unfortunately temporary farewell to a clingy Skalli. Standing Crane, as she had warned, was far too busy even for a quick drink at Gaston's. Spock, Uhura and McCoy of course were so deeply entangled in the peace negotiations that they could barely spare a moment to chat, although Spock had told him that things were progressing surprisingly well. Sulu, lucky devil, had his own ship now and was off somewhere captaining it. Kirk had messages in to both Chekov and Scotty, but so far, they hadn't responded.

Everyone, it seemed, was terribly busy. Except for one James T. Kirk. He rattled the ice in his Scotch and took another sip.

His door buzzed. Kirk glanced at the chronometer. It was after midnight. Who could it be at this hour?

Whoever it is, he thought grimly, *is welcome . . . unless it's Skalli.*

"Come in," he called, not bothering to see who it was.

The door hissed open and two handsome blond men stood in its frame. One was in his mid-thirties, well built and solid looking. The other, who hung back a little, was younger and slighter. They looked familiar, but Kirk couldn't place them at once.

Then the older one of them smiled, and the memory clicked into place.

"Hi, Uncle Jim," Kirk's nephew, Alexander, said.

"Good Lord," Kirk said, feeling a smile stretch across his face. "Alex . . . Julius . . . come in, come in! Is it really you?"

They stepped inside. "Nice place," said Julius, the youngest of Kirk's three nephews. How old was he now—twenty-seven? Twenty-eight?

A long, uncomfortable moment ensued as the three men regarded one another. Had they been the youngsters Kirk remembered, he'd have known what to do—fold them into a big, avuncular hug. But they were men, not boys, and it had been so long since he'd seen them. . . .

It was Alex who broke the ice by suddenly laughing and embracing his uncle. Alex was now bigger than Kirk, taller and broader, and Kirk felt a distinctly odd sensation that was both familiar and completely strange. Slowly, he reached up and returned the hug. He had a sudden, painful flashback to when he had first embraced his son David. He forced that memory down. David was dead, killed by—

—*(Klingons)*—

41

—a madman. Alexander and Julius were here, alive, and it felt very, very good to see them.

Julius forestalled an embrace by extending his hand, smiling stiffly. Kirk grasped the hand.

"I suppose it has been a bit too long for you to want to hug your Uncle Jim, Julius," he said as gently as he could.

Julius's smile froze on his lips. "I wasn't trying to—" he began. Kirk held up a hand, forestalling his comment.

"You look good, both of you. I saw your brother just recently." Peter, the eldest son of Kirk's late, beloved brother Sam, was active in Starfleet Diplomatic Corps. While not part of the group that had been selected to travel to the Klingon homeworld, Peter was nonetheless heavily involved in the peace process. He and Kirk had managed to grab a few moments for a cup of coffee together before their respective duties had called them away. It was, unfortunately, a very typical encounter for both of them.

Julius didn't react, but Alex brightened visibly. "Peter! How is he? We don't hear from him much."

Kirk heard the unspoken word "either," but ignored it. "He's doing very well. Quite active in the peace negotiations. Have a seat, both of you. What can I get you?"

Julius nodded at the small glass of amber fluid Kirk was carrying. "That Scotch?"

"Indeed it is. A parting gift from my chief engineer. You can practically cut the peat."

A quick, genuine smile flitted across Julius's sharp

features, softening them for an instant. "Sounds perfect. Neat, please."

Kirk turned to the bar and poured Julius two fingers' worth of the twenty-four-year-old Bunnahabhain. "How about you, Alex? Scotch, wine . . ." He turned with a smile. "Romulan ale?"

Alex looked puzzled. "I thought that was illegal," he said.

"It is, but you don't look official to me." A thought crossed his mind. "And if you are, that was just a joke."

Alex laughed. "No, we're not official, Uncle Jim. I'll just have some ice water with lemon, thanks."

Kirk finished preparing the drinks, then handed them to his nephews. "To family reunions," he toasted, lifting his glass. Both young men did likewise, and then each took a sip. Kirk sat in a chair opposite Alex and Julius.

"I must confess, I'm quite surprised to see you two, especially at this hour," he said. "To what do I owe the pleasure?"

The Kirk brothers looked at each other. Julius, who was sitting on the arm of the couch, sat back a little, swirling his scotch. Alex put his glass of water down on the coffee table and leaned forward.

"I didn't think you'd think it was just a social call," he said. Kirk smiled faintly and took another sip. Alex ran a hand through his thick fair hair and laughed uneasily. "For months I've rehearsed this, and now that I'm here, it's all gone right out of my head."

"We're all family here," Kirk said. "Speak from the heart, Alex. It'll come out all right. Trust me."

Alex licked his lips and looked down at his entwined

hands. He took a deep breath. "We, uh, didn't see much of you after Mom and Dad died. And I know that it wasn't your fault. I mean, you were a captain of a starship, and they don't let you take families with you on those. We couldn't go with you, even if you'd wanted us, and we know that. Peter was at the starbase for so long and then went back to Earth with Grandma and Grampa. And we stayed with the Pearsons on Rigel VI."

Kirk regarded his nephew steadily. "I know all this, Alex. Why are you mentioning it now?"

"Because the Pearsons treated us like cattle," said Julius unexpectedly. "And we've been on our own for the last several years. Something you might have known if you'd bothered—"

"Julius!" snapped Alex, his mild face flushed and angry. At once, his younger brother subsided.

Kirk was immediately attentive. "Alex . . . were you and Julius abused in any way?"

"Oh, no, Uncle Jim, nothing like that. But it was clear that we weren't wanted. I don't think they realized how much of a handful we would turn out to be! So when I was twenty I . . . well, I just took Julius with me and left. They didn't seem to care too much. Anyway, that's not the point. The point is, we've been doing a lot of traveling, and over the years we realized what we really wanted: a home."

Guilt warred with indignation within Kirk. Alex had been right—even if he'd wanted to adopt his three nephews, which he was unhappily certain he hadn't, he wouldn't have been able to. There was no place for children aboard a starship. And then one thing led to another, and the next thing he knew he had contacted the Pearsons and they told him that Alex and Julius were all grown up and striking out on their own as young men.

He'd sent a message on each of their birthdays, every year, along with what he hoped were suitable gifts. Every time he'd been near Rigel VI, which wasn't often, he'd arranged to visit them. He had adored his big brother, George Samuel Kirk, but even they had fallen out of touch once they had reached adulthood. The Kirks just weren't a close-knit family, that was all there was to it, especially with their divergent interests that took them all over the galaxy.

But this revelation about the Pearsons disturbed him greatly. "I didn't know that you weren't happy," he said. "You were visiting the Pearsons when your parents died, and it seemed the right place for you. You have a home here, with me, if you want it."

"It's all right, Uncle Jim. We don't want to move in!" Alex forced a laugh. The turn of the conversation was clearly as uncomfortable to him as it was to Kirk. "We want our own home. Our own place. And we've met with many others who share our vision."

He leaned forward, his eyes sparkling. "Uncle Jim, we want to found a colony."

Now I understand, Kirk thought. *They want me to pull some strings and find them a suitable place.* The thought that they had sought him out not for his own sake, but what he could do for them, pained him a little, but he supposed he couldn't blame them. Clearly they, too, thought of him not as a person, not as Uncle Jim, but the Great Captain James T. Kirk.

"I'll see what I can do," he began. "Most of Starfleet's attention is on this conference, and they're not going to be able to spare a lot of people to help you find a place."

"Oh, no, you've got it all wrong," Alex said. "We've found a planet already."

"Really? Where?"

"It's in the Besar system, very remote, freely donated as a goodwill gesture by a race that is negotiating with the Federation for admittance. I call it . . . Sanctuary." His face softened and his eyes lost focus. "It's beautiful, Uncle Jim. We're going to make it our own little corner of paradise. Here's a list of those who have already agreed to go."

Alex handed Kirk a padd and Kirk quickly scanned the names. The list of scientists and engineers was lengthy, and most of them were renowned for their cutting-edge discoveries and developments. Whatever else this colony might be, it would certainly be very high-tech.

"Alex, I'm impressed. You seem to have the cream of the crop here."

"Yes, we do," Alex continued eagerly. "There aren't that many ideal places out there anymore, as I'm sure you know."

"How fortunate that these . . . who's donating the planet?"

"Falorians."

"That's the second time this week I've heard their name crop up," Kirk said. "A friend of mine greeted their diplomatic delegation. Very friendly, very curious, is that correct?" He tried and failed to get Standing Crane's story of the Falorian scooping out a fingerful of every spice in Starfleet Headquarters' banquet kitchen out of his mind.

"Oh, yes," Alex said. "So open-handed."

"There's no such thing as a free lunch," Kirk reminded him.

"I know that," Alex said, and bridled a little. "It's obvious that they're hoping to win favor for their admittance by letting us have the colony. And we've negotiated certain rights to anything we might learn. Not all, of course," he hastened to add. "They've never had any desire to colonize it themselves or else they'd have done so centuries ago. It works out to be a good thing for everyone involved."

"How did you manage to snag this gem of a world?" Kirk wanted to know.

"It's all thanks to Julius," Alex replied, turning to regard his brother with affection. "He's been amazing. I've been working hard to get people to sign on for it, but he's been the one out there talking to all kinds of alien races to find us our Sanctuary."

Julius flushed a little—that pale coloring didn't serve him well—and looked down at his empty glass as if he wished there were more Scotch in it.

"Really?" Kirk said, trying to not sound too surprised. "Starfleet has a whole section with dozens of people devoted to that kind of wrangling. How did you manage it on your own?"

Julius's jaw tensed almost imperceptibly and Kirk wished he could rephrase the question. "This is the culmination of many years of discussions with many different species, Uncle Jim. Let me assure you Alex and I have had our share of false starts and deals falling through. We were able to contact the Falorians at the right time, when they were trying to look good to the Federation."

"So, luck, skill, and hard work, is that what you're saying?"

Julius shrugged. "Pretty much."

"A wise man once said, the harder you work, the luckier you get," Kirk said. "It sounds to me as if you are both very lucky, from that standpoint. Tell me a little more about . . . about your vision, Alex."

Those were apparently the magic words, for Alex lit up immediately. "You've seen the list I gave you. You know these people, what they're known for, their personalities."

"Iconoclastic geniuses might not be too strong a term," Kirk said.

"Individualists," Alex insisted. "Dreamers who can back up their dreams with concrete realities. But we don't want to just hand over the results of our hard work to someone else—we want it for our own. We'll share everything, for the betterment of all peace-loving species, but we won't just surrender what we know, what we've made, without long, careful thought. And we'll make sure it's all used for the right purposes. We'll make sure our knowledge doesn't ever fall into the wrong hands."

Kirk felt a quick stab of pity for Alex's naïveté. He'd been that idealistic once. He thought of Oppenheimer, of

Lu Wang Hu, of the Vulcan teacher Sekur. All of them had used their genius to break barriers; all of them had eventually seen their creations turned into weapons of mass destruction. He hoped this wouldn't happen to Alex.

"We're taking as our inspiration the Amish and the Quakers," Alex was saying. "They've made it through centuries still holding onto their ideals of nonviolence. So can we."

"The Amish don't exactly approve of cutting-edge technology," Kirk reminded him.

Alex laughed. "No, that's true. But we don't have to be Amish to respect them and learn from their wisdom."

Kirk gestured with the padd. "And all these famous people have agreed to this?"

"Absolutely. We are committed to this, Uncle Jim."

Kirk looked at him for a long moment. "Your father would be so proud," he said quietly. "Of both of you," he added, including the more withdrawn Julius as well as the open, talkative Alex.

"I wish you both all the luck in the universe," Kirk continued.

Alex and Julius exchanged amused glances. "He hasn't figured it out yet," Julius said with a slight smirk.

"Figured what out?"

"Uncle Jim," Alex said, "We didn't come all this way and show up at your door at midnight just to *tell* you about our colony. We came to ask you to come with us."

Chapter Five

"**O**ut of the question," Kirk said automatically. "I have responsibilities here. I can't just go galloping across the galaxy as if I were your age again."

"Why not?" The question was uttered in absolute innocence and Alex seemed genuinely puzzled by his uncle's abrupt refusal. "You could help us so much. You have so many years of experience!"

"Experience in captaining a starship, yes," Kirk said. "Experience in protecting and defending a colony from hostile forces. But I don't know how much use I'll be to you and your people. What could I possibly do?"

"You could give me excellent advice," Alex said promptly. "You could help Julius with the Falorians." He grinned sheepishly and added, "And if I may be frank, having someone with your reputation join the colony will be a real feather in our cap. It would give us a great deal of legitimacy in the Federation's eyes, some nego-tiating clout when it comes to that."

"Please come, Uncle Jim." Surprised, Kirk turned to

look at his youngest nephew. "We've worked so hard. It would mean so much to Alex . . . to me . . . if you would come with us."

"Worried about your old uncle, is that it?" Kirk asked. "I appreciate your concern, but I'm not ready to be farmed out to pasture just yet, thank you very much."

"Then what are you doing right now?" Julius challenged. He leaned forward. His blue eyes were intense in his lean face, his body taut with emotions Kirk couldn't quite decipher. "Don't you think we've been keeping tabs on you? We needed to know if you'd be in a position to even consider our offer, and you most certainly are."

"Juley—" began Alex, worried.

"Don't 'Juley' me, not now, Alex," Julius shot back. "We're too close to let him stop us."

Kirk began to speak. "Julius, I can understand—"

"Shut up!" cried Julius, startling both his brother and his uncle into a momentary silence. "You have no idea what we've been through the last few years, Uncle Jim. No idea. You don't know the, the begging and pleading Alex has had to do, the crawling through mud and getting sick and being literally scared for my *life* half the time that I've done to get this thing to fly. We've got names, we've got backing, we've got a beautiful, unspoiled world owned by friendly aliens, and the last piece of the puzzle is *you*."

He paused, swallowing hard, then continued. "It was part of the dream from the beginning, having us all together again. We know we can't get Peter. We know what he's dealing with and as peace-loving people our-

51

selves we have respect for that. But you're done, Uncle Jim. You're hanging around Starfleet hoping they'll toss you a bone, and all they've done is given you classes at the Academy. I heard about your "Command Decisions and Their Consequences" class. The kids loved it, but I bet it rankled, having to stand up in front of a class and just talk about the glory days instead of living them."

Kirk had gone from startled to angry to amused. "Please, don't stop now, Julius. Keep telling me how I feel."

The youth was too wrapped up in his own emotions to take offense at the gibe. "You're a legend. And your career speaks for itself. You like to act, to be involved, to do things, just like we like to do things. Just like Alex tells me Dad and Mom liked to. I have to take his word for that; I don't have any memories of them. I think it's in our blood, this—this love of doing. And I can't believe that you're happy with these so-called responsibilities.

"Tell us, Uncle Jim. Look us in the eye and tell us that you are happy where you are, teaching eighteen-year-olds ancient history, when you could be part of an experiment working alongside your own blood to bring about things that can change the universe. You tell me this and we'll go away and not try any more to drag you out of this early grave you've dug for yourself. Can you do it, Uncle Jim? Huh? Can you?"

The amusement had faded and the anger had surged back. Coolly, but with an edge to his voice, Kirk replied, "It's been good seeing you both. I wish you luck with Sanctuary."

For a moment, Julius stared. He seemed more distressed than Alex at Kirk's blunt refusal.

It was Alex who finally broke the taut silence. "I told you he wouldn't come, Juley," he said heavily. "But you were right about one thing. We had to try."

Julius still seemed to be in shock. "I can't believe it," he whispered. "I can't believe you'd just . . . without even . . . ah, the hell with it. And the hell with you, *Captain*." He slid off the back of the sofa and strode toward the door. It hissed open and he was gone, without a backward glance.

"I apologize for Julius, Uncle Jim," Alex said. He was still seated on the couch. "You'll have to forgive him. We really have been through a lot in getting this colony pulled together, and it would have been the jewel in the crown if you could have been part of it. He was so insistent that we come talk to you in person about it. I think he really thought we'd be able to convince you."

"You didn't seem so sure," Kirk said softly.

"No. I figured you were pretty well entrenched in whatever it was you were doing. We'd have to catch you at just the right moment, and that would be hard." He rose and smiled awkwardly. "Admiral Karen Berg is one of our sponsors. She'll be able to contact us if . . . if you change your mind."

"Alex, I'm sorry. I think Julius believes it has to do with you, but it doesn't. It has everything to do with my responsibilities."

"Oh, sure, Uncle Jim. He'll understand. Well, I better get going if I'm to catch up to Julius." He smiled sadly, and again reached out to his uncle. But there was a resignation in the hug that had not been there the first time.

They drew apart and looked into one another's eyes. "I'm sure Sanctuary will live up to its name with you as the leader, Alex," Kirk said.

Alex seemed about to say something, then apparently thought better of it. He smiled, squeezed Kirk's shoulder one last time, then turned and followed his brother into the night.

The silence was absolute. Slowly, Kirk picked up the discarded glasses, took them to the sink, washed them, and went to bed.

It was still dark out when his door chimed. Kirk bolted upright and glanced at the chronometer. Who would possibly be at his door at 5:30 A.M.? Maybe it was Julius and Alex, back to try to convince him again. For some reason, he was pleased at the prospect.

He fumbled for a robe, hastily sashed it closed, then stumbled into the living room. He glanced up to see who it was and groaned softly. It was not Julius and Alex. It was not anyone he had any desire to see.

Steeling himself, he opened the door. "Good morning, Skalli."

She bounced a little, standing in the doorway with a big grin on her lively face, then scampered inside. She carried a large basket, which she summarily plopped down on the kitchen table.

"Good morning, Captain Kirk! I brought us breakfast before our hike."

Kirk sighed. "Skalli," he began, "it's really not appropriate for you to be here at all, especially at this

54

hour of the morning." *Let alone,* he thought, glancing down at his black terrycloth robe, *when your instructor is wearing just a bathrobe.*

Skalli had turned and followed his gaze. "Oh, you mean because of the possibilities of sexual relations between student and teacher. Don't worry. You are absolutely *not* of interest to me sexually."

Kirk didn't believe it, but he felt himself blushing at her frank conversation.

Skalli's hand flew to her mouth. "I didn't mean that to sound the way it did . . . oh, dear . . . Not that you're not attractive . . . I mean, in your own human way, but to Huanni aesthetics humans aren't . . . there's not a *chance* that—"

Kirk held up a hand, growing slightly desperate to change the subject. "That will do, Cadet. All questions of impropriety aside . . . what *are* you doing here at five-thirty in the morning?"

She tilted her head in the expression that he had come to recognize as confusion. Her large ears flapped twice, then stood at full attention. "I thought I told you . . . I brought breakfast—"

"Before our hike, I got that. Didn't you think that perhaps I might have made my own plans about how I wanted to spend my day?"

"No," she said. "*Do* you have other plans?"

"No, but that's not the point. Why are you here?"

"For breakfast and—"

"I got that part," Kirk almost bellowed. "But why are we having breakfast and hiking? And you are not permitted to say because it will be healthy."

"But, you're my personal advisor. I thought we should get started immediately. Now that I have you all to myself, I have so many questions!"

Kirk ran a hand through his hair. "Skalli, that's during the semester."

Her ears sagged slightly and drooped like dying flowers down either side of her head. "You . . . you don't want to see me. Oh. I understand. I'm sorry. I'll go now."

He caught her by her long arm as she headed for the door, tears brimming in her enormous eyes. "It's not that, it's just . . . There are certain protocols and etiquette we have in place that you'll need to familiarize yourself with. One of them is, cadets don't interact with faculty members except during the school year. Another is, you schedule your meetings, which usually last about an hour. A third is, you never show up at a faculty member's home even if you're not sexually attracted to them."

He paused. That somehow hadn't come out quite right.

She listened with an earnestness and an intensity that was a bit unnerving. "I understand, Captain," she said firmly. "I apologize for my breach of protocol."

Kirk dropped his hand. "Apology accepted, Cadet." She still looked so distressed that he softened. "Tell you what. Since you went to all the trouble to make us breakfast, let's not let it go to waste. Let me get dressed. We'll eat, talk, then say good-bye, and I'll see you in September when the semester starts."

Her smile lit up her face. "That sounds great, Captain!"

It was a long breakfast, but it was delicious: blueberry muffins, fresh-squeezed orange juice, fresh fruits that Kirk didn't recognize but were delectable, and a thermos of a wonderfully aromatic beverage that was a kissing cousin to coffee but even tastier. Skalli talked incessantly, pummeling Kirk with questions, as the sun rose.

Finally, after every last crumb had been devoured, Skalli sadly slid off the chair and packed up the basket. "Let me apologize again, Captain."

"No need, Cadet. Thanks for breakfast. Have a good summer."

Her ears drooped. "You too, sir." The very personification of dejection, she slumped to the door, looked back at him sadly, and was gone.

The door had scarcely closed behind her when Kirk was at the computer. "Computer, contact and leave a message for Admiral Karen Berg. Please inform her that Jim Kirk needs to contact his nephews as soon as possible."

Shortly after Kirk had showered and shaved, a soft chime from his computer told him that someone was trying to contact him. It was Alex, managing to look both wary and hopeful at the same time.

"Got your message, Uncle Jim. What's going on?"

Kirk smiled. "You and Julius were right. There's nothing for me here that can't be resumed later. I'm not ready to make a long-term commitment right now, but . . . is the offer still open for me to come for a few months?"

He heard a faint whoop from somewhere in the room,

and Alex's face split into an enormous grin. "You bet, Uncle Jim! Stay as short or long a time as you want. I'm sure though once you're there, you'll never want to leave!"

Kirk didn't share Alex's certainty, but he did know one thing: He was dying a slow death here, teaching classes and putting up with Skalli's boundless enthusiasm. He needed to be away, out there . . . *doing* something.

"You've got a great list of people, but you could probably stand to use a few old hands. Mind if I bring along some friends?"

"Absolutely not! Any friend of our Uncle Jim is a friend of Sanctuary," Alex said. "Who did you have in mind?"

Chapter Six

"I'm afraid not, Pavel," said Admiral Gray. "There's been no change since our last conversation."

"I see," said Commander Pavel Chekov, striving not to let the disappointment show.

"Captain Sheridan keeps asking about you," Gray continued, his dark face expressionless. "That first officer position is still open."

"Yes, sir. I know, sir."

"Pavel, I really suggest you take it. With all the hullabaloo going on with the Klingons, there aren't going to be many changes in the upper ranks. I don't think a captaincy is going to come along any time soon, and in the meantime, you're just sitting at that starbase wasting your time."

Part of Chekov thought that Gray was absolutely right. He was going mad here at Starbase 14, twiddling his thumbs. Ostensibly he was there as a "Starfleet presence," whatever the heck *that* meant. He was coming to the conclusion that it meant twiddling one's thumbs.

But he knew that he was ready for a captaincy. His last job as first officer of the *Reliant* had been a trying one. He'd distinguished himself very well since, but the thought of going back to the same position when his old helmsbuddy Sulu had been given the *Excelsior* felt to him like he was giving up. It was just a bad time, that was all. He'd ride it out and surely something would turn up.

"Please tell Captain Sheridan that I am flattered by his obvious respect," he told Gray. "But I can't accept."

Gray sighed. A handsome man of African descent, he'd been doing a lot of string-pulling on Chekov's behalf recently, and Chekov doubted he'd continue to do much more.

"I appreciate everything you've done for me, sir," he said. "But I know I'm on the right path."

Gray smiled wryly. "That makes one of us, Pavel. You're a good man, but you're like that former captain of yours. Stubborn as they come."

"Any comparison to Captain Kirk I will take as a compliment," Chekov responded, bridling a little on Kirk's behalf.

"As well you should," Gray said, still smiling. "Gray out."

Chekov leaned back in his chair, took a deep breath, puffed out his cheeks, and exhaled. He laced his fingers at the back of his neck and cradled his head, thinking hard. Was he really on the right path? Or was he on a wild goose chase? Gray might come back with one more offer, but that would certainly be it.

If only he had some kind of a sign—

His computer beeped, indicating a message. Chekov tapped it. "Commander Chek—*Captain!*"

On the viewscreen was an image of Captain Kirk. "Hello, Pavel," he said. "How are you doing? I thought you'd have a command of your own by this time."

"Thanks for the vote of confidence," Chekov answered, grimacing a little. "But, strangely enough, Starfleet doesn't seem to share our opinion. How is your class going?"

"Over and done with," Kirk said, "as is my tenure at the Academy. I've got a proposition to make, if you're in a position to think it over."

Chekov felt his mouth curve into a smile. Hell, it stretched into a grin. Anything Jim Kirk was going to get him into was going to be exciting, and he could use some excitement along about now. Sooner or later, there'd be a captaincy for him. In the meantime, he'd listen to what Kirk had to say.

"I'm all ears," he said, seeing in his mind's eye Spock's reaction to the colorful phrase. Ah, those were the good old days.

Commander Montgomery Scott was freezing his rear off.

It had been decades since he'd been home to bonnie Scotland, and while for the first few weeks it had been a true delight, he was forced to admit that he'd forgotten just how cold, wet and, if one were to be honest, miserable the place could get.

Now, mind, that wasn't when one was sitting back in a cozy pub with the fire burning, sipping on a dram of the finest alcoholic beverage in the galaxy (Romulan ale, bah!), playing a round of darts. Or on a summer's day, strolling happily through Edinburgh. Or dancing at a ceili with the fair-skinned, rosy-cheeked lasses . . . ah, now that was Scotland at her sweetest.

But fishing in the high country . . . now that was a wee bit different.

Even in summer, storms would arise and the temperature would plummet. As now. Scott's little boat, *Highland Lassie,* rocked furiously. Scott looked at the gray, choppy water, the gray, cloudy sky, the gray, frigid rain that was suddenly starting to pepper him with cold wet droplets. He had worn rain gear, of course—one never ventured outside for any length of time without wellies and macs—but the thermos of hot spiked coffee he brought for just such occasions wasn't going to get him through this one. Grumbling and muttering to himself, he tapped the controls and took *Highland Lassie* back to the rocky shoreline. The rain and wind picked up and he barely managed to get his little boat safely ashore and secured. Cursing roundly, Scott stumbled up the rickety steps that led from the shoreline to his cottage. He'd thought it quaint and charming that sunny day he'd decided he had to have it; now nearly every day he cursed its antiquated "quaintness." What he wouldn't give for an upscale apartment in Edinburgh right now. . . .

He stumbled inside, his gray hair plastered to his skull, and began shedding clothes as he made his way to the bathroom. A hot shower steamed up the bathroom and revived him, and by the time he had wrapped himself in an old, beloved robe and started water boiling for a pot of tea he was feeling almost human again.

The rain pounded on the roof and lashed at the windows. He gazed at it for a moment, sluicing down in gray sheets, and then gave it a rude gesture.

He turned back to check on the kettle. Out of the corner of his eye, he saw a green light flashing. It was the computer alerting him that he had received a message. He hit the controls and finished toweling his hair dry as the Starfleet insignia filled the screen.

Then a familiar visage took its place. "Captain Kirk!" Scott cried delightedly, even though it was a recorded message and Kirk couldn't hear him.

"Hello, Scotty." Aye, but it had been a long time since Scott had heard that particular affectionate nickname. "I hope you're out on that boat you bought, landing one that's this big." He spread his arms wide, and Scott chuckled. "I don't know how well retirement is treating you, but if you're anything like me, you're bored silly."

Scott sighed, shaking his head ruefully. "Too true, lad," he said.

"I've got a proposition for you. My nephews Alexander and Julius are getting ready to depart for a planet they call Sanctuary, to found a new colony."

"A game for the young," Scotty said, still speaking aloud as if he were addressing Kirk. "I've no time nor back strength for diggin' in the dirt."

"It's going to be a site where cutting-edge technology is going to be developed," Kirk said, as if anticipating Scott's response. "I've sent you a list of names of those who have already committed. Its mission is completely one of peace—we'll have no weapons being developed here of any sort." Scott punched a button and a list of names began scrolling across the screen to the left of Kirk's image. His eyes widened.

Kirk leaned forward. "Think of it, Scotty. All this new technology, and you'll get to be an intrinsic part of its development. You'll have a chance to work with some of the most famous people in the galaxy, not just the Federation. And they'll have the chance to work with you." He smiled. "We have to resign ourselves to being living legends, my friend. Let me know if you're interested. Kirk out."

The list continued to scroll across the screen even though the image of Kirk had gone. Scott couldn't believe it. His heart began to quicken at the thought of getting his hands on this stuff. . . .

But what about *Highland Lassie?* Bonnie Scotland, home of his birth?

He looked out the window again, at the storm that continued to rage.

"Hell with the boat," Scott said.

They met for a pre-departure dinner at a banquet hall in one of San Francisco's finest hotels, a scant three weeks later. Kirk had barely had enough time to get his affairs in order, and was mildly amused at how easy it had been to talk Scotty and Chekov into coming. They must be itching for action, just as he was.

The banquet hall was lavishly decorated and the drinks flowed freely. Some of the faces were familiar, and it was obvious that he was recognized. When eye contact was made, Kirk smiled pleasantly. Many of the future colonists introduced themselves. They seemed all of a type to Kirk, regardless of gender or species: young, eager, bright-eyed and oh so very sincere.

It was a petty thought, but he figured that a few weeks on an alien world they'd have to build from scratch would take some of the shine off them.

"Captain!"

Kirk, who had just taken a refill of scotch on the rocks from the cheery female Bolian bartender, cringed. Oh, no. It couldn't be. Not here, not now. . . . The Bolian winced sympathetically.

"Ooh, that bad, huh, sweetie?" she whispered.

"Yep," Kirk said quietly, forcing his features into a pleasant expression. He turned around. "I didn't expect—"

He should have seen the bone-crushing hug coming, but he didn't, and all the air rushed out of his lungs in a *whoosh*.

"Are you surprised to see me?" Skalli chirped.

He stretched his lips into a rictus of a smile. "'Surprised' doesn't even begin to describe it," he said.

She let him go and jumped up and down, her large ears flapping excitedly. The other soon-to-be colonists, including both nephews and his old *Enterprise* crewmen, stared.

Kirk ignored them. "It was . . . kind of you to come see me off," he said.

Skalli laughed. "I'm not here to see you off, Captain. I'm here to join the colony!"

"What?" Kirk realized he had raised his voice and

quickly lowered it to a more conversational tone. "Skalli, you don't mean to tell me you dropped out of the Academy to follow me?"

"I sure did!"

He groped for words. "Skalli, you're putting your whole future at risk. You want to be an ambassador. You'll get so much out of Starfleet Academy that will—"

"I can always reenroll later," she said, dismissing his argument.

"How did you even find out about this?" Kirk had kept news of his departure close to his chest. Only a few people knew.

"Well, when I learned that you weren't going to be teaching next semester, I got worried. I went to our embassy and had someone find out what was going on. Then I got to thinking, well, Skalli, why don't *you* go along with the colony? There are so many reasons for me to go! For one thing, you're getting older, and who knows how much longer you'll be around for me to learn from."

"Thank you, Skalli, I feel so much better now."

She beamed, clearly not recognizing sarcasm when she heard it, and continued. "And second, what a unique chance to really learn from and bond with such a variety of people! Finally, it's almost in my own backyard. I'll get the chance to meet a Falorian!"

Her revelation distracted him from the innocent insult she'd delivered earlier. "You're in neighboring star systems and you've never met a Falorian?"

"Never. We're . . . a bit distant, the Huanni and the Falorians."

Kirk was now completely alert. "Were there hostilities between your people in the past?"

"Oh, no. Neither of us is an aggressive people." She wrinkled her nose at the thought of violence. "That's another reason I wanted to join the colony—their ideology is so profound. Technology can mean lasting peace, ways to help people, grow better crops, and provide shelter. It doesn't have to lead to war. Why do we always have to manufacture weapons? Why—"

Kirk steered her back to the subject of Huanni and Falorian relations. "It's hard for me to understand that two species in neighboring star systems didn't interact without there being some hostility between them."

Skalli sighed. "There was contact, many centuries ago. We developed on the same world—my world—but the Falorians wanted their own planet. So they left, went to another hospitable planet the next system over, and became Falorians. As I understand it everyone was pretty annoyed with everyone else, so there followed a custom of noncontact. Now that we have applied to the Federation and they are considering it too, though, we'll have something to talk about!"

Her expression had been unhappy when she began speaking, but by the end she had brightened back to her normal, almost unbearably cheerful self. Kirk didn't know whether to be pleased or regretful; the sad Skalli was much quieter.

The tinkling of a bell sounded, and the buzz of conversation in the hall quieted. Alexander and Julius were at the front of the room. Alexander stood behind a podium, while Julius hung back, off to the side and slightly behind his brother. Not for the first time, Kirk wondered at the difference between the three of his nephews. There was a definite physical resemblance between them all, but there the similarities stopped. Each had his own distinct personality.

Alexander almost glowed. Even when he tried to look more serious, it appeared as though it was impossible for him to wipe a delighted smile off his face.

"Good evening, ladies and gentlemen," he said. "I hope you've been enjoying the event thus far. We'll be heading in to dinner soon, but before we do, I would like to take this opportunity to thank you for your faith in Project Sanctuary. This has been a dream that my brother Julius Kirk and I have shared for many years. It's taken a lot of work, and the road has been far from easy. But we've done it.

"In approximately two weeks we will arrive on the prettiest planet I think I've ever laid eyes on. We will enjoy the natural beauty of Sanctuary. We will do our best not to despoil this lovely place. But we will also gracefully welcome her gifts. Those gifts, combined with our own skills and technology, will bring forth a society that exemplifies the best the civilized worlds have to offer. Nature and technology do not have to be opposed. Peace and progress can go hand in hand, if the minds and hearts of those who create them will it so.

"You'll have plenty of time to meet and get to know one another when we depart. The *Mayflower II* departs spacedock at oh-eight-hundred sharp. We'll all be eager to get underway and we won't be happy to wait for stragglers, so be on time!"

He grinned, and the crowd chuckled kindly, not so much at Alex's humor as at his obvious excitement and eagerness.

"Before we sit down for dinner, there is someone I'd particularly like to thank. Uncle Jim, where are you?"

Damn, Kirk thought. *More living legend nonsense.* Nonetheless, he forced a smile on his face and waved. Alex's lit up even more, if such a thing was possible.

"Folks, I'd like to introduce you to my uncle, James T. Kirk. Most of you have heard of him. I'm delighted to say that he will be joining us for at least a few months. Let's see what we can do to convince him to stay longer, shall we?"

And to Kirk's utter chagrin, Alex began to applaud. Julius joined in. For an uncomfortable moment, they were the only ones clapping, but slowly the others started to applaud as well, though with an obvious lack of enthusiasm. Kirk smiled graciously, waved a bit, and waited for the noise to subside.

He was beginning to regret this. He had a feeling he was in for a long several months.

Despite Alex's warning, the *Mayflower II* left spacedock late at 0934. It settled into a steady warp five and soon left the Sol system behind.

Shortly afterward, a cloaked Klingon bird-of-prey, careful to keep its presence undetected, began to follow.

Chapter Seven

Kirk hadn't been aboard for fifteen minutes when the trouble started. He, Scott, and Chekov were unpacking in the cramped quarters that would serve as home for the duration of the trip. None of the three had shared such close quarters with anyone else for a long time, and there was much joking and bumping of elbows. They left the door open and at one point Scott was looking down the corridor.

"Ah, looks like there's someone coming to see us," he remarked.

Kirk's head came up. "Female?"

"Aye."

Kirk swore underneath his breath. Would Skalli never leave him alone? He backed off to the side and said in a whisper, "Tell her I'm not here." Damn it, she ought to at least let him unpack before she came to harass him.

Scott and Chekov looked at him oddly, then Scott shrugged. He stepped into the doorway and leaned against the frame, effectively blocking Skalli's entrance. Kirk flattened himself against a wall.

"Hey," said a voice that was definitely not Skalli's. "Name's Kate Gallagher."

"The captain's not here," Scott said, and at the same time, Kirk stepped forward to greet the new visitor. There was an awkward silence. Kirk smiled faintly, embarrassed at having been caught trying to duck someone.

The human female who stood just outside the doorway had short brown hair, wore the loose khaki pants and white sleeveless shirt that served as an informal uniform here, and had no jewelry or cosmetics on. Her frame was lean and wiry, and judging by the collection of freckles on her face she'd spent a lot of time in the sun. She stuck out a callused hand.

Kirk hesitated for just a moment at the incredible informality, realized he'd better get used to it, and shook the proffered hand. "I'm Jim Kirk."

"Yeah, I know. Looks like you are here after all. Nice to meet—" Gallagher broke off in midsentence, staring past Kirk at the half-unpacked suitcase on the cot.

"Is there a problem?" Kirk asked.

"Yeah," she said, as if he were stupid. Gallagher pointed at the phaser. "That. We don't allow weapons. I'm surprised you were able to smuggle it aboard."

Kirk bridled at the implication that he had sneaked the weapon on. "Alex knows I have it. He gave us special permission." The ship, of course, had ample defense technology, but regarding additional weapons Alex had made it clear that as far as he was concerned there was no need for them, not even to protect themselves from the planet's native creatures, and to arrive in a place called Sanctuary bristling with tools of violence would only send the wrong message to the Falorians. Kirk's nephew had relented, very reluctantly, for the three Starfleet men only because Kirk had told him that he and his two friends would either have handheld phasers or they wouldn't come.

"This is a peaceful mission," Gallagher said, her eyes going hard and flinty. "We don't need weapons where we're going. Biggest predator there is a *miyanlak*. It's about the size of a coyote and very shy."

"Look, Kate," Kirk began in a placating tone, but Gallagher had obviously found something else about which to wax wroth.

"Oh, my God," she said, "is that *fur?*" She pointed at something furry and plaid in Scott's bag.

"Aye, that's rabbit fur. It's a sporran," Scott said defensively. "It's been passed down in my family for almost two hundred years. It's part of my formal dress uniform."

Kate laughed, but it wasn't a friendly sound. She crossed her hands over her chest in a defensive posture. "You know, I was going to give you guys the benefit of the doubt. I thought you'd at least try to respect our beliefs, work with us. You bring weapons, dead animals—I just don't know."

She turned and stalked out. Kirk stared after her, hardly believing the whirlwind of rudeness and aggression that had just swept through the tiny cabin.

"Well," Chekov said, "I feel so welcome now."

"Ah," Scott said, as if he'd just figured that out. "That's Kate then, is it?"

"What do you know about her? Other than that she's blunter than a Klingon," Kirk asked.

"Great lover of peace, that one. And beasties. I remember reading her bio—she's devoted to figuring out ways to protect endangered species. Can't suppose I blame the lassie. In this day and age, we don't need to make coats out o' their fur. But I tell you, Captain, this wee bunny would have been dead a long time ago o' natural causes."

"Don't let her get to you, Scotty. We knew we'd rub some people the wrong way. I'm sure that once we get to know these people, it'll all work out."

He was sure of nothing of the sort.

During the trip, the old *Enterprise* crew members did indeed get to know some of the colonists. A few seemed approachable: Dr. Leah Cohen, an oceanographer; Alys Harper, a linguist and communications expert; the head geologist Mark Veta; and Dr. Theodore Simon, the medical doctor for the colony. Others, like Gallagher, the Talgart botanist Mattkah, and the taciturn engineer Kevin Talbot, seemed to take an instant and permanent dislike to the three Starfleet officers. The rest fell into a swirl of names and faces that never particularly stood out. They would come to the mess hall, eat quickly, and scurry back to their quarters.

The only exceptions were, of course, Skalli, who ambushed Kirk for chats repeatedly, and Alex. Alexander alone sought out his uncle and his friends. When he was with Kirk, the others all relaxed and risked friendly smiles and hellos. They followed his lead almost like dogs awaiting commands from their master. They might clash with one another—and Kirk was witness to a few arguments, particularly between Mattkah and Gallagher—but they all turned toward Alex like flowers to the sun. Kirk realized that Alex was, like George Washington on Earth in the eighteenth century, the "indispensable man." One thing he seemed to do with ease was bring disparate people together and focus them on a mutually beneficial goal.

Kirk, Scott, and Chekov found themselves seeking out one another's company almost constantly. At first, Kirk thought it was his imagination, but when both Scott and Chekov ruefully reported their own litany of polite refusals and occasional downright snubs, Kirk realized something he should have seen before: Among this group of peace-loving scientists and engineers, Starfleet's comparatively martial presence just wasn't welcome.

"How ironic," Kirk mused over lunch one day. As usual, he, Chekov, and Scotty were sitting by themselves. "I can't count the number of times that I've said the words 'we mean you no harm' or 'we are a peaceful people' in various alien encounters over the years, but that seems to count for nothing here."

"When I was first officer aboard the *Reliant*," Chekov said, "I had to work closely with the scientific types. They are not easy to get to know, but they are good people."

"And an engineer is an engineer," Scott said between mouthfuls of reconstituted stew-like substance.

"Scientist, Starfleet, peace lover, what have you. Scratch the surface of an engineer, and you'll find a heart of dilithium." His eyes crinkled at his joke, and even Kirk smiled a little.

"I'm certain we'll find that we have more in common than we think once we reach Sanctuary and get to work," Kirk said. "We'll be living together, working alongside one another. Our differences won't seem so great once we're working toward a common goal."

He knew his voice rang with assurance, but he had his doubts. And he was to be proved right.

The enormous transport that was the *Mayflower II* settled with surprising gentleness on the planet's surface. Kirk had had plenty of time alone to familiarize himself with what to expect.

Sanctuary was a Class-M planet, with all of the attendant climates that usually included. They had landed in the northern hemisphere in a temperate zone that would be pleasantly warm in the summers and occasionally snowy in the winters. Small teams utilizing the single shuttle called the *Drake* would explore in detail other climates, some of which, such as the desert area with its deadly sandstorms, were hostile indeed. That in-depth level of exploration and possible expansion was slated for what the colonists called Year Two. Today, the landing, was Day One of Year One. Kirk thought this new numbering of days and years was a bit silly, but the colonists liked it, so he said nothing.

There would be plenty of time to settle in before the winter approached; it was late spring, and when Kirk stepped out onto Sanctuary's soil for the first time, the smells that teased his nostrils made him smile. For the first time since they'd left Earth, he felt excited and hopeful about the project's success again. It was truly a beautiful place.

Standing ready to greet them were six beings that Kirk assumed were Falorians. Standing Crane had been right. They did resemble the Huanni, which of course made sense if indeed both species had originated on the same planet, as Skalli had said. But they were different, too; stockier, less animated in their movements. He smiled and automatically stepped forward, but a gentle hand on his arm stayed him.

"Julius has had the dealings with the Falorians, Uncle Jim," Alex said softly. "He should be the one to address them first."

Of course, Alex was right. "Sorry," Kirk said. "Old habits die hard."

He stood next to Alex, taking his cues from his nephew, as the colonists, all 108 of them, exited the *Mayflower II.* He expected them to form a line, but instead they all clustered together, talking animatedly. Kirk frowned to himself. This was hardly the way to greet one's host. A more formal appearance was called for. He bit his tongue.

Julius was the last one out. Kirk was certain this wasn't accidental. The young man ran lightly down the steps and stretched out a hand to one of the Falorians.

"Kal-Tor Lissan," Julius said. "It is good to see you again."

"And you, Julius Kirk," the Falorian leader said

politely. Kirk assumed Kal-Tor was a title, but not a military one, much like "chieftain" or "leader" or "head." "We have long looked forward to this day."

Lissan was speaking with Julius, but his large, dark eyes were scanning the crowd. "Permit me to introduce my brother," Julius said. "Alexander, this is Kal-Tor Lissan, the person I've been in negotiations with."

"Julius speaks of you often and highly, Kal-Tor," Alex said, stepping forward to shake the alien's hand. "We are so grateful that you have entrusted us with Sanctuary. We will take good care of her."

"I'm certain you will," Lissan replied politely. His eyes fell upon Kirk. "Forgive me, but . . . do I detect a family resemblance with this person here as well?"

"You do," Alex said. "This is my uncle, Captain James T. Kirk."

"Ah," Lissan said, nodding. "Even out here on the edge of Federation space, we have heard of the famous Captain Kirk. We are honored to have you here, Captain."

"It's an honor to be here, Kal-Tor," Kirk replied. "I understand you are in negotiations to join the Federation. I wish you every success. You have shown good faith thus far."

Lissan seemed flattered and inclined his head. "We are eager to become a part of such a fine organization of worlds. Your people will see that we have much to offer." His eyes narrowed a little as he regarded Skalli, who was practically jumping up and down. "I see that you have brought a neighbor. What is your name, Huanni child?"

"I'm Skalli Jksili, Kal-Tor," she said, bowing deeply. "As a member of this colony, and especially as a Huanni, I look forward to getting to know you and your people better." For her, it was an extraordinarily restrained response. Kirk was surprised.

"We will be visiting from time to time, to discuss how things are progressing," Lissan said. "Perhaps there will be a chance for us to converse then. In the meantime, I see that you have much to do. Julius, you know how to contact us if you have problems."

He touched a bright button on his robe. "Please transport," he said, and he and the others vanished.

"Wow!" Skalli yelped, her composure evaporating like dew beneath a strong sun. "That was a Falorian! A real, live, Falorian! I can't believe it!"

"Believe it," Kirk said, putting a restraining hand on her slim shoulder. "Come on. Let's unpack and make this place home."

Despite the assurances of Kal-Tor Lissan, the colonists did not see a great deal of the Falorians, and most of them seemed to like it that way. The first few days were filled with the practical necessities of simply getting the colony up and running.

Most of the *Mayflower II*'s vast storage space had been devoted to materials that were now put to good use in constructing sound, stylish shelters. Part of the ship itself was broken down as well. They would need to keep her in flying order in case of an emergency evacuation, of course, but she could be largely stripped and much of her parts utilized. No rustic log cabins here; all was new, gleaming, and very high-tech.

In keeping with Alex's sentiment that he wanted this colony to feel like a family, there was only one large building. In the center was a room that could accommodate all the colonists with ease. Here was where reports on progress would be given and where weekly meetings would be held. Right off this room was a mess hall, with a large pantry to store food harvested from Sanctuary's bounty and top-of-the-line equipment for preparing it. The entire left section of the compound was composed of labs and testing areas; the right-hand side, of living quarters. Kirk was quite relieved when he learned that he would have a private room, although when he saw it, he thought it smaller than his ready room aboard the *Enterprise*.

A staggering quantity of delicate, complex equipment was hauled out and set up in the testing areas. Scott, who was finally actually able to get his hands on some of these technological beauties, was openly in awe of them. This endeared him to his fellow engineers, most of whom had had a hand in creating the obviously admired technology.

There was a wide-open field right in front of the building. When there was time, people dragged out chairs to watch the sunset before heading in to dinner. It had gotten the name of the Courtyard, although it wasn't one in the real sense of the word, and as names often do, this one stuck.

There was a new sense of camaraderie as the colonists worked together to build their new homes and workplaces. But once they had finished construction, the colonists dove for their laboratories like gophers for their holes, and Kirk again felt the discomfort he had experienced while they had traveled to get here.

He had expected that Skalli would be a complete nuisance, but she turned out to be only a moderate one. With her eidetic memory and the staggering rate at which she was able to absorb information, she quickly became rather popular among the Sanctuarians, as the colonists had taken to calling themselves. She flitted easily from engineering to chemistry to medicine to geothermal mapping, and was clearly enjoying herself immensely. Her eyes still lit up whenever Kirk entered a room, however, and whenever she had a free moment she would seek him out. But she was in great demand, and her time was rarely her own. Kirk imagined that eventually, once they had learned to control their emotions to some degree, the Huanni would be very valuable contributors to the Federation.

Even his old friends Scotty and Chekov were less frequent companions than he had expected. He wasn't surprised that Scotty had been so taken with the bright and shiny new engineering technology that was going to be experimented with and perfected here on Sanctuary; this was, after all, the man who had been delighted to be confined to quarters because it gave him a chance to catch up on his technical journals. It was Chekov's interest in, and proficiency with, scientific research that had surprised Kirk. He had clearly learned much as first officer aboard the *Reliant,* and despite his protests about wanting his own captaincy, was clearly enjoying himself.

For the first few nights, once they had erected such things as private quarters, Kirk and his nephews had dined together. It had been awkward and strained, more so than their midnight encounter a few weeks ago when they had turned up on Kirk's doorstep. This, however, did not surprise Kirk.

Up until this colonial venture, Kirk had been in command, wherever he was. Over many years he had come to accept, embrace, and excel in his role as a natural leader. Now, he wasn't sure *where* he fit in. Alexander was the founder and head of the colony, and clearly everyone adored him.

He had no particular interest in science or medicine, and any knowledge and training he had was hopelessly outdated when compared to the "it was just discovered last week" experience of this group. He had learned his way around the engine room of a starship, but he couldn't even begin to guess what those coils, pulsating colors, and humming sounds meant.

Alex had insisted that having the family together— what they could cobble together of it, anyway—was important to him, and Kirk had no doubt that Alex had meant it at the time. Alexander Kirk was like his father, nothing if not sincere and earnest. But the reality was that with Kirk present, Alex would be upstaged if he didn't assert his authority often and clearly. Kirk didn't blame the younger man; he'd have done the same in his position. An expedition like this needed a clear leader.

As for raising their profile with Starfleet and the Federation in general, Kirk had already done all he could. Now they were stuck out here on this rock, lovely though it was, and Kirk realized he wanted nothing more than to go back home. Even his apartment in San Francisco would be better than here; at least there, he was surrounded by familiar and loved things.

But Jim Kirk liked nothing better than a challenge, and so he determined that he would win over some of the people who seemed the least likely to befriend him. His first target was Kate Gallagher. He had downloaded her bio from the computer, and had to admit she was impressive. She was only thirty-four and had already won seven major awards, including the coveted Peace Star for Humanitarian Achievement. Gallagher was deeply passionate about her work, and Kirk figured that that much, at least, they had in common.

She kept the lab door open all the time, but Kirk knocked gently on the wall nonetheless. Kate turned from the computer, saw who it was, and a look of irritation crossed her sharp features.

"Thought even you would figure out that if a door was left open you could come in," she said.

"Just trying to be polite," Kirk said. "I've been reading your bio, Kate."

"It's a free colony," she said, keeping her eyes on the screen. Her short-nailed fingers flew over the keyboard as she entered data.

"I'm very impressed. Why didn't you tell us you had won the Peace Star?"

"I know stuff like that matters to you Starfleet people, but I don't give a damn about it," she said.

"You give a damn about protecting innocent creatures," Kirk said, refusing to rise to the bait. "You were the only one who believed the Vree rats were sentient. You saved an entire species from being relocated—which would have led to their extinction."

Now she did turn and look at him. "Yeah," she said. "The rest of the team wanted to clear them out to study the other flora and fauna. Wanted to transport them across the planet to a comparable temperate zone."

"And you proved that doing so would remove them from their sole source of nourishment—insects that had fed on a certain type of honey. You believed, against every available shred of evidence, that those small rodents were intelligent."

"Thank God there was a Vulcan in the group willing to do a mind-meld," she said.

"Ever heard of the Horta?"

Kate looked down. Her cheeks were red. "Yeah."

"Kind of a similar situation, don't you think?"

"Jim, I've read your bio, too. About the Horta . . . and about all the space battles in which you participated."

"I'm not in battle now, and I don't want to be. Truce?"

She glowered, but she didn't say no. Encouraged, Kirk asked, "I hear you're working on something quite remarkable. Something that could protect endangered species all across the galaxy."

"I call it the Masker," Gallagher said. Was Kirk mistaken or was that the beginning of a smile playing at the edge of her lips? "Hundreds of years ago we tagged animals with primitive means, to keep track of their progress. We still do it now, though, of course, with a much less invasive method. There are so many animals that are being poached across the galaxy it just makes me sick. We can only do so much, but I got to thinking—today's poacher finds his prey by scanning for its signs on a tricorder. What if we tagged animals so that their signal was masked? It wouldn't be that hard—just insert a small chip under the skin that sends out a signal that confuses a tricorder. Suddenly, they're invisible."

"Of course, each species has a different type of tricorder," Kirk pointed out. "A signal that would confuse a Federation tricorder wouldn't protect an animal from a Klingon using his people's tricorder."

Her thin shoulders sagged. "Yeah, and that's the problem."

"Kate, I think it's a brilliant idea," Kirk said, and meant it. "Our Mr. Scott might be able to help you out a bit, if you'd let him know you were interested."

She hesitated. "I'll think about it." She turned back to the computer and Kirk knew he'd been dismissed. He turned to leave.

"Hey, Jim?"

He turned around. "Yes?"

She smiled, fully this time. "Good job with the Horta."

Chapter Eight

Encouraged by his progress with Gallagher, Kirk then tried to warm up to some of the others. He eventually was able to talk pleasantly with Cohen and Harper. The geologist, Mark Veta, also warmed up to him. Kirk tried, but couldn't share the man's enthusiasm for discussing the cave system that apparently riddled Sanctuary. Although at one point, when Veta asked if he was interested in spelunking, Kirk felt the first rush of pleasure he'd had since they had left Earth. Mattkah had apparently taken an extreme dislike to Kirk and Dr. Sherman's cool, formal demeanor did nothing but remind Kirk of how much he missed his old friend McCoy's folksy good humor.

Kirk's help was apparently not welcome in graphing the weather patterns, something of vital import in a world that had sudden flooding and sandstorms that could come out of nowhere and scour bones clean in five minutes. It was not welcome in charting this world's stars. It was not welcome in biology or botany or geology or engineering.

After the third week, when most of his attempts to assist had been politely but obviously rebuffed, Kirk learned that the Falorians were coming to visit and discuss the colony's progress. *I'm not much of a diplomat, but I've had more experience than these boys,* he thought. Perhaps this was a way he could contribute. Hell, Alex had even suggested as much.

The Falorians were to materialize in the same spot. Julius was already there to meet them, his hands clasping and unclasping as he paced back and forth. Kirk raised an eyebrow. Impatient boy, that one. He stepped forward. Julius froze in midstride and whirled to look at him.

"Uncle Jim," he said, clearly surprised. "What are you doing here?"

Kirk smiled. "I'm an old hand at negotiations," he said as mildly as he could. He didn't want to step on Julius's toes, and wasn't certain that his expertise would be welcomed. "I thought I might be able to assist."

Julius continued to glare, the surprised expression on his sharp features turning into annoyance. "I've been negotiating with the Falorians for some time now. I doubt I'll need any assistance." As an afterthought, he added, "Thanks, though."

Kirk decided to be as honest as possible. "Julius, I respect your familiarity with this matter. But," and he laughed a little self-deprecatingly, "I'm finding it hard to find a place here where I can contribute. You asked me to come here. You all but demanded it," he reminded his nephew. "So, I'm here. I came, as you wanted. Let me help."

Kirk couldn't read the myriad of emotions that flickered across Julius's face. Finally, the young man opened his mouth to answer. At that moment, Kirk heard the distinctive hum of a transporter and Lissan, along with two others, shimmered into existence.

Lissan blinked and drew his head back slightly. "Captain Kirk," he said. "I did not expect to see you here. My meeting was with Julius."

Before Kirk could say anything, Julius interjected smoothly, "My uncle and I were exchanging pleasantries. He was just leaving." He turned and smiled. "I'll see you back at the colony for dinner this evening, Uncle."

The smile was pleasant, kind even, but Julius's blue eyes glittered like chips of ice. Kirk forced a smile onto his own face.

"Certainly, Julius. Until then."

It was obvious that Kirk's expertise would not be welcome in dealing with the Falorians.

After that conversation, Kirk decided he would benefit from a walk around the perimeter of the colony. The sun was just starting to set and it was quiet and peaceful. He shrugged into a light jacket against the chill of the evening and strode forth.

He moved briskly, not wanting to run for fear of spoiling the quietude but wanting more than a stroll. It smelled so fresh out here. He was reminded of his many camping trips and an idea occurred to him. Perhaps he could be useful as part of a scouting trip. All he'd need would be a tricorder, shelter, a knife and a pan to cook in. It would be a challenge to learn how to find and harvest the abundant foodstuffs Sanctuary offered, and sleep under the stars of this new world.

The more he thought about it the better the idea seemed. He breathed deeply of the cool twilight scents and felt himself calming down. These weren't Starfleet personnel; they were scientists, researchers, engineers. People who had spent most of their lives *avoiding* contact with people just like him. It was only natural that they'd take some time to warm up. In the meantime, he thought he'd finally come up with a way to contribute.

He was striding through a field now, and the heady scents of meadow flowers wafted up to his nostrils. He was disturbing some of them, and pale little spores flew up into the cool air, drifting to another spot upon which to settle and root, continuing the circle of life. Grinning a little, he created more breezes with his arms, sending them flying away to their new homes.

He felt better by the time darkness fell and he returned to the encampment. He'd missed dinner, so he went into the mess hall to see what he could rustle up. Mattkah, the irascible botanist, was there. Did the fellow ever stop eating? He knew that Talgarts had an unusually high metabolism, of course. Once he'd overheard another colonist refer to Mattkah as "the giant shrew." He was downing an enormous bowl of oatmeal and as Kirk entered was drizzling at least a cup of honey on it.

Kirk bit his tongue against a sarcastic remark and instead said simply, "Good evening, Mattkah," as he searched the cupboard for something quick, tasty, and nutritious.

Mattkah looked up with a surly expression on his flat face and then his eyes widened in horror. "Oh, no!" he yelped.

"What?" asked Kirk. "What's wrong?"

Mattkah had risen and was now pointing directly at Kirk. "The spores! You're completely covered with them!"

Kirk looked down and saw that indeed, his jacket and pants were dotted with tiny white spores from the little plants he'd walked through. He chuckled ruefully.

"It seems I am," he agreed. "Don't worry, there's nothing dangerous in any of the plant life that we—"

"It's ruined! You clumsy oaf, you've completely ruined the experiment! We started this on the second day we were here and now it's all for nothing." Mattkah had sunk back down in his chair, his head in all four of his hands. "We'll have to start all over again. Didn't you see the markers?"

Kirk closed his eyes briefly. Clearly, the flowery meadow through which he had so blithely trod was actually an outdoor laboratory. He had seen no markers in the darkling twilight, and even if he had, he wondered if he would have noticed them.

"Mattkah, I'm sorry, I didn't know. I would never have walked through the meadow had I known you were conducting research there."

The sour look Mattkah shot him told Kirk that the Talgart didn't believe him. Clearly, in his mind, Kirk was a lumbering elephant that had nothing better to do than to go gallivanting through delicate research areas, rendering weeks of work entirely useless. He gulped the rest of his oatmeal, helped himself to an armload of native fruits, and stormed out of the mess hall.

For a long moment, Kirk just stood there. Then he slowly returned the juicy, yellow-red fruit he'd been about to bite to the bowl on the center of one of the tables.

He'd lost his appetite.

He returned to his small, cramped but at least private quarters. Lying on the small bunk, he stared at the ceiling, counting the days until the next resupply ship would arrive and he could go home, where he belonged.

There was no place for him here.

Kirk's door chimed. He blinked awake, startled, and glanced at the chronometer to see that he'd slept through breakfast. He reached for his robe, sashed it, and called, "Come in."

The door hissed open. "Well, good morning, Mr. Chekov. I apologize for my present state. What can I do for you?"

"Sorry to intrude, sir, but there's something I think you should see." Kirk smiled wryly as he observed that although he was no longer in command, he was addressing Chekov, and Chekov was responding, just as they would have aboard the *Enterprise*.

"Sit down . . . if you can. It's tight quarters here on Sanctuary," Kirk said. Chekov took one of the two small chairs and Kirk took the other one. "What is it?"

Chekov frowned. "It may be nothing," he said.

"Or it may not," Kirk said.

"Well, I'm not particularly trained to contribute scientifically, although I have been helping out. Most of the time I've been assisting Alys in downloading and sending messages," Chekov said. "You know, to loved ones back home."

Kirk nodded. He hadn't sent a single message. He had friends and acquaintances scattered throughout the galaxy, but unlike most of the colonists, there was no one on Earth—no one "back home"—he really felt like talking to.

"Subspace traffic has dramatically increased over the last four days," Chekov continued. "And I'm not certain of this, but I think . . . Captain, I believe our communications are being monitored."

"What makes you think that?"

Chekov shrugged, clearly troubled. "Nothing I can point to for certain. Little things. Echoes, blurry images, things like that."

"That's a pretty slender thread to hang charges of eavesdropping on, Lieutenant."

"I know, sir. I probably shouldn't have troubled you with this, but I didn't know who else to take it to."

Kirk leaned back, thinking. "For now, take it to no one. I want you to spend as much time as you can on sending these messages, and I want you to document every glitch you encounter. If this keeps up, we'll tell Alex about it. It could be nothing more serious than the system needing to be fixed."

"Aye, sir." Chekov rose.

"And Chekov?"

"Aye, sir?"

Kirk grinned. "Thanks for thinking of me."

Chekov returned the smile. "You were the only one I did think of, Captain."

After he had gone, Kirk showered and dressed, thinking hard. One was trained to look for the most likely answer to any problem. Chances were, the equipment simply hadn't been set up properly and there was a glitch in the system. As for subspace traffic being heavy, well, maybe this was a hot time for space travel in this sector.

Still, he trusted Chekov, and he knew the younger man wouldn't have come to Kirk about this if he hadn't had some kind of feeling that there was something wrong.

Just like the feeling Kirk was starting to have.

Scott was thoroughly enjoying himself. He was having a "day off," as he put it, though others on the engineering team would have called it a day of hard labor. He, Alex, and Skalli were going to traverse the entire planet and tune up the monitoring posts they had set in each of the Sanctuary's ecosystems. This was done once a week, whether it was needed or not, as so much of the colony's research came from these posts. In Year Two, there would be much more extensive visitation of the areas, but for now, this sufficed.

There were eight of them: One in each icy heart of the arctic circles, two along the planet's equator, and one on each continent. Oceanographer Leah Cohen had bemoaned the fact that they didn't have the technology to put a few on the ocean floor, to which Scott had gallantly replied that in a few years he was certain the brilliant engineering team would figure out a way to do so. The bonnie lassie had rewarded him with a sweet smile.

The posts retrieved data from the surrounding area twenty-seven hours a day, data that was carefully analyzed. Each week (of course, the weeks here were a long nine days and three hours) someone would come and make sure everything was functioning correctly, and now it was Scott, Alex, and Skalli's turn. Today, they were having problems with what Scott called The Desert One. Technically, it was Monitoring Post AE-584-B2, stationed in the arid climate of one of the major continents, but Scott preferred to keep things simple.

Alex was piloting, humming happily to himself, while Skalli was talking animatedly with Chekov, back at Sanctuary Heart, as the base itself was called, as the little shuttle *Drake* flew over the brown-yellow sands. Not for the first time, Scott admired the sleek design of the craft, the ease with which Alex was able to maneuver her. Aye, she was a bonnie one, all right.

His stomach rumbled. When they'd finished with this one, it would be time to take a break for lunch.

"Where's a nice spot to have our picnic?" he asked Alex. Alex grinned over his shoulder.

"There are the most spectacular waterfalls near the top of the continent," he said. "We stop for lunch every time we check out the post there and have never been disappointed yet. But you've got to keep the secret— don't want everyone volunteering for post-check duty!"

"Ooh, a waterfall!" cooed Skalli, her eyes wide with anticipation. She was oblivious to the glares Alex and Scott were giving her. "Yes, Chekov, you heard right— we're going to a waterfall for lunch when we finish. Won't that be fun!"

Scott and Alex exchanged rueful glances. "Looks like somebody let the cat out of the bag," Scott muttered.

"Yes," Skalli was saying. "We only have—Chekov? Pavel, are you there? Hello? *Drake* to Sanctuary Heart, come in. Uh oh." She turned to look at Alex. "It sounds as though we lost him."

"Skalli, come in," Chekov said urgently. "Skalli— Sanctuary Heart to *Drake,* please come in." Silence. Damn it. Once again, they'd lost communications. In frustration, Chekov slammed his fist on the console.

"Hey, take it easy," said Alys Harper, the blond human female who was serving communication duty along with Chekov. "No need to break it more than it already is."

Chekov gnawed his lower lip, then made a decision. "Alys, go find Captain Kirk."

"Kirk?" He couldn't see her expression, but he didn't need to. She managed to cram a great deal of distaste into the single syllable word. "Why? Julius is in command whenever—"

"Just go find him, all right?"

"Okay, okay, calm down, sheesh." Muttering under her breath, she left to do as he had asked. Chekov found himself longing for the days when orders were given and followed without commentary, critique, or discussion.

He took a deep breath, calmed himself, and methodically began to check everything that could possibly be wrong on his end with the communications.

He had a gut feeling he wouldn't find anything.

"Hello? Hello? Hmmm," Skalli said. "Looks like we've lost communication for some reason." She frowned, turning the problem over in her mind, then seemed to dismiss it. "Oh, well. We're almost at the post anyway."

Scott was rather more disturbed at the abrupt termination of communication than Skalli was, but she was right about one thing. Alex was already beginning their descent. He could see the landing area now, the only flat rock in a sea of sand and jagged peaks.

Alex eased the craft down smoothly and they gathered their tools, putting on their protective glasses and gloves. The sun's glare was almost unbearable, and the post would be far too hot to touch with bare hands.

"One quick check before we go," Alex said. He nodded. "Good. No sandstorms in the vicinity. We've got a window."

When Scott opened the door, a blast of heat hit him with almost palpable force. For a brief moment, he recalled with longing the chilly rainstorm that had driven him to embrace this mission. Then he took a cautious breath of the hot air and jumped down into the sand.

They had a long walk ahead of them before they would see those waterfalls.

Kirk listened attentively as Chekov described the problem and everything he'd tried to fix it. On a whim,

Kirk opened his communicator. "Kirk to Julius." Nothing.

"Our communicators aren't even working, then," Chekov said. Kirk shook his head. Chekov pointed to the screen. "This is closing in on their area and we can't even alert them to it."

Kirk looked at the monitor and his grim mood worsened. A sandstorm was starting to form. Here on Sanctuary, that was a dangerous thing indeed. "If they're still in the shuttle, they'll detect it," he said.

"But if they're not, they could be caught in the open," Chekov said. Kirk knew what the team would be wearing: the usual Sanctuary garb of comfortable pants and shirts that permitted easy movement, boots, gloves and glasses. Nothing more. Nothing that would remotely protect them from the whipping winds of a sandstorm. Not for the first time, he wished that they had a second shuttle. There would be no time to get the *Mayflower II* prepared to fly.

"Keep trying to raise them," he told Chekov. "I'm going to go find Julius."

Several long minutes were wasted in searching, since the communicators weren't working. Kirk finally found Julius in his quarters. The door chimed several times before Julius answered the door. He was tired-looking and unshaven, and seemed surprised to see Kirk.

"What is it, Uncle Jim?"

"Your brother and two other members of this colony are about to be bombarded with a violent sandstorm, and we can't reach them," Kirk said bluntly.

Julius snapped to attention. "What the—what do you mean?"

"Communications are completely off-line," Kirk said. He flipped open the dead communicator. "Even these. There's a chance that they're still in the shuttle but if they're outside in this—"

"Oh no," Julius breathed.

After a ten-minute walk—more of an ordeal than a stroll, considering the terrible heat—the team reached the post. Although they had erected a protective physical shielding around it, it was obvious that the grit of the desert's sand was taking its toll. Scott proceeded to quickly clean the internal workings and then put it through a test run. This would take about twenty minutes. It wasn't enough time for them to hike back to the shuttle, so they resigned themselves to being hot for a while. They leaned up against a rock formation and waited. Scott closed his eyes.

"Hey, what's that?" Skalli asked. She pointed to a flurry of motion in the distance.

"Uh oh," Alex said. "That looks like a dust devil." He removed his communicator and flipped it open. "Alex to Sanctuary Heart. Hey, how come you didn't warn us about this sandstorm we're . . . damn it. It's dead!"

Scott felt a chill despite the severe heat. It was conceivable that the communications had been damaged on the shuttle, but for the individual communicators to quit working meant that something had occurred on a much larger scale. He rose, staring at the dust devil that was rapidly becoming a sandstorm.

"Alex, is there anyplace we could take shelter?" he asked. *Because if there isn't,* he thought grimly, *then all a rescue party will find will be three scoured, bleached skeletons.*

Alex didn't reply. He was fiddling with the communicator, still trying to raise Sanctuary Heart. Scott's eyes flicked from the youth and his communicator to the encroaching storm.

He reached out and shook Alex by the shoulder. "Lad, we've got to take shelter!" he said, raising his voice to be heard above the rising wind.

Alex looked up at him wildly. *Poor lad,* Scott thought with a twinge of sympathy. *This is his first real crisis.* Alex had the charm and charisma to get people to follow him, but he didn't seem to know a damn thing about how to lead when the chips were down.

"Over here!" It was Skalli, jumping up and down and waving her long arms. Scott hadn't even noticed her get up, but she had clearly done so and found them protection against the storm. Scott shifted his grip to hold Alex's upper arm and hauled the young man to his feet.

The sandstorm was beginning. As they stumbled to where Skalli stood, Scott was intensely grateful for the goggles. Grit scoured his face and even though he covered his mouth and nose with his hands, he felt the fine, powdery sand slip past his lips and into his nostrils. Alex was hacking violently by the time they squeezed into the crevice. It was easy enough for Skalli, but Scott reluctantly admitted to himself he'd had one too many desserts as he nearly got wedged tight. By sheer stubbornness he forced his way inside.

There was no light save what filtered in from the crevice, and they needed to get as far away from that as possible as wind and sand continued to find their way into their shelter.

"This way!" cried Skalli. "Follow my voice!"

Alex was able to stand on his own now. Coughing and gasping for air, both men stumbled toward the back of the cave. It grew darker and darker until finally Scott could see nothing. He still walked forward as quickly as he could, arms extended to feel his way, until Skalli's slender, gloved fingers closed about his hands and guided him forward to sit on the floor.

They could still hear the wind crying and moaning like a wounded beast. Pressed together for warmth, for the cave was cold after the unforgiving heat outside, Scott felt Skalli shiver.

"It's scary," she said, voicing something that would probably have gotten her kicked off Kirk's bridge. "It sounds like a monster or something."

Scott was not inclined to reprimand her, as she was directly responsible for all of them surviving this in the first place. "Good job, lass," he said, squeezing her shoulder.

Alexander Kirk, who had coaxed over a hundred people to pack up and move in pursuit of a dream, and who had completely panicked at the first sign of a real problem, said nothing.

Chapter Nine

"I don't care if Lissan isn't scheduled to return for three days, I want him here *now*." Kirk was aware that he was close to bellowing but frankly didn't give a damn. They still hadn't been able to communicate with the away team and had watched in quiet apprehension as the fierce storm had settled directly over the monitoring post for almost two hours. Kirk and the others knew that if the party had been caught outside, they'd be dead by now.

"But you don't understand," said Julius, flushing a little. "I can't just order them to—"

"Fine. Then I will," Kirk shot back.

"Hey," snapped Julius, stepping in toward Kirk and looking him in the eye. "I'm the one who deals with the Falorians. You keep your Starfleet nose out of it."

Kirk smiled without humor. "I seem to recall that my Starfleet nose—or at least my Starfleet self—was one of the things you and your brother desperately wanted to get to Sanctuary."

He took a deep breath and calmed himself. He reached to put his hands on Julius's shoulders but the youth angrily shook them off.

"Julius, listen to me. Something is going on that is causing our communications to be disrupted. Because of it we weren't able to warn the team about the sandstorm. They could be dead as a result of that. It's your own brother. Aren't you worried?"

Julius's blue eyes continued to bore into Kirk's, but a muscle in his jaw tightened. "It could be equipment malfunction," he said, sounding to Kirk's ears like a stubborn child.

"We've checked everything out. Besides, that wouldn't take into account the communicators," Kirk replied. "Something external is jamming the frequencies. I'm not accusing the Falorians of anything. I'm sure they don't even realize what's going on, but I'm also sure that they are the ones responsible, even if it's indirectly. Now, will you contact them or shall I?"

Julius's shoulders drooped slightly. "I'll do it," he said. "Once we have communication again."

Uncle and nephew stood side by side in the communications room for the next twenty-three minutes, arms folded across their chests in almost identical poses, until with a burst of static a welcome, lively female voice was heard.

"—Heart. Come in, Sanctuary Heart. Repeat, we have minor injuries and are returning to home base, do you copy?"

With a relieved grin, Kirk leaned forward to reply. Julius's hand blocked the motion and the younger Kirk said, "We read you loud and clear, Skalli. What is the nature of your injuries? Is everyone accounted for?"

"We're fine, Juley," came Alex's voice, turning warm with affection. "We lost communications and were right at the monitoring post when the storm hit. I've no doubt you saw it on your sensors."

"We did indeed," Julius said. "Pretty big one."

"We have some minor dermal abrasions but were able to find shelter in time," Alex continued.

"Thank God for that," Julius said, sounding more sincere than Kirk had ever heard him. He glanced at his nephew and saw that Julius was pale and shaking a little. And were those tears he was blinking back? For the first time, Kirk realized just how deeply these two brothers were bonded.

"Did you figure out what was causing the malfunction?"

Julius, who was leaning over the console, looked up at Kirk. The cautious, hard mask was back in place. "Not exactly," he said. "We think perhaps the Falorians may have accidentally jammed the signal. We're going to try to talk to them."

"Good thinking, Julius," Alex said approvingly.

Julius scowled.

When the shuttle finally arrived, Julius hurried to embrace his brother. Six engineers scuttled out to attend to the *Drake,* looking for all the world like busy ants. Kirk felt a strong hand on his arm and glanced up to see Scott propelling him to a quiet corner.

"What happened out there, Scotty?" Kirk asked.

"Your nephew cracked," Scott said. "He's a good lad,

mind, and I'm not passing judgment, but he panicked."

"You were the one who found the shelter, then?"

"Och, no, can't take that credit. Young Skalli kept her wits about her and found it for us."

Surprised and impressed, Kirk looked up to see Skalli talking with Chekov, waving her arms, flapping her ears, and pointing back at the shuttle.

"Good for her. How bad was Alex?" he asked quietly.

Scott shrugged. "Och, he'll be fine for the most part. But let me say I'm glad we're here if there's any real trouble."

Julius was able to reach Lissan, who showed up by evening the next day. Kirk, who had agreed to let Julius do most of the talking but had insisted on being present, was champing at the bit but managed to restrain himself. Communications continued to be erratic, and Kirk knew it was by sheer luck that he hadn't lost three crewmen, including his nephew, the first Huanni to attend Starfleet Academy, and one of his oldest, dearest friends.

Lissan materialized in the Courtyard. "Good evening," he said. "Julius, it is good to see you again. Alexander, let me express my pleasure that you are all right. Ah, and Captain. It is good to see you again as well. Julius has informed me of your communication difficulties. It's rather embarrassing, but . . . well, I'm afraid they're not going to end any time soon."

"Why not?" Kirk said, before he could stop himself. Julius glared at him.

"We are planning to reopen an old facility on the

other side of the planet," Lissan continued. "You have inspired us with your colony, you see. We realized that we, too, could make use of Sanctuary."

"It was my understanding that you had given Sanctuary to us, freely, as a goodwill gesture," Alex said.

"And so we have! We will do nothing to hinder you, Alexander. You won't even know we're here."

"Well, it's difficult not to know you're here when your facility is interfering with our ability to communicate with anyone off world," Kirk said. He was just going to ignore Julius. "What kind of facility are we talking about?"

"Merely a resupply base for trading with various cargo ships."

"That accounts for the increase in subspace communication," Julius said, as if it explained everything.

"What about the problems in our communications?" Kirk pressed.

"We have erected a shield over the trading facility, and it appears to be that which is interfering with your communications," Lissan said.

"A shield? To protect you from what?" Kirk continued.

Lissan looked embarrassed. "Well, you see, Captain . . . some people with whom we trade are . . . one hates to say it . . . not entirely trustworthy, and might attempt to take cargo on without paying for it. The shield prevents them from absconding with anything of value. They have to be let in and out, one at a time. There is no chance of anyone attempting a quick transport that way."

It made sense, but there was still something wrong about the explanation to Kirk. Julius had given up trying to interrupt and now simply leaned back in his chair, arms folded across his chest, and an obvious, open scowl on his face. Alex leaned forward, clearly interested in following the discussion.

"I see your predicament," Kirk said, hoping to put the alien at ease.

"Not everyone is as honest as the Federation and the Sanctuary colonists," Lissan said generously.

"Clearly you need this shield. Equally clearly, we need to communicate with our friends and families. Is there any way you can change the shield's frequency so it doesn't interfere with our signals?"

Again, Lissan looked uncomfortable and apologetic. "Our technology is not nearly as advanced as yours. I regret to inform you that for now at least, we can only operate the shield on this specific frequency."

Keeping an open, honest expression on his face, Kirk spread his arms in an all-encompassing gesture. "It is my understanding that the reason you were willing to host this colony is to promote open exchange. Isn't that right, Alex?"

"Oh, yes!" Alex said eagerly. "We'd be happy to help you! It would be an honor to be able to assist our benefactors."

"We have a dozen or more highly skilled engineers, including one I can personally vouch for," Kirk continued. "We'd be happy to send them over to your . . . facility . . . and make whatever adjustments are necessary."

"Captain, you and Alex are most generous," Lissan

said warmly. "But you have set us a challenge, you see."

"You mean, this is something you want to do on your own?" Julius said before either Alex or Kirk could speak.

"Precisely," Lissan said. "You are an inspiration to our own scientists. We would like to tackle this problem ourselves."

"But it would be so much quicker if—" began Alex, but his brother interrupted him.

"Come on, Alex! The Falorians have been so helpful to us in getting us Sanctuary and as Lissan says, we've been an inspiration to them. You don't want to take the thrill of discovery away from them, do you?"

"Please don't," Lissan said. "Trust us—when we are, how do you put it, at the end of our rope, we won't hesitate to contact you! In the meantime, we will enjoy figuring this out on our own."

"How long will it be until you reach the end of your rope?" Kirk demanded.

For the first time since Kirk had seen him, Lissan appeared to be caught offguard. "I really have no idea. I—"

"Give me your best guess."

"A—a few weeks," Lissan said.

Kirk had more to say—a lot more. But Julius stepped forward quickly. "Then it's settled," Julius said firmly. "The Falorians will work it out on their own and they'll ask for help if things don't look promising. Thanks, Uncle Jim, Alex. Lissan, I do have some questions on the specifics of something. A word?"

The two walked away together, chatting quietly. Alex smiled. "Well, that problem is solved."

"I hope so," Kirk said, but as he watched the alien and his nephew bow their heads together in close conversation, he had his doubts.

"So," Alexander said to his brother as they dined together late that night on leftover salad and pasta, "Everything *is* okay, isn't it?"

Julius sopped up some tomato sauce with his bread and popped it into his mouth. Chewing, he replied, "Oh, yeah. Everything's fine. The Falorians aren't as technologically advanced as we are, you know, so there are bound to be some glitches when they try something new." He twirled spaghetti around his fork. "Plenty of time to help them out when they get stuck and ask for our help."

"I never would have thought about it that way," Alex said. "But I suppose that's part of diplomacy, isn't it? Helping the other species save face."

"They're a good people, but are a little embarrassed about their personal lack of technology," Julius said facilely, pouring his third glass of robust red wine. "It's best to let them try everything they can first."

"You're right, as usual," smiled Alex. "You really do know these people well, don't you?"

"Yes," said Julius. "I do."

That night, as he lay in bed, Julius couldn't sleep. He tossed and turned, alternately sweating and chilled.

It had been close, today. Far too close for comfort.

Alex could have died out there, and the Falorians hadn't said anything to Julius about jamming their communications.

He knew their messages were being monitored, of course. They had been since the beginning, but earlier, at least, Lissan and his cohorts had been very careful to disguise it. If Kirk hadn't brought that Russian along on the trip, Julius doubted if it would ever have been detected.

Damn Kirk! Always getting in the way, always acting so smug and superior with his "Starfleet does it *this* way" attitude. *Well, I've got news for you, Uncle Jim. You're not in Starfleet anymore. You're out here, in the wilderness, all alone.*

Julius groped for the cup of water on the bedside table and downed a large gulp. He badly wanted something alcoholic, but was smart enough to know that he'd drunk enough at dinner and would be feeling it if he didn't switch to water.

Lying back down on the pillow, he thought about his childhood and Kirk's part—or lack of a part—in it. Alex hadn't lied to Kirk about their boyhood with the Pearsons, but he hadn't told him everything, either. There had been no abuse, as far as it went. Neither foster parent had laid a hand on them. But they hadn't needed to in order to break them sufficiently.

They left the boys alone almost all the time. They ignored Alex and Julius when they could, said sharp, cruel things to them when they couldn't. Alex tried everything to get the Pearsons' attention and love: taking good care of Julius, earning excellent grades, taking on odd jobs. Nothing worked. Julius's tactics, which consisted of cutting classes, getting into trouble, and offering what Mrs. Pearson called "sassy backtalk" did get attention, but the wrong kind.

Alex had made the meals and told Julius bedtime stories. Alex had protected him from the bullies, and helped him with his homework. Alex had listened with a loving smile when Julius went through agonies about which little girl liked him and which didn't. Alex was the sun around which Julius revolved.

And every now and then, their Uncle Jim would show up. He was a kindly, but distant presence. He often brought gifts that served only to show how little he knew what his nephews were interested in. Julius hated him, because he knew—he *knew*—that life with Uncle Jim raising them would be sweeter and happier than life with the Pearsons, and Uncle Jim never offered to take them away and care for them.

Alexander had a forgiving nature, and he never blamed Uncle Jim for not saving them. *He's a starship captain, Juley. They can't have kids on starships.*

But Julius never forgot, nor forgave. And now Uncle Jim was here. Damn the Falorians! Why had they made that the deal-breaker?

He'd done everything they wanted. Even served some time in a pretty bad alien prison getting the things they had asked for. A few times, he'd try to talk to other species about colonies, but those were all dead ends.

He reached for the water again. He was getting the shakes just thinking about some of the places he'd been. Places he had willingly gone into for Alex's sake, places that Alex would have died rather than have Julius enter.

Gunrunner. Though the weapons to which the name referred were obsolete, the name had stuck through the centuries. It had sounded exciting, romantic, and as far away from anything the Pearsons represented as it was possible to get. And at first, it had been fun.

Why the hell had he gotten involved with the Orion Syndicate? The answer came back, *because they were the only ones who could get me what I wanted—a colony for Alexander.* Looking back on it, he could see each step down that dark path had led him to the next, and the next. He couldn't believe he was now trading in illegal weapons and information when the goal had been to found a colony of peace and technology.

God, if Alex ever found out. . . .

Julius reached again for the water and this time knocked it over. He swore, grabbed a towel, and began mopping it up. He realized he was shaking.

He kept replaying the conversation he'd had with Lissan today. *What the hell is going on?* he had demanded, forcing a smile so false his mouth hurt. *My brother almost got killed today! And what kind of facility is really going up? You said nothing about that!*

Lissan had looked at him with those large, cold eyes, devoid of any emotion save perhaps a flicker of amusement. *The danger to which your brother was exposed was not intended.*

It damn well better not have been. I won't budge on that. No harm comes to Alex, and he never knows about us. He was not the best of liars and he knew it, and it was a real struggle to appear to be having a pleasant chat with this alien when he really wanted to rip his throat out. But the appearance must be maintained. . . .

What is going on with this facility?

Lissan had smiled. *The less you know, the better.*

Julius swore an old, ugly Anglo-Saxon word. *I got you everything you wanted. Weapons. Information. Technology. Even Kirk, damn it. I gave my own uncle to you. I have to know what's going on.*

Lissan's unpleasant smile had widened. *No you don't, Julius. No you don't.*

And Lissan had stepped away, ending the conversation. Julius had stared. To follow him and pursue it would have tipped Kirk off. Alex, bless him, wouldn't have noticed, but Kirk would. Kirk would.

Julius didn't know what this mysterious facility was really for, but from what he knew of the Falorians and their goals, he knew its purpose wouldn't be that of innocently catering to trading vessels.

He had finally thought himself safe for the first time in his life. Safe and sound at last, on Sanctuary, with his brother. He'd sold his soul to pursue Alex's dream for him, and damn it, that ought to have been enough.

But it wasn't.

Julius Kirk didn't fall asleep until the small hours of the morning, and when he did, he dreamed of Alexander looking at him with sorrowful disillusionment in his eyes just before a cackling Lissan, firing the very weapons Julius had obtained for him, killed them both.

Chapter Ten

The representative of the Orion Syndicate known to Lissan only as 858 looked around speculatively at the spartan quarters that served as a conference room. There was only a single desk covered with padds and a computer, two chairs, and a dented old box shoved into a corner. His green lips curved in a smile that was more condescending than appreciative.

"Nice place," he said, and Lissan could hear the sarcasm in the words.

"It suffices," he said, his voice clipped.

"Aren't you going to offer me anything to drink? A little local delicacy to snack on, perhaps?"

"No," Lissan said.

"All right then. Let's get to business." He leaned forward and the humor had vanished. "You're behind schedule."

"It's been unavoidable," Lissan replied.

858 sighed. "You've been telling us that for too long already."

"It was the Syndicate's idea to have Captain Kirk come along," Lissan reminded him. "He's been nothing but trouble."

The dark, steady gaze of the Orion male was unsettling. "Let us hope," 858 said softly, "that he does not suspect. Otherwise, *you* are going to be in a great *deal* of trouble."

As if we weren't already, Lissan thought sourly.

"Kirk doesn't suspect because we have been as cautious as we have," Lissan said. Even as he uttered the words, he knew they were a lie. Kirk suspected something, all right. Julius had promised he'd be able to keep his uncle under control, but clearly this James T. Kirk was more than anyone had bargained for. Pushing as hard as he had for getting the "communications problem" solved. . . .

"We are too close to success for us to risk being discovered before we are ready."

"But, Lissan, old friend," 858 said in a falsely comradely voice, "when *are* you going to be ready? We've been very patient. We've waited years, now, without seeing a single payment. But patience does run out."

The words sent shivers across Lissan's body, but he kept his face neutral. He was grateful for so many centuries of stoicism. A Huanni would be a blubbering heap right now.

He decided to play the Orion's own game. "We are very grateful for all your help and your remarkable patience," he said, forcing his voice to sound as sincere as possible. "But you must admit, when you will be paid, it will be quite the treasure for something that required relatively little effort from the Syndicate."

"It is the value of that treasure," 858 agreed silkily, "that made us agree to be paid later rather than sooner."

Lissan's mind raced. There was still so much to be done before they were ready, and yet 858 was quite right about one thing: Time was running out. The window of opportunity, which had yawned so wide for such a long time, was closing rapidly. All depended on them leaping through that window while they still could.

He decided to go on the offensive. "Part of the reason that time is so short is because the Syndicate failed to keep Huan out of the Federation. That's made everything incredibly difficult."

"The Syndicate agreed to do what it could," 858 said icily. "It did. The problem is yours, not ours. Our problem is, we need a timetable from you. And it needs to be a timetable we agree with. When can we begin?"

"We still have so much—"

"You know," 858 interrupted, a green hand reaching down to his waist, "I really wasn't the best contact for this job. I don't have a lot of patience, personally. And I have to be frank with you, Lissan. I need a specific and firm date. And if I don't come out of this meeting with one, you don't come out of this meeting at all."

In his long green fingers was a small disk, with an opening aimed directly at Lissan. He didn't recognize the weapon at all, but that was hardly surprising. Of course, agents of the Syndicate would be equipped with the latest technology that could be bought or stolen.

"You're bluffing," he stammered, then looked up from the weapon to 858's cold eyes.

The Orion wasn't bluffing.

"A date," 858 repeated, softly.

"Two months," blurted Lissan.

Almost sorrowfully, 858 shook his black head. "Not good enough, I'm afraid." His thumb moved.

"One month!"

The thumb paused a millimeter from a red button. "Two weeks."

"Yes, all right, two weeks, curse you!"

858 smiled pleasantly. The little weapon vanished into the folds of his clothes. "I do so enjoy the give and take of negotiation."

Kirk hadn't served in Starfleet for as long as he had without learning when to trust and when to be suspicious. And right now, he was suspicious.

He voiced his concerns only to his old, trusted friends. Alex was a good man, clearly, but the colony was his baby. And Julius . . . there was something about Julius that Kirk didn't like, something that went deeper than the obvious resentment of perceived past neglect. Skalli was Starfleet, but Skalli was also . . . well . . . Skalli.

The old comrades met each day for lunch. With their history, that wouldn't be noticed, but any more frequent encounters might. Spring was giving way to summer, and Kirk knew of a few places where they could dine al fresco and not be observed.

Kirk lay on his back, watching clouds move slowly across a blue sky. He bit into a carrot, looked over at Chekov, and said, "Status report?" He was not unaware of the incongruity of the conversation and the setting.

Sitting cross-legged on the blanket, Chekov replied, "Communications have cleared up slightly. We are able to communicate with one another here on Sanctuary, but I don't think we can successfully send or receive messages outside. And I still think someone is listening in."

Kirk finished the carrot and moved on to a roasted native bird of some sort. He bit into a drumstick and thought wryly, *tastes like chicken.* "Are you certain the messages aren't getting out?"

"No," Chekov replied. "In fact, they do appear to be getting out, but the fact that we have never received any response makes me think that they really aren't being transmitted."

"Spock would praise your logical deduction," Kirk said approvingly. "As do I."

"One thing Chekov and I did notice," Scott added, "was that it looks like the Falorians are able to get messages through. We detected a narrow band subspace carrier wave in that facility of theirs. It's able to punch through their shield just fine, thank you very much."

"Curiouser and curiouser," Kirk said. "What's the engineering buzz?"

"They're so busy with their noses in the engines that they don't stop to look up," Scott said. Kirk thought the same could be said of Scotty from time to time, but he said nothing. "We're getting flyovers almost daily. Sometimes more than once a day. There's a lot of traffic up there, Captain."

"If the Falorians are telling the truth, then that would

make sense," Kirk countered. "It's a resupply base. Of course there'd be a lot of ships coming to Sanctuary now."

Scott raised an eyebrow. "If the base is over on the other side of the planet, they wouldn't be needing to fly quite so directly over our little colony, though, now would they?"

"So we're being watched," Kirk said. His friends exchanged glances, then nodded their agreement.

Kirk permitted himself to finish the drumstick, then announced his decision.

"Gentlemen, I think this base needs to be investigated. Either of you like to accompany me?"

It was 0134 the following morning that Kirk, Chekov, and Scott rendezvoused at the *Drake*. The air was heavy with dew and they were all shivering in the early morning chill.

"Let's go," Kirk said. Quietly and quickly, they entered. With a deft touch born of years of coaxing obedience from delicate machinery, Scott started the atmosphere shuttle. Seconds later, they were aloft.

Chekov shook his head, smiling in amazement. "I can't believe it," he said. "I thought for certain we would have been noticed and challenged."

"I knew we wouldn't," Kirk said with just a touch of superiority.

"How?" For the briefest of moments, Pavel Chekov looked like the brash young ensign Kirk remembered from thirty years ago as he stared at Kirk in wonder.

"He asked for the shuttle," Scott said. Kirk grinned like a wolf, and Chekov threw back his head and laughed.

"Alex thinks we are on a research mission to document the cycle of a rare, night-blooming flower. Said mission is headed by you, Mr. Chekov, so you'll need to be able to answer any questions."

Chekov made a face.

"Coincidentally," Kirk continued, "it happens to grow in profusion very close to where Lissan's mysterious base is located. We'll just have to remember to get a few samples before we head back home."

While the little atmosphere shuttle was not designed to explore space, it excelled at what it was designed to do and sped along quite nicely. As they approached the continent, all three of them instinctively quieted and focused on the tasks at hand.

"There it is," Scotty said.

"It doesn't look big enough to be a resupply base," Chekov said.

"That's probably because it isn't," Kirk said. Resupply bases were enormous. They had to be, in order to house sufficient supplies and provide ample docking for those ships that could land planetside. They were sometimes the size of small cities. The facility he was looking at was hardly a full kilometer. Whatever it housed was protected by a shield that not only prohibited examination via a ship's computer, but any visual appraisal as well. It was a ghostly blue color and arched over the whole like an eggshell.

"Any sign we've been detected?" Kirk said, leaning

over Scott's shoulder to look out through the *Drake*'s large windows.

"Negative," said Scott. "There's very little in the way of scanning equipment."

"They apparently assume that no one will come looking for them," said Chekov. He didn't comment about how this directly contradicted Lissan's comments about erecting the shield as a precaution against the untrustworthy. He didn't have to. It was obvious that the entire story was one enormous lie, and with each new bit of information they gleaned that lie unraveled further.

Scott's fingers flew over the controls. He shook his gray head. "Their technology is a lot more sophisticated than they'd like us to believe," he said. "I've tried all the tricks in the book and I can't penetrate that shield."

Kirk made a decision. "Land us."

Scott and Chekov didn't bat an eyelash. They'd served with him long enough to know that any protest would go unheard by Kirk. It was one thing to just fly over and claim they were researching flowers. It was another thing to actually land the shuttle near the facility and do what Kirk was planning on doing. Scott maneuvered the small shuttle close to the earth, skimming along until he found a large copse of trees with a meadow in its center. With a surgeon's grace, he dropped lower still and eased the shuttle into the clearing. The *Drake* hovered, then settled gently down onto the grass.

"They'll find us if they do any scans," Scott warned,

"but with any luck, the trees'll at least provide visual camouflage."

"Well done, Scotty. You need to stay with the shuttle."

Scott's mustache drooped. "But Captain, I—"

"No buts. I need your expertise to get that shield down long enough for us to get inside. Once Chekov and I are in, bring the shield back up immediately and get out of here fast. I think we'll be able to figure out a way to get the shield open from the inside when we're done." He smiled wryly and added teasingly, "That's of course assuming that you've been doing your research."

"Ah, now, Captain," Scott scolded gently, his eyes sparkling.

"You *think* we'll be able to get the shield open?" Chekov exclaimed. "But if we can't—"

"Then Scotty will have to lead a rescue team," Kirk said wryly. "I'm not sure how much time we'll need, so keep monitoring for our life signs outside the shield. We'll head back for this copse. We won't be able to communicate with you once we're inside, so it's up to you to keep a sharp lookout and get us out of here. Go to our original destination—the flower field. It's within transport distance and a few seconds away at top speed. You may have to pick us up very quickly."

Obviously, Scott was disappointed. But he saw Kirk's logic and reluctantly nodded. "Aye, it's a good plan. But I'm not going to be likin' just leaving you here."

"There's less of a chance you'll be discovered than if you just stay in this copse," Kirk pointed out. He placed a hand on Scott's shoulder. "We need you with the shuttle, Scotty."

"Aye," Scotty said, straightening. He turned back to the computer and for a while the three old friends sat in silence, waiting. Finally, Scott grunted approvingly. "So that's how we do it, eh?"

With a flourish, he touched a few more controls, and then the screen began to display a series of complicated graphics and code.

Scott turned around to explain what he was doing to Kirk and Chekov. "All right. Here's the situation. I've been able to piggyback on that subspace carrier wave and I can disable their entire security system from here. Any monitors, screens, scanners—they'll all go out. The only thing you two will have to worry about is being physically seen. And the beauty of it is it'll look like a common, garden-variety glitch. They'll never know it was us."

"Scotty," Kirk breathed, "you're a genius!"

Scott inclined his head modestly. "You and Chekov go on, Captain. I'll have that thing open and shut for you in the blink of an eye. And unless anyone is actually looking at the controls at the time I do it, they won't notice *that*, either."

Kirk grinned, clapped the miracle-performing engineer on the back, and opened the shuttle door. He and Chekov dropped quietly down to the earth and sped for the Falorian "resupply base."

It loomed ahead of them, its pulsating blue glow eerie in the dark night. Kirk's eyes flicked from the approaching shield dome to his tricorder. No sign of humanoid life. So far as he could tell, they were still undetected.

He didn't slow as they drew closer, and Chekov matched his pace easily. Kirk trusted Scott completely, and just as it appeared that they were both about to slam into the shield and probably be killed, the shield disappeared.

They kept running.

Already aloft, Scott watched without blinking as the two dots that signified Kirk and Chekov entered the facility. The instant they had cleared the shield radius he jabbed a button and the shield was reerected.

They were in.

Smoothly, Scott maneuvered the little vessel toward the field of white flowers. "Godspeed," he wished his two friends, and began the wait.

Chapter Eleven

Commander T'SroH had never been more bored in his entire life.

Intellectually, he knew that he had been given a great honor: to assist his noble Chancellor in carrying out her vow of *DIS jaj je*. When Kerla had first contacted him and informed him of this important task, T'SroH had puffed his chest out with pride.

And then Kerla filled him in on the details.

The destruction of Praxis had been a disaster on a scale that most Klingons were only now truly beginning to appreciate. T'SroH, like Kerla, had not at first approved of Gorkon's peace initiatives, but with each day that passed, the unpleasant reality revealed itself more clearly: The Klingons needed peace if they were to survive as the passionate, proud people they had always been. The events at Khitomer regarding one James T. Kirk had startled T'SroH and many others, and when he learned that Kirk was the subject of Azetbur's *DIS jaj je*, he was not surprised.

If only Kirk had willingly accepted the great honor that Azetbur had bestowed! Then T'SroH would not be bored, as he was now. It was not the fact that he now owed a year and a day out of his life to fulfilling his chancellor's honor debt, but the manner in which he had to spend that year and day.

He had followed the large, ungainly ship called the *Mayflower II* to this planet, nauseatingly named Sanctuary. His ship, the proud and noble *K'Rator,* had maintained its cloak the entire time, running undetectable while any other ships were in the vicinity and scanning quickly, cautiously, when they were not.

Why had Captain Kirk, by all accounts an adventuresome human, come to this wretchedly peaceful place? The Klingon had been brought up to speed, of course, and knew that there was a blood bond between the starship captain and the younger colony founders. But what purpose would it serve? From what he knew of Kirk, T'SroH suspected the human was as bored as he.

Weeks had gone by in this manner. T'SroH was beginning to think he might go mad. His crew was beginning to grumble as well. At this rate, the entire Year and a Day would pass before Kirk would do so much as stub a toe.

At least there was *some* activity to break up the monotony. T'SroH had watched with mild interest as the Falorians worked without ceasing to build a spacedock close to Sanctuary. He had made note of the vessels that came and went. Many were large cargo vessels; some were sleek, dangerous-looking fighters. Still others were strange hybrids, clearly cobbled together of many dif-

ferent vessels from many different peoples. One or two
T'SroH thought he recognized as belonging to members
of the Orion Syndicate, but, of course, he could not be
certain unless they chose to display their symbol of a
circle and a lightning bolt. Which, naturally, they would
be reluctant to do. He made a mental note and let it go.
If the Falorians chose to deal with the scum, let them.
His sole focus, his reason for being locked in orbit
around this miserable place, was James Kirk. All else
was extraneous.

To that end, of much greater interest were the daily
flyovers the Falorian ships made of the colony. T'SroH
kept hoping for some kind of attack to break the monotony, but none came.

T'SroH had also hoped this mysterious facility the
Falorians had built on the far side of the planet would
prove of interest, but thus far, the shields had only been
lowered for the briefest of moments. There had been no
time to execute an order to scan so they might discover
what that shield protected.

The Klingons had long since adapted to the cycles
of this planet's days and nights, and it was the small
hours of the morning on Sanctuary. T'SroH lay in his
bed, unable to sleep, although sleep would be an excellent way to pass the time that appeared to be on his
hands.

There was a sharp whistle of the communications
system. "Commander," came his second-in-command's
voice.

"Speak," T'SroH grunted.

"Captain Kirk and two others have left the colony. I

thought you would wish to be informed," continued Garthak.

At this hour? That was indeed unusual. T'SroH sat up in his bed. "What is their destination?"

"Uncertain." A pause. Then, his voice laced with excitement, "They are heading to the facility."

T'SroH growled his pleasure and leaped out of bed. *This* should be interesting. Perhaps the time had finally come to pay the *DIS jaj je*.

He hastened to the bridge just in time for Garthak to say, "They are right outside the perimeter."

T'SroH found himself breathing shallowly, his blood racing. Had it really been so long since anything had happened that the sight of two humans outside an alien facility would make him catch his breath so? He made a mental note to challenge Garthak to a good *bat'leth* practice later today.

But T'SroH was not the only one watching with excitement; he could feel the tension on the bridge. There he was, the famous James T. Kirk. He knew, as Kirk could not, how secure the Falorians were in the impenetrability of their base. Clearly, they thought the colonists would behave like good little Earth sheep and stay where they were supposed to; stay where the Falorians could keep watch over them.

He found himself doing something he thought he would never do—rooting for a human.

"I have heard of his Engineer Scott as well," T'SroH said. "If he is the one in the vessel, then it is likely that—"

He fell silent as in front of his eyes, the shield went

down and the two humans raced inside. T'SroH caught only the briefest glimpses of the shapes of buildings before the blue, pulsating shield went back up.

The shield had only been down for half a second. With any luck, if it was even noticed by whatever security the Falorians had, the brief shutdown would be assumed to be a technical error.

He leaned forward in his command chair. After weeks of waiting, T'SroH wasn't about to miss a moment of this.

There was a low hum and a crackle as the shield went down. Phasers at the ready, Kirk and Chekov charged in. A fraction of a second later, the shield was back up. They remained tense, alert for any sign that they had been discovered, but all was quiet.

Kirk looked around while Chekov studied the tricorder. In the distance was a large tower. Scattered about were six or eight outbuildings, all small, utilitarian looking and single-story. There were a few lights on, but not many. The perimeter was only sparsely lit as well.

"Clearly, they put a lot of trust in that shield," Kirk said. "Scott said their security systems were a bit lax."

"I see no cargo areas, no ships, nothing that even remotely resembles a vessel," Chekov said. Sarcastically he added, "I wonder why that is?"

"But I do see the source of that subspace carrier wave," Kirk said, stepping forward and craning his neck to look up at the tower. "It dominates the entire area."

"It's a subspace relay, all right, but . . ." Chekov

frowned. "This is a Starfleet issue relay, I'm certain of it."

"What?" Kirk looked with renewed interest at the relay. "No cargo areas, pirated technology . . . it's not looking very good for the Falorians' trustworthiness. Come on."

Carefully they moved toward the mostly darkened buildings. Scotty might have disabled the security system for the next few hours, but there was always the chance that they'd run into the old-fashioned security system—a guard. But the Falorians were diurnal, as were humans, and it looked as though most of them had gone to bed for the night.

Kirk heard a slight noise and, grabbing Chekov's arm, pulled him up close against the nearest building. Several meters away, a single bored-looking Falorian guard, carrying a Starfleet-issue phaser, strolled past.

"If that's their security system, I think we're a match for it," Chekov whispered.

"Did you see the phaser?"

"I'm holding one just like it."

Quietly, they moved on. A window was open across a wide patch of grass, and Kirk squinted, trying to see inside. He saw what appeared to be a bed and a desk, and then the room went dark. These were living quarters, then.

But who lived here?

"Captain," Chekov said quietly, "There's a large entrance into the soil at the center of the area. It seems to be a tunnel of some sort. I'm detecting more evidence of high-level technology there than in any of these outer buildings."

"Then that's where we should be," Kirk said. This area was better lit than the perimeter, but Chekov was able to pinpoint the presence of any Falorians. When all was clear, they sprinted for the tunnel.

The mouth was several hundred meters wide and narrowed as it went further into the ground. Kirk could catch glimpses of the technology that Chekov's tricorder had revealed. His eyes widened slightly. Lissan's claim that they didn't have the level of technology that the colonists possessed was clearly a lie of the most elaborate sort. At the end of the tunnel, there was no dirt or stone to be seen. All was metal and alloys, lights and gantries and lifts. Kirk caught a glimpse of similarly clad Falorians scurrying along corridors here and there, carrying padds and looking focused.

Quickly they stepped down onto a gantry and pressed back against cold metal. Chekov was still reading the tricorder.

"I'm detecting very little indication of weapons," he said as Kirk continued to take their bearings. "This may be a research facility."

"Let's find out what it is they're researching." It was clearly an enormous complex, and they were only two humans. With the security system disabled, luck ought to be with them. They hopped onto a lift and rode it down. Despite himself, Kirk felt his imagination stir at the sight of all the unfamiliar technology, much of it obviously new. It was probably just as well Scott wasn't with them. The engineer might have fallen in love.

The lift clanged to a stop. The corridor was empty and they jumped off, ducking into a darkened room. Chekov glanced at the tricorder and nodded that all was clear. Phasers drawn, they proceeded down the corridor.

"What are we looking for?" Chekov whispered.

"We'll know it when we see it," Kirk hissed back. Even as he spoke the words, he wondered if they were true. What they were looking for was some reason why the Falorians had woven such an extensive web of lies. Why had they given up an entire planet to an alien race, with the only stipulation being a share in the technology the colony developed, when it was clear they had advanced technology themselves? Why had they erected a shield over nothing more dangerous than a research facility, and called it a "resupply base"? Why were they lying about jamming the colony's frequencies, and why did they not want the colonists communicating with the outside world? What was a pirated Starfleet subspace relay system doing here, and how had they gotten a hold of it in the first place?

Answers were what he and Chekov were looking for. He only hoped they would indeed know them when they saw them.

Many of these rooms were storage facilities for equipment. And much of this equipment was Starfleet issue. It solved at least one problem. Kirk leaned over and whispered in Chekov's ear, "The Orion Syndicate."

Chekov nodded. "Cossacks," he muttered. Then, wordlessly, he hauled Kirk down behind a cabinet full of beakers of various shapes and sizes.

"Lights," came a voice. Footsteps passed them, hesitated. They heard the clink of glass, then the footsteps moved away. "Lights off," called the Falorian, and all was quiet again.

The next room into which they ventured was obviously a laboratory. Kirk looked around, then spotted what he was searching for—access to a computer.

"Start downloading anything you can," he said. "I'll look around."

Chekov nodded, and immediately began configuring the tricorder to link up with the computer.

Kirk could have made a fair guess at navigating an alien bridge, but here in an alien laboratory, Kirk felt out of his element. Too bad Spock wasn't here. He'd know what to make of this confusing jumble of equipment and—

Notes.

A padd lay tossed on the table next to a cup of something that had been poured and forgotten and was now growing some kind of mold. That in itself would be an interesting project, but Kirk was certain that was only an accidental side effect of too many hours spent in painstaking research. It was funny how similar scientists were, whatever their species. He picked up the padd, careful not to accidentally erase any information. Of course, it was all written in Falorian, but translation would be easy once they got back to the colony.

"Captain, look at this," Chekov said. He was glancing back and forth from his tricorder to the screen. Kirk looked up to see a graphic of various shapes parading across the screen.

"What am I looking at?" Kirk asked, deferring to

Chekov's greater familiarity with all things scientific.

"I'm not certain, of course, but I've got a general idea of the focus of their research. At least one focus. Nanotechnology."

Kirk watched, fascinated, as what he now realized were infinitesimally tiny machines marched about their business. "That covers a lot of ground," he said. "What are the nanotechs doing? Is the focus on medicine, repair, what?"

"They're not repairing anything," said Chekov. "I don't have enough information yet, but my guess is they're going to be used as some kind of weapon."

Kirk's stomach clenched. "I want you to go to the deepest level of information they have in the computer," he said.

"That could take time."

"If they're formulating a weapon, then the clock's ticking already, Mr. Chekov."

"Aye, sir." He hesitated. "So far, I've only downloaded basic information. If I try to break into their encrypted files, I could alert someone to our presence."

"That's a risk we have to take. We must know what they're planning."

Chekov bit his lower lip. This wasn't his area of expertise, but he was still more familiar with something like this than Kirk would be. With clear reluctance, he sat down and began to try to bypass the security system around the computer.

Kirk's mind was racing. Everything was starting to make at least some kind of sense now. He looked down at his tricorder. This complex was enormous and extended for several hundred meters into the earth. It wasn't anything new, nor was it anything that had been abandoned long ago and recently reoccupied. The Falorians had to have been working on getting it up and running for some time now. How could Alex not have known about this?

The answer came to him almost immediately, but it was an answer that he almost would rather not have had.

Julius.

Julius had always been the liaison to the Falorians. It wasn't inconceivable that he had known what was going on from the very beginning, and had conspired with them to conceal evidence of this mammoth facility from any scans and reports.

Kirk's mind went back to that middle of the night conversation when Alexander and Julius had first shown up on his doorstep. How long ago it all seemed now. *It's all thanks to Julius,* Alex had said. *He's been amazing . . . he's been the one out there talking to all kinds of alien races to find us our Sanctuary.* And Julius's own words: *You have no idea what we've been through the last few years, Uncle Jim . . . the crawling through mud and getting sick and being literally scared for my life half the time that I've done to get this thing to fly.*

He thought of the Starfleet technology generously peppered through the complex. *Oh, Julius. I think I do know what you've been through . . . and what you've done.*

"I've done as much as I dare do," said Chekov, breaking into Kirk's thoughts.

"Good job. We've got one more stop on this pleasant little tour of the resupply station."

According to the tricorder readings there was an enormous cavern at the very bottom of the facility. They had seen dozens of labs, conference rooms and storage rooms, but nothing like this.

Kirk had to shake his head at how easy this all was. The shield and the system Scott had so easily cracked had lulled the Falorians into a false sense of security. Doors hissed open as readily for them as for the aliens, and after taking a long ride down on a lift, they stepped into what was clearly the heart of the complex.

Like everything they had seen thus far, this cavern was entirely Falorian-made. There was no glimpse of stone walls or dirt anywhere. Every wall was lined with panels, monitors (most of which, Kirk noticed appreciatively, were blank), switches, buttons, and blinking lights of every variety.

"We're in a control center," Chekov breathed, awe in his voice. "A very, very *big* control center."

Kirk had moved forward and was now looking at some of the images on the screens. Most of them were of places he didn't recognize.

But there was one he did, and his heart began to pound fiercely in his chest.

He was looking straight into the formal reception hall of Starfleet's headquarters in San Francisco.

Chapter Twelve

"That's . . ." Chekov's voice trailed off as he stepped beside Kirk and looked at the banquet hall.

"Yes," Kirk said grimly. "My friend Admiral Standing Crane told me that the Falorians were very curious people. They wanted to visit every starbase and member planet, tour every ship. And they were so pleasant, so charming about it that no one suspected anything. Not even Standing Crane, who's as sharp as they come. Whatever the Falorians are planning, there's a good chance it's going to affect the entire Federation." He nodded to one of the enormous consoles, and Chekov hastened up to it.

He touched the tricorder, and then frowned. "They have a heavy encryption on the data here, much more than they had in the labs."

Kirk knew what he was saying. Chekov had been able to break into the computer system fairly easily. It would be harder now, and every minute they lingered here meant a greater chance of discovery. Also, the deeper encryption clearly guarded information of greater import. Chekov wasn't an expert at this, and an attempt to access the information could trip some kind of security system.

"Continue, Mr. Chekov."

Chekov's eyes searched his for a moment, and then he nodded. He turned, took a breath, and touched the computer. His fingers flew over a few soft pads, and then the tricorder began to hum.

"It's work—"

A shrill alarm cut him off. And at the same time, he snatched his hands back with a cry of pain. His fingers were blackened and smoking. White bone peeked through. Kirk swore. He rushed forward and grabbed Chekov's tricorder and phaser.

"Let's go," he cried. They rushed back up the way they had come. Kirk heard Chekov trying and failing to stifle the occasional whimper of pain and he cursed himself. He knew that breaking into secure systems could be dangerous. Why hadn't he been the one to take the risks? Why had he put Pavel in jeopardy?

As they raced for the nearest lift Kirk heard a clatter of booted feet echo down the hallway. He looked around and saw metal rungs extending up as far as the eye could see. Despite Scott's efforts, Kirk had managed to trip the security system, and he knew that all the lifts would be shut down now. There was only one way out.

He glanced over at Chekov. The younger man's handsome face was twisted in a grimace of agony. His fingers were now black and swollen. Blood and pus crested and broke through the burned flesh.

"Can you climb?" Kirk asked.

Chekov forced a smile. "Do I have a choice?"

Despite the direness of the situation, Kirk smiled. "I don't think so. Go on. You first."

"But I'll slow us down—"

"That's an order, Mister," snapped Kirk. Chekov nodded, and set his teeth against the pain as he began to climb, slowly and in obvious agony.

Kirk followed, glancing down. Below him he saw a handful of guards come running into the corridor and into the chamber Kirk and Chekov had just vacated. It was huge and there were a number of places people could hide. With luck, that would keep them busy for a while.

They kept climbing. Chekov was deathly silent, but as he followed him, Kirk could feel the smear of fluid on each metal rung. Chekov began to breathe heavily. He alternated hands and tried to use his lower arms instead of grasping the rungs directly. Kirk looked up. They still had such a long way to go.

"You can do it, Pavel," he said, softly and urgently. "One rung at a time."

"Captain," gasped Chekov raggedly, "You should leave me behind. There's no point in both of us getting captured."

"I won't leave you. Keep going."

It seemed to take an eternity to get to the next level. Kirk ducked his head into the corridor and pulled back quickly. Guards. He touched Chekov on the leg to silently signal that he needed to keep going. After the briefest pause, Chekov gamely continued. Kirk wished that he could help Pavel, but he could do nothing except let him set the pace and be below him on the ladder to catch him in case he slipped.

Kirk didn't know how long it took, but they made their slow, agonizing way up ladder after ladder. When they could, they ducked into corridors and labs to catch their breath and give Chekov a respite, albeit a brief one, from the pain. If only the lifts hadn't been shut down! At the very least, they seemed able to avoid capture.

Finally, Kirk saw that they were close to the top. There were only two or three more ladders to climb. He checked the tricorder. All seemed clear in the nearest corridor, and he silently signaled Chekov that they should take a break. Before they could scramble over the lip and head to freedom, they had to get the shield down.

He leaned back, thinking. Next to him, he heard Pavel hissing softly through his teeth as he stretched his damaged hands out in front, keeping them as still as possible. Where would be the best place for security posts? In the center area, of course, since it appeared that the control room was the most sensitive area. And right near the top, to prevent exactly what he and Chekov had managed to do.

He checked the tricorder and nodded as it confirmed his logic. The top floor, which ran the circumference of the tunnel, was filled with weapons, technology, and Falorians.

"Here's the plan," he told Chekov.

Once Chekov was in position, Kirk stepped close to the edge of the corridor, aimed at a piece of equipment several meters below, and got off a single, rapid shot. At once he heard a commotion. Had anyone been watching, they would have seen the direction from which the phaser had been fired and could easily have traced him, but as it was, they didn't realize what had happened until it was too late and now congregated around the smoking, blasted piece of equipment.

While their attention was diverted, Kirk sprang onto the nearest ladder, scaled it swiftly, and ducked into the first security room he came to. He surprised a guard, who lifted a weapon in one hand even as he reached for an intercom button with another, but Kirk was faster. He fired and the guard crumpled. Kirk whirled and fired again, taking out two more guards. He leapt over the bodies and scanned the equipment.

Damn it, he had no idea what he was looking for. He'd relied on Chekov to do that. His pulse racing, Kirk examined alien lettering and various colored buttons. Pulsing lights in red, yellow, orange, indigo, and—

Blue. The same pale blue as the shield. Would it be that simple, that obvious? Kirk thought about the overconfidence the Falorians had, how easily their systems had been disabled, and decided that the gamble was worth it. He flipped open his communicator.

"I'm in. I'm going to press a button, Chekov. Let me know what happens."

"Aye, sir."

Without a moment's hesitation, Kirk pressed the blue button.

"It's down!" came Chekov's excited voice.

"I'm right behind you," Kirk said. He snapped the

communicator closed and headed for the ladder.

But now he was spotted, and he heard shouts. A directed energy weapon blast struck inches from his head. A few centimeters above him was the lip of the tunnel and—

Kirk almost lost his grip as a booted foot kicked him in the face. Gray and white swirled in front of his eyes, but he refused to lose consciousness. He reached up in the gray swirl, grasped the leg attached to the boot that had kicked him, and pulled. Screaming, the Falorian hurtled down into the depths.

Bleeding from a broken nose, Kirk pulled himself over the lip of the tunnel. The shield was still down, and the stars arched above the complex. Their calm, cold twinkling was strangely incongruous to Kirk. He got to his feet and took off running.

He dematerialized in mid-stride.

Kirk treated his own and Chekov's more serious injuries with the medikit on board the *Drake,* filling Scotty in on what had transpired.

"I can't believe getting the shield down would be that easy," Kirk said. "You were right, Scotty—the Falorian security system is amazingly lax. Push a blue button, a blue shield comes down."

"Um," said Scott, looking uncomfortable.

Kirk looked up sharply from Chekov's hands. "What?"

"Well, um . . . the shield . . . I was fiddling with the signals and—"

"*You* got the shield down?"

"Um . . . aye, sir. Though I'm sure you would have

been able to figure it out yourself had you had the time."

Kirk grinned weakly and turned back to Chekov. "It's good that you got that information, laddie," Scott said to Chekov, clearly trying to change the subject, "and we'll be able to translate it for sure. But if it's encrypted, I doubt there's anyone sufficiently trained back at the colony to break the code."

Kirk's heart sank at the words, but he didn't let his disappointment show. "We have at least three Starfleet officers here," he said. "Between us, we'll come up with something."

"I was never trained in such things," Scott said. "And unless you two have taken some courses I don't know about, neither were you."

"Damn it, we have to try!" Kirk cried. "The entire Federation could be at risk!"

At that moment, there was a crackle and then Alex's voice filled the little shuttle. "Uncle Jim! We're under attack! Repeat, we're under attack!"

Even at top speed it was several minutes before the *Drake* could reach the colony. They saw the brutal orange and crimson glow of the fire while still several kilometers away. There had been a few injuries, none of them serious, and no fatalities. The only true casualty had been the *Mayflower II* herself.

"They came out of nowhere," Alex had told them, his voice high-pitched with panic. "They came out of nowhere and just started firing on the ship!"

"But not on the colony itself?" Kirk had wanted to know.

"No, not on us. But the ship's gone, Uncle Jim. There's no way to repair this kind of damage."

Kirk had hoped his nephew had been wrong, but as they skimmed over the burning wreckage, he had to agree with Alex's assessment. As they settled in for a landing, Kirk saw the flames dying as chemicals were sprayed on them. As soon as they stepped out of the shuttle, Alex rushed up to them.

He looked dreadful. He was wild-eyed and sweating, and reached to clasp Kirk's arms. "I'm so glad you're back, Uncle Jim, we— What happened to your face?"

Kirk waved it off. "A little accident. Chekov is more in need of treatment than I am. A . . . wiring accident, which we've already taken care of."

He didn't particularly enjoy lying to his nephew, but it was obvious to him that the Falorians had fired on the colony in retaliation for the break-in. The less Alex knew, the better, at least until Kirk could better assess the situation. Alex ran his finger through his soot-darkened hair, his eyes drawn inexorably to the inferno.

"Did you see who did it?" Kirk asked.

"Huh? Oh. We've got their signal, but no one actually saw anything. We were all asleep. We don't recognize the ships at all."

Skalli came rushing up, her long legs carrying her swiftly across the dewy grass. "Oh, Captain Kirk!" she exclaimed. Tears of sympathy welled in her huge eyes. "Your face! What happened? Oh! And Mr. Chekov, your hands, your poor hands!"

"Pavel, go with Skalli to see Dr. Sherman. Skalli, stay with him." It would keep her out of his hair. "Alex, let's you and Scotty and I go look at the records."

Before they left, Kirk took a quick look back at the crowd that was busily damping the flames. Among them was Julius, bare chested and clad only in pajama bottoms. His torso glistened with sweat and looked orange in the light of the dying fire. As if feeling Kirk's gaze upon him, he turned. Their eyes locked, and Kirk saw a brief expression of anguish cross Julius's face before the younger man turned away quickly.

Kirk thought about the pirated equipment he'd seen in the complex, and then turned to follow Alex.

"See? It's nothing we know," Alex said as they looked at the images on the screen.

Kirk could make a pretty good guess, and so could Scott. They exchanged glances. Kirk wondered how much he ought to reveal at this juncture. He decided to start with the truth.

"That's a vessel built by a species that is known to have dealings with the Orion Syndicate," he said. "See that shadow on the hull?" He pointed to a thin, dark line. "That indicates a false panel. They can remove it to display the mark of the Syndicate when it serves them, and hide it when it doesn't."

Alex's eyes widened. "Really? Do you think they're dealing with the Falorians?"

Surprised, Kirk said, "Yes, we do."

"No wonder they wanted that shield," Alex said. "I'm sure they don't trust the Syndicate at all. Maybe they stopped dealing with them and the Syndicate retaliated by attacking our ship."

Kirk sighed quietly. Alex still bought Lissan's story about the facility being a resupply base. And now was not yet the time to disillusion him. Alex was not a liar, and if Lissan returned to the colony and Alex understood fully what was going on, Alex would give them all away.

"Maybe you're right," was all he said.

The cool night winds blew away the smoke, and the colony awoke to a crisp, bright dawn. Its cheerful roseate glow made the ruins of the mighty colony ship look even more stark and desolate. It was black and twisted, a dark skeleton silhouetted against the morning sky.

Kirk was up early, helping everyone scavenge what they could. According to Alex, all the damage had been caused by a single strafing run of the unknown vessel. It had not made a second pass, which would have utterly destroyed everything. Clearly the attack had been to simply make sure they had no means of escape. Utter destruction had not been deemed necessary.

Scarcely had he begun pitching in when he heard the hum of a transporter. Kirk glanced over to see Lissan materialize in the Courtyard. He choked back a wave of anger. If he had any hope of discovering and thwarting the Falorian plans, he had to maintain a façade of trust. He would let Lissan set the tone for this meeting.

"What happened here?" exclaimed Lissan, staring at the remains of the *Mayflower II*.

He was good. If Kirk hadn't known better, he'd have

bought it hook, line, and sinker, just like Alex did. Alex and Julius stepped forward to greet the Falorian.

"It happened last night," Alex said. "This ship came out of nowhere and just started firing. It was awful. Do you have any idea who it might be?"

Lissan shook his head, looking pained. "Regrettably, I do. It appears we are both victims. You see, last night our facility was broken into. Whoever it was did a great deal of damage and even stole some things. I would imagine it is those same people who destroyed your vessel."

He turned to look Kirk directly in the eye as he said this, and Kirk felt a chill. Lissan knew, all right. He knew who had broken into the facility and what they had taken. The stakes in this dangerous game had just gotten higher.

"Why?" Alex asked, all earnestness. "We've done nothing to anyone."

"I told you that we were dealing with some very unsavory people. We did our best to keep the riffraff out, but sometimes one fails." This was most definitely aimed at Kirk. Out of the corner of his eye Kirk saw Julius glancing from Lissan to Kirk.

"I don't suppose you'd be able to help us with repairs?" Kirk said, looking innocent.

"As I have told you, our technology is nowhere near your level," Lissan lied smoothly. "We have our hands full simply repairing our own damage."

"I see," Kirk said, and smiled gently.

"Please let us know if we can help," Alex said.

Lissan inclined his head. "You are most kind. I am

certain that at some point you will be very helpful indeed to us. Farewell."

He touched a button on his chest and dematerialized. Kirk gave his nephews an avuncular smile and put a hand on each of their shoulders. He felt Julius stiffen beneath his touch.

"Let's go inside," he said. "There's something I need to talk to you about."

"I have to—" Julius began, but Kirk squeezed his shoulder. Once they were safely inside Alex's quarters, away from prying eyes, Kirk whirled. He seized his youngest living relative by the front of his shirt and shoved him into a chair, hard.

"I want to know what the hell is going on, Julius," he demanded. "You're going to tell us everything."

Chapter Thirteen

Julius's pale face flushed bright red. "I don't know what you're talking about!"

"Uncle Jim—" Alex interrupted, but Kirk pressed on.

"Come on, Julius. Alex may only want to see the good in you, but I'm a little more detached. I know you're involved in something, but I want to know just how deep it goes."

Julius laughed shakily, turning to Alex for support. "I don't know what's got into him."

"Yes you do. You know where we were last night, just like Lissan knows where we were. Did you tip him off, Julius? Were you happy to sell your old uncle down the river? You're damn lucky that Lissan decided to attack just the *Mayflower* and not the colony."

Julius said nothing, only glared at Kirk with an intense hatred.

"Uncle Jim . . . where were you last night?" Alex, his voice soft, pained.

"Tell him, Julius. Tell him where I was and what I saw."

"How the hell should I know?"

"Because you're in this so deep that you're about to drown," Kirk shot back. "I can't believe that my own nephew—"

"Oh, yes," Julius sneered, "your own nephew. The nephew of the great Captain James T. Kirk. God forbid that any of us should do anything to sully your spotless reputation. Well, you taught me better than you know, Uncle Jim. I'm not the first person in this family to break a few rules in order to get things done!"

The accusation stung, because Kirk knew Julius was right. "Yes, I've bent the rules. Sometimes I've even broken them. But I never would have sacrificed my own family—"

"I didn't know why they wanted you so badly!" Julius shouted. "They just—it was part of the deal, and we had to have Sanctuary, so—"

Alexander had gone pale. "Juley," he said, his voice alarmingly steady and calm, "Juley, what have you done?"

And like a twig snapping beneath a fierce wind, Julius Kirk broke. His body sagged, and all the tension drained out of him. Moisture filled his eyes and he wiped at them with the back of his hand. When he spoke, his voice was low and ragged with pain.

"I did what I had to do to get you Sanctuary," he said. "They wanted technology. I gave them technology. Then they wanted information. I got it for them. Then they wanted weapons. I got those too. Finally, they wanted you, Uncle Jim. That was the deal-breaker. I had to get you here, and now they're preventing us from communicating with the outside and have destroyed the only way we have to get off this damned planet. Oh, God, I'm such a fool."

Alex stared, open-mouthed. "Julius," Kirk said gently, laying a hand on his shoulder.

Violently, Julius wrenched away from the hand that was meant to comfort. "Don't touch me, you bastard!" He was sobbing now. He turned his wet face to Alex and reached out a hand to his brother. "Alex, I'm sorry, I'm so sorry, but I had to do it. We spent years looking for a place. You know that. I didn't mean for it to . . . first it was just a little technology, nothing classified, and then some weapons . . . a couple of phasers or so . . . then they were going to leave us alone. We got the colony, just like you always wanted. I got it for you, Alex. I did everything for you, just like you used to do everything for me. I never forgot that."

Kirk's heart ached in sympathy for Alex as he stared at his brother. "Juley, my God, did you really think I wanted you to become a—a *gunrunner* for me? Do you think I wanted to buy Sanctuary at the price of the lives of innocent people? Am I that much of an obsessed, single-minded monster to you that—"

"Alex!" The anguish in Julius's cry would have melted the hardest of hearts, but Alex, dealing with his own pain of betrayal, turned away from his brother.

Slowly, Julius looked to his uncle. "This is all your fault," he said between clenched teeth. "You let us rot. You came just long enough to make yourself feel that you'd done your duty and then left again, whereas we had to—God, Uncle Jim! Why didn't you even *try* to find out what was really going on?"

"I'm sorry," Kirk said. Julius blinked, startled at the ready apology. "I didn't know, and you're right, I didn't try to find out. I had my career, and I thought I was doing something important, something useful for the betterment of humanity. I tried to be a good uncle to you, but I see now I didn't try hard enough. Maybe one day you'll forgive me. But right now, if you want to help, you have to tell me everything you've done and everything you know."

Julius took a deep, shuddering breath and wiped a final time at his wet eyes. He stole a quick glance at his brother, who still stood facing the wall.

"Okay," he said. "Okay." He paused, gathering his thoughts. "It started a few years ago. I'd tried to talk various alien species into giving us a planet, but without the backing of the Federation they weren't interested. I began to realize that I had to have something more to offer them than what Alex had authorized, so I started keeping my ears open for any edge I could find."

Kirk thought that Julius's obvious need and desperation must have made him an easy target. He could see Julius in his mind's eye now, frantic to help his brother fulfill his dream, and burning with a bitterness that made him seize the first opportunity that came along.

"It never seemed exactly innocent, but at first, they didn't seem to want a lot."

"They who?" Kirk suspected, but he had to know.

"The Orion Syndicate," Julius said. Alex made a small sound in his throat and shook his head. He still hadn't turned around to face his brother. "They said they could help, and they did. They helped me get what the Falorians wanted."

"Last night," Kirk said, deciding the time for his own confession had arrived, "Scott, Chekov, and I went to check out this so-called facility. Have you been there, Julius?"

The young man shook his head. "I didn't even know about it until they told us." His voice was filled with self-disgust.

"It's some kind of laboratory and research facility. In the very heart, deep in the earth, is an enormous control center. They're monitoring hundreds of places scattered throughout the Federation, including Starfleet Headquarters itself."

Alex had turned around now and stared at Kirk with wide eyes and parted lips. Julius's flushed face had paled again, and he looked slightly ill.

"Their technology level is much higher than they're letting on," Kirk continued. "And part of the reason is that this research facility is crammed with Starfleet technology. They even fired a standard-issue phaser at us."

Julius rested his elbows on his knees and cradled his head. Mercilessly, Kirk plowed on.

"Chekov was injured when we downloaded some information from their computer systems. I took this." He held up the padd, which he had safely ensconced in a jacket pocket. "We were able to determine that the research is centered around nanotechnology. They're planning something big, gentlemen. Something that could potentially harm the Federation. But we don't have enough information yet."

Kirk caught and held Alexander's gaze. "Alex, you've got some of the best minds in the quadrant assembled here. We've got to put them to work. The Falorians obviously don't have any intentions of letting us leave."

He glanced at Julius. "Was that it, Julius? Were we supposed to be hostages?"

Julius finally looked up, and he seemed to have aged a decade. Kirk had always thought the saying that one's eyes were "haunted" was a cliché of the worst sort, but now he vividly understood what the phrase meant. Julius did look haunted, by ghosts of his obviously rough childhood and the fear of what he might inadvertently have done to his own people.

"It never occurred to me, Uncle Jim. When they wanted you so badly, I assumed it was just to wave it in the faces of the Huanni. They hate them so much. I would never have put Alex in harm's way. Never. I'd die before I'd do that."

Kirk latched on to what Julius had said. "The Huanni—they hate them? Even now? Why?"

"I don't know. Some ancient racial thing, I think. I— I thought that's what they wanted the weapons for, but they never asked for anything big enough to start a war with." A muscle twitched near his right eye. "At least, not from me. Guess I wasn't a big enough fish. Uncle Jim, it's obvious to me that I was just some kind of stepping-stone. They've cut me out of the loop, and from here on in, I swear to you, I don't know what they're planning."

"I believe you, Julius. Come on. We've got a job to do."

T'SroH stared at the images of flickering fire. "The colonists remain unharmed? Particularly Kirk?"

"It appears so," Garthak replied. "But their ship is completely destroyed."

"The colonists' ship is destroyed," T'SroH mused aloud. He drummed his sharp-nailed fingers on the arm of his chair. "Their communications are being monitored and all outside messages are not being transmitted. When the shield of this facility was lowered, we detected signs of advanced technology and not a few weapons. These Falorians have built an enormous spacedock about which the colonists know nothing. They are in contact with the Orion Syndicate. Kirk obviously knows something. He yet lives, which means that the Falorians deem his life has value to them."

He made his decision. "Contact the chancellor." He had enough to warrant alerting her to the situation. She might have a chance to complete her *DIS jaj je* sooner than anyone had expected.

Spock sat alone in his quarters, absently plucking the sweet-sounding strings of his Vulcan lyre. The act soothed him, though he was well aware that what he was doing was much more akin to what humans called "jamming" than performing the demanding, rigid, thousand-year-old Vulcan songs traditionally played on the instrument.

He permitted himself to continue. He found that this action busied his fingers while simultaneously freeing his mind. His thoughts turned now to the last, nearly disastrous meeting between himself and the High Council.

Gorkon's dream, even now, was far from universally shared among the Klingons. Spock had found Gorkon to be a reasoned, far-sighted individual, particularly so for a Klingon. While his daughter shared her father's dream, she did not have his temperament. Loud shouting matches often erupted when she spoke, in which her council eagerly joined. The cacophony was offensive to both Spock's ears and sensibilities, both of which were delicate. Yet he knew that peace was possible, and he recognized, as far too few of his contemporaries did, how much the Klingons could contribute to the Federation if they ever decided to officially seek membership.

Spock was pleased, however, with how well things were working on the less political front. McCoy's medical staff interchange was weeding out those who were far too biased to be effective ambassadorial doctors and bringing to the forefront those who might have fewer commendations but more open minds. And he had to confess, he personally was enjoying the rehearsals of Earth music and Klingon opera. Uhura had obviously greatly impressed the explosive Karglak. Wars had been won by less.

His door chimed. Spock raised an eyebrow. This was

his private time, and he had left orders not to be disturbed. Curious as to who would violate his order for privacy and why, he called, "Enter."

The door hissed open. Chancellor Azetbur quickly stepped inside. The door closed behind her.

"Chancellor," Spock said pleasantly. "What may I do for you?"

"I have a favor to ask," Azetbur said, "and perhaps an even greater one to offer."

"Indeed? Please continue." With a wave of his hand, he indicated a chair. She moved toward it, then apparently decided not to sit and began to pace. Spock sat patiently, letting her take her time. She knew he was supposedly out of contact at this hour; there must be a pressing need for her to have sought him out.

Finally she stopped, planted her feet squarely, and regarded him with an intense gaze. "I have reason to believe your friend James Kirk is in danger," she said.

"I am curious as to what makes you come to that conclusion."

"A few weeks ago, I took the oath of the *DIS jaj je.*"

"The Year and the Day," Spock translated. "Klingons have many rituals to appease the honor code. This one stipulates that the one who swears the oath will protect the other for an entire Klingon year and a day."

"You have indeed familiarized yourself with our customs," she said, and there was a note of approval in her voice.

Spock inclined his head. "It seemed the logical thing to do. What does not seem logical to me, knowing the captain as I do, is that he would accept such a commitment."

"He did not," said Azetbur. "Not knowingly, at least. But I took the oath and I would not be forsworn, so I have sent one of my most trusted men to guard Kirk without his knowing."

"This way, honor would be satisfied, and Kirk's pride would not be affronted," Spock said. "Brilliant, Chancellor. You are a better diplomat than you think. I take it then that this trusted man of yours deems that the hour has come for you to assist Captain Kirk?"

"He does. Kirk and a few others are on a planet called Sanctuary. My ship has been monitoring the situation." Briefly, Azetbur told Spock of the blocked communications, the increased presence of the Orion Syndicate, and the destroyed vessel.

Spock digested this in silence, doing everything he could to brush aside the distracting, illogical thought: *Jim never told me he was leaving.* He endeavored not to show his surprise, and apparently was successful.

"I have no wish to cause an incident by sending my own ships to Sanctuary," Azetbur said. "The colonists are members of the Federation, if not Starfleet. It is my thought that perhaps it would best be handled by the Federation."

"Thank you for your information, Chancellor. I will contact Starfleet immediately."

"You will let me know what transpires?" She struggled not to appear too anxious, too eager to fulfill her honor debt.

"Of course."

"I thank you." She nodded once, then left. Spock sat for a moment, his fingers steepled, thinking hard. Then, before he did what he had promised Azetbur he would do, he tapped the computer. "Dr. McCoy, Commander Uhura . . . please report to my quarters immediately. I may require your assistance."

Chapter Fourteen

"I understand how you must be feeling, Captain, but there's really nothing I can do." Admiral Standing Crane looked terribly apologetic, and Spock knew that much of her concern stemmed from genuine caring. She had known Jim Kirk almost as long as Spock had. "All you've given me thus far are unverified rumors and suppositions. I can't possibly get authorization to get a starship out there on just that."

"I understand your predicament, Admiral."

Standing Crane didn't seem content to just let it lie there, and continued, "You of all people know about the dozens of little fires we're putting out right now. Every single ship is spoken for. If we're to pull them off their already established duties, we'll have to have a lot more proof than what you've given me."

"As I said, I do understand."

Standing Crane sighed. "Listen, Spock. You know I trust your judgment and I believe everything you're telling me is true. But that's not enough. What I can do is give you my personal authorization to go and check it out for yourself, if you can find a way to get there. You give me proof that Jim and those colonists are in real danger, and I'll get you starships so fast it will make your head spin."

"Your hyperbole is exaggerated, but I appreciate the confidence you are displaying in my discernment, Admiral. I will do what I can. Spock out."

"So what do we do now?" asked McCoy. He and Uhura stood behind the console. They had agreed it would be wisest if Standing Crane hadn't known they were all involved. "We can't leave Jim and the others there!"

"Indeed we cannot," said Spock. "The Klingons prize honor above all things. I trust Azetbur to tell me the truth as she knows it. The *DIS jaj je* is an ancient and revered tradition; she would not feign it if she had not actually sworn it. But Admiral Standing Crane is correct. It would be unwise to authorize a Starfleet vessel to depart without further proof."

"Like the doctor said, what do we do now? We don't have a ship of our own anymore," Uhura said.

Spock raised an eyebrow and looked at each of them in turn.

"Of course," said Azetbur. "My only regret is that I cannot accompany you myself."

"To the best of my admittedly limited knowledge," said Spock, "there is nothing that says that the *DIS jaj je* must personally be carried out by the invoker, as long as she is at least indirectly responsible for its completion."

Azetbur smiled faintly. "Your knowledge is not as limited as you think, Captain. I have a duty to see it carried out, yes, but I have an equally important duty to my people to be here, on our homeworld, to see that peace is achieved."

"Agreed."

"The *Kol'Targh,* a *K't'inga*-class battle cruiser, is under your command, Captain," Azetbur said. "Her crew is to obey you as they would obey my own word. You should encounter no resistance. Do not hesitate to contact me if you require anything further. Azetbur out." Her image disappeared from the viewscreen.

"I'm getting mighty tired of spending time on Klingon ships," McCoy muttered.

"We do seem to be doing an awful lot of it," Uhura said. "I hope we're not gone too long. I can't stomach food that looks back at me while I eat it."

"Then you should be about setting in what you can eat, Commander," Spock said. "I fear that this trip might be longer and more dangerous than we might desire."

"What did they get away with?" The green face of the Orion on the screen revealed no emotion, but Lissan shrank inwardly from 858's image nonetheless. "And do not think to lie," 858 added. "We know more than you think."

Which was, mused Lissan, either a very good bluff or the truth. "You know they broke in and you know what they must have seen," Lissan said. "Whether they understand what they witnessed or not, I do not know."

"Then what do you *think* they learned?" 858 said in a voice of exaggerated patience, as if talking to a child.

"They downloaded some information, but they have no cryptographer. It is highly unlikely they will be able to break the code at all, let alone do so before we are ready to begin the operation."

"You are right about that," 858 said, "because the operation will begin in three days."

"Three—" Lissan almost choked. "That is simply impossible."

"What a shame. Because if we're not ready to go within three days, you know what will happen."

Lissan did. Bitterly, he recalled the dozens of times 858 had made that threat: *We will descend upon your facility and take everything, then blast it, and you, out of existence.*

They had the ability to do it. Not for the first time, Lissan wished he had never set eyes upon the human known as Julius Kirk. Young Kirk had brought in the Syndicate, and they had wooed Lissan like he was a shy little girl. He closed his eyes briefly.

"We will be ready," he said, and in a fit of spite terminated the conversation.

He leaned back in his chair, feeling a wave of nausea crash over him. Things were getting very bad very quickly.

There was no way they were going to be ready in three days. His mind went over the various options. There was, of course, the obvious: move in and take the colonists, especially the very high profile and highly vexing James Kirk, hostage. It would buy them time, granted, but it could also alert the Federation that something was amiss.

He could show 858 how very close they were to being ready at the end of the three-day timetable. The Syndicate had been patient for years; surely they would not risk all so close to achieving their goal.

Or at least, thinking they were going to achieve their goal.

The third option was the one that Lissan personally liked best. It involved destroying a Syndicate ship and having a dead Orion pilot at the helm.

He smiled contentedly at the little fantasy, and then the smile faded. This was not what his heritage had bred him for. He was descended from a long line of proud people, who disliked violence and used it only as a last resort. Murder was the Orion's passion, not his. Lissan's was only to help his people get what they should have been given a long, long time ago.

He rose and went to an ancient wooden box, shoved with seeming carelessness into a corner of the room. It was scratched and dented, completely unassuming. To look at it, one would have no idea of the value of its contents. It had come here hidden, and to all but a few, it remained so.

Gently, reverently, Lissan lifted the lid. He reached a respectful hand to touch the gleaming stone's rough surface, caressing it, connecting with the past that it represented now and the future it would embody.

Somehow, his ancestors had known the true value of the yellow-hued Great Stone. As time went by and the Falorians began to interact with other worlds, they

learned exactly how precious this stone was. It was valued beyond measure in other worlds, and could have
bought the Falorians freedom long ago. But now, it was
going to bring Lissan and his people more than that. It
was going to bring them justice.

With great affection, Lissan stroked the largest, most
perfectly formed dilithium crystal in the known universe.

After Scott had thoroughly swept the conference
room for any bugs, Kirk ordered that everyone assemble
there within an hour of his confrontation of Julius. They
came, annoyed at having their research interrupted, and
sat down none too graciously.

Alex addressed them first. "My friends," he began,
"what my uncle and I have to tell you is devastating.
There is no other word for it. I ask for your patience in
hearing Captain Kirk out. What he has to say will sound
unbelievable, but it's true. I also ask that everyone
remain calm, as what he has to say is . . . unsettling, to
say the least."

He stepped back and indicated that Kirk proceed.
Kirk quickly glanced at Julius, who was seated in the
back of the room. Kirk had recommended that, for now,
Julius's role in their present situation not be mentioned.
It was not out of a desire to shield his nephew, but rather
an overriding need to maintain calm. If these people
knew what Julius had done, there could be a riot. Right
now, he needed their cool heads, concentration, and
unquestioned genius.

He spoke briefly, telling of his, Scott's and Chekov's

trip to the facility. There were murmurs of indignation at first from the crowd, then a stunned silence as he proceeded to inform them of what he had seen. Kirk played on their sympathy, asking Chekov to rise and show his still-unhealed hands.

"I am now asking . . . begging . . . for your help," he finished. "We obtained this information at a great personal cost. It's up to you to help us determine what the Falorian plot really is." He looked at the assembled crowd and smiled at them. "We've got something going for us that the Falorians don't have—some of the best minds in the quadrant are seated in this room today. I don't think I can overstate this: not only do our lives depend on you right now, but possibly the lives of untold millions, perhaps even billions, of innocent people. The Falorians could descend at any moment. We have to use what precious time we have to the best of our ability."

He paused to take a breath in order to continue speaking, but the crowd of scientists and doctors began to pummel him with so many questions he couldn't even distinguish between them.

"When will the Falorians come for us?" Leah Cohen cried, her dark eyes large and frightened.

"What kind of plan should we put into action?" Of course Kate Gallagher would ask that. She was always ready to act.

"Should I prepare the hospital wing for casualties?" Dr. Sherman's voice was high and frightened, though he tried to look calm.

"Please!" Kirk cried. "We've got to do this in an

orderly manner! You're disciplined scholars and researchers, start behaving like it!"

Alex shot him a look but Kirk ignored it. There was no time to coddle these people. He was painfully aware of every second that ticked past.

"We've already instructed the computer to translate the data we obtained," he continued. "But it's encrypted so deep that we haven't been able to break the code. Is anyone here trained in encryption?"

Not a single hand went up. Kirk felt his heart sinking. "Anyone have any experience at all?" Still no hands.

The silence was palpable. Then, shyly, Skalli raised her hand.

"Captain Kirk? Would you let me try?"

Kirk opened his mouth to form a polite refusal but the words seemed to stick in his throat. The Huanni were shockingly quick and intelligent, and retained everything they learned. And unlike a computer, Skalli had hunches and guesses. Who knew but that her ancient link to the Falorians might serve them well now?

"All right," Kirk said, and he could see by the way her ears stood up that he had surprised her. "Give it the old Academy try, Skalli. Impress me."

She did.

At her own request, she sequestered herself in a room with a computer, a stack of sandwiches, and a pot of Vulcan spice tea ("I love this stuff!" she had gushed when Kirk himself brought her a full pot). The rest of the colony puttered about, waiting, looking at the chronometers, ready to spring into intellectual action the minute Kirk gave them the signal. Kirk himself paced in front of the door. No one was foolish enough to try to gain admittance.

After fourteen hours and twenty-two minutes, the door hissed open and Skalli emerged. She was trembling and looked exhausted, but there was a smile on her weary face. She extended a padd to him.

"I did it," she said, her voice tired. "It was pretty hard too. They had triple-encryption sequences that relied on a familiarity with their regional dialects and slang terms, which is why it took me so long. I had to go back through the database and cross-reference with everything we knew about the Falorian language and customs. I got a break in that their Taskirakti region has fourteen different terms in common with Huan's Urhark province, or I'd *never* have been able to do it."

"That's . . . very fortunate indeed," Kirk said.

"You're telling me! Glad I don't have to do that every day!" She grinned, and her normal cheery self emerged for a moment despite her obvious exhaustion.

"Skalli. . . ." Kirk began. He gestured with the padd. "This is amazing. I'm in awe of you, and I'm very, very proud. Well done, Cadet."

Skalli blushed and bounced up and down.

They made multiple copies of the decrypted information and handed them out to several different groups. The way the scholars greedily snatched at the information and hastened off to study it made Kirk think of handing off the baton in a relay race. Gallagher, Veta, and Talbot were the first in line. For the moment, until these little clusters of scientists reported back with their findings, there was little he could do. His part of the race was over, for the moment.

He poured himself a cup of coffee and went outside, suddenly craving the feel of real sun and air on his face. It was a beautiful day. The sun shone brightly in an azure sky, and soft white clouds drifted slowly by. The warm breeze was filled with the scent of flowers, and stirred his hair gently. The only thing that marred the vista was the blackened hulk of what had once been a proud ship. Kirk's hazel eyes lingered on the wreckage and he sipped his coffee slowly, thoughtfully.

The colony was on what would be called red alert if it were a Starfleet venture. Those who were not involved in analyzing the Falorian data were constantly monitoring the skies as best they could. Kirk knew, though, that even that would be little enough defense if—no, when—Lissan and his buddies decided to swoop down and make their hostage situation a formality. Alex's insistence that this be a peaceful colony with no weapons, not even for defense, would prove to be their downfall. He, Chekov, and Scott had discussed this briefly earlier today. The only weapons in the entire colony were their three handheld phasers, which Kirk had ordered that they wear at all times from here on in.

"Uncle Jim?" The voice was soft, hesitant—uncharacteristic for its owner.

"What is it, Julius?" Kirk took another sip of coffee and kept his eyes on the horizon. He heard Julius move toward him and stand next to him.

"I, uh . . . I can't get Alex to talk to me."

"I'm not surprised."

Julius took a shaky breath. "I guess I'm not, either. Which is why I never wanted him to find out. Why'd you have to tell him, Uncle Jim? Why couldn't you just have confronted me in private?"

Now Kirk did turn, slowly, and regarded his nephew with a mixture of pity and contempt. "With all that's going on right now, with the Federation itself possibly at stake, that's all you can say?"

"Frankly, I don't give a damn about the Federation," Julius said, sounding more like his old, sullen, hostile self. "Let the Federation rot. What I care about is the only person I've cared about since the day I was born." His voice caught. "I know what I did was wrong, but I did it all for him. I can't—if he hates me for this, I don't know what—"

"This isn't cheating on an exam, Julius. You deliberately and knowingly gave technology and weapons to a race of people who are clearly planning to use these things against someone else."

"The Falorians aren't aggressive, they've never—"

"They've never had the kind of an edge that you gave them," Kirk continued. "You don't know what they'll do now that they've got it. You've admitted that they've already double-crossed you, and God knows what they've got in mind for the Federation. Alex has every right to feel angry, betrayed, and disillusioned." His voice softened. "But I doubt very much that he hates you."

Julius didn't look at him. His jaw tightened and his throat worked. "I wish there was some way I could undo this. I wish I'd never laid eyes on this place, or the Orions, or Lissan."

"We can't do anything but wait until the scientists come back with their report," Kirk told him.

Julius groaned. "I hate waiting. I want to be doing something."

"Now that," Kirk said, "is one thing we have in common."

Scott stifled the urge to wrap his hands around Kevin Talbot's throat and throttle him. It was this desire, he mused, that had kept him from going into research and development and placed him in the engineering room of a starship instead. He was used to accomplishing his miracles quickly and under the sort of pressure that made today's situation feel like a day at the beach.

Despite Scott's efforts to keep up to date on the latest technological breakthroughs, he knew that Talbot was about three steps ahead of him in that respect. But och, it was agonizing watching him put the pieces together, slow as a bear in midwinter.

Finally, he could take it no longer. He leaned over and touched a few panels.

"Hey, what are you—" Talbot stopped in midsentence. "Oh. Oh, my." He, Scott, and the rest of the engineering team leaned over the screen, barely breathing, as they watched the nanoprobes dance across the screen.

They were witnessing a test, and as Scott began to understand exactly what was transpiring, he felt the skin at the back of his neck prickle.

"Lord ha' mercy on us all," he said, quietly.

Chapter Fifteen

"**D**ilithium crystals," was the first thing Scott said to Kirk, Chekov, Alex, Julius and Skalli as they entered the secured "debriefing room."

"What about them?"

"Think for just a moment about how important they are," Scott said, obviously savoring his knowledge even though his face was pale.

"Oooh!" Skalli waved her hand as if she were still in class at the Academy. Kirk winced. For all her staggering intelligence, she was still such a youngster. Such a *Huanni* youngster. "I know!" She cleared her throat and began to recite, word for word, information that had been printed in the Academy textbook on the subject. "Dilithium is a crystalline substance used in every warp propulsion system on every known type of starship. Its unique composition regulates the matter/antimatter reactions that provide the necessary energy to warp space and therefore travel faster than light. Dilithium in its natural state is extremely rare and is found on only a few planets.

In 2286, Captain Spock traveled back in time and discovered a means of recrystalizing dilithium by exposing it to gamma radiation, but this technology is still in its infancy. The purer the form of naturally occurring dilithium, the more valuable it is because it will require less processing in order to render it usable. It will also last much longer than lower-grade dilithium because—"

"Thank you, Skalli, that will suffice," Kirk said. Skalli settled back in her chair, her ears flapping gently with satisfaction.

"The short version is," Scott said, "without dilithium to power our ships, the entire quadrant would slow to a grinding halt. Under those circumstances, he who has dilithium would be lord of all he surveys."

"So you're saying that the Falorians have found a way to destroy the present deposits of dilithium?"

"Not destroy, exactly. We've had a look-see at the nanotechnology they've developed, and judging by our computer simulations, the Falorians have concocted a nasty virus that will render dilithium crystals inert by altering their molecular structure. They'll be just as pretty to look at, but they'll no longer be suitable for regulating matter/antimatter reactions."

"And from the sound of it," Chekov said tiredly, "those Falorians have planted this virus everywhere."

"How stable is the virus?"

"Unfortunately for us, very stable," Scott growled. "It's smaller than a dust mote and can adhere to skin, clothing, damn near anything. So you'll be taking it with you when you go to check on your dilithium crystals."

"Or when the miners go into the dilithium mines,"

Kirk said, the memory of his own recent visit to Rura Penthe still quite vivid.

"Like I said," Chekov said, "it's everywhere."

"At least it's not weapons," Alex said. Everyone stared at him. "I mean, we were thinking that the Falorians were going to start a war or something. We thought millions of people might die."

"They may not die initially," Kirk said, "but when it's learned that every starship, every major mining colony, every hunk of dilithium is now not worth a damn, then there'll be violence, all right. A hell of a lot of it." He looked up at his old friend. "Scotty. Tell me there's something you can do about this."

"Right now," Scott said grimly, "there's not a bloody thing. But I'll keep running the computer simulations. There could be a flaw somewhere, something we haven't thought about yet."

"Julius, do the Falorians have a lot of dilithium stockpiled?" Kirk asked.

"Not that I know of, but as we've learned, I certainly don't know everything about them."

"But that doesn't make sense," Kirk said, thinking aloud now. "The Falorians have been a spacefaring race for some few centuries now. If they had access to dilithium, they would have used it before now. We'd have known that Falor or a Falorian-owned planet would yield dilithium, it's easy enough to scan for. The Falorians could have been wealthy for hundreds of years. Why wait?"

"Maybe because they're just greedy," Julius said. "I mean, that I know. They are greedy little—well, they might have been willing to postpone immediate gratification for longer-range riches."

"Do they have that kind of patience, Julius?" asked Kirk.

Julius thought. "They do have patience, but we're talking the kind of patience that is going to take generations to see fulfillment. I don't know that many species have that."

"And it's a devil of a gamble," Kirk said, continuing to follow this train of thought. "Too many things would have to occur in exactly the right fashion for this to work out to their advantage. Call it a gut feeling, but I think they've only recently come into this dilithium. Or they may not even have it yet. Maybe that's why the Orion Syndicate is involved—to help them get this one last cache of dilithium."

"One thing that I did notice," Scott said, "was that the grade of dilithium the Falorians utilized in their testing was amazingly pure. About ninety-nine-point-nine-eight percent pure. I've never seen that level of purity before in my life. It must be a pretty bauble indeed to look at. And the value of such a thing on the black market would be staggering. I'll bet that's it, Captain. They've teamed up with the Orions to get a hold of and control this cache of pure dilithium."

"So, they have weapons, they have the Syndicate, and they have a target that's rich in dilithium," said Chekov. "The question now is, where would they strike?"

"Oh, no," Skalli breathed. Kirk looked over at her. Her ears drooped and she was trembling. "This . . . this can't be. . . ."

"Skalli, what is it?"

She turned a frightened gaze on him. "I can't tell you. I'm not allowed to tell."

"On whose orders?"

Tears welled in her eyes. "We are never supposed to speak of it, never, never. I'm sorry, I can't. . . ."

Kirk reached over and grabbed her arms, shaking her gently. "Skalli, listen to me. You've remembered something that clearly might have an impact on what we've just learned. Don't you think you need to tell us what it is?"

"You don't understand!" she cried, gulping hard. "My people . . . I can't, I just can't!"

Kirk released her. "Maybe you didn't understand the full impact of what Mr. Scott has just said. Your people have recently joined the Federation, presumably because they share its ideals. Those ideals will be shattered like broken glass once dilithium becomes useless. Anyone who has any amount of dilithium will have the sort of power that could make him a god in some peoples' eyes. Everything the Federation has worked for will disappear overnight. The galaxy will be a place where those with dilithium rule with an iron fist over everyone else. It'll be absolute chaos, tyranny of the very worst sort imaginable. Is that the kind of galaxy your people want, Skalli?"

"No," she whispered.

"Then tell us." He reached for her again, very gently this time. "Help us."

Her eyes met his and she swallowed hard. "All right," she whispered. She took a deep breath and began.

"You have been told that the Falorians wanted to leave Huan," she said. "That's not true. We—the Huanni—banished them. They had labored for us for centuries as slaves, growing our crops, mining the soil, building our cities. When we had sufficient technology that we no longer needed them, the last thing we wanted was to be reminded of them. So we put them on a ship and put them down on Falor."

Kirk stared at her. Her lip trembled. "It was a lovely planet," she said, defensively. "It had everything they needed to thrive. It wasn't cruel to leave them there!"

Kirk said nothing. The whole room had gone silent, everyone no doubt sensing, as did Kirk, that they were witnessing a powerful revelation.

"They did just fine on Falor," she continued. "None of us held grudges. We were happy in their success. We even extended the hand of friendship to them, but we were refused. They hate us, Captain. You can't imagine how much they hate us. That's why I wanted to become an ambassador, and why I was so excited about getting to meet a Falorian. I wanted to be a part of a new chapter in history, to help Falorians and Huanni be allies, even friends. We're the same people, we ought not to let something that happened hundreds of years ago stand between us!"

"But Skalli," Kirk said quietly, "no one ever told us that you had enslaved the Falorians."

"We were ashamed," she whispered, tears pouring unheeded down her face. "Wouldn't you be?"

"You know my planet's history. Until very recently, slavery, unfortunately, wasn't at all uncommon. We were able to see that it was wrong, admit it, and move on," Kirk said. "We didn't pretend it didn't happen. You can't heal what you don't acknowledge, Skalli."

"We were afraid the Federation wouldn't take us, that if they found out, they'd ask us to leave."

Kirk had nothing to say to this. Skalli was right, but for all the wrong reasons. It wasn't the fact that Huan had enslaved and then abandoned half its population centuries ago that was the problem. There were many Federation member planets that had a far nastier and bloodier history. What mattered was who those people were now. The problem was, the Huanni had lied about their past to the Federation. That was more than sufficient grounds for expulsion if such drastic action was desired.

"What does this have to do with the dilithium?" he said at last, hoping the change of subject would help.

"I'm not sure, but there used to be stories. They're now—what was the human term for them—folk stories, fairy tales. Tales about beautiful, powerful gems deep in the earth. You know the sort of stories, where the hero finds them and all kinds of good things happen. You wanted to know if the Falorians had access to dilithium. Maybe they don't have any on their planet, but maybe we do. Huan. Maybe those folk tales are real, and the Falorians, who used to dig in the earth, knew it. And it's a perfect excuse to attack *us,* to hurt *us,* as they feel we hurt them. They'd become very wealthy and exact revenge at the same time."

Kirk's thoughts churned. At first, he wondered—how could the Huanni not know that they had dilithium deposits? As he had just said a moment ago, it was easy enough to scan for, and the Huanni weren't foolish. They'd have scanned for it.

But what if something prevented the scan from reading correctly? Such things happened. Radiation, soil composition—there were more than a few things that could make a scan inaccurate. It wasn't beyond the realm of possibility.

It all made sense now. If the Falorians did indeed have ancient knowledge about hidden deposits of dilithium buried deep within Huan's soil—knowledge of which even the Huanni themselves were ignorant— then of course they would want to control the dilithium trade. Destroying the efficacy of dilithium across the quadrant would make what few unaffected deposits there were fabulously rare. Thanks to the weapons and technology provided by first Julius and then the Orion Syndicate, the Falorians would easily be able to take Huan while the Federation limped along, crippled to the core. Eventually, of course, this "gold rush" of dilithium would fade. They already had the technology to recrystalize dilithium, but as Skalli had stated, they were still working on it. It would happen, yes, but it would take time. Perhaps years.

And in the meantime, the Falorians and all who associated with them would become wealthy and powerful beyond their wildest dreams.

He was so lost in the dire scenario that he didn't hear Scott's comments. "Sorry, Scotty, what was that?"

"I said, I'll want to run some more computer scenarios." Scott frowned darkly. "Something's bothering me,

Captain. I don't know what it is, but I'll not be happy until I've figured it out."

"In the meantime, what do we do?" asked Alex. "We're stranded, we've got no way to warn anybody—"

"It looks bad, yes," Chekov spoke up. "But Captain Kirk has gotten us out of worse situations." He turned to give what he doubtless thought was a reassuring smile of utter confidence to his captain. But to Kirk, it was only a mocking grimace.

It didn't just look bad, it *was* bad. And he didn't have the faintest idea what they were going to do about it.

Kirk lay awake in bed, thinking furiously. It had been almost two full Sanctuary days since he'd broken into the facility. At any moment, the Falorians could come for them. Right now, everyone was very carefully entertaining the fantasy that nothing was really wrong. But after seeing the research facility and learning about the truly diabolical plan the Falorians had come up with, Kirk was not about to make the mistake of underestimating Lissan. Lissan knew very well that they were hostages; he just hadn't made the situation formal yet.

Chekov and Harper were frantically doing everything they could to try to get a message out, but Kirk knew in his heart that it was just a way to keep spirits up. Scott was running his additional scenarios, for whatever good that might do. Conceivably, he could come up with some way to reprogram the nanoprobe virus, but even miracle worker Scotty needed time and resources to perform his special engineering magic. And those were two things that were in very short supply.

His door chimed. He glanced at the chronometer. It was 0214. He reached for a robe and donned it. "Enter," he called.

The door hissed open and Skalli stood there. She looked terrible. "Captain Kirk? I'm so sorry to bother you."

"It's no bother," he said, and it wasn't a lie. Anything was preferable to being alone with his dark thoughts right now. "What's the matter?"

"You know!" And she put her head in her hands and sobbed. "I'm so ashamed . . . of my people, of myself . . . Captain, I've been less than useless to you. I'm sure you regret the day we met."

"That's not true." Again, the comment was no lie, and it slightly surprised Kirk. He'd gotten more used to Skalli's highs and lows, and they didn't bother him nearly as much as they used to. "You have been invaluable. We'd still be stuck wondering what the Falorians were up to without your code-cracking skills."

She waved a hand in angry dismissal. "Any Huanni could have done that."

"I doubt that, but even so, no one else here could have." He sat down next to her in the chair. They were both facing straight forward, and Skalli determinedly avoided his gaze and wiped at her wet face. "And as for your ancestors' treatment of the Falorians, that's hardly your fault. I bet you've never enslaved a single Falorian in your entire life."

He said it lightly, but her eyes again filled with tears. "But we should have taken responsibility for what our ancestors did. You were right. We shouldn't have pretended it didn't happen, even if we did want to be friends. Especially if we wanted to be friends. Friends apologize wh-when they're wrong."

She couldn't know it, but her words stung. Kirk had been very wrong about Skalli. While she was still terribly emotional, she was intelligent, competent, and capable. She'd been the one to keep her wits about her and find shelter during what could have been a fatal sandstorm. She'd been the one to lock herself away with only sandwiches and Vulcan spice tea until she'd cracked a completely new code. And as for her outbursts, well, Kirk knew more than a few humans of her age who were that emotional.

"Well, then, let me be a friend," he said, gently. "I misjudged you, and that was both wrong and foolish of me. You're doing a marvelous job in a very stressful situation, and you have been a great asset to this colony."

Now she did look at him. She swallowed hard. "R-really? You're not just saying that?"

"Not at all. I mean every word." He punctuated the comment with gentle pokes on her shoulder until she smiled and ducked her head. Her long ears crept upward from where they had been plastered against her head. Then she sobered.

"If we do get out of this alive," she said, "then I will have been responsible for Huan being asked to leave the Federation, won't I?"

"No. The Huan Council of Elders, who made the decision to lie about their past to the Federation advisory board, will be responsible, if that even happens. What you will be responsible for is helping us figure out how to stop the Falorians from essentially taking over the quadrant."

Now her ears were fully erect, and she beamed at him. He squeezed her shoulder affectionately. "Feel better?" he asked.

"Oh, very much!" She hugged him vigorously. He supposed he should have expected it. He endured the embrace, and smiled at her as she rose and left.

He went back to bed, feeling oddly better, and was just drifting off to sleep when his communicator chirped. Groaning, he flipped it open. "Kirk here."

"It's Scott. You'd best get here right away."

The clipped, tight sound of Scott's voice put Kirk on red alert. He hurried into his clothes and fairly ran.

Alex, Julius, Talbot, and Gallagher turned to him when he entered, their faces pale and drawn. He imagined he could smell the fear.

"It's bad, Captain. It's very, very bad."

"Show me."

Scott swiveled the computer screen so Kirk could see it. "What am I looking at?" he asked.

"Remember when I told you that all the testing the Falorians did was with an incredibly pure chunk o' dilithium?" Kirk nodded. "That got me to thinking. You and I know that most of the dilithium crystals in operation out there are much less pure. When it comes right down to it, all dilithium crystals really are are hunks of stone. They therefore can be expected to have varying degrees of impurities in them—other minerals and so on. Processing can clean them up a bit, but most of the crystals we use have a certain amount of impurity to them."

Kirk nodded. "Go on."

"This is the test scenario utilizing a crystal of the purity that the Falorians used, over ninety-nine percent pure." Kirk watched as the animated nanoprobes descended. He saw the molecular structure of the crystal altered. The image shrank, pulling back until Kirk was looking at a crystal about the size of his hand inside a warp core. Nothing happened.

"When the virus alters the molecular structure of the crystal, it's as if you put a diamond in the matter-antimatter chamber," Scott said. "Nothing happens. But watch what happens with a crystal that's not quite so pure."

He tapped the keys and the simulation played again. A second time, Kirk watched as the virus went to work and the image pulled back.

The light from the explosion was so bright that he had to close his eyes. "What the—"

"The virus weakened the molecular structure so much that the crystal shattered," Scott explained. He looked ten years older. "The fusion of matter and antimatter without the intervention of the crystal resulted in a warp core breach."

Kirk stared at the screen, which had reset and was replaying the deadly scenario. "How impure was the crystal?"

"About eighty-seven percent. We ran a few more scenarios. If you want to avoid a warp core breach as a result of this virus attacking the crystal, you'd need at least a ninety-two percent purity."

Kirk didn't want to hear the answer, but he had to

ask. "I know you don't know exactly, but give me your best estimate. How many starships out there have crystals that will fracture if they're infected with this virus?"

"About nine out of every ten, if we're lucky," Scott replied, grimly.

"So if this virus is released—"

"Nine out of ten starships, of every make and model, of every fleet in the quadrant, will be destroyed," Scott replied grimly.

Kirk's mind reeled. The Falorians weren't just going to invade Huan and dominate the dilithium trade.

They were going to kill billions of innocent people while doing it.

Chapter Sixteen

For a long, dreadful moment, no one spoke. What words could there be, to voice one's horror? Finally, Julius broke the silence.

"I can't believe it," he said, his voice soft.

"You're not calling my scenarios into question, now, are you, lad?" said Scotty softly, with a warning in his rich Scottish burr.

"No, no, I'm sure they're correct, but. . . ." Julius ran a hand through his sandy blond hair. "I'm just having a hard time believing that the Falorians are going to commit mass murder. I thought I knew—"

"We don't know anything about them!" cried Alex, speaking directly to his brother for the first time since Julius revealed his treachery. "*You* don't know anything about them! They're probably reveling in the knowledge of what they're about to do. You think you know someone, and then they go and do things. . . ." His voice trailed off.

"It's one thing to steal something, to hatch a plot to

make yourself rich," Kirk said. "It's quite another to cold-bloodedly set about the murder of billions of innocent people who have never done you harm."

Julius physically shrank from Kirk's words. Kirk knew what he was thinking, because he was thinking it too: *Julius began this. If he hadn't introduced them to the Syndicate, they would never have been able to put this plan into action.*

But attacking Julius wouldn't solve anything. Kirk took a deep breath and changed the subject slightly. "Is the virus presently active?" he asked Scott.

"No, and that's a blessing for sure, at least for the moment," Scott replied. "I can't be certain without more information, but I'm betting that each probe will be remotely activated at some point, probably simultaneously. Whenever the Falorians decide the time is right."

"That makes sense," Chekov said. "They don't want a single probe to be detected until they're ready to wreak havoc with all of them at once."

"Thank heaven for small favors," Kirk said dryly. The disaster had not yet struck, and might yet be averted. The question was, what could they do? How did they go about warning the Federation, and incidentally, saving their own hides?

"Scotty, I don't suppose you could adjust the *Drake* so that it could leave the atmosphere?"

"Not without a lot of parts we don't have, and probably not even then," Scott answered grumpily. "She's a remarkable little atmospheric vessel, but she's not designed for space flight."

"The only ones able to get information out are the

Falorians," Kirk said. "You were able to piggyback onto their signal once, to raise their shield and shut down their security systems. Do you think we could get a signal to Starfleet the same way?"

Scott looked thoughtful. "It's possible, but I doubt I could do it without actually being inside the complex."

"Then it sounds like we'll have to get you inside."

"Why haven't they attacked yet?" Gallagher wanted to know as Kirk gathered them together for their final round of instructions. For someone who advocated peace so strenuously, Gallagher always seemed to be itching for a fight.

"On Earth, we have an old saying: don't look a gift horse in the mouth," Kirk answered. "The Falorians may feel that we didn't escape with anything significant, or assumed we'd never be able to decode the information even if it was important. Under normal conditions, they'd be right, but they hadn't counted on Skalli."

From where she sat in the front row, Skalli beamed.

"We've been very careful about where we've discussed our plans," Kirk said. "Or at least, I hope we've all been careful. The Falorians have seen to it that we can't communicate with the outside, and that we can't leave. Whatever it is we do know, we can't spill the beans to anyone. There's no need for them to attack us quite yet. Which is completely to our advantage."

He outlined his plan while they listened attentively.

The weather cooperated, and over the course of the next nine hours, small groups of threes and fours left the perimeter of the colony. They carried testing equipment and food, and moved without haste toward the areas they were studying. Mattkah and his crew went to their flower field and began running tests. Veta went to a cave he'd been mapping. Gallagher went to a forested area, where she'd been conducting tests on the wildlife. Others went to different areas. There were several shuttle runs that dropped off research teams.

In short, the colonists all appeared to simply be going about their business of research and study. Three times, Falorian ships flew over, and Kirk knew they were all being carefully watched. It was perhaps the hardest thing he had asked yet of the Sanctuarians—to pretend that everything was normal when it wasn't. A few of them were tense and harried-looking, and their "conversations" were designed to be overheard. But Kirk was counting on the Falorians doing a quick sweep, not moving in tightly to get facial expressions and overhear words. He only hoped that they wouldn't notice that instead of the usual groups of about three or four, every single colonist was now casually departing the base allegedly to do research.

Each team of "researchers" carried with them emergency ration packs and as many useful tools as possible. The one piece of equipment they didn't have were communicators. Mark Veta's careful, meticulous mapping of the caves over the last few weeks was now invaluable. Everyone had a map of the cave system thanks to his diligence, and that meant a place to literally go to ground and hide. Veta's work could help save lives.

Kate Gallagher had worked with Scotty on refining her "Masker." They had identified the frequency at which it worked to block Falorian tricorder readings. What had been created as a way to protect endangered species from poachers was now being turned to protect endangered colonists from kidnappers. The Masker worked in the lab, but they had no idea just how effective they would be in the field.

"Humanoids are the ultimate predators," Gallagher had said as she was the first to be injected with the subcutaneous chip. "How ironic that we're the hunted now." She had rubbed her sore arm and glared at Dr. Sherman. "You need a better bedside manner, Ted."

The entire plan was a huge gamble, but it was the only way to get people out of harm's way as quickly as possible.

"I want you to go too," Kirk said to Alex, as the last team was getting ready for departure.

"No way," Alex said. "I'm coming with you."

"I don't think that would be a good idea."

Alex flushed. "Why not? Because I'm incompetent? Because I'm not a leader like you? I saw him watching me," he said, jerking his head in Scott's direction. "I know he saw me crack, during the sandstorm. But I've learned so much, Uncle Jim. I could help you."

Kirk put his hands on his nephew's shoulder and looked him right in the eye. "I know you could help me. But they need your help more than I do. The fewer people who try to break into that complex, the greater the likelihood that we'll succeed."

Anguished, Alex cried, "You're taking *him* with

you, and he's the one who got us into this mess!"

Julius paled. "You know why Julius is going," Kirk said before tempers could flare further. "He knows the Falorians better than any of us, and he's more familiar with their equipment. We'll need his knowledge when we get inside."

Alex stubbornly refused to reply. Kirk tried again. "Alex, you're not Starfleet. You're not trained in the sort of things you'll be required to do. What you are, is head of this colony. These people trusted you enough to uproot themselves and follow you halfway across the galaxy in pursuit of a dream. That dream is in danger. You owe it to them to be with them. You promised to protect them. Keep that promise."

Alex looked over at the group slipping on backpacks and checking their equipment. They looked back at him intently. Kirk hoped Alex could read their body language as he could: *Come with us, Alex. We need you. We're afraid.*

Kirk removed his phaser and extended it to Alex. The younger man recoiled as if Kirk had offered him a cobra. "I don't want it."

"You might need it," Kirk pressed. "Take it."

"No," Alex said firmly, straightening. For the first time in days, he seemed to have his old sense of confidence back. He was again the intense, persuasive dreamer. "Things have fallen apart, Uncle Jim. A lot of things have spiraled out of our control. But the one thing I can control is how I behave in this crisis. Sanctuary was founded on high principles, foremost among them being a desire not to harm anyone. You're right, the Falorians do need to be stopped. But the minute I take that phaser and fire it at one of them, I become just like them. Don't you see?"

"No," Kirk said, honestly. "I've never seen anything wrong with defending yourself, and the phasers can be set to stun." He smiled. "But this is your colony, Alex. Your people. You have to do what you think is best to protect them in a way that honors all your beliefs."

Alex looked back at the group, as if for confirmation. They were all smiling and nodding. Kirk admired their resolve to adhere to what they felt was right, even in the face of injury or death. Personally, he always felt more comfortable with a phaser in his hand, but one of the reasons he'd used a phaser as often as he had in his life was to protect just such ideals as Alex and the other colonists fervently believed in. He wouldn't force Alex to take a weapon if he didn't want to.

"Besides," Alex said, forcing a smile, "We're just quietly hiding. You five are going into the tiger's lair. You'll probably need all the phasers you've got."

Kirk agreed with him. Frankly, he wished they had more. But three would have to suffice.

Alex's group was the last one to depart. As he had done with each of the others, Kirk shook everyone's hand. Leah Cohen actually pulled him into a quick hug, while Mattkah did little to hide his continuing dislike. Kate Gallagher grasped Kirk's hand firmly, as was her wont, and he hesitated.

"Your Masker is going to save lives today," he told her. "Perhaps not the way you envisioned, but it won't be abused." That, he knew, had been her biggest worry:

that somehow her talents would one day be put to destructive use.

She smiled, and her face softened. "Thanks," she said. She didn't let go of his hand for a moment. Then she said, "Hey, Jim, if we ever get out of here, I'd like to show you my thesis one day." Gallagher squeezed his hand and let it drop.

When this last group departed Sanctuary, Kirk nodded to Skalli, Julius, Scott, and Chekov.

"Let's go," he said, and they climbed into the *Drake*.

In the end, Lissan knew that he was glad that 858 had forced the timetable up. Like the Orion, Lissan too was growing impatient. The scientists had had their day. Now, it was the time of those who would act.

Lissan was a direct descendent of Takarik. On a planet where there had been no indigenous peoples, it was fairly easy to keep track of one's ancestry from the hour that the Huanni had abandoned them. While the Falorians did not believe in royalty per se, one's ancestral lineage was considered to be important. So when Lissan had decided to follow politics and eventually become one of the Kal-Toreshi, the governing body of Falor, no one was too surprised. For years, he had been aware of the plan, and despite the warnings of the scientists clamoring for more time to do more thorough testing, he was ready, even eager, to plunge forward.

The Falorians and the Huanni had long been silent enemies. When forced to interact, both sides had been unfailingly polite, but the Falorians had never bothered to disguise their hatred. And why should they? They had been the wronged, the innocent, forced into harsh physical labor for centuries and then discarded as inconvenient and unwanted. And the arrogance of the Huanni! No mention of what they had done, no offers of regret or apology, nothing.

It had been a racial triumph for the Falorians to have kept the precious secret for as long as they had. It was hard to keep from gloating, but they had managed. Centuries ago, when the Huanni had almost offhandedly deposited their own brethren on Falor, Lissan's ancestor had stolen a single precious crystal—one of uncountable millions yet to be mined. Physical labor had uncovered them, and to this day, the Huanni remained cheerily ignorant of the riches upon which they were squatting. Deep mineral layers under the soil prevented scanners from discovering the unbelievably pure deposits. Technology would not reveal them; only the difficult digging of generations of slaves had done so.

It had been a terrible irony: the Huanni had the means to mine the dilithium, but no knowledge that it was even there, whereas the banished Falorians knew of its presence, but had no means to recover it.

Until now.

Now, the Falorians had weapons, allies, and technology. They could descend upon Huan and quickly, efficiently subdue it with a minimum loss of life. Life was precious to the Falorians, even Huan life; the fewer who died in the coming conflict, the better. Lissan was not after blood, he was after riches, power and acknowledgment, curse them, *acknowledgment* of the wrongs the Huanni had perpetrated upon his people.

Once he had that, the Falorians would move in and harvest every kilo of the precious crystals, sharing, of course, with their good friends and comrades the Orion Syndicate.

Lissan couldn't resist a smile. This was the sweetest part of a delicious, infallible plan.

Oh, yes, the Orion Syndicate would help them subdue Huan and mine the dilithium. They would even take almost half of the staggeringly pure crystals. Then they would go away, the deal completed to everyone's satisfaction.

And then, Lissan would order the nanoprobe virus activated. The precious dilithium the Syndicate thought they had all but stolen from seemingly gullible Falorians would be worth nothing more than any other rock. Nearly every ship in the quadrant, including Syndicate ships, would be hanging dead in space.

No Syndicate, to come looking for revenge. No Huanni to attempt a retaliatory strike on Falor. And probably no Federation to send their mighty starships, to protect their newest member planet of Huan.

And even if they did, mused Lissan, he had—oh, what did the humans call it—the trump card.

One James T. Kirk.

He was glad of 858's suggestion, now. From what his infiltrators had told him of humans, they regarded the lives of their own as highly as Falorians did. They would do anything to protect their colonists, especially when among that number was a man as honored and revered as Kirk apparently was. Soon, it would be time to—

"Kal-Tor!"

Jarred by the intrusion, Lissan whirled angrily on the youngster who had dared enter in so unseemly a fashion. "What do—"

But Jasslor didn't even let him finish. "Kal-Tor, they've fled!"

"What—who has fled?"

"The colonists! Look!" Completely tossing aside any semblance of protocol, the underling rushed past his Kal-Tor and quickly activated Lissan's monitor. Jasslor called up several cameras, and each one showed the same dreadful image: an empty room. Empty mess hall, empty labs, empty research stations, empty fields.

Empty, empty, empty. . . .

"The pilot conducting the fourth daily flyover reported that he hadn't seen anyone. That aroused our suspicions, so we activated the cameras and . . . and saw what you see. What you don't see." Jasslor looked confused and frightened, as well he should be.

"Right out from under us," muttered Lissan. "They slipped out from right under us like. . . ."

Kirk. This reeked of him. A growl formed deep in the back of Lissan's throat and erupted as a roar of shame and fury. He curled his fingers into a fist and slammed it down on the console. Sparks flew.

"Find them!" he shrieked. *"Find them now!"*

Chapter Seventeen

There were not many Falorians on Sanctuary who could be spared for the search, but Lissan called up every last one of them. He had thought it would be simple, but again, the unexpected cleverness of these humans foiled his plans.

He went over the recordings that the flyover ships had made. Even in his anger and frustration, Lissan felt a certain amount of compassion for the pilots. No one was rushing to safety; the colonists were all walking, carrying their equipment and chatting, as they had done every single day since their arrival. There was nothing to alert any pilot that there was anything amiss.

The only indication as to what was really going on—a mass exodus—was that each of the flyovers saw the same thing: four to five groups of five to ten people going out to do research. Had they compared their recordings, they would have been on to the ruse much earlier, but there was no reason to take that time-consuming step. Alone, each recording looked innocent. Together, they spelled trouble.

Precious time was wasted in simply trying to track them down. Lissan had thought it would be easy. The signatures of all the colonists, even the nonhuman ones, were greatly different than that of the Falorians. Eventually he realized that the colonists had hidden in the not inconsiderable cave systems that ran through the planet. Further, the trackers were reporting that they weren't picking up any humanoid lifesigns at all. Lissan closed his eyes against the wave of fury that rushed through him. This search would have to be done on foot, and they had utilized the *Drake*.

But he had no choice. He had to get those colonists back. Each life was another reason for Starfleet to refrain from attacking.

He gave the order, and the search began.

"They'll find us," Mattkah said morosely. "You heard what Kirk and them said about the level of their technology. These things under our skins aren't going to throw them off."

Gallagher bridled and opened her mouth to report.

"We don't know that," Alex said swiftly, trying to prevent a fight. "I prefer to hope."

"Of course you do," Mattkah said, in a voice that dripped contempt. "Live in hope, die in despair, isn't that the Earth quote? 'Come with me, we will build a place called Sanctuary, and we'll all live happily ever after.'" Mattkah made an appalling sound and hawked up a huge gobbet of spit and expelled it in Alex's direction.

Alex was on his feet at once. Adrenaline pumped

through him and his face was red with a dangerous combination of embarrassment and anger. Mattkah laughed harshly.

"And I've got you all riled now, haven't I? You're just like your brother underneath that complacent surface. All you humans are hotheads."

Alex took a long, deep, slow breath, forcing his pumping heart to slow. "Yes, you did get me riled. And that's my fault, for rising to the bait like that." He was still edgy, nervous, and began to pace.

"Alex," said Leah Cohen, staring at her fingers, "are they going to find us?"

"I don't know," he said honestly. "But I do know that we are doing all we can. We knew there would be dangers on this journey. We knew we'd be far away from anything safe." He laughed, sadly. "What we didn't know was that the danger would be coming from the one group of people we thought we could rely on for help."

"I hope Kirk gets that message out," Mattkah said, "and after they've done that, I hope one of the Falorians rips Julius's head off. Damned betrayer."

Alex paled. "What do you mean?"

Gallagher sighed. "It's a small colony, and it's hard to keep secrets, Alex. We know about Julius."

She didn't seem particularly angry, nor did any of the other colonists. Save for Mattkah, they all appeared to have forgiven Alex's wayward brother. If only Alex could, too.

Alex warred with conflicting emotions. He was furious at Julius, and terribly, terribly hurt. But no matter what his brother had done, Alex still loved him. He would always be little Juley to him, frightened and clingy and seeking reassurance. Even seeing Julius confess had not changed that.

Once, Alex had lived for Julius. If he now had to die for that, so be it.

"Perhaps Julius made it easier for the Falorians," Alex acknowledged. "But they would have found someone else if it hadn't been him."

"Yeah, but maybe then we wouldn't be stuck hiding in these caves and fearing for our lives," Mattkah said.

"Maybe. But don't blame Julius for that. Blame me. You're my responsibility."

"All right," Mattkah said with an evil cheeriness. "I will."

At that moment, they heard a sudden noise as of dozens of running feet. A powerful bright light blinded them.

Unable to see, Alex still rushed toward the sound. "My responsibility," he cried, and then fell backward as a blast caught him in the chest.

It had been a particularly long day for Laura Standing Crane. She had processed two more requests for Federation membership, joined together in a remote conference with Chancellor Azetbur to come up with a . . . well . . . *creative* reason as to why their chief negotiator was unable to continue with the conference, and heard about sixteen more annoying incidents with the Falorian delegates on no fewer than twelve Federation planets.

She stood for a long time in the shower, letting the hot water beat down on her hair and breathing in the steam. Too bad she couldn't spare an hour for a massage; she could certainly use it. Standing Crane got out of the shower and toweled herself dry, lighting a smudge bundle to help purify the environment of her small apartment in which she barely spent five hours a night, if she was lucky.

The pungent, calming scent soothed her somewhat, but not completely. She extinguished the smoldering bundle in an abalone shell and let the smoke curl around her. Her thoughts were on Jim. She combed out her long, thick, silver-shot black hair, not seeing her own reflection as she stood in front of the mirror.

Spock was not the sort of person to overreact, even given his love—yes, love, though he'd die before using the word—for his former captain and friend. And Azetbur was hardly one to put herself out for a human. Despite what she had said to Spock, Standing Crane completely believed everything he had told her. There was no doubt in her mind and heart that Jim, beloved friend for so many years, was in danger.

But she had responsibilities that extended beyond her own personal thoughts, fears and affections. She had told Spock the only thing she could—that she couldn't authorize the use of a starship based on rumors and innuendos. Azetbur had sent her a brief, mysteriously worded note that had convinced Standing Crane that the chancellor herself had arranged for a ship. Standing Crane was glad of it. She hoped to hear at any minute that Spock had found out that the whole thing was a mistake and there was no trouble at all. Failing that, that he'd gotten proof that the colony was in actual danger, because she would like nothing more than to get a starship out there, pronto.

Her computer made a soft beeping noise. Spock? Standing Crane wrapped a towel around herself and sat down in front of the message.

The image of the president of the Federation, not Spock's impassive visage, filled the screen. Great Spirit, more work, then. She smiled tiredly. "What's the trouble now, sir?"

Standing Crane had always thought that the president looked more than a bit like the famous author of several centuries ago, the humorist Mark Twain. But there was nothing light about his expression. He looked as strained as she had ever seen him, and worry shot through her.

"Get dressed and prepare for transport *now*," was all he said.

Four minutes later, a four-star admiral stood clad in a hastily donned uniform with dripping hair in the president's office in Paris. She felt the wetness along her back spread with each second, but paid it little heed.

"We've got a message from one of the Falorian Kal-Toreshi. Calls himself Lissan. He particularly asked for you, Laura," the president said.

Standing Crane nodded once. She took her place alongside four other admirals and various high-ranking Federation civilians as the president signaled the screen to be activated.

The face of Kal-Tor Lissan smiled pleasantly. "Thank you for attending. It is my understanding that the hour is late on your planet. I apologize."

"Kal-Tor," said the president, "you didn't roust us all out of bed to exchange pleasantries. I gather your message is of some import. Do you have concerns about the way your delegates were treated? Because we were just about to offer you membership upon certain—"

Lissan interrupted him with a hearty laugh. "Oh, the timing is too amusing. We have no desire to join your little club, Mr. President."

Standing Crane felt heat rise in her face. What game was this arrogant creature playing?

The president stiffened beside her, but he kept his voice calm. "If you no longer desire membership in the Federation, rest assured, we will not pursue you. But if that's not the reason for your contacting us, then may I inquire as to what is?"

"I must admit, that from everything I have heard from our delegations, the planets of the Federation have shown us great hospitality. And for that, we thank you. Soon I will tell you how valuable those gestures were to us. But first, out of gratitude for the kindness you have shown us, I am going to give you a warning."

Lissan leaned forward until his face filled the screen. "We are poised to take Huan. Our vessels and those of our . . . allies . . . are moving even as I speak to you. This is a quarrel that goes very deep, its dark roots extending into the shadows of the past. It has nothing to do with you, and you will be well advised to stay out of it."

"Huan is a Federation planet!" snapped the president. "We will come to the aid of one of our own!"

"A noble sentiment, but quite misplaced," Lissan continued maddeningly. "I will say this once, as clearly as I can, out of respect for the lives and safety of your people. Listen well. We have set up buoys around Huan. If any vessel, Federation or otherwise, violates that perimeter, then we will activate a virus that will leave every ship you possess hanging dead in space. No Federation vessel will be able to engage warp drive. Think about that, Mr. President. Think about all the ships on deep-space missions far away from any hospitable planet or starbase. It would take them years to get anywhere under impulse power. Some ships would do just fine, but others wouldn't. Even if they did get home, the crews of many ships would be old and gray before they ever again saw their loved ones. This is not something I would see happen to innocent people. Do *you* want that to happen, Mr. President? For the sake of a few million worthless Huanni?"

A young man named Parkan had been listening intently to the conversation, and out of the corner of her eye, Standing Crane had been watching him just as intently. Now she saw the color drain from his face, his breath catch, and his eyes widen slightly. Standing Crane closed her dark eyes briefly. She thought she knew what Parkan's reaction meant, and she prayed she was wrong.

Instead of firing more questions about the threat, the president chose a different tactic. "It is clear to me that you have a great enmity toward the Huanni."

"You choose pallid words, Mr. President."

"The Federation has long been known for its ability to fold in different cultures and create harmony," said the president. He looked over at Standing Crane.

"Even now, we are making peace with a people who have historically been our worst enemies," Standing Crane said, picking up her cue. "It has been a hard road, but when they were in need, we came to their aid. We are helping preserve the Klingons as the proud, powerful people they are. We are not trying to make them just like us. Perhaps we could help you initiate negotiations that could lead to peace between both your peoples. War may not be the only option."

Lissan looked at her searchingly. "Tell me, Admiral, have you ever been owned?"

"What?"

"Have you ever been owned," he repeated. "Has anyone ever owned your ancestor, made him work hard labor, and then tossed him away like so much trash when his usefulness was done? Has anyone—"

"I have such a history," spoke up Admiral Thomas Mason. He stood tall, proud, and handsome, his dark brown skin slightly shiny with beads of perspiration induced by the incredible tension in the room.

"A few hundred years ago, I would have been her property," he said, nodding in the direction of Admiral Anastacia Cannon. The younger woman met Mason's gaze evenly. They stood side by side, her short blond hair and pink complexion a contrast with his dark brown skin, hair and eyes. "And Standing Crane—her people were once herded like cattle onto reserved chunks of land, their histories diminished, their language all but destroyed. So you aren't telling us anything that we haven't experienced and overcome right here on this single planet."

He reached and grasped Cannon's hand, and their fingers entwined, the dark and light merging into a single strong unit, yet retaining their individual differences. Together they raised their joined hands.

"This is what we are all about now," said Cannon. She looked deceptively delicate, but Standing Crane knew there was fire in her heart. "Unity. Working together. The past is the past. We learn from it, and then we move on. The Falorians and the Huanni can do the same."

Lissan seemed stunned. Clearly, whatever research he had done on human history hadn't included checking for such disharmony. He'd have found it easily enough; nothing was covered up. But neither was it anything that anyone thought of on a day-to-day basis anymore. There were too many other important things going on for long-gone racial conflicts to be an issue.

"I . . . I would I had learned of this sooner," Lissan said. Then he shook himself slightly and his old demeanor returned. "But now it is too late. You have my warning. Perhaps you need another."

He turned and gestured to someone off screen. Another Falorian moved into view, roughly pushing a bound human who was obviously a prisoner in front of him. The Falorian spun the human around to face the screen.

"Alex," breathed Standing Crane.

Alexander Kirk stared at her, his face puffy and bruised and bleeding. His blue eyes were large and despairing.

"Tell them," Lissan said.

"I . . . won't. . . ." Alex growled between clenched teeth.

Lissan sighed and nodded to the guard, who curled his fingers into a fist and landed a solid punch to Alex's abdomen. As one, every person in the president's office instinctively moved forward.

"Tell them," Lissan repeated.

"The *Mayflower II* has been destroyed," whispered Alex, struggling for breath. "They've captured some of us, of the colonists. They say they have Uncle Jim, too, but—"

The guard moved forward menacingly, but Lissan raised a hand. "I do not enjoy cruelty," he said, "and I would much rather not have to hurt my hostages further. If you stay away from Huan space, your ships and your people will be safe. This is my warning to you. Heed it, or face the consequences."

He abruptly terminated the conversation. When the screen went dark, everyone in the room sagged a little.

The president turned to Parkan. "Tell me he's bluffing," he almost pleaded.

Parkan turned a stricken face to the president. "He's not. At least, not about most of it. They are indeed moving toward Huan, and the desire for revenge is very powerful in him. There's a tremendous sense of righteousness about him. He's telling the truth about what this virus can do as he knows it, I'm certain of that. He also isn't comfortable with hurting the hostages. But he's hiding something. He hasn't told us everything yet. What is your human phrase . . . something about waiting for a dropping shoe? That's what I'm sensing here."

There was no doubting Parkan's conclusions. His people had a proven ability to accurately sense such things as emotions and falsehoods. The only hope lay in the slim chance that Lissan himself had been misled.

"There's so much about this I don't understand," said the president, shaking his white head. "How is it they were able to plant this thing so well? And who was that young man, and who is this Uncle Jim he spoke of? You seemed to recognize him, Admiral."

Standing Crane swallowed hard. She straightened and turned to face the president. "I claim responsibility, sir," she said in a formal voice. "I am the one who gave permission for the Falorian delegations to have the access they did."

"Standing Crane," the president said softly. "You must have had a reason."

"They seemed so harmless, sir," Standing Crane continued, knowing how pathetic the words sounded. "We did our research. We never heard anything from either the Falorians or the Huanni about this history of slavery. Neither species seems inclined to violence, and it appeared as though the delegates were merely curious. Of course, I never let them into classified areas," she hastened to add. "They were only permitted in areas that are generally available to all promising candidates for membership. The trouble is, they were insistent about visiting *every* permitted area, not just some."

"Tell me," said the president.

In an emotionless voice, but feeling misery and fear roiling inside her, Standing Crane recited the lengthy list. It included starbases, Starfleet and Federation headquarters, large ships, small ships, planet capitals, and research centers. With every word, it seemed to Standing Crane that the mood in the room dropped lower and lower.

"No one suspected," she said. "I discussed this with the Vulcans, the Makorish, the Andorians—all of us were *amused* by their curiosity."

The president merely nodded. "And the young hostage?"

"His name is Alexander Kirk," Standing Crane answered. "He is the nephew of James T. Kirk, the former captain of the *Enterprise* who—"

"—saved my life a few months ago," the president finished. "This is a damn bad business we've got here. Parkan, Alexander seemed to indicate that they might not have Kirk. Your opinion?"

"The mention of the name roused a great deal of anger in Lissan, but I couldn't tell whether or not they had captured him."

"We must proceed as if they have," the president said grimly.

"One thing in our favor," Standing Crane said. "If they do have Jim Kirk, he's giving them hell. And if they don't, he's doing everything he can at this very moment to contact us and free those hostages. I'd bet my life on it."

"Let us hope you're right. Now, can anyone—"

"Sir," Standing Crane said, "there's more. A few days ago, Captain Spock came to me with rumors that the colonists might be in trouble. I said I couldn't authorize a starship on nothing more than rumors, but

I did give him permission to investigate on his own if he could find a ship to take him to Sanctuary."

"Sanctuary? Is that the name of this colony?" When Standing Crane nodded, the president blew angrily through his dangling mustache. "We didn't need that irony on top of everything else. Anything more you wish to tell me, Admiral?"

Standing Crane licked her lips. "No, sir. I think that's about all."

"It's enough." At her barely perceptible wince, the president added, "You couldn't have been expected to guess that all this would unfold the way it has, Admiral. No one could." He turned to face the rest of the group. "We've got work to do. Send out orders to every civilian and Starfleet vessel to head for the nearest habitable planet or starbase at top speed, and wait there for further instructions. I won't have our people stranded in the cold of space. We'll have to think of some other way to help Huan. About this virus . . . I want everyone who. . . ."

He continued speaking, but Standing Crane didn't hear him. *I should have trusted Spock,* she thought, with an anguish that she would never let show on her dark face. *He wouldn't have come to me if he didn't think there was a good reason. Damn it, Jim, I just hope I was right about you being able to handle yourself. If I never see you again, how will I sleep, knowing I might have saved you?*

Chapter Eighteen

Scott knew exactly how high the *Drake* needed to fly in order to evade Falorian scanners. Visual contact was still a possibility, of course, but they had to hope that if they were indeed spotted, the Falorians would merely think them colonists out on another research mission.

"I wish there were some way to find out if they were on to us yet," Kirk said, thinking aloud. "I'd feel better if I knew the colonists were still safe."

Scott craned his neck and looked back at his captain. "Och, we can do that. I'd have done it before but there's a slight risk it'd be detected."

Kirk leaned forward. "I'll take that risk, Scotty. How did you manage that?"

"Well, it was a wee bit tricky getting into their communication system once," Scott said. "I didn't want to have to do it all over again if we needed to, so I installed a back door while I was waiting for you and Mr. Chekov. Kept me from getting bored." There was a slight twinkle in his eye as he spoke.

"Back door?" Chekov said, confused.

"Oh, aye. It's an old computer term. It means I've got a way back in. Half a moment. . . ." Scott fiddled with the panel as only he could, and then the small screen on the console sprang to life and Lissan's arrogant voice filled the shuttle.

"—to take Huan," he was saying.

"No," whispered Skalli fiercely, and crammed her knuckles into her mouth in order to keep from sobbing aloud.

"Our vessels and that of our . . . allies . . . are moving even as I speak to you," Lissan continued. The five watched intently. "This is a quarrel that goes very deep, its dark roots extending into the shadows of the past. It has nothing to do with you, and you will be well advised to stay out of it."

"Scotty," Kirk said urgently, "can we get a message out ourselves?"

"Huan is a Federation planet!" It was the president of the Federation. Kirk knew the voice, although he could not see the President's visage. "We will come to the aid of one of our own!"

"We'd definitely be detected," Scott warned.

"A noble sentiment, but quite misplaced," Lissan smirked. "I will say this once, as clearly as I can, out of respect for the lives and safety of your people. Listen well. We have set up buoys around Huan. If any vessel, Federation or otherwise, violates that perimeter, then we will activate a virus that will leave every ship you possess hanging dead in space. No Federation vessel will be able to engage warp drive. Think about that, Mr.

President. Think about all the ships on deep-space missions far away from any hospitable planet or starbase. It would take them years to get anywhere under impulse power. Some ships would do just fine, but others wouldn't. Even if they did get home, the crews of many ships would be old and gray before they ever again saw their loved ones. This is not something I would see happen to innocent people. Do *you* want that to happen, Mr. President? For the sake of a few million worthless Huanni?"

"I don't understand," Chekov said. "They would be more likely to comply if they knew they would die otherwise. What's this nonsense about being old and gray?"

Kirk waved him to silence. "Do it, Mr. Scott. If we can get a warning out it'll be worth it."

The president was speaking again. "—that you have a great enmity toward the Huanni," he was saying.

Lissan's eyes flashed. "You choose pallid words, Mr. President."

"The Federation has long been known for its ability to fold in different cultures and create harmony."

"Scotty. . . ." Kirk said, his voice tense.

"I'm trying, Captain, but it's not as easy as you might think!" Scott retorted, his fingers flying over the console.

"Even now, we are making peace with a people who have historically been our worst enemies," came a new voice. Kirk instantly recognized it as Standing Crane. "It has been a hard road, but when they were in need, we came to their aid. We are helping preserve the Klingons as the proud, powerful people they are. We are not trying to make them just like us. Perhaps we could help you initiate negotiations that could lead to peace between both your peoples. War may not be the only option."

"Pray God he listens to you, Admiral," Scott muttered.

Lissan's reply shouldn't have been unexpected, but it was, and Kirk felt a stab of pain at the Falorian's words. "Tell me, Admiral, have you ever been owned?"

"What?"

"Have you ever been owned," he repeated. "Has anyone ever owned your ancestor, made him work hard labor, and then tossed him away like so much trash when his usefulness was done? Has anyone—"

"I have such a history," came yet another voice.

"Who's that?" Chekov asked.

"Admiral Thomas Mason," Kirk said. They listened intently as Mason described the institution of slavery that had once haunted humanity, and spoke eloquently of the shameful acts perpetrated on indigenous populations all over the planet.

"I've almost got it," muttered Scott. "A few more minutes. . . ."

"Listen to him," said Skalli, as if Lissan could hear her. "Please, listen."

"The past is the past," Mason was saying now. "We learn from it, and then we move on. The Falorians and the Huanni can do the same."

Lissan stared, his mouth slightly opened. For a moment, he was silent.

"That shook him," Kirk said. "He doesn't realize that

the Falorians aren't the only species to have endured slavery."

Beside him, Skalli sniffled loudly and wiped her nose on her sleeve.

"I . . . I would I had learned of this sooner," Lissan said. Then he shook himself slightly and his old demeanor returned. "But now it is too late. You have my warning. Perhaps you need another."

Kirk suddenly felt a knot of apprehension in his gut. When Lissan turned and motioned to someone off screen, Kirk knew what was going to happen next.

"Alex! God, no. . . ." Julius turned his face away from the screen and wiped at his eyes.

Kirk kept watching with narrowed eyes, taking it in swiftly. Alex had been roughed up some, but he didn't appear to be seriously injured. He had a few shallow, superficial cuts and some bruising, but that was it. Kirk had a sudden, swift realization: *This is for show.*

"Tell them," ordered Lissan.

"I . . . won't. . . ."

Kirk winced as the guard punched Alex. Maybe that was for show, too, but it clearly hurt.

"Scotty. . . ."

"I'm going as fast as I can, Captain!"

"Tell them," Lissan repeated.

"The *Mayflower II* has been destroyed," whispered Alex, gasping for air. "They've captured some of us, of the colonists. They say they have Uncle Jim, too, but—"

Lissan intervened before the guard could land a second punch. "I do not enjoy cruelty," he said, "and I would much rather not have to hurt my hostages further. If you stay away from Huan space, your ships and your people will be safe. This is my warning to you. Heed it, or face the consequences."

His image disappeared. Scott uttered a blistering oath.

For a long moment, there was silence in the shuttle.

"Another second or two and I'd have had it," Scott said bitterly. "We could have gotten a signal out on their signal, but now they've terminated communication, the only way we'll be able to talk to the Federation is to get into the Falorian stronghold and sit ourselves right down at the console."

"It's all right, Scotty. We'll just continue with our first plan. Keep monitoring their communications," Kirk said calmly. "Let me know if you learn anything significant."

"Aye, sir," Scott said, subdued.

Suddenly Julius uttered an incoherent cry and slammed his fist against the ship's console.

"Hey, that's delicate equipment!" Scott snapped angrily.

"I don't give a damn," snarled Julius. "I want Lissan! That son of a bitch hurt my brother, and damn it all, it's my fault. Alex," he said, and fell silent.

Thoughts were racing through Kirk's brain at a kilometer a second. "Something's just not adding up," he said. "Lissan warned the Federation not to intervene or else they would activate the virus and strand millions."

"But that's a lie!" Skalli's voice was thick with

unshed tears. "They know that once the virus is activated that all the warp cores involved will breach!"

"I'm not so sure they *do* know," Kirk continued. "They warned the Federation about the virus instead of just going ahead and activating it, so we could bring our people to safety. Did you see how shaken Lissan was to learn that other species had dealt with being enslaved? And the cuts on Alex's face—he wasn't tortured. All the injury was to his face—where it would be visible, where we'd be sure to see it. Lissan didn't even let the guard punch him again. Does all this sound like the behavior of a butcher who's knowingly planning on cold-bloodedly murdering billions of innocent people?"

There was silence in the shuttle. No one spoke.

"Lissan doesn't know," Kirk said firmly. "I'm sure of it."

"Doesn't know what?" snapped Julius.

"He doesn't know what the virus can do."

"Oh, come on, Uncle Jim, his people *created* the damn thing!"

Kirk ignored his nephew's outburst. "Scotty, what was it you were saying—that the dilithium the Falorians used for testing was incredibly pure?"

"Aye," said Scott. "Over ninety-nine percent pure. I've never seen the like."

"And you saw no indication that they ever used a crystal that was less pure."

"None at all. It looked as if all the tests were run with samples from the same crystal. They all had the exact same level of purity." Scott glanced back at him, his brown eyes curious. He was wondering what Kirk was getting at.

"Is it possible, in theory," Kirk continued, reaching for the thread, "that the Falorians really believe that all this nanoprobe virus is going to do is render the crystals inert? That they have no idea that it could cause a warp core breach?"

Scott's eyes brightened. "All the tests they ran on that one crystal would verify their theory that the virus would make the dilithium useless, but not dangerous."

"They'd be taking advantage of the whole quadrant, but they don't think they'd be killing anyone," Chekov said.

"Oh, they'll be killing people, all right," Skalli said with a harshness that surprised Kirk. "They're getting ready to kill *my* people so they can take Huan's dilithium."

"Skalli's right," Julius said. "And part of that blood is going to be on my hands."

"I'm not saying that the Falorians have suddenly become the good guys," replied Kirk. "And I'm certainly not trying to pretend that an attack on Huan is trivial. What I'm saying is it sounds to me as if they don't know that their virus is lethal. We have to tell them that."

"Somehow I don't think Lissan is going to sit down over a nice cup of tea and let you talk to him about his virus," said Julius.

"I'm certain he won't," Kirk said. "We've got a job to do, but informing Lissan about the virus is part of that. Scotty, take us in."

* * *

Standing Crane didn't think she'd ever seen so many famous dignitaries gathered together in one place. Many of these people she'd never even met, and wished that they were mingling at a banquet over drinks and not around a table discussing the possibility of the entire galaxy being plunged back into the dark ages.

The president called the meeting to order. The assembled group watched as the conversation between the president and Lissan was replayed. There was utter silence in the room. When the lights went back up, the president continued.

"We have had the best scientists in the Federation working on this," he said. "Samples have been obtained from every known area in which the delegates from Falor were present. Unfortunately, it appears that Kal-Tor Lissan was telling the truth. We have discovered a nanoprobe virus at every site."

Soft groans and winces went around the table. The president pressed on.

"Even worse, the technology involved is quite beyond our present understanding. We're not sure if we could deactivate even the samples we have, which are but a fraction of what's out there. As I understand it, this is a true virus, even though it's comprised of tiny machines. If you shook hands with a Falorian delegate, if he was on your ship, at your space station, visiting your capital or being entertained in your banquet halls, he left the virus. Then anyone who walked through that banquet hall, or brushed up against you, or stopped at that space station—they, too, would have the virus. It's on your clothes, your hands, in your body."

"Have any of our esteemed scientists learned what this virus will actually do?" The question was asked by Sarek, his face as calm as ever.

"Lissan said it would render all our ships dead in space, unable to engage in warp drive, and Parkan has told me that on this, he did not lie," the president answered. "Of course we'll have to confirm that independently. There's a chance Lissan might have been lied to, but I personally doubt it. Our next concern is to determine if other machinery will be affected, and how. Preliminary investigation into the nature of the nanoprobe reveals that it is harmless to organic beings, which is a small blessing."

"I have been doing my best to be constructive," the Huanni ambassador, Ullak, said. His expressive face worked as he clearly tried to get a handle on his emotions. "But I cannot sit quietly by while we discuss the virus without voicing the needs and fears of my people! Huan is a Federation member in good standing. What is the Federation going to do to prevent this undeserved attack?"

"Ambassador," the president said quietly, "your planet is currently not in good standing, as you must know. You have admitted that you lied to us regarding Falor. Had we known of your . . . past relationship . . . with the Falorians, steps might have been taken to bring you both to the negotiating table at that time. This whole tragedy might have been averted."

"Whatever we did in the past," Ullak cried, "surely you cannot sit here and tell me that the living Huanni deserve to die for it!"

"Of course not," replied the president. "But neither can we move to stop the Falorians until we know exactly what their virus will do to us. It's not just Huanni lives at stake here, Ambassador. It's the lives of people on ships throughout the quadrant."

He looked suddenly weary, and nodded to Standing Crane that she take over at this point. She cleared her throat.

"Lissan's threat was very specific: If we violated the space that they had designated with the buoys, they would activate the virus. What we can therefore do is bring at least a few ships right up to that point and have them wait there for further instructions. Every other ship is to be recalled to the nearest starbase or planet, just in case this thing does go off. At the present time, the closest vessel capable of defending the Huanni is the *Excelsior.* I've notified Captain Sulu about the situation and he's en route at this very moment."

"Good," the president approved. "In the meantime, we wait . . . and hope the scientists will learn something useful."

From the expressions on the faces of those seated around the table, this was an unsatisfactory resolution. She shared their sentiments, but at the moment, there was nothing else to do.

She envied Spock and Sulu at the moment. At least they were getting to do something.

Chapter Nineteen

McCoy was frustrated at being unable to do anything except sit back and twiddle his thumbs. Why in God's name had Kirk's nephews ("Alexander" and "Julius" indeed, factor in "Tiberius" and it was clear that the whole Kirk clan had an unhealthy obsession with ancient empires) gone gallivanting halfway across the galaxy for this Sanctuary? Was it that hard to find a nice little planet closer to home?

They had only been able to acquire a handful of rations, and those were now gone. Spock had said coolly that they would be able to survive on what the Klingon crew ate; the digestive systems of human and Klingon were sufficiently similar. Those were his exact words—"sufficiently similar." However, the writhing mass of worms on the plate in front of him was not "sufficiently similar" to spaghetti or indeed *anything* McCoy had encountered and recognized as an edible foodstuff for him to want to pop it into his mouth.

"I'd sell my soul for a nice, thick steak along about now," he muttered.

"Heck, I'd swap mine for a ham sandwich," Uhura said. She poked and prodded at the squiggly mess, an expression of distaste on her lovely face. Finally she put her fork down and delicately pushed the plate away. "You know, a water fast is great for slimming down," she said, "and I've got a performance in a week or two. Provided we get home by then."

McCoy was in high dudgeon now, though, and simply pushing the plate away was not a "sufficiently similar" option to complaining loudly.

"And why is everything always red or black with these characters?" He gestured theatrically. "Red lighting, black walls, blood wine, black armor. Damn boring color scheme if you ask me."

"I do not recall anyone aboard this ship asking your opinion on their decorating choices," Spock interjected mildly as he joined them in the mess hall.

"So what are you going to have?" McCoy asked, scooting on the bench to make room for the Vulcan captain. "Some red and black, spiky, dangerous-looking Klingon version of rutabagas?"

"I am joining Commander Uhura in her fast," Spock said. "The Klingons do not eat vegetables."

"Well," McCoy said, "Aren't we going to be the lean, mean fighting machine when we reach Sanctuary."

"Take heart, Doctor," Spock said. "We should be there shortly."

"You must eat!" bellowed a jovial voice. McCoy tried and failed not to roll his eyes as Karglak entered, carrying a tray loaded to the gills with slimy, purple-black, moving items that the Klingons called "food." He caught Uhura's gaze and stifled a laugh. Poor thing. She sure hadn't asked for this.

When Uhura had informed Karglak and Lamork that she had been called up on an emergency mission and the concert might have to be postponed, Karglak had been horrified. He had insisted that he be allowed to accompany her. Apparently, opera singers had a lot of clout, for sure enough he'd been in the transporter room ready to depart with the rest of them. The Klingons on the ship treated him like a sort of deity. When McCoy had pressed for something resembling a logical reason as to why, Captain Q'allock had replied, "Why, his honor is double. He is a warrior and a performer. Therefore, he can perform glorious deeds *and* sing about them."

It was an answer, McCoy supposed, but it didn't clear up a damn thing for him. Uhura had been doing her best to duck him, but the fellow clung to her like a burr. Karglak hadn't declared his feelings openly, but it was obvious to anyone that he had a bit of a crush on the lovely human woman who, like Karglak, could hold her own in a battle *and* sing about it afterward.

"Captain Q'allock to Captain Spock."

"Go ahead, Captain."

"Chancellor Azetbur would speak with you." McCoy thought Uhura looked relieved.

"Patch it through to the mess hall," Spock said, turning to the wall where the large screen was located.

It came to life, and Azetbur's face, tense and angry-looking, filled the screen.

"Captain Spock," she said. "Your errand has taken on a new urgency. Stand by to receive a transmission. This is what we recently heard from Kal-Tor Lissan."

All thoughts of food—even of fresh-baked chocolate chip cookies and deep-fried chicken—fled McCoy's mind as he and Uhura rose to stand beside Spock. Not to be left out, Karglak left his tray of quivering foodstuffs and hastened to Uhura's side. They all listened to the conversation in utter silence, absorbing the sobering message. When it was over, Azetbur's face reappeared.

"I see your point," Spock said.

"The *Kol'Targh* has been in space for several months," Azetbur said, "so the chances that it has been infected with this virus are practically nonexistent. You can probably assume that you are safe."

"Now there's a comfort," McCoy said. Spock said nothing.

"The captain of the *K'Rator* assures me that James Kirk has not yet been captured," she continued. "We have been able to monitor his unique signal throughout this entire ordeal. We should yet be able to fulfill the *DIS jaj je.*"

McCoy brightened, and gently squeezed Uhura's shoulder. Karglak grunted, but it sounded like a happy grunt. "It is good to satisfy honor," he growled.

"It seems your suspicions that Captain Kirk and the colonists were in danger were completely validated, Chancellor," said Spock. "But the nature of our mission has now changed, I would think. The reason we are all here is to ensure Captain Kirk's safety, but now it appears the stakes are higher. May I ask how you wish us to proceed?"

Azetbur's eyes flashed, and McCoy almost took a step backward. Damn, Klingons could be intimidating, even the best of them.

"Planting a virus to cripple a foe's fleet is a coward's way of fighting," she said, contempt dripping from every syllable. "Some of the Federation members are happy, pleased that Lissan was thoughtful enough to warn us. He may indeed not activate the virus if we don't violate his space and give up Huan without a fight. He may keep to his word. Or, he may do it anyway, now or at any time. The Federation is proceeding with caution and much wringing of hands."

"You have not answered my question," Spock said. "Perhaps I should ask another. How would a Klingon proceed?"

A predatory smile curved her lips, revealing pointed teeth. "We would find the laboratories that created and controlled such a virus, blast any guard ships out of the stars, free our people, and bombard the base until nothing but the barest specks remain."

"It is therefore unfortunate that the incident is not your problem," Spock said.

"If the virus is as widespread as Lissan claims, then it is everybody's problem," Azetbur retorted. "Do what you will."

Spock raised an eyebrow. "There is an old Earth saying: When in Rome, do as the Romans do." He looked around. After so many years together, McCoy could read the Vulcan's mind. Spock was looking at the Klingon ship, sponsored by the Klingon government, operated by a Klingon captain.

And he was doubtless thinking, *when on a Klingon ship. . . .*

The battle cruiser approached the badly misnamed Sanctuary under full cloak. Spock settled into the command chair, which was quickly vacated by Captain Q'allock.

"Report," Spock asked. McCoy and Uhura had accompanied him to the bridge. And, of course, where Uhura went, there went Karglak also. Spock wished he had been able to dissuade the singer from accompanying them, for many reasons. The mission was likely to be dangerous, and if the best-loved opera star of his generation were slain, it would seriously affect the peace negotiations.

Or would it? Perhaps it might buy them yet more honor. With Klingons, such things were hard to predict.

McCoy came to stand by his chair, as he had so often done with Kirk, and Uhura moved almost without thinking to the equivalent position of her old post, Karglak following as unobtrusively as it was possible for an enormous Klingon to do. Spock was glad his former *Enterprise* colleagues had accompanied him, for reasons other than their excellence at their duties.

"We are still several parsecs away," the navigator informed him. "The *K'Rator* has informed us that the Falorians have constructed a spacedock."

"What ships are currently docked there?"

"Seven—no, eight small attack ships. They are built for speed, not for lengthy battles."

"Weapons?"

"Phasers only."

Spock nodded. Although he did not know the specific ship, he knew its type. It was designed for surprise attacks rather than sustained battle. Eight of these small vessels posed little threat to a Klingon battle cruiser and bird-of-prey.

"Any sign of any larger vessels on the long range scanners?"

"Negative, sir."

"From what Azetbur told us, I'd guess that all their battleships are either at Huan or en route," Uhura said.

"Brilliant!" exclaimed Karglak, gazing fondly at her.

"A logical conclusion, Commander," Spock said. "Obviously, we were not expected here at Sanctuary. They do not think this is where the conflict is. They are mistaken."

He felt McCoy's surprised gaze on him, but did not turn to look the doctor in the eye. If McCoy chose to infuse the statement with emotion, that was his interpretation. Spock was merely stating a fact.

As far as he was concerned, this was where the real fight would be.

"It won't be as easy as it was the last time," Scott said. "They'll be watching for us for sure."

"Especially if they've gotten all the other colonists and we're the only ones missing," Julius said.

Kirk laughed a little. "Easy, Mr. Scott? I didn't think it was easy the last time." He sobered. They were within a few hundred kilometers of the base.

"All right then," Scott said, more to himself than the others. "They still could take a few lessons on how to watch for intruders. There are no ships or guards at the base."

Julius made a small, happy sound in the back of his throat. "They're probably scattered, chasing the rest of us."

"Long-range scanners would seem to indicate that," said Scott.

"There were never very many Falorians here to begin with," Julius said. "Even considering Lissan was lying to me about a lot."

"Most of them are probably in their warships attacking Huan right now," Skalli said morosely.

Kirk said nothing, but he assumed that Skalli was correct. Most of the Falorians here on Sanctuary would be the researchers who had created the virus. There would be a few guards, but considering that Kirk and company by all rights ought to have been met with everything Lissan had, their tactic of having the colonists scatter was proving to be a boon. He was deeply sorry Lissan had found Alex, but oddly reassured by the targeted beating. Kirk had witnessed, and even experienced, real torture; compared to what brutalities could be inflicted upon the fragile human body, Alex had gotten little more than a slap on the wrist.

"It would seem that Lady Luck is with us," he said. "Let's do our best not to offend her."

But Lady Luck was a fickle date, and Kirk wondered how much longer she'd hang around them before seeking entertainment elsewhere. The small group of five grew silent as they approached the base.

"Still no sign that we've been noticed," Scott said, his eyes on the screen. "I'm sorry I couldn't tap into the conversation in time for us to contact the president while we had him, but there's an up side. We'd have given ourselves away and they'd be on us like a duck on a June bug."

"That's hardly a Scottish saying," Kirk said.

"No, I got it from Dr. McCoy."

Kirk felt an unexpected, quick pang. He'd been so engrossed with first his nephews, then the colony, then the disaster that was threatening to descend that he hadn't realized how much he missed his old friends.

Bones. Spock. Uhura. Sulu. He permitted himself a brief moment of nostalgia, and wondered what they were doing now. Spock, Uhura, and McCoy, he knew, were involved with the Klingons. He had heard something about a medical forum, and hadn't Spock hinted at a musical program? And Sulu, lucky Hikaru Sulu. Captain of his own ship, off having adventures like he, Kirk, used to have.

And just what is this, Jim? he thought. *Breaking and entering a secret enemy facility in an effort to save a few billion lives is hardly a walk in the park.*

But anyone could do this. Even Alex, if he had to. Kirk desperately yearned to be on the bridge of a starship again, to be in charge, to make the decisions that could help bring peace to the galaxy. And, yes, to give the order to fire when all avenues had been exhausted in the name of that peace.

Along about this moment, Lady Luck decided she'd had enough.

"Three small ships approaching, Captain," said Scott.

Chekov muttered something vicious-sounding under his breath.

"Hang on," Scott grunted.

And with no more warning than that, Scott pulled the little atmosphere shuttle up at top speed. The Falorian ships followed, keeping close on the *Drake*'s tail. Scott frowned and the ship veered down and to port. Beside Kirk, Skalli gasped and dug her fingers into the seat.

"I'm . . . not very good with rapid movement like this. . . ." she said, gasping a little and turning an odd lavender color.

"This would be a particularly bad time to get sick, Skalli," Kirk said as noncommittally as he could. She nodded, and began trying to breathe slowly and deeply.

The shuttle now lurched violently to starboard and then seemed to go straight up. Kirk was slammed against the back of his chair and saw only sky in the windows.

"Clumsy big things," Scott sniffed. "Can't outrun my sleek wee bairn." He patted the console affectionately. "I like her better than the boat, I think. Maybe I'll get one when we get back to Earth."

"I'll help you pick one out myself if you can get us through this," Kirk said.

Scott didn't reply. He was too busy doing a complete

loop and heading back the way they had come. Kirk looked out the window to see two smoking wrecks on the ground. Even as he watched, the doors to one opened and an obviously shaken Falorian crew emerged.

He breathed a little easier. The fewer casualties on any side in this strange battle, the better.

The ship rocked suddenly. Kirk remembered belatedly that there were three ships, not two, and apparently one had managed to stay aloft sufficiently to fire on them.

"Julius, this thing have any weapons?" Scott asked.

"No," Julius said, sounding a little disgusted. "Alex ordered the weapons system disengaged when we arrived. Said we'd have no need for it."

"You know, I respect Alexander's pacifism," Chekov said, "but I really wish that he'd forgotten about disabling the *Drake*."

"That makes two of us," Scott said grimly, again performing evasive maneuvers that made Kirk just as glad he hadn't eaten for several hours. Beside him, Skalli whimpered, just a little.

Whoever was on their tail was good, Kirk had to give them that. The Falorian vessel refused to be shaken.

"Mr. Scott," Chekov said, "would you be willing to let an old navigator have a try?"

Scott's strength was technical, and everyone knew and respected it. Kirk had him at the helm so that he'd be in a ready position to counter any attempts by the Falorians to fix on their position, and also so they wouldn't waste a moment trying to break into the facility.

But Chekov had spent years, together with Sulu, in handling the *Enterprise*. Scott looked at Chekov's still-healing hands even as the *Drake* shuddered again from a glancing blow.

"Your hands, lad," Scott said softly.

"Don't worry about that. Let me try," Chekov said. Scott glanced back at Kirk, who nodded.

Chekov swiveled his chair to reach for the console as Scott leaned back to give him room. Kirk saw the muscles of his face twitch in pain as his injured fingers moved across the lighted buttons, but Chekov didn't slow down. With amazing speed he programmed a sequence of movements.

"Now!" Chekov cried.

The shuttle seemed to take on a life of its own. It shot upward, then sped downward so close that Kirk could see each individual petal on a single flower. It then swung violently to the left, then right, then up, then down again. Beside Kirk, Skalli clapped one hand to her mouth. With the other, she clutched the chair as if for dear life.

Kirk heard the sound of the ship that was in pursuit plowing into the ground behind them. Smoke billowed past them as the *Drake* began again to gain altitude.

"Good job, lad!" Scott enthused, again taking the controls as Chekov leaned back in his seat. He permitted himself a grimace as he placed his bandaged hands gingerly in his lap.

"Well done, Mr. Chekov," Kirk said. Chekov gave him a faint smile.

"Now we just come a'calling as we planned," Scott

said. "There's no sign of any more pursuit. Let's get this thing open and us inside."

"Captain Spock," the Klingon helmsman said. "I am detecting explosions and several moving craft around the Falorian base."

"Onscreen."

The pleasant image of the slowly turning blue and green planet was replaced by that of a glowing hemisphere of softly radiating blue light. The research that Commander T'SroH had done had provided some information about what was inside the facility. It was little enough—indications of labs, some weaponry, advanced technology. But with what Spock knew now, it became clear to him that the Falorians had chosen Sanctuary to be the place where their nanoprobe virus would be developed and honed.

Even as Spock watched, a small atmosphere shuttle approached. With no warning, the shield went down and the shuttle landed.

"Now who in blazes would—oh." McCoy's question was immediately answered when Kirk, Scotty, Chekov, a younger man that McCoy didn't recognize, and a Huanni female clambered out of the shuttle and high-tailed it for a large entrance that obviously led to a subterranean shelter. Of course it was Jim. Who else would fly right into the lion's den to rescue over a hundred Daniels?

"Such courage!" exclaimed Karglak. "When we return, I will commission an opera about this adventure." He straightened. "And I shall play the intrepid Captain Kirk."

At any other time, Spock would have been pleased at the honor Karglak was offering to a human, but right now, more immediate problems pressed.

"Closer on the captain," Spock said. Jim's image filled the screen. Spock nodded. "Hail Captain Kirk," Spock said. "I see he still has his communicator."

"Captain, with respect," Q'allock growled, "that would give away our position!"

Spock swiveled in the chair and, McCoy would later swear, *glared* at Q'allock. "Hail him," he repeated, his voice as cold and hard as the doctor had ever heard it.

When the Klingon at the communications console still seemed to hesitate, Uhura stepped in. Brusquely and with the efficiency of one who'd been doing this for years, as indeed she had, her long, sure fingers flew over the console. "Cap—"

She wasn't even able to finish the first word. The security field had sprung back up and any attempt to speak with Kirk or anyone else inside was now impossible.

Uhura and McCoy's eyes met, and though Uhura conducted herself like the professional she was, McCoy felt a surge of sympathy at the expression of anguish in those beautiful brown eyes. Karglak, standing by her side, reached to pat her shoulder reassuringly.

A sharp whistle shattered the moment. "Captain Spock," Uhura and the Klingon communications officer said at the same time. Glowering, the Klingon sank back in his chair and crossed his arms across his broad chest.

"Captain Spock," Uhura said, "we're being hailed."

"I told you!" the Klingon captain bellowed. "You've thrown away any element of surprise we possessed—our best weapon!"

"Captain Q'allock," Spock said, "your silence will serve us all best now. Uhura, onscreen."

The visage of the Falorian Kal-Tor known as Lissan appeared, and he grinned malevolently.

"Captain Spock, I presume?"

Chapter Twenty

"Kal-Tor Lissan," Spock replied.

"I have done my research," Lissan said. "I know of you, Captain. And Dr. McCoy and Commander Uhura, as well. How touching, that you rush so eagerly to the rescue of a friend. But am I not correct in assuming that this is hardly a Starfleet-issue vessel?"

"What this vessel is or is not is not under discussion," Spock said.

"And what precisely *is* under discussion?" Lissan asked. "What do you want from me, Captain Spock?"

"These games do not become the representative of such an intelligent species," Spock said. "We have knowledge of your recent communication with the president of the Federation and your threat. We have come for the hostages, as you must know."

"We have them all, you know," Lissan said. "Including Scott, Chekov, and James T. Kirk. Surely you can't imagine that we'd turn them over simply because you asked nicely?"

"My Starfleet training compels me to pursue the diplomatic option first," Spock said.

The words seemed to anger Lissan. Before, he had been lounging in his chair, sneering. Now he bolted forward, his hands on the desk in front of him.

"Always the diplomats, you Starfleet and Federation types. Well, my people are at war, Mr. Spock, and frankly, as we both know, the fleet presently on its way to Huan is no match for your powerful vessels over the long term. However, I have two safeguards—the virus, about which you already know, and the hostages. I won't hand them over, and if you don't depart Sanctuary space within ten of your Earth minutes, I will begin killing them one by one. I know your kind, Mr. Spock. You Federation types are soft. As long as I hold the hostages, I have the upper hand. You'll back down."

Desperately McCoy tried to read the face on the screen. He didn't know Lissan or his people from a hole in the ground. Some species would indeed start killing the hostages without a care in the world. Others would be bluffing, preying on the human respect for life in order to get what they wanted, but also sharing that respect. Which one was Lissan? A killer, or a good poker player?

"You have made an error in judgment, Kal-Tor," Spock replied. "While a professional Federation negotiator might indeed back down, as you put it, I will point out that I am a Vulcan. Under these circumstances, I find backing down illogical. I am aboard a Klingon ship. Klingons find backing down dishonorable. Commander Q'allock, fire at will."

Kirk's communicator sounded. Even as he ran, phaser in hand, firing as he went, he fished for it and flipped it open. It crackled, and a sound that might have been a voice and might have been a high-pitched squeal of static issued forth. Then, dead silence.

A phaser blast whizzed past, almost hitting him. Kirk whirled, communicator still in his left hand, and fired in the direction from which the shot had come. The five of them kept running, in a close-knit group, all three phasers being put to good use.

Even as he defended himself, Kirk's mind raced. What had just happened? Had some of the colonists disobeyed orders and taken communicators? They had discussed this and decided it was too risky. If Lissan had been able to get a hold of even one communicator and had had his wits about him, he could have tricked any of the colonists into revealing themselves. But Kirk knew that these independent idealists couldn't always be trusted to obey orders to the letter. It wouldn't have surprised him if someone thought they knew better than James T. Kirk and was now trying to contact him.

Or was it just a burst of static, an accident? Given all the signals being broadcast here, it wouldn't surprise him in the least if his communicator had inadvertently gone off.

Regardless, it was irrelevant. There would be no way to talk to anybody until they got to the precise console and could send a message out. Still running, he smoothly returned his communicator to its holster. Looming ahead was the entrance.

The Klingon crew currently under Spock's command had clearly been itching for just such orders. Barely had the words left Spock's mouth than the weapons officer, uttering a cry that made the humans' hair stand on end, fired phasers.

The eight small attack ships had their shields up, but even so they took damage. They zoomed from the spacedock with startling speed, their quickness an advantage over the larger, but more heavily armed, battle cruiser. As they zipped past, they fired. The ship rocked.

"Report," Spock ordered.

"Slight damage to the port nacelle," the Klingon bridge officer cried. "Decks one and three are staunchly carrying on."

Spock and McCoy exchanged glances. While McCoy's expression remained appropriately serious, there was a twinkle in his eye at the words the Klingon chose to describe the ship's damage.

"Lock phasers on their weapons and fire again," Spock said.

The Klingon gleefully did so. He struck one of them a good blow. It slowed and stopped, dead in space.

The ship rocked again. "Target weapons systems and engines of all vessels and fire at will. Helm, maneuver as necessary. I suggest everyone grasp a secure hold of a railing or chair."

Shrieks of victory filled the bridge as the Klingons obeyed. One voice rose over all the others, and Spock recognized the famous aria "Bathed in Blood, I Stand Victorious."

Red phaser fire screamed across space, hitting target after target. For a moment, the ship pretended it was a little skiff, moving so rapidly that even Spock became slightly disoriented. There was a half roll and a dive. Ship after ship took damage. Despite Spock's orders, he suspected that the Klingons were not being terribly scrupulous in their targeting. He supposed he could not blame them.

After what seemed an eternity of Klingon curses and song, a rolling ship, and the yellow light of fire filling the screen, the ship steadied.

"We have Kahless's own luck," Q'allock announced. "All ships have either been destroyed or disabled."

Spock sat back in his chair, thinking. If there had been any weapons on the planet, Lissan would have put them to use by now. It was indeed too bad that Vulcans did not believe in luck.

"I believe we are safe for the moment," he said. "We must now focus on destroying the force field and retrieving Captain Kirk and the others."

Standing Crane was halfway through the list of people she had to contact when she received a top-priority incoming message. Her gut clenched. What now?

"Yes, Mr. President?" she said as his visage filled her screen.

"We've gotten some preliminary results back from

the first round of tests," he said. "Lissan was correct. This virus will indeed prevent any infected vessels from going to warp."

She could tell by his expression that there was more, and her heart began to thud rapidly. "And?"

"The virus targets the dilithium crystals. Any attempt to introduce matter and antimatter causes them to shatter."

"Great Spirit," Standing Crane breathed, her hand coming to her mouth. Shattered crystals meant a warp core breach, and that of course meant . . . "H-how many ships would be affected?"

"Our best guess is only an extrapolation. Taking into account all the ships and docks and starbases actually visited by the Falorians, and assuming a certain number of cross contaminations, we're looking at upward of six thousand vessels. Delaney tells me that it's a conservative guess. She thinks it's more likely to be in the tens of thousands. And with each minute that ticks by, the likelihood of further contamination doubles."

Tens of thousands of vessels, not people. Thousands of ships that would try to go to warp and end up as atoms floating in space. Millions of people who'd end up the same way.

For a moment, she couldn't speak. She stared numbly at the president, knowing that her horror was written plainly on her face.

"I know. It took me several minutes to calm down sufficiently to tell you," the president said, sympathizing. "It appears that most of the planets that are mining dilithium have been infected, too, so it's not a matter of swapping out the crystals. Laura, we're looking at the worst disaster the Federation has ever faced."

"And because of the very nature of that disaster, we can't do a damn thing about it," she finished, nodding her head. She forced herself to breathe deeply and slowly, to regain control. She would not serve well if she broke down. "So, what do we do now?"

"Delaney is trying to figure out how to counter the virus, but she's not making much progress. Most of the ships have docked safely, but there's a lot of them still out there."

"The only way then for us to remain safe is to permit no ships to go to warp until we've figured this out," Standing Crane said. "Lissan and his buddies are going to walk all over Huan, and there's not a thing we can do about it."

"There are some days when it just doesn't pay to get up in the morning," the president said dryly, and Standing Crane forced a smile.

If she didn't laugh, she'd cry. And she knew if she started to cry, she might not stop.

Kirk took back his comments to Scotty about their previous attempt not being easy compared to this second one. Every inch of ground they got was hard won. They tried to keep Julius and Skalli in the center, as there were only three phasers between them. They did a good job, but even so, at one point Kirk heard Skalli cry out and turned to see that she'd taken a hit. She clapped a hand to her smoking, burned shoulder and grimly continued, though her expressive face was contorted in pain.

Once, Julius stumbled and hit the ground hard, face-first. In one smooth motion, Kirk leaned down, hauled his nephew up by the arm, and pushed him forward. They had to keep moving. Julius's face was a mask of blood. It looked as though he'd broken his nose and knocked out a few teeth, but they were almost there.

Ahead, looming over all, was the Starfleet-issue subspace relay tower, the source of the carrier wave. Kirk knew that the controls were inside, deep underground. Briefly, Kirk wondered if this was part of the black market equipment Julius had helped the Falorians smuggle in, or if this was something they'd obtained on their own. Angrily he cut off that line of thinking. Whatever Julius had done was in the past, and now that the Falorians had shown their true colors, Kirk felt certain his nephew would do everything he could to help them. It was the reason he'd brought the boy along.

Under heavy fire, they kept going, until they were at the entrance of the tunnel. Skalli, who had been checking her tricorder despite her injury cried out, "Wait! They've got a field up!" The group skidded to a halt and ducked behind one of the small outbuildings. It wasn't much, but it offered temporary shelter while they weren't moving targets.

"Julius, you got them this equipment," Kirk said. He knew how harsh it sounded, but it was the truth, and there wasn't time to dance around Julius's feelings. "What frequencies do they use?"

A phaser blast struck the building. Kirk leaned around the edge, fired quickly, and was rewarded by a harsh cry of pain.

Julius spat out a mouthful of blood. He leaned in close to Skalli and together they adjusted the tricorder to the same frequency as the shield.

"Got it!" cried Skalli.

"Watch out—they'll have guards down there!" Kirk got off a few more shots and then they ran hell for leather for the tunnel entrance. They were greeted by phaser blasts. Kirk, Chekov, and Scott took careful aim and picked their attackers off one by one.

They scrambled down inside, all clinging as best they could to the gantries. "Skalli, change the frequency and get that force field back up," Kirk cried, gasping for breath. It wouldn't last for long, but any second of reprieve would be welcome.

He looked around, phaser at the ready, and was stunned to find they encountered no further resistance. Apparently the guards who had attacked them on the surface, plus the four or five who had fallen defending the entrance, were all the security Lissan could summon. It was a lucky break, and Kirk intended to make the most of it.

"Shield's up, Captain, and the frequency has been reconfigured," Skalli said. "I threw in a few things to make it harder for them to crack it. They'll figure it out eventually, but it should buy us some time."

Kirk paused for a second to regard Skalli with respect. She continued to astonish him. If they got out of this alive, he wouldn't just be her advisor, he'd be her damned sponsor through Starfleet, and count himself lucky to have the privilege.

"Everyone all right?" he asked.

"We can all walk," Scott said grimly. It wasn't exactly a direct answer to the question, nor was it encouraging, but Kirk took it. He nodded, gulped for air, and then they began to descend.

Somewhere down there were the controls to get a message out to Starfleet about the true scope of the disaster they were facing. Kirk would get that message out, or die trying.

Chapter Twenty-one

Lissan was at his wit's end.

It had all been going so well. Everything had unfolded as it should. The Federation had reacted precisely as Lissan had predicted. The Orion vessels were taking up position around Huan, waiting to swoop in on the dilithium like *taggors* on a dead animal once the Falorian fleet had conquered Huan. Although Lissan and the other members of the Kal-Toreshi realized that Huan's fall might take a while, even with the Orion-provided weaponry and ships, early signs were promising. Lissan was sweating every single minute until that longed-for hour when the virus would be activated, and the entire quadrant would be begging for the largest cache of pure, uncorrupted dilithium in the known galaxy. It would all be all right then, but until that time, things could go wrong.

Things like two Klingon vessels showing up here at Sanctuary and blasting all eight of his ships out of the sky. Things like one of those vessels being captained by a famous Starfleet figure known to be Kirk's best friend, somehow allied with a species Lissan knew to be hostile to Vulcans and humans alike. Things like the wiliness of the aforementioned James Kirk.

Lissan and his people were now as stranded on Sanctuary as the colonists were. Once the battle for Huan was over and the Falorians victorious, of course, they would come for him. But until then, he was not pleased about his forced isolation.

Precious resources and time were being squandered in chasing down the scattered colonists. Now that Lissan had moved to take them hostage, he had to do so, or the whole plan could collapse. His troops, what few there were, were all over the planet trying to find them. Only a handful had been captured to date. He knew he had been exceedingly fortunate that Alexander Kirk was among the few they had found. He'd seen the reaction when the youth's bloody face had been presented to the Federation.

The beating had been 858's idea. Actually, killing and mutilating Alexander had been 858's idea—"Nothing convinces someone you mean business like a dead body"—but Lissan had been so appalled by the suggestion that the Orion had backed up a step.

"Verbal threats are good," the green-skinned alien had said, "but physical evidence is better. You can lie about what you might do, but when they see what you've already done, what you're willing to do, well, your threat becomes that much more effective."

They had argued about just what that beating should consist of. 858's dark eyes had brightened when he described cutting off digits, inserting sharp implements in nostrils and ears or under finger- and toenails, or peeling off skin. Lissan fought desperately to conceal his disgust and horror. He seized on what he thought might convince the Orion, which was that Alexander might be of more use to them alive and ambulatory than not. Even so, he had not enjoyed watching Alexander's face get pummeled.

And now word had just reached him that Kirk and a few others, including Julius, were loose in the facility.

His computer made a sound and Lissan sighed. He was certain he did not want to talk to whomever might be trying to contact him, but resolutely tapped a button. When 858's green visage filled the screen, Lissan cringed inwardly but kept his face impassive.

"I understand that there might be a problem. A very, very big problem."

"I don't know what you're talking about," Lissan lied. "We had a deal. You gave us the vessels we needed to attack Huan. We hold off the Federation long enough to access the dilithium, and you get paid. Well paid. You then go away and leave us alone while we handle the wrath of the Federation. How difficult is that for you to comprehend?"

"What kind of idiots do you think we are?" 858 asked. "Did you really think we wouldn't be monitoring your communications? You've got a nice setup, I'll admit, but we finally cracked your conversation with the Federation president, and we are very interested in learning more about this virus of yours."

Lissan made a dismissive gesture. "A lie, a trick," he said.

"You've never been a good liar, especially not to me," 858 said. "And we have found traces of this virus on our own ship."

Desperately, Lissan wondered if half-truths would save him. "All right. There is a virus." True. "And you probably tracked it onto your vessel yourself." Untrue—it had been quite deliberately placed. "It's all over here, too." True. They had a way to ensure the nanoprobes harmlessly self-destructed by transmitting a simple signal accompanied by the correct code. "It's totally inert—the nanoprobes don't do anything." That was as great a lie as anything Lissan had ever uttered. "The Federation will figure this out in the not too distant future, but it won't matter. It will stall them long enough for us to take Huan and you to get paid. Once the Federation realizes that they've been tricked, yes, they will come after us. But we will be entrenched on Huan, thanks to you, and will be fighting from a position of strength."

Please believe this, Lissan thought frantically. *Please believe this.* Surely there was enough truth to it to make it sound plausible. They'd find him out, of course, but maybe he could hold them off just long enough.

858 met Lissan stare for stare. "I should have called this off sooner," 858 finally said, obviously disgusted. "I never believe in advancing credit to begin with, and this—well, I didn't agree to it, just to enforce it. All right, Lissan. I will take what you've told me to my superiors, and do rest assured, we will be testing your so-called inert nanoprobes. And if you have lied to me—if what you told the Federation is true—then rest assured, I will come for you and carry out your execution myself."

He smiled a slow, predatory smile. At any other time, it would have chilled Lissan to the bone. But for a brief, wild moment, the Falorian wanted to laugh. 858 was millions of kilometers away. One push of a button, and his ship would stop dead. It was hard to execute someone when you couldn't get to him. Still, it wouldn't do to gloat.

Not yet. Later, perhaps.

So Lissan looked appropriately serious when he replied, "You'll find that all is as I have said. I only hope you're not so busy checking up on your ally that you miss your window of opportunity. The Federation won't be fooled forever, and I'd hate to see you embroiled in a battle with them without your share of the dilithium."

He heard it, even as he tried to stifle it—that burbling pleasure in his voice. 858 looked at him sharply, then the screen went dark.

Lissan sagged in his seat, the odd burst of pleasure gone. What was he thinking? The Federation had probably already confirmed what Lissan had told them about the virus. The Orion Syndicate didn't put the value on scientific research that the Federation did, true, but it certainly had access to scientists and labs. They, too, would find out in fairly short order what the virus could do. And they would know they had been double-crossed.

With his forefinger he stabbed a button. "Any word on Kirk?" he demanded.

The head of security looked chagrined. "Nothing, sir. They were able to penetrate the force field and are presently unaccounted for."

"You had better account for them soon," Lissan said.

"It's—difficult, sir," Jasslor stammered. "They have some kind of technology that masks their bio signs. It's the reason it's been so hard to find the colonists. The only thing we can tell for certain about their location is where they *have* been—when someone doesn't report in, or a security field is breached. Where they are is another matter."

Lissan summoned patience. "Can you give me your best guess?"

"We think they're still in the upper levels, judging by the activities reported. At least we hope so, because that's where the guards are. If they're not, if they've gotten deeper into the complex, there will be only about five people capable of stopping them. After that, you're going to have to think about arming your scientists—and yourself."

"Where to, Julius?" asked Kirk.

"How should I know? You've been here before, you tell me." Kirk was mildly amused at the still-rebellious tone Julius used.

"You know the types of equipment they have better than we do," he said.

"Yeah, I know, I know, because I sold it to them. You've made your point." Nonetheless, Julius examined Chekov's tricorder and looked around him. "They're very orderly, very meticulous," he said. "They'd probably have a special section for everything. We wouldn't find communications mixed in with labs. We've already passed the security level. And this entire floor looks like research to me."

It looked familiar to Kirk. "Chekov, do you remember this section?"

"Aye, sir," Chekov replied. "This upper level was where we found the test labs and where we almost ran into the scientists."

"We took a lift down several stories," Kirk said, the details coming back to him. "We saw quite a few storage rooms. About twelve stories down was where we found the padd in that small lab."

Chekov nodded. "I was able to get onto the computer. Perhaps we could try it there again, find out where the main communications area is located."

"Too risky," Scott said. "They didn't know you were here that time. They do now."

"Captain," Chekhov said, trying to keep his voice from sounding too excited, "I'm detecting human life signs."

"Where?" Julius cried.

"About two stories down, halfway across the tunnel," Chekov said.

"Then let's go!" Julius was halfway down a metal ladder when Kirk stopped him with a sentence.

"We can't," Kirk said.

Julius looked up. He looked frightening, his blue eyes blazing against the smear of drying maroon blood on his face.

"You give me one damn good reason why I'm not going to find my brother," he said, his voice deep and intense.

"I'll give you several," Kirk said, refusing to be drawn into Julius's vortex of pain, guilt, and anger. "We wouldn't be able to rescue them, not with just a few phasers. Even if we did manage to free them, we couldn't get them to safety. Attempting to do so would give away our position, and if we get caught, then the Falorians get five more valuable hostages and no one gets warned about the real danger of that virus."

The muscles in Julius's bare arms tensed and his chest moved rapidly. His eyes never left Kirk's. "He's my brother," he finally said, softly.

"I know exactly how you feel."

"How can you—"

"I know what it's like to lose a brother," Kirk said. "I'll never forget beaming down to Deneva and finding his body. I loved your father, just as you love Alexander. I know what I'm asking of you, and I don't ask it lightly. But if we play our cards right we'll all get out of here alive, and we'll be able to save other lives as well. Millions of other lives. Help me, Julius. We need you. You've got a chance to correct the mistakes you've made. Not everyone gets that kind of opportunity."

For a long moment, the two Kirk men locked gazes. Finally Julius uttered a long, quavering sigh.

"Damn it," was all he said. "Damn it." But he climbed back up the ladder.

They continued downward. On their previous reconnaissance of the area, Kirk and Chekhov had discovered that the deeper they went, the more security systems they encountered. It was a good bet that communications, which was clearly vital to the implementation of the Falorians' plan, would be here, where it could be well protected.

It was harder this time; the Falorians had beefed up their security. Julius was not patient with the time it took to deactivate each force field or break into each area. Kirk sympathized, but he knew where his duty lay.

Although the time seemed long to Julius, Kirk was frankly amazed at the speed with which Scott deactivated seemingly complex systems.

"In another lifetime, Mr. Scott, I'm sure you had a successful career as a safecracker," he said at one point, remembering how Scotty had enabled an escape when they were prisoners at Sybok's hands.

On his hands and knees, tinkering with the tricorder, Scott laughed. "Oh, aye," he said. "But don't you be holding that against me, Captain."

"On the contrary. I'm counting my blessings even as we speak," Kirk replied.

Level by level, door by door, the five wound their way into the heart of the Falorian complex. While Scott worked, Kirk and Julius hung back, keeping an eye out for guards. More than once, they surprised a few; more than once, unconscious Falorian bodies lay sprawled in the corridors.

Finally, Scott uttered a long, happy, satisfied sigh. "Gentlemen," he said, his burr more pronounced with pleasure, "We're in."

Chapter Twenty-two

Approximately twenty-three minutes and thirty-seven seconds had passed since all eight Falorian vessels had been destroyed. Spock had issued orders that the field surrounding the complex be analyzed, the data prepared, and presented.

The Klingons had grumbled. They felt such a dispassionate, measured approach was, if not precisely dishonorable, at the very least not something about which one would boast. But they had obeyed, and now Spock, McCoy, Uhura, and four Klingons, including the ubiquitous Karglak, sat around a table in the captain's ready room.

Spock steepled his fingers and listened intently to the information they had been able to gather. Finally, he nodded.

"I regret that we seem to have but one option," he said, rising and going to the screen that displayed a graphic of the shield. "Although I anticipate that my crew will, on the contrary, be quite pleased with the order I am about to issue." He indicated the glowing blue shield. "This is not a large area. We can see no noticeable generators. From what little information we have been able to obtain about this facility, most of it is located well below ground. It would seem quite secure, perhaps impregnable. We have little knowledge of the Falorians which would enable us to disable the field by manipulating the frequency."

He lifted an eyebrow. "We must therefore take a more Klingon approach to the problem. We have disabled all the adversaries who lay in wait to attack us. We know that it is unlikely that the Falorians will spare any vessels from Huanni space to engage in conflict here. Therefore, as I see it, the only option we have is to fire steadily upon the shield and hope that, eventually, it weakens."

Captain Q'allock let out a roar of approval, and he and the other three banged their fists on the table repeatedly until Spock held up a hand for silence.

"I do not believe it will fall easily, but at the very least we can be an annoyance. A steady attack will busy their computer and people, and with luck cause various outages throughout the complex. It will probably not do any serious damage, but it might provide Captain Kirk with a welcome distraction."

McCoy's craggy face spilt into a grin. "No-see-ums, by God!" he exclaimed.

Both of Spock's eyebrows reached for his hairline. McCoy often uttered colorful phrases that Spock did not quite understand, but this one was truly bizarre.

"I beg your pardon, Dr. McCoy?"

"No-see-ums," McCoy repeated.

"Your answer does not offer clarification," Spock said.

"No-see-ums are these little bugs that plague you in the summer, specially in the warmer climates," McCoy continued. "They were the bane of my existence when I was growing up in Georgia. Gnats, or something, I don't remember exactly what the little devils are properly called, but they travel in a cloud. They're very tiny, and you don't see them until you're smack dab in the middle of a whole slew of them."

"Hence the name," Spock said, nodding. "No-see-um. One does not see them."

"Knew you'd catch on eventually," McCoy said. "They're not dangerous—no bites or stings—but boy, are they annoying! They get in your eyes, your mouth, your nose, your hair—they'll stop you dead in your tracks and have you dancing around and waving your arms until you're clear of the cloud." He sank back in his chair, satisfaction writ plain on his face.

Spock considered McCoy's words, and then nodded. "It is perhaps an overly enthusiastic, but nonetheless apt, analogy," Spock said. "We shall be like these insects of Dr. McCoy's. We shall have very little bite, but undoubtedly we can do a superlative job of aggravating the Falorians. Also, Commander Uhura, I want you to do everything you can to block any communication that might originate from the facility."

Karglak puffed up with pride on Uhura's behalf, but Uhura herself frowned. "With respect, Mr. Spock, that means that if Captain Kirk tries to contact us, we won't know it."

"If we succeed in forcing them to drop the shield, we will be able to contact the captain via his communicator," Spock said. "If we do not, it is highly possible that the order to activate the virus will be given from this facility, since it is where it was created. I cannot risk—"

The door hissed open. "Captain Spock." It was Captain Q'allock, who had the bridge in Spock's absence. "An urgent message from the Federation president is coming in."

"I will speak with him," Spock said, rising.

"Sir, it's a recorded message, sent to all Federation vessels. And us," he added, clearly feeling a need to distance himself from the "Federation."

"Patch it through to here," Spock said. His curiosity was aroused, and though he would not admit it, he felt apprehension stir as well.

Spock felt a start of surprise, quickly suppressed, at the haggard appearance of the president. His white hair was in disarray and there were hollows under his eyes. His body posture sent a clear message of hopelessness even before his words confirmed it.

"Attention all Federation vessels. Before anything else, let me say that you are not, under any circumstances, to engage warp drive until further notice. Consider this as inviolable an order as you have ever received. You have heard about Kal-Tor Lissan's threatened virus. Our scientists have learned that the Falorians told us only part of the truth. If any infected ship attempts to engage warp drive, the dilithium matrix could destabilize and the crystals may fracture or shatter. An instantaneous warp core breach would occur."

The president paused and took a deep breath. McCoy and Uhura exchanged glances. Spock kept his eyes on the recording.

"Obviously, not every ship is infected, and there are a very few of you who know with certainty that you are not. We ask you few to hold your positions. It may well be that when this is all over, you will be the only vessels in the Federation capable of warp drive, and as such you will be precious indeed to the cause of unity and freedom in the galaxy."

"My God," McCoy breathed. Karglak growled.

"We have the top scientists in the Federation working around the clock to find a way to counter this virus, and we have every hope that they will succeed," said the president, although Spock noted that his body language belied his confident words. "Stand by until further notice."

The screen went dark.

"Captain Q'allock," Spock said, sounding exactly the same as he had before this message had been played, "is this vessel one of the few of which the president spoke?"

"We've been nowhere near the *pahtk* who did this," the captain said, and turned and spat on the carpeting. "We have been in space for many months. You are the only passengers we have taken on."

"Your homeworld was one of the sites visited by the Falorian delegation," Spock said. "We therefore must assume that we, too, have been contaminated."

"Do you mean to tell me," Q'allock said, rising anger in his voice, "that you have brought us out here to strand us in orbit around this pathetic planet for the rest of our lives?"

Karglak sprang to his feet. "You shame yourself with those words! We are here on orders from our Chancellor, to fulfill the Year and the Day!"

"It is my understanding that Klingons are willing to die to see an honor debt satisfied," Spock said calmly. "Are they unwilling to live to see the debt paid?"

The Klingon had no response to that. He folded his arms and glowered.

"We came here to satisfy the *DIS jaj je*," Spock continued. "Let us be about it."

Lissan stood straight and tall as he reported to his fellow Kal-Toreshi. Even as he spoke with an easy confidence, he felt a brief pang inside. Lying had once been something he had abhorred. Now, it seemed to come to him far too easily. The falsehoods rolled glibly off his tongue. No, the Federation would be no trouble at all. Yes, 858 might have gotten wind of the plot, but Lissan had been able to put him off. No, the colonists weren't being any problem, and of course Lissan had been able to capture them all. No, 858 had exaggerated the skirmish with the Klingon vessel. The eight ships suffered minor damage but were victorious. Could they see Kirk? Not at the moment, the pesky human was being interrogated. Soon, Lissan promised. On schedule? Of course everything was on schedule. This had been planned down to the last second, why wouldn't everything be on schedule?

On their end, unless they were lying too, the Kal-

Toreshi had very good news to report. Lorall, the aged female who was the head of the small group, fairly radiated pleasure.

"The Huanni are putting up a good fight, but they are no match for our enhanced fleet," she enthused. "The first few hours have gone well. There is no reason to believe that the planet will not eventually fall to our forces."

"That is wonderful and welcome news," Lissan said, and for the first time since the conversation began, knew those words to be the unvarnished truth.

There came a deep rumbling sound, and the image of the Kal-Toreshi was shot through with static. "Lissan?" Lorall's voice was harsh and buzzing, and her image was fuzzy. "We are having trouble—"

Panicked, Lissan turned off the screen and contacted his head of security. "What is going on?" he demanded, his voice high.

"The Klingon vessels are firing on the shield," Jasslor reported.

"What's the damage?"

"Insignificant, sir. We think the shield will hold through several hours, perhaps days, of such bombardment. However, they are also firing into the ground around the shield. There is a great deal of energy rolling off the shield into the surrounding area. The soil and rock is grounding most of it, but we're still getting power spikes and are going to have to take some systems closer to the surface offline." Inwardly, Lissan groaned. Security was located immediately below surface level. The chief hesitated, and then added, "It looks like they are also successfully jamming our communications."

"We are in the final stages of activating the nanoprobe virus," Lissan said, hissing the words. "We need to be able to communicate. We need to transmit the order that will ensure our victory. We need to not lose data. What are you doing about this?"

"Sir, as I've told you, we are very short on security personnel, and with the problems caused by the bombardment—"

"I know, I know, security systems are being taken offline. Then leave the cursed colonists in their hidey-holes. Call all security back in," Lissan ordered. "It looks like we need them here more."

Jasslor hunched his shoulders and managed to look more miserable than he had earlier. Lissan had not thought such a thing possible.

"Sir," he said, "With the communications systems jammed, we can't contact them to have them report back."

Lissan was so horrified at how rapidly and severely the situation had deteriorated that for a moment he didn't even have breath to reply. For the briefest of moments, he felt sheer panic stalking him like a wild beast. No. He would not yield. Wild, uncontrollable emotions were a Huanni trait, not a Falorian.

"Here is what you will do," he said, calmly. He leaned forward into the screen. "You will find a way to get external communications working again. You will contact all personnel currently searching for the colonists and call them back. You will stabilize the field so that these attacks do not disrupt it further, and you will find Captain Kirk and his comrades and bring them to me. Do I make myself clear?"

Jasslor swallowed. "Yes, sir," he said.

The minute they were inside, alarms began to ring shrilly. At once, they slammed the door shut. There was no time to let Scott work his magic and reactivate a scrambled security device; Kirk simply fired at the controls. If anyone wanted to get in, they would have to blow open the door or phaser it open physically.

Unfortunately, if they wanted to get out, they would have to do the same.

"We're in it now for sure," Julius said.

"Were you ever not?" Kirk asked sharply.

Unexpectedly, Julius smiled. "Once," he said, "but not anymore."

Kirk looked around and assessed the situation. They were again in the enormous control center, the very heart of the place. He felt a brief stab of anxiety as he looked at the screen that had once showed the formal reception hall of Starfleet Command. All the screens were blank. No doubt that hall was presently empty, of course; no time for entertainment or festivities now. Here was where Kirk first grasped the vastness of the Falorian plot, although the details had not yet been revealed. Here also was where he had given the order that had caused Chekov's hands to be so badly damaged. He wouldn't make that mistake again.

"Let's find out which of these is the communication console," he told Scott. "And make sure you disable any security precautions. I don't want anyone else injured."

At that moment, they heard sounds from outside. Someone was banging on the doors.

They had been discovered.

"Time's a-wasting, gentlemen," Kirk said. He took up a position at the door, phaser at the ready. The guards might eventually break through, but Kirk was going to stop at least a few of them. Chekov, too, stepped beside him and lifted his phaser.

Scott and Julius went from console to console, trying to find the right one. Skalli trailed behind them, craning her long neck and wringing her hands, but keeping silent.

"I think that's it," Julius said. "Some of the readings look similar to other communications devices I've seen the Falorians using. What do you think?"

The banging stopped. A new sound could be heard faintly over the shrill alarm; the high-pitched whine of a phaser adjusted to a fine cutting edge.

Scott didn't reply, but glanced from the console to the tricorder and back. Finally he nodded his nearly white head. "Aye, that looks about right. I'll take it from here, lad."

"Maybe I can help?" Skalli said.

"You've been useful indeed, lass," Scott said. "Step in here and have a look."

A tiny hole appeared in the heavy metal door, surrounded by a shower of sparks. Kirk and Chekov exchanged glances. They still had some time, but not much. Kirk adjusted his grip on the phaser.

"Uncle Jim?" Julius's voice was surprisingly quiet, devoid of its usual surly undertones.

"I'm a bit busy, Julius," Kirk replied.

"I'd like to help. Scott and Skalli are busy at the console. Let me have a phaser. I'll stand with you."

Kirk glanced at him sharply. The blood had dried on his now-swelling face, but for the first time since Kirk had seen him his expression was almost tranquil. He knew they could all die here. And he knew what he was asking.

"All right, Julius. Take Mr. Scott's phaser. It will be an honor to have you at our backs."

Slowly, despite the pain it must have caused his damaged jaw, Julius smiled, and for the first time, Kirk saw the boy in the face of the man.

The black line had grown to an inch now.

The howling siren stopped. Kirk's ears felt hot from the cessation of the sound. Then came another sound.

"Captain Kirk," came Lissan's voice. "So, I have found you at last."

Chapter Twenty-three

"Kal-Tor Lissan," Kirk said. "I have some information for you."

"Unless it is where you have hidden all your colonists, I have no interest in anything you might say," Lissan said. His voice echoed in the chamber, quiet save for the Kal-Tor's voice and the steady, high hum of the phaser continuing to cut through the door.

"We know about your plot to destroy all dilithium crystals except the stash you are planning to take from the Huanni," Kirk said.

"You figured that out? Very clever. Did the Huanni female help you out? Did she tell you what her people had done to ours?"

"There's no time for this, Lissan," Kirk snapped. "Your scientists have made a fatal mistake. There's a flaw in your research. I believe your only desire was to control the flow of dilithium in the galaxy. But you're going to kill thousands, maybe millions, of people doing so."

Harsh laughter rang through the room. The cut in the door was now a vertical six-centimeter gash, and as Lissan replied, the unseen guard on the other door moved his phaser horizontally. The cut continued in a straight line to Kirk's right.

"We have been planning this for years," Lissan said. "We have run every test imaginable. There is no flaw. You would say anything to try to halt our triumph and keep the Federation's advantage in the quadrant's affairs."

"We studied your data," Kirk said urgently. "We know that you utilized an extremely pure crystal, that indeed all of your tests were performed using splinters of that single crystal. Did you do any tests on any other crystal? One with more impurities?"

"There was no need. A dilithium crystal is a dilithium crystal. This is nonsense, Kirk. I am not cruel. If you surrender now, I give you my word you will not be harmed."

Kirk glanced over at Scott, who was still working frantically. Skalli shook her head; the engineer hadn't been able to get a message out yet.

The cut was now three centimeters across. The angle again went down. Sparks sputtered.

"We ran simulations on our dilithium crystals," Kirk continued. "Crystals of only about seventy-five percent purity. They shattered like common glass, Lissan. If that had been a real crystal in a real matter-antimatter chamber, it would have caused a warp core breach. You know what happens then."

Lissan was silent. The cutting sound continued.

"That's not possible." There was hesitancy in the Falorian's voice.

"Think about it, Lissan. If you activate this virus and a ship goes into warp, you're going to be responsible for the deaths of every single person on that vessel. Is that really what you want? Is that the legacy you've dreamed of for the Falorian people? To go down in history as the worst mass murderers of all time?"

"We are not killers, Kirk."

"I don't think you are, Lissan," Kirk said truthfully. "I don't think you knew that this would happen, but it will."

"All we want is what was rightfully ours!" Lissan cried. "We died in the mines on Huan. We discovered that dilithium, we *earned* it. This story you have fabricated—you just want to help your precious Huanni. You lie, James Kirk, and promise to the Federation or no, the moment my guards break into the control center I swear, we will activate that virus!"

Kirk glanced at the door. The cutter was making steady progress.

"Let me talk to him," Skalli said unexpectedly. Kirk looked at her sharply. "Please," she said. "Let me talk to him."

"This is a very delicate situation. What are you going to say?" Kirk wanted to know.

"Something that should have been said a long time ago," she replied.

Kirk hesitated, then nodded. Skalli cleared her throat and spoke more loudly. "Kal-Tor Lissan? This is Skalli. The Huanni."

A long, cold silence. "There is nothing you have to say that I could possibly want to hear, Huanni. Save your dignity and don't beg for your planet."

"I'm not going to beg." Her chest hitched with short, shallow breaths. "I want—I w-want—" She gulped and wiped at her eyes, cleared her throat, and squared her narrow shoulders. "I want to apologize."

Again, silence. Then, shockingly, laughter. It was malicious and sent shivers down Kirk's spine. Skalli visibly shrank away from the sound.

"I had no idea Huanni had such a sense of humor," Lissan said. "Of course, that makes everything all right, now, doesn't it? Centuries of laboring under Huanni domination, of taming a world to which we were never born simply because you got tired of us—well, we'll just put that all behind us because one Huanni child practically still slick from her mother's womb says she's *sorry*."

Skalli was crying so hard that tears spilled down her face from all four corners of her eyes. Kirk reached to put a hand on her shoulder.

"Stop," he said softly, for her ears alone. "There's no sense in torturing yourself." She wrenched away from his comforting touch.

"Oh, listen to the little Huanni girl, so sad she's crying. Poor little thing. Too bad you're not on your home planet, you'd really have something to cry about."

Kirk winced at the venom in the words. He knew that he was hearing more than one individual's words. He was listening to centuries of pent-up hatred stream out. Skalli swallowed and somehow summoned the wherewithal to reply. Her voice was so thick that her words were almost unintelligible.

"I . . . don't th-think this will change anything," she cried. "B-but that doesn't make any difference. This is something I need to say, and I need you to hear w-whether you believe it or not. Lissan, I *am* sorry. So terribly, terribly sorry for what my people did to yours." She laughed shakily. "It's not even as if we're different people, we're the same, and yet the people from whom I'm descended did terrible things to the people from whom you're descended. We never speak about it because we're so ashamed. We think that if we don't say anything, then it's almost like it didn't happen. I don't blame you for rejecting our offers of friendship. How can we truly think to be your friends when we can't even admit we did anything wrong?"

She dragged a sleeve across her streaming nose. "So now you're doing something just as bad to us, but at least you've got a reason. I just wanted you to know. That there was someone, at least, who is able to acknowledge what the Huanni did to the Falorians and say it was wrong, and I am very, very sorry."

Again, a long silence. Finally, Kirk broke it. "Lissan, are you still there?"

"It was you, wasn't it, Kirk? You put her up to this."

"Skalli is her own person, Lissan. I'm as surprised as you are by what she just said. It's not too late. Promise me you won't detonate this virus and we will arrange for negotiation between you and Huan. Maybe we can—"

"This conversation is over."

"Lissan? Lissan!" But the Kal-Tor was gone. "Scotty, how far are you—"

"It's no use, Captain. We can't get a message out," Scott said glumly. "Someone's blocking it. This was all for nothing."

Kirk stared at him, feeling the horrified gaze of everyone else upon him. This couldn't be! They couldn't have come this far and not be able to at least warn the Federation. But Kirk had known Scott for decades, and he knew every expression that flitted across that face. There was nothing Scotty could do.

"This isn't *fair!*" wailed Skalli, finally surrendering to her grief and sobbing into her hands.

The Falorian guard was done with his second vertical cut. He moved to complete the rectangle. Once that was done, they'd be in.

"Scotty, give me something. Anything."

Scott remained silent. Kirk's thoughts raced. He looked around the vast room again, seeing it with fresh eyes.

"We're in the control center," Kirk said. "The *control center.* Julius, you said the Falorians were very organized. Do you think they would create this virus and then put the ability to launch it anywhere but here?"

Julius's blue eyes glittered. "Not a chance," he said firmly. "This is where it was made, this is where it will be activated. I'd bet my life on it."

"You may well be doing exactly that," Kirk said. If they had time, maybe even a few more minutes, they could probably determine which console controlled the activation of the virus and destroy it. But they didn't have time. Time was running out. They had a few seconds remaining, a moment or two at the outside.

"You've broken into the communications system, right, Scotty?"

"Aye," Scott said. "But I told you, we can't—"

"We can't get a message out, I know. But within the complex, can this system talk to the others?"

Skalli's tears were drying and now her eyes gleamed. "I think they can," she said, clearly seizing onto the merest shred of hope.

"We don't have time to find out where the activation of this virus is centered," Kirk said. "But if this entire complex is destroyed, the Falorians won't be able to send the activation signals to the nanoprobes. The virus will remain dormant."

The faces that turned to him were grim, but unafraid. Everyone knew what was at stake here. Even Julius didn't offer a protest.

"I can link up all the consoles throughout the facility so that one short will send the whole kit and caboodle sky-high. This whole pit will be one big ball o' flame. We won't be needing to worry about what our relatives will do with our remains."

"I don't give a damn about what happens to me," said Julius. "But the other colonists—Alex—how can we justify making this decision for them?"

"Alexander knows what's at stake here," Kirk said. "What do you think he would want us to do?"

Slowly, Julius grinned. His eyes were shiny. "Stop these bastards," he said.

"Then that's what we'll do. Scotty, get on it now."

Kirk had never seen the engineer move so quickly. Kirk glanced from Scotty's flying fingers to the cut in the doorway. For the moment, it seemed to have stopped. They had reached some kind of bolt or barrier within the door, and the cutting was taking longer.

"Got it, Captain." Scott edged out from under a console. "I crosswired with the security system that blew up Mr. Chekov's console the last time. Press that blue button up there and it'll send a command to all the consoles to self destruct."

Kirk nodded to show he understood. He took a deep breath.

"Commander Sabra Lowe," Skalli said softly. She had stopped crying and had a strange, calm expression on her face.

"What?" asked Chekov, but Kirk understood immediately what Skalli was referring to.

"Yes, Skalli," Kirk said. "We are indeed in the same situation as Commander Lowe was so long ago. It seems the more things change, the more they remain the same."

"You have the same choice as she did, Captain," Skali said. "Continue to fight and eventually be overwhelmed, or destroy this control center now, sacrificing all our lives to save the lives of millions of other innocents."

She smiled softly. "A true command decision, just like hers was. I believe that Commander Lowe did the right thing then, and I believe that what you are about to do is the right thing now. It's funny, but up until this moment I always thought of Commander Lowe as a hero. But I guess she felt just the same way as we do now—scared, worried, hoping this is the right thing, hoping it'll work."

Kirk gazed on her with pride and affection. "Skalli," he said, "you would have made a wonderful ambassador."

Her ears pricked up and her eyes shone.

Kirk heard the whirring noise and knew that the Falorians had gotten past the obstacle. In a matter of seconds, the guards would be in. Kirk looked from face to face, taking them in at this last moment of his life.

Scotty, his face weathered and his eyes bright. How very many times had he saved Kirk's life before? But now, there was nothing even he could do.

Chekov. Kirk had watched this man mature from an enthusiastic boy into an intelligent, experienced man, one Kirk was proud to have served with and to now call friend.

Skalli, who had grown more than he had imagined possible. She was so young, had had so much to offer.

And Julius. As he locked gazes with his nephew, Kirk saw no reproach, no regrets, only a steady determination. Julius had many black marks against him, but in a moment, his selfless sacrifice would wipe that slate cleaner than the youth could have dreamed. Kirk regretted that only now, in these last few hours, had he felt truly close to Julius.

It was time. Push the button, Scott had said, and the threat to the Federation, to innocent lives, would be over.

He moved calmly, his finger steady. But when he was

only an inch away from the glowing button, Kirk suddenly paused.

He was thinking about that strange, brief burst on his communicator as they fought to enter the complex. What had that been? Or rather, *who* had it been? Kirk knew that Starfleet was aware that he and the others were being held hostage. What if they'd sent out a rescue ship? Under the circumstances, it wasn't logical, but Kirk knew at least one friend who, despite his professed devotion to logic, would have come if there had been any possible way. He would have done the same for Spock and the others—*had* done the same in the past. Would they do less than he?

Kirk felt keenly that he had not particularly distinguished himself recently. He'd botched experiments, gotten in the way, been responsible for a severe injury to Chekov, alerted Lissan that they knew about the complex and caused Lissan to destroy their only escape vessel, failed to prevent his nephew's capture and beating, failed to convince Lissan to stay his hand, couldn't get a message out, and was now about to be responsible for the deaths of both Kirk brothers.

His time on this planet had been one failure or problem after another. He was fine commanding a starship— he knew what to do there. He'd done it for years, and no amount of false modesty would make him feel that he didn't deserve the accolades he had achieved for his service on the bridge of a starship.

But here, it seemed that all he'd done was make one mistake right after the other. Every time he'd tried to act, all he had done was make the situation worse.

Maybe he shouldn't act.

Maybe his command decision would be to decide *not* to destroy the complex.

Maybe he should trust his friends.

Slowly, Kirk leaned back, and curled his extended finger into a loose fist.

Skalli uttered an incoherent cry and sprang forward, determined to push the button herself. Quick as a snake, Kirk seized her wrist.

"What are you doing?" Skalli shrieked.

"Trusting," Kirk said. The door burst open.

And the room dematerialized around him.

Chapter Twenty-four

When his environment again solidified, Kirk found himself face to face with a Klingon.

Before he could react, a familiar voice said, "Welcome aboard, Captain. Chancellor Azetbur will be pleased to see that her vow of *DIS jaj je* was successfully completed."

Kirk whirled to greet Spock, noticing as he did so that Skalli, Chekov, Julius, and Scott had also made it safely to the bridge of this Klingon ship. The Vulcan stood with his hands clasped loosely behind his back, his head cocked at an angle that Kirk knew very well indeed. Kirk stifled his impulse to hug the Vulcan and instead said, "Mr. Spock. Have I ever told you that you have impeccable timing?"

Spock lifted an eyebrow. "We await your orders, Captain." The Vulcan indicated the command chair. Kirk eyed the Klingon who was probably the real captain of the vessel, received an almost imperceptible nod, and took the proffered seat.

"We've got some hostages down there who—"

"We have already transported everyone in the complex, including the Falorians, to this vessel and our accompanying bird-of-prey," Spock said.

So Spock had come riding over the figurative hill with not just one, but two Klingon ships? This *DIS jaj je* was obviously of great importance to Azetbur. Kirk supposed he should be grateful.

"Very good. I can assume that the Falorians are all in custody and the injured hostages are being attended to?"

"You may indeed," Spock said.

"The rest of the colonists are hiding in the cave system. Kate Gallagher rigged up a system to block their life signs from the Falorian tricorders, but the Klingons should—"

"We have already scanned for and located them, Captain."

Kirk wondered if there was anything that *hadn't* already been efficiently taken care of.

"That complex is the heart of the Falorian plan," Kirk informed his former first officer. "But I don't think it ever included mass murder." He sought out the Klingon captain, figuring the biggest, meanest-looking of the bunch would hold that rank. "Captain . . . ?"

"I am Karglak," the Klingon said. The opera singer? Here? "That is Captain Q'allock."

Kirk turned to face the real captain. "Captain Q'allock. I need you to send down your finest crewmen to secure that complex. Mr. Scott, you will accompany them. Sanctuary is in Federation hands now."

The Klingon saluted. "It is already done," he said.

"What?" Kirk said, amazed.

"Not actually," Spock said. "It is a figure of speech. A slight exaggeration."

"I'm glad to hear it," Kirk said. "I'd like to think I had something to contribute." He swiveled in his chair, speaking as he did so. "Communications, open a channel to—Uhura!"

The elegant, beautiful African woman gave him a slow, wide smile, positioning her long dark fingers expertly on the console. For a second, Kirk grinned stupidly, then composed himself and said, "Contact the president of the Federation. Use every encryption key in the book. This conversation needs to be completely secure."

Turning to her console, Uhura said teasingly in her warm voice, "It is already done." Karglak moved to stand by her side, looking at her affectionately.

"Any more surprises up your sleeve?" Kirk asked Spock. The Vulcan looked slightly nonplussed at the phrase and was about to reply when the unmistakable voice of Kirk's favorite country doctor came through the intercom on the chair.

"Jim!"

"Bones?"

"Got my hands full here, but I wanted to make sure they'd really managed to get a hold of you."

"We're all fine, Bones. My nephew. . . ."

"We've got Alexander here, he's fine." A pause, then in a more sober tone, McCoy continued, "He keeps asking for his brother. What should I tell him?"

Kirk looked over at Julius. Julius glanced away, fidgeting, trying to hide his emotions beneath his don't-give-a-damn exterior. But Kirk knew him better now. Come to think of it, the boy needed to see the doctor, too. "Tell him that Julius will be right down."

"He'll be glad to hear it."

Kirk hoped so. "Mr. Chekov, you go with him. I'll feel better about those burns if I know Dr. McCoy has looked at them."

"Aye, sir." Chekov, Scott and Julius stepped briskly toward the turbolift.

Kirk's eyes followed Julius. "Commander Uhura, open hailing frequencies throughout both Klingon vessels."

"Hailing frequencies open, Captain."

"This is Captain James T. Kirk to the crew and passengers of the Klingon vessels—" Kirk suddenly realized he didn't know their names.

"The *Kol'Targh* and the *K'Rator*," Spock said helpfully.

Nodding his thanks, Kirk said, "—the *Kol'Targh* and the *K'Rator*. The colonists of Sanctuary and I are profoundly grateful for your assistance here today. You have quite literally saved all our lives, and we thank you. It is my understanding that many of the colonists successfully eluded capture by the Falorians. I know that many of you took with you valuable information regarding the present danger we all face. I would like for you to upload all information you have to the Klingon computer databanks, and make sure that both ships have complete copies of this information. Captain Spock was put in charge of this mission—" it was a guess, but as

Spock didn't make any move to naysay him, Kirk knew it had been a good one "—and upon my arrival, has passed command on to me. You are to take everything I have said as an order. Kirk out."

"Captain, I have the president," Uhura said.

"Onscreen." The image of Sanctuary slowly turning in space was replaced by the reddish skin and white hair of the Federation President.

"Captain Kirk," he said. "It is a great pleasure to see you alive."

"You'll be even happier when I tell you that Sanctuary and its Falorian research facility is under Federation control," Kirk said. "I have a group of Klingons securing it even as we speak."

The president brightened visibly. "That is the best news I have heard in a long, long time."

"This virus is more dangerous than we thought. The Falorians did all their testing with extremely pure crystals. Anything less pure would shatter and—"

"Yes, and cause a warp core breach. We found that out ourselves." Kirk tried not to show his disappointment. He should have known that anything he'd been able to learn, Starfleet would have been able to learn.

"What is the status of the virus?" continued the president.

"As far as I know, it hasn't yet been activated, and I believe that it can't be as long as we're in control of that facility."

"That's part of the problem solved, but not all of it," the president said. "If the nanoprobes remain dormant, someone could learn how to activate them. We must find a way to render them completely useless."

Kirk nodded his agreement. "And if they remain intact, someday someone could learn how to recreate the virus. I don't believe it was intended to be used as a method of mass destruction, but as we've discovered it certainly could be. If the nanoprobes aren't completely destroyed, the danger exists that this could happen again. What's the status on Huan?"

The president sobered. "Not good. They've been bombarded for eleven hours now. So far it's mainly infrastructure that's been destroyed—their fleets, military bases, and so on. Minor casualties, but that could change at any minute."

"Who's at the perimeter of Huanni space?" Kirk asked. "You can safely give them orders to attack now."

"Them? Kirk, the only ship close enough to do any good that we could be certain wasn't infected was the *Excelsior*. We'll of course notify every ship we can now, but it will take them hours to get there, perhaps even days."

"Do you mean to tell me there's only one Starfleet vessel standing ready to defend Huan?"

"I'm afraid so."

Kirk digested the news, then said, "Inform Captain Sulu of the situation."

"Kirk, he's only one man with one ship."

"Respectfully, Mr. President, I served with Hikaru Sulu. He'll think of something. In the meantime, we'll be doing our best to make sure this virus is obliterated."

"Good job, Captain. Best of luck." The image disappeared.

Kirk turned to Spock. "You said that the Falorians were all in custody?"

Spock nodded. Kirk rose. "You have the bridge. Captain Q'allock, I'm less familiar with the layout of your vessel than you might think I would be. Could you escort me to the brig?"

Q'allock snarled. "It would give me great pleasure to behold the quailing scum with my own eyes."

Kirk took that as a yes.

The confines of a Klingon brig made those of Starfleet ships look like luxury suites. Dozens of Falorians, most of them clearly confused and frightened scientists, were crowded together so tightly that Kirk wondered how they could breathe. Dim red lighting provided little illumination. Kirk scanned the crush for Lissan and was about to give up, thinking that the Falorian leader had been transported to the other vessel, when he spied the Kal-Tor in the back.

"Him," Kirk said, pointing. The guards looked at Q'allock for confirmation. *DIS jaj je* or no, Kirk wasn't their captain. The Klingon nodded, and the guards deactivated the force field. One pointed a disruptor at the crowd while the other one shoved into the press of Falorian flesh, seized Lissan, and pulled him out roughly.

For an instant, Kirk could hardly believe that this was the selfsame being that had strutted about Sanctuary so arrogantly. He was bruised and cut, his once-crisp uniform wrinkled and soiled. Then Lissan straightened, and Kirk realized that even though everything had changed, nothing had changed.

They eyed one another for a moment, then Lissan spoke. "I suppose this is the part where you either beg me to cooperate and save your precious dilithium, or you set your hired thugs on me and bully me into submission?"

"Neither," Kirk said shortly. "Which one of these people is your top scientist? The one who had the greatest part in creating the virus?"

Lissan folded his long, thin arms across his narrow chest and said nothing.

"If you want to play it that way," Kirk said. He turned to the crowd of Falorians. "Which one of you is the top scientist?"

"Say nothing, any of you!" cried Lissan, and before Kirk could stop him, a Klingon had slammed the butt of his disruptor into Lissan's gut. The Falorian doubled over. The Klingon drew back for a second blow.

"Stop it!" Kirk cried.

The Klingon shot him an angry look. "These people are dishonorable! They would see us all dead!" he spat. "They deserve far worse than this!"

"That's not for you or me to decide," Kirk said. "The Falorians will be tried fairly. Until then, you will treat them with care and respect."

The Klingon reluctantly subsided. Kirk turned again to the prisoners. "I ask again—Who among you is the top scientist?"

They simply stared at him with large, frightened eyes. Kirk sighed. He had started to turn away when a small, timid voice said, "I'm the one you want."

Kirk glanced over to see a small, slender fellow push

his way to the front. Judging by Lissan's expression of annoyance and disgust, Kirk felt that this was indeed the man he wanted. The force field was again deactivated and the scientist stepped out.

"What is your name?" Kirk asked.

"Don't tell him," Lissan warned.

The scientist swallowed, and then said quietly, "I'm Kalaskar."

"Well, Kalaskar, I have a few things I want you and Lissan to see."

Under heavy guard, Kirk and the two Falorians entered the engineering section of the ship. While the layout was different, the huge pulsing warp core was familiar to Kirk. He asked for and was given a tricorder.

"This vessel is a Klingon *K't'inga* class battle cruiser. It's one of the finest ships in the Klingon fleet. Wouldn't you agree that such a vessel would be equipped with the highest-grade dilithium available?"

Lissan only glowered, but the more timid Kalaskar said, "That would make sense."

Kirk tossed him the tricorder. "Scan it," he ordered. Hesitatingly, Kalaskar did so. He frowned. "What poor grade," he said, with a hint of Lissan's arrogance.

"What's the quality?" Kirk asked.

"A mere ninety-one percent," Kalaskar said.

The chief engineer bridled. "Ninety-one percent is excellent! Our ship is equipped with a superior grade crystal. Better than ninety-five does not exist!"

"But it does," Kirk said. "It exists on Huan. But the rest of us have to make do with a purity rate of sometimes as low as seventy-two percent. You're the scientist, Kalaskar. What do you think this crystal would do if your virus was activated?"

"I—don't know," the Falorian stammered. "We didn't know that a crystal this impure even existed."

"Don't give me that," snapped Kirk. "You're a spacefaring race, you've used dilithium crystals in your ships!"

"We have only been a spacefaring race for two centuries, Captain," Lissan said, his tone equally as sharp. "And even for that, we have had to subsist on the *charity* of the Huanni. What ships we have, they gave us, along with the crystals to power them. We never examined their purity; we assumed that they were all the same. All like the single crystal we have kept since the day we were stranded on Falor."

Kirk searched his eyes. In them he found coldness and dislike, but no lie. He nodded to himself, convinced of Lissan's truthfulness. Kirk waved them over to a console.

"Some information about the virus was recently downloaded to your computers," he told the chief engineer. "We ran several simulations. Call them up."

The engineer complied. Kirk had seen the simulations before; he was more interested in watching the reactions of the two Falorians. Both of them looked upset, but Lissan continued to mingle his distress with defiance. The scientist had no such constraint.

"This is terrible!" He turned to his superior. "Kal-Tor, we never intended this. The virus was only supposed to make the dilithium useless, not destroy it!"

"I told you, I never thought you were a killer, Lissan,"

Kirk said quietly. "Julius seems to think that the virus can only be activated from that site down on that planet. I'm betting that only you know the command codes. Am I right?"

Lissan didn't answer. Finally, Kalaskar could stand it no longer. "You are right," Kalaskar said. "There's no way to activate the virus except from Sanctuary. And yes, only Kal-Tor Lissan has the command code."

"Is there any way to get the nanoprobes to self-destruct?" Kirk pressed.

"Oh, yes," Kalaskar said. "It was one of the safeguards I insisted we have, just in case the virus got tracked onto one of our own ships. It, too, can only be executed from Sanctuary, and again, Kal-Tor Lissan is the only one that knows the correct code."

"Lissan," Kirk said, "You see what's at stake. If those nanoprobes aren't destroyed, someone with less conscience than the Falorians could figure out how to activate them. What would happen if that level of technology fell into the hands of a race like the—" Kirk stopped himself. He had almost said *Klingons*. "The Orion Syndicate, or the Romulans, or another racist species? Someone who thinks every other species is beneath them?"

"As I see it, Captain," Lissan said coldly, "that is your problem, not mine. We are a dead race now. You have utterly ruined our chance to gain the wealth that should have been ours from the beginning. You will halt our attack against our ancient enemies, the Huanni. The Syndicate knows that we tricked them, and do not think for a moment that we will escape their wrath. The Federation will never consider us as potential members now and will probably not permit us to conduct any kind of outside trading. We've lost everything. I don't care what becomes of you."

He folded his arms and held his head high. "I wish to return to my cell now."

Kirk stared. "You can't mean this," he said. "You know that someone will figure it out. The Falorians may yet be indirectly responsible for wiping out half the galaxy!"

Lissan's eyes glittered. "The corpse cares not who follows him, Kirk. My people and I are as good as corpses. And soon, you will be, too."

Chapter Twenty-five

Wordlessly, Kirk escorted the two Falorians back to their crowded cell. Lissan vanished into the crush of bodies without a backward glance. Kalaskar wasn't as certain, but he too went silently.

"Guards, these two may speak with me at any time," Kirk said. "Lissan, I hope you change your mind."

"You may rot, Kirk, and all your Federation friends with you," was Lissan's retort.

He returned to the bridge and met Spock's gaze. He shook his head. "Any word from Mr. Scott?" he asked.

"Negative," Spock said. "The complex is quite large. It will take even our Mr. Scott some time to determine how the controls work."

The door to the turbolift hissed open. Skalli stood there, her tall, willowy frame looking desperately out of place aboard the sharp angles and shiny metal of a Klingon ship's bridge.

"Captain? May I speak with you?"

He opened his mouth to say no, but then thought better of it. She'd proved herself many times on Sanctuary. If she wanted to talk to him, she probably had a good reason. It amused him to think of how much his attitude toward her had changed.

"Of course." He indicated what served the Klingons for a ready room, and they entered. The door hissed shut behind them. "What is it, Skalli?"

She hesitated, her ears flapping. Finally, she said, "You did not act."

For a second he was confused, then understood what she was saying. "In the control center? You're right, I didn't."

"I watched you. We talked about Sabra Lowe and agreed that destroying the complex was the right thing to do, and yet you didn't do it. You gambled that there would be someone to rescue us, which made no sense. You didn't know anyone would even be looking for us. It was an illogical decision."

Kirk smiled. "Illogical," he agreed, "but the right one. There are always . . . possibilities. Commander Lowe did the right thing. She had a choice, just as I did. Her decision was the best choice she could have made, the one that would save the most lives. Going out in a blaze of glory is noble, but death is a rather final option."

She cocked her head, trying to make sense of it. "Then . . . you are saying that sometimes it takes more courage to live, to find another option, than to die."

"Exactly. Had I pressed that button, we'd have destroyed the complex, certainly. And we'd have destroyed the Falorians' ability to activate the virus. That would have stopped the immediate threat. But you know and I know that as long as those nanoprobes are out there, someone is going to figure out how they work. Oh, we'd do as much cleanup as possible. We'd find most of the probes, but we wouldn't find them all. And one day, maybe not tomorrow, but in a year, or two, or ten—someone will discover how to activate the virus and we'll be right back where we were. But as it stands, because the facility is still intact, we now have the chance to determine how to completely destroy the nanoprobes once and for all."

She brightened. "We do?"

"There's a signal and a code. If I could just convince Lissan to give it to us." He sighed.

Skalli was silent for a time. At last, she spoke. "I have decided that I need to know more about these things, these command decisions and why they are made. I'm going to return to the Academy and continue my training. A diplomatic career will no doubt be full of such . . . options."

"I'm glad to hear it. Anything else?"

She thought about the question carefully. "No," she said at last.

Kirk opened his mouth to dismiss her, and then he paused. The words died in his throat. *There are always possibilities. . . .*

"You really want to be an ambassador?" he asked.

"Oh, yes!"

"How'd you like to start right now?"

"What do you mean?"

"Lissan is refusing to assist us. You might be able to get through to him."

She recoiled as if he'd struck her. "Oh, no! I tried, down on the planet . . . and he was so mean to me. . . ."

"He was so mean because something you said affected him," Kirk said, pressing his point.

Her ears flapped wildly and her eyes bulged. "I'd mess everything up . . . I'd get him angry with us again. . . ."

"Skalli, he's not willing to help us as it is. You can't possibly make anything worse. And you might very well make it better. You're the same species. He's got more reason to talk to you than to anyone."

He could tell she wanted to believe him. "But I . . . oh, Captain, what would I say? What would I do?"

Kirk smiled and squeezed her shoulder. "Trust," he said. "Trust yourself."

She was silent, then said, "If I do this, you have to promise me something. I don't want the conversation monitored. He needs to know that I am the only one who'll hear what he has to say."

Kirk was confused. It would be safer if they could keep tabs on Lissan. "I'm . . . not sure where you're going with this, Skalli."

"Neither am I, but it feels like the right thing to do." She looked at him, her large eyes pleading. "You said trust."

"So I did. All right. But I will post guards. And if you are in any danger, I want you to call for help."

"Aye, sir." She saluted smartly. "I'll do the best I can, Captain."

As she left and he returned to the bridge to give the peculiar order, Kirk desperately hoped he was doing the right thing. He walked down with her to the room the guards had secured, and for a moment, they stood together outside. She shuffled her feet. She looked very, very young.

"He can't physically hurt you," Kirk reassured her. "The minute you call for help these two gentlemen," and he indicated the towering, muscled Klingons on either side of the door, "will be in immediately."

"I know," she said.

"But he can and very likely will say some very hurtful things. I know your people are very sensitive."

"If I ever want to be an ambassador, I'll have to learn to live with people saying hurtful things." She placed a hand on his arm and squeezed, then took a deep breath. "I'm ready."

The guards tapped the controls that unlocked the door and it hissed open. In the back of the room, Lissan stood staring out the window at the stars. His hands were clasped behind his back, and he faced away from the door.

Skalli stepped forward. Slowly, Lissan turned. Their eyes met, and then the door closed behind her.

"What have you got for me, Scotty?" Kirk asked.

Scott's face filled the screen. "Well, I've figured out how they were going to do this, at least," he said.

"Let's have it."

"It looks as though your little scientist told the truth. The signal was to be sent from this console through the main subspace relay tower. It consisted of a certain code and a keyword that apparently only Lissan knew. Now, that signal's not strong enough to go very far on its own, but there's a series of subspace amplifier buoys scattered throughout Falorian space," Scott said. "And they just happen to be Starfleet issue."

"One of the things that Julius got for them. All the better to penetrate Federation space," Kirk said grimly.

"Aye," Scott said. "The signal would hop along from buoy to buoy, and every single nanoprobe in the area would be told to turn its little self on. The good news is—"

"The self-destruct code works the same way," Kirk finished. "Keep working on it, Mr. Scott. I want to be able to send the signal immediately if we can convince Lissan to aid us."

Scott gave him a dubious look. "The difference between the two orders is probably nothing more than a single word, Captain. Even if you could get Lissan to agree to give you the code, there's no telling if he'd give you the one to activate the nanoprobes or order them to self-destruct."

Kirk nodded. "Understood. Kirk out." He glanced at the chronometer. Skalli had been in with Lissan for over twenty minutes. The guards had reported no sounds of violence. Kirk could only hope that somehow, the Huanni could get through to him.

All their lives depended on it.

Hikaru Sulu, captain of the starship *U.S.S. Excelsior,* sat alone in his ready room, sipping tea and thinking furiously. A few moments ago, he had learned that the immediate threat posed by the Falorian nanoprobe virus had been halted. While at the present time the *Excelsior* was the only vessel in the area, the president had assured him that more were on their way. The first should arrive within forty-eight hours. In the meantime, Sulu was to use his own best judgment as to how to proceed.

He drank his tea without sugar, lemon, or cream, and the slightly acidic flavor mixed with the sweet jasmine scent never failed to both calm and stimulate his thinking.

Sulu's mind raced. He desperately wanted to charge forward, phasers blasting, to defend the Huanni. But that would only result in every Falorian vessel targeting him and, probably, blowing him right out of the sky. No help to the Huanni from a destroyed ship.

He reached forward and tapped a button. Instantly he saw what was on the main screen on the bridge: an image of a green, pleasant-looking planet being bombarded by a hodgepodge of vessels. Apparently the Falorians dealt in trade; there was no uniform look to the ships. Debris from the destroyed Huanni fleet floated in space. As Sulu watched, a ship approached a vessel that appeared to be only slightly damaged and locked a tractor beam on it.

Sulu frowned as he gazed intently at the scene. He hadn't seen that before.

He kept watching, the tea growing cold, as another ship approached and did the same thing to another small vessel.

And then Sulu figured it out. "Sulu to communications," he said.

"Aye, sir?"

"I need to send a message out. Top security clearance. Stand by for coordinates."

A few moments later, a face appeared on Sulu's screen. The green-skinned Orion wore a mask to hide his features, but his species was obvious.

"Well, well. Hikaru Sulu. It's been a long time. The console signature says, *Excelsior.* So, what are you, captain now?"

Sulu nodded. "I am indeed the captain. Otherwise I'd never have the authorization to initiate this pleasant chat." He leaned forward. "And pleasant as it is, I'm afraid we have some serious matters to discuss."

"What is it you want, Sulu?"

"I just saw some of your scavengers hard at work in Federation territory," Sulu said. "Around a nice little planet called Huan which, incidentally, is under severe attack."

"I'm sure you're mistaken," the Orion said.

"I'm sure I'm not." Sulu shook his head in mock sympathy. "I have to say, it looks pretty bad for the Syndicate. I'm well within my rights to open fire, seeing your people brazenly operating in Federation territory like this."

The Orion, Sulu knew, liked playing the game almost as much as he did. But this time, Sulu knew that he was the one with all the cards.

"So why aren't you attacking?" Sulu's contact pressed.

"You know violence isn't what the Federation is about," Sulu said. "I'm actually contacting you to do you a favor . . . even though *you* still owe *me* one." He smiled. "But who's keeping count?"

"Who indeed?" Sulu had him on his guard now. Good.

"You see, the people attacking Huan just tried to get a corner on the dilithium market by creating a virus that would kill anyone aboard a ship that launched into warp drive. Now, with those Syndicate ships waiting around to pick up what the Falorians leave, it sure looks as though you're involved. And if it comes out that you've assisted a mass murderer. . . ." He let his voice trail off and sighed deeply in false sympathy. He spread his hands. "Much as I'd like to help, you know I'd have to report what I saw here. Unless. . . ."

The Orion's face didn't move a muscle, but his eyes gleamed behind the black mask.

"You always were a good bluffer, Sulu."

"Hey," Sulu said. "I'm sure you've got someone working on it, but let me send you the information we've got. You'll be able to see that it's genuine. Get back to me if you're interested in talking further."

Sulu had barely gotten himself a fresh cup of tea when his Syndicate contact reappeared. He looked utterly furious, which was exactly what Sulu had hoped for.

"The Falorians are no friends of the Syndicate," the Orion snarled.

"I take it you were able to verify my information?" Sulu said smoothly, taking a calm sip.

The Orion, unsure as to what to say, said nothing.

"Look," Sulu said. "Your organization is not allowed

to traffic in Federation space. I've caught your people red-handed. Further, I've got a feeling that you weren't here by accident. I'm betting you allied with the Falorians and they've double-crossed you. And I'm also betting that that makes you pretty mad."

He put down the cup. The delicate china clinked against the saucer.

"If indeed we were ever working with the Falorians," said the Orion, and by his choice of words Sulu knew that the Syndicate had been, "you may rest assured that we knew nothing about the virus." In a quieter voice, he said, "They would have, as you said, double-crossed the Syndicate. On the level, Sulu, we would not have participated in a scheme such as that. Dead men can't pay their debts, and mass murder is bad for business."

Sulu believed him. The Syndicate was all about money, and while murder didn't particularly disturb them, he knew better than to think they'd risk the ruination of their carefully crafted empire.

"Federation heat would be pretty bad for business too, I'd imagine," Sulu said. "I have a proposal for you."

Kirk couldn't take it anymore. He had just arrived at the room in which Skalli and Lissan were closeted when the door hissed open. Skalli staggered out. She was pale and exhausted and almost collapsed into Kirk's arms. Her face was streaked with tears, but she was smiling.

Behind her stood Lissan. His face was a mixture of emotions, and he trembled violently.

"Skalli," Kirk said, helping her stand. "What happened?"

She gazed up at him with pure happiness in her large eyes. "Kal-Tor Lissan will help us," she said in a thick voice.

"Yes," Lissan said. "The Huanni child . . . Skalli . . . has convinced me that I cannot be part of something that will claim so many lives." His voice was hoarse and cracked a little. If Kirk didn't know better he'd think Lissan had been crying. He looked more closely and saw the Falorian's eyes were wet.

"Good God, Skalli," Kirk said, unable to believe the turn of events. "What did you do?"

She steadied herself against him and extended a hand to Lissan, who grasped it swiftly. Squeezing the hand of the being who had hours ago called her a sworn enemy, she smiled.

"You were right. I needed to trust what I felt, and I did. I listened," she said simply.

And then Kirk understood. Skalli was a Huanni, a highly emotional creature. Lissan was descended from the same genes. For centuries the Falorians had lived in isolation, nursing grudges both real and imagined, while the Huanni tried to cover their wrongdoings by simply pretending they hadn't happened. And now, a Huanni sat and listened as a Falorian poured forth the pain of those centuries, listened with her wide-open heart and taking Lissan's anger and pain as her own, healing them both as she did so. It would take more than this to completely mend the rift between the estranged cousins, but it was one hell of a start. It was a tactic that would never have occurred to Kirk, and it was the only tactic that had a prayer of working.

"You'll give us the codes to order the nanoprobes to self-destruct?" Kirk asked.

Lissan met his gaze evenly. "I will," he said.

"Then let's go."

Chapter Twenty-six

They materialized in the control center, and Kirk couldn't help but think that although the room looked exactly the same, things were now very, very different.

He knew he was taking an enormous gamble in trusting Lissan. Spock had been against the idea from the outset. He claimed there would be time later for the Federation to meet with the Falorian government and discuss the nanoprobe technology. Kirk had argued that every moment was one in which someone, somewhere, was analyzing the tiny machines. They had a chance to forever remove the possibility of the virus harming anyone, and he wasn't going to miss it.

Spock had then offered to perform a mind-meld, but Lissan refused, looking frightened. Skalli had intervened, tearfully insisting that to force Lissan to submit would be to cause him extreme torment. Despite their open emotions, Huanni possessed brains with natural barriers that prohibited easy telepathic contact. Falorian brains would likely be constructed in the same way. Spock might eventually be able to tear down the barriers, but at a cost to both him and Lissan.

"We have to show him that he can trust us, and that we trust him," she had pleaded.

Kirk had been saved by his intuition more times than he cared to admit. He was a big believer in building bridges between peoples, and he knew what happened when a Vulcan forced a mind-meld.

It was a time for trust. And the stakes had never been higher. If he gambled incorrectly—if Lissan was playing both him and Skalli for fools—millions could die.

Lissan seated himself at a console while Kalaskar busily went about entering an obviously lengthy list of code. Finally, the scientist sat back. For a long moment, no one moved.

"Lissan," Kirk said. "Now would be good."

"It is not so easy, Kirk," the Falorian Kal-Tor said. "When I enter this code, I will have willfully destroyed all chance of my people ever rising to their rightful place."

"That's not true," Kirk said. "There'll be an investigation. Some of you will be imprisoned. But we'll not hold an entire race responsible. And what you are about to do will go a long way toward mitigating our response."

"Imprisoned," Lissan echoed. "I am sure I will be. How long do you think, Kirk? Forever?"

Kirk wanted to lie, but he couldn't. "I don't know, Lissan," he said honestly. "I'll do what I can for you and your people. As will Skalli. But I can't stand here and tell you that there won't be consequences for what you tried to do."

Slowly, Lissan nodded. "Good," he said. "Had you lied to me I would have known that none of you were to be trusted, and that you would probably have decimated my world. I would have entered the activation code."

He turned and looked at Skalli. She gave him a tremulous smile. Returning his attention to the console, his fingers flew as he entered a series of code almost as lengthy as that which Kalaskar had.

"Preparing to activate self-destruct sequence," the computer said in a clipped male voice. "Awaiting proper authorization."

"Lissan, series one one four one seven one eight eight four two."

There was a long moment where lights chased each other around the console. Kirk realized that every muscle in his body was tense, expecting betrayal. Had he made the right choice? He was gambling now with lives other than his own.

Then, "Self-destruct sequence activated. All nanoprobes destroyed. Virus rendered harmless."

And Kirk permitted himself to breathe. He clapped Lissan on the back. Skalli wriggled happily in her seat. Kirk flipped open his communicator.

"Report."

"The chief engineer informs me that the nanoprobes have harmlessly imploded," came Spock's calm voice. "Apparently, there is not a sufficient amount left of them for analysis."

"That is . . . exactly what I wanted to hear, Mr. Spock. Beam us up and let's get to Huanni at top speed to give Captain Sulu a hand. I'm sure he'll appreciate the assistance."

Sulu was practically humming when he stepped onto the bridge. Ensign Tuvok, the junior science officer on duty, regarded him with barely concealed contempt. Sulu stifled a grin. For someone who claimed to have no emotions, Tuvok certainly gave the appearance that he had quite a lot of them. More than once, Sulu had received what could be called a "dressing down" by this very Vulcan Vulcan. He'd never put the fellow on report; he enjoyed teasing him too much. In a way, it was a very familiar relationship. Sometimes, Sulu could imagine Kirk's voice coming from his own lips, and hearing Tuvok utter Spocklike retorts. No, he'd not chastise a Vulcan for simply being who he was.

He settled into his chair and gazed at the screen. Huan was still under attack, but as Sulu watched he saw several of the mismatched Syndicate ships stop their scavenging. In a few moments, they were joined by several others. More and more odd, cobbled-together ships appeared.

Sulu's first officer, an elderly woman named Janine Clark, looked over at him. "Captain, care to let us in on what's going on?"

"There's an old saying," Sulu said. "The enemy of my enemy is my friend. The Falorians right now are our enemies. And those ships out there—well, they're the Falorians' enemy too."

"I don't understand," Clark said. "Aren't they all Falorian vessels?"

"Patience," Sulu said. It was obvious to him that the Falorians had obtained the shoddy looking but actually well built ships from the Syndicate. Such ships were typical of the Syndicate, but they were also typical of small, independently owned vessels. It was one of the reasons that the Syndicate was so hard to track down. Sulu thought of the early days of sailing, about which he enjoyed reading. Back then, pirates prowled the seas. They didn't have clearly identifiable "pirate ships." They had ships they stole, like the Syndicate did. It was part of what made them so dangerous. A captain would see a ship in the distance that appeared to be a member of his own country's fleet. The hapless captain wouldn't know he was about to be attacked by pirates until and unless they flew the famous skull and crossbones.

At that moment, a dark spot began appearing on the hulls of some of the vessels around Huan.

"What the hell . . . ?" Clark's voice trailed off as the *Excelsior*'s crew stared. Sulu knew what was happening and in a moment they'd figure it out too. A false panel covered those hulls, which was now being retracted to reveal something painted beneath. Gradually the dark blot formed itself into a clearly recognizable shape of a circle with a lightning bolt shot through it—one of the recognizable symbols of the Orion Syndicate.

"But—but—" Clark began.

"Skull and crossbones," Sulu said.

"Those ships are members of the Orion Syndicate,"

Tuvok said crisply. He apparently did not suffer from Clark's present inability to find the words.

"I'm glad you can identify them so promptly, Mr. Tuvok," Sulu said.

More clearly marked Orion ships had appeared. Sulu waited . . . waited. . . .

"Shields up," he ordered. "Lock phasers on the weapons and nearest Falorian ship. Those are the ones without the Syndicate symbol."

"Sir," said Clark, "our orders are to—"

"On this ship, my orders are the only ones that count. Lock phasers."

"Phasers locked, sir."

"Fire."

The minute red phaser fire hit the Falorian ship, every single Orion vessel began to attack as well. Once the order had been given to fight, the *Excelsior* crew dived in with gusto. Sitting here waiting had taken its toll, and now they were more than eager to take action.

The Federation ship rocked. "Shields down fourteen percent," Sulu's tactical officer said. "Some damage to decks eight and nine."

"Return fire," Sulu ordered. It was a direct hit, and the Falorian ship that had damaged them spun slowly and then came to a halt, hanging dead in space.

The battle continued, but the tide had definitely turned. The Orions knew all the weaknesses of the vessels they had sold to the Falorians, and exploited them mercilessly. More than once, Sulu felt a stab of pity for the Falorian fleet. He targeted only weapons and engines, but the Orions aimed to kill.

Finally, Sulu turned to his communications officer. "Open hailing frequencies and send this message: This is Captain Hikaru Sulu of the *U.S.S. Excelsior* to the Falorian vessels. Several dozen Federation ships are on their way, and the Orions and I can certainly keep you here until they arrive. Surrender at once, or prepare to continue to fight."

A pale, female face crowned with long ears filled the screen. She was bleeding from a cut on her forehead. "This is Commander Yalka," she said, gasping. "The Falorian fleet surrenders."

"Stand by for terms. Jackson, reenter the coordinates I gave you a few moments ago and put it onscreen." Time to let these children know just how roughly their captain was willing to play.

The masked face of the Orion filled the screen. "So, are there really Federation ships on their way, or was that just a nice bluff?"

"Oh, they're coming, all right," Sulu replied. "Which means that your people should probably clear out."

The Orion cocked his head. "You didn't let me off so easily the last time," he said.

"I didn't let you off at all, as you'll recall," Sulu said. "You—er—left the party early."

"So why are you doing so today?"

"Let's just say that I'm glad the ships of my fleet can go into warp without going into the next world," Sulu said. "I imagine your people are, too. And we'll leave it at that." He grinned. He held up the first two fingers of his right hand. "That's *two* favors you owe me now. Sulu out."

The image of the Orion was replaced by that of a now-safe Huan. The Orion ships covered their telltale symbol again and went into warp.

Stunned silence reigned on the bridge. It was, predictably, Tuvok who found his voice first.

"Sir . . . you collaborated with known criminals, and permitted them to escape."

"Yes, Tuvok, I did. As captain, that decision was mine to make. We've saved countless innocent Huanni and had the entire Falorian fleet delivered right into our hands."

He smiled softly, a fond memory in his mind. "And besides—it's what Jim Kirk would have done."

"Good God," Kirk said, as the *Kol'Targh* dropped out of warp. He hadn't realized the odds had been this bad. There were dozens of dangerous-looking ships, and the *Excelsior* sat exposed. He had just opened his mouth to order the shields up when Uhura said, "Captain, we're being hailed. It's Captain Sulu."

"Onscreen."

For someone who was clearly outnumbered, Sulu certainly looked calm and relaxed. "Hello, Captain Kirk. Glad you could make it."

"Captain Sulu," Kirk said, puzzled, "do you require assistance?"

"Indeed I do. We've got an unconditional surrender and we'll want to interrogate some of the commanders."

"You've . . . got an unconditional surrender," Kirk repeated. "I see." He groped for words, then simply said, "Very well done, Captain."

"I had a little help," Sulu smiled. "And I see you did too. Why is it I'm always seeing you on a Klingon ship?"

"I've no idea," Kirk said, and meant it. "It looks like you have everything under control, Captain. I'll send some people over to give you a hand, and then I'd very much enjoy it if I can transport over and ask you . . . how you did it. Kirk out."

He leaned back in his chair and looked over at Spock. "Well," he said. "Nothing like racing to the rescue and arriving just in time to help with cleanup. Mr. Spock, you know the crew better than I. Send someone over to Captain Sulu. I'll be in sickbay."

Sickbay was crammed full, with many people all talking at once. Yet over the din, McCoy's distinctive voice could be heard: "Good God, man, do you people still use *needles*? You'll punch a hole right through his arm with that thing! I'd pay real money for a decent hypospray along about now. Yes, I know I was supervising the medical exchange, but we were still working on anatomy when Spock high-tailed it out to this godforsaken part of the galaxy. Now show me how to use that."

It was music to Kirk's ears. He threaded his way through the crush of colonists, most of whose injuries appeared quite minor, and tapped McCoy on the shoulder.

"Alex, I told you to—Jim!" McCoy laughed brightly and embraced his old friend.

"Sorry Spock dragged you out to this godforsaken part of the galaxy," Kirk said.

"Nah, wouldn't have missed it for the world."

"How are my nephews?"

McCoy sobered a bit. "Physically, they're fine, but emotionally—well, you probably know better than I do what they've been through."

"They both down here still?"

"Yep. Told them to stay put until whatever was happening happened. Sounds like we dodged a phaser blast today."

"We did indeed." Kirk searched the crowd, then caught a glimpse of two fair heads at the far end of sickbay. He made his way toward them. They were sitting on what passed for a Klingon diagnostic bed. Physically, they were almost touching, but by their expressions and body language, they were trying to put light-years between them. Julius's face was still slightly swollen, but the blood that had turned his handsome face into a ghoulish mask had been washed off and the lacerations were healed. Alex looked fine; as Kirk had thought, the wounds the boy had incurred during the staged beating had been minimal and easily treatable.

"What are a couple of nice boys like you doing in a place like this," Kirk said lightly.

As one, they glanced up at him, and their expressions were so similar Kirk almost laughed. Why hadn't he realized before how much they resembled one another, despite their great differences? He'd been so busy patting Alex on the head and worrying about Julius's sullenness, he'd missed how very much alike they were.

"The doctor says you're both going to be all right. How do you feel?"

Neither one answered. Kirk sighed. "All right, boys, this is your Uncle Jim speaking, and he's a starship captain. You're both very lucky to be alive. You ought to realize that."

"It's all ruined," Alex said. "I was such a fool. It's all ruined now." He ran a hand through his thick fair hair. His father Sam had had that same habit, and for a moment he looked so much like Kirk's dead brother that Kirk's breath caught. "God! How could I have been so stupid! I put everybody in danger because I was too blind to see what was right before my eyes, that the Falorians were just using me and that my own brother . . ."

He closed his jaw with an almost audible snap and looked down at the floor.

Julius swallowed hard. "That your own brother was dealing with criminals in order to get you the colony," he finished. "You're kicking yourself because you believed in me. I've always been good at lying, Alex. You know that."

"But I never thought you'd lie to *me*." Alex's voice cracked on the last word.

"I'd have done anything to help you realize your dream. I'd have killed for you. I'd have *died* for you."

"Don't you get it, Julius?" Now Alex did look at his baby brother, raw pain in every line of his body. "I never wanted anyone to suffer, to, to get hurt, to die for what I wanted. I wanted a peaceful colony, one where technology could be invented and used to benefit everyone. Instead because of this damned colony technology nearly killed millions of people. I'm a failure."

"You didn't fail, Alex," Kirk said, softly so as not to shatter the moment. "Your dream was and still is a worthy one. So what if this one venture didn't work out? Do you know how many times colonies had to be founded before they hit on the right combination of ideas, resources, and people? I'm certain there would be many species willing to fund another attempt. Technology for peaceful, humanitarian means is a noble and brave ideal, one from which you and your people never deviated. You could have fought, and you didn't. You always sought a peaceful solution. That's going to resonate with a lot of people when the story gets told."

Julius snorted. "Yeah, and when the story gets told, Julius Kirk is going to be a big black mark against his uncle's legacy. Piracy, information trafficking, theft—"

"Courage," Kirk said. "A willingness to own up to his mistakes—mistakes that he only made in the first place because of a deep love for his brother. True remorse and every effort to help correct the wrongs he'd done. And an uncle who's very proud of him, and who would be honored to stand by his side during his trial."

"Nice pep talk, Uncle Jim," Alex said. "But a pep talk isn't going to make everything all better."

"I know," Kirk said. "Just like I know that showing up once or twice a year for a few hours wasn't really being any kind of an uncle to you. I've made my mistakes, too. But mistakes don't have to scar you forever. Life's too short, too precious. What happened on Sanctuary can be a beginning, not an ending, if you let it."

He looked at them for a moment longer, then sighed and turned away.

But out of the corner of his eye, he saw Alex slowly lift an arm and put it around his brother's shoulder. And he saw Julius wipe clumsily at suddenly full eyes.

Chapter Twenty-seven

"You're a sight for sore eyes," Admiral Laura Standing Crane said as she smiled at Kirk from the viewscreen.

"The feeling's mutual," Kirk said. "You still owe me that drink."

"After what you've done, I think I owe you dinner *and* a drink," Standing Crane said. "Although that will have to wait until I get back from the Huanni/Falorian conference."

Kirk uttered a mock groan. "That could take years. I'm getting old, Laura, I don't have that much time left!"

Now she laughed aloud. "Jim Kirk, you're the youngest man I know."

"I'm not sure how to take that."

"Take it as a compliment."

"All right, I will. I don't envy you, Laura. The Federation's got a big job ahead of it in trying to sort out the Huanni/Falorian mess."

"Truer words were never spoken," she admitted, "but it's not as bad as it could be. A lot of lives were lost in the Falorian campaign against Huan, but far fewer than it could have been. I'm a little fuzzy on the details—how did Captain Sulu manage to defeat the fleet?"

Now that was a sticky issue. Kirk kept his face carefully neutral as his mind raced, trying to come up with an answer for that one.

"You'll have to talk to Captain Sulu about that. I'm not sure about all the details myself and I'd hate to tell you something that might not be correct." The response was so smooth that even a Romulan would have been proud of it, he thought.

"Fair enough. Regardless, the Huanni infrastructure took a lot of damage and it's going to take time and resources to get them on their feet again. And there's going to be an inquiry, of course."

"About the fact that they enslaved the Falorians and pretended it didn't happen," Kirk said.

"You have to admit, that's a big omission."

"If Skalli's a fair representative of the Huanni, then they're a good people."

Standing Crane nodded her dark head. "I'm inclined to agree with you, but we can't let this pass without notice."

"What about the Falorians?"

"They're being extremely cooperative. Good job on coaxing Lissan into destroying the nanoprobes, Jim. That's a big point in their favor right now. They might be great actors, but I'll tell you, the Kal-Toreshi seemed stunned by how close they came to mass murder. On their own, before we could even request it, they destroyed all information relating to the development of the virus, so that such a threat might never again occur."

"I assume you're trusting but verifying," Kirk said.

"Of course. We'll have our own teams there to make sure of it. For the present, the planet's under martial law."

Kirk nodded. He had expected as much. All the members of the Kal-Toreshi, including and especially Lissan, had been detained and would be brought to Starfleet headquarters for questioning and, most likely, some term of imprisonment.

"Sounds like it's all over but the shouting," Kirk said.

"Just about. I've got to get going, Jim, but I wanted to see with my own eyes that you were all right."

"I'm fine. But I'm hungry. Don't be too long on that dinner."

She smiled. "I'll do my best. Standing Crane out."

Kirk leaned back in the torture device the Klingons called a "chair" and touched a button on his personal recording device.

Captain's personal log, addendum:

Despite the messiness and the scope of this situation, I have high hopes that the two separated people will be reunited. If not, then at least they will be able to live in peace. Skalli's courage in repeatedly extending the hand of friendship to Lissan, despite his initial harsh rebuffs, is largely responsible for this development. I'm glad she's coming back to finish her education, though it might take a while since both Huan and Falor have requested her involvement in future proceedings.

My nephew Julius is also returning for trial. While I cannot condone his actions, his subsequent behavior will count in his favor. He's a good man. Sam would have been so proud of all his boys. And I understand that despite what they went through, all the colonists, down to the last man, have assured Alexander that if he can get them another opportunity, they will be willing to sign up again.

Kirk didn't want to talk about the rest. It all still irked him. He turned off the recording device and sat back in the hellishly uncomfortable chair in his private quarters.

There was a harsh, grating buzz, and Kirk realized that someone was requesting admittance. "Come in," he called, and the door hissed open. Spock and McCoy stood there. McCoy grinned and lifted an amber bottle.

"I invited the rest of the old gang, but they're all busy. Good thing, too. Scotty would have wanted us to drink his Scotch instead of this sweet stuff."

"Well, let's not let that fine Kentucky bourbon go to waste," Kirk said, waving them in. As he located three of the hefty mugs the Klingon used to drink a beverage called "blood wine" he noted with amusement that he was becoming used to Klingon ships.

"Boy, the Klingons don't do things by half measures, do they?" McCoy said, eyeing the massive steins. He poured a little into each one. What would have been a generous shot in any other glass barely covered the bottom.

"So I assume Scotty's busy reading up on what is left of the Falorian technical information," Kirk said. Spock nodded. "Where are the rest?"

"Commander Chekov's over talking with Sulu," McCoy said. "I wouldn't expect him to return with us if

I were you, Jim. Seems Sulu's first officer is due to retire in six weeks and he needs a first officer."

"Chekov was holding out for a captaincy," Kirk said.

"Chekov has always valued service and friendship above the advancement of his career," Spock said. "I believe he would serve Captain Sulu well and loyally."

"I know he would. And I understand the multitalented Uhura is going to be performing in less than a week."

McCoy chuckled. "You should see how she handles that Klingon opera star," he said. "She's got him under her thumb, that's for sure."

"I saw a little of that on the bridge. I've never seen a smitten Klingon before. I don't suppose the feeling's mutual?"

"I doubt it," McCoy said. "Uhura's a tough cookie, and she's admitted that Karglak's voice makes her weak in the knees, but I just can't see her walking around wearing all that armor and eating *blech*."

"The term for that particular food item is *gagh*," Spock said.

McCoy fixed him with a gaze. "You call it what you want, I'll call it what I want."

"Looks like Uhura has developed some unique negotiating skills," Kirk said. "Perhaps we should permit her to conduct all negotiating sessions with the Klingons."

Spock looked a tad offended. "I do not think that would be appropriate."

Kirk and McCoy looked at each other and grinned a little. "I propose a toast," McCoy said. "To old cowhands on the last roundup. May they always bring their charges safely home."

"Cowhand?" Spock asked, raising an eyebrow.

"Shut up and drink, Spock," McCoy growled. Spock did.

Kirk swirled the liquid in the mug and sipped, trying to ignore the strange, musky scent that still clung to the mugs. "The last roundup," he mused. "Is that it? And are we the cows or the cowhands? Going back to the bunkhouse or going out to pasture?"

McCoy set his glass down and stared at Kirk. Spock, too, looked sharply at his former commander.

"Captain," Spock said slowly, "I perceive that you feel unhappy with the level of your involvement in recent events."

"Damn right I do." Kirk knew he was bone-tired, or he wouldn't have let the words spill out so freely. And again, it could be the strength of Bones's bourbon mixed with whatever might still be in the bottom of the mug. "I've done nothing right since the *Enterprise* was decommissioned. I'm . . . lost without her, Spock. I don't know how to be anything other than a starship captain. I feel useless and worse, I feel like I'm a hindrance.

"I didn't do anything. I didn't save the colonists—they saved themselves. Veta and Gallagher came up with the technology that allowed them to disappear into the cave system. You and Spock saved us when I was just about to blow up the control center. I didn't save the Huanni from Falorian attack—Sulu did. I didn't convince Lissan to cooperate—Skalli talked him into it. Hell, even the *Klingons* played a more active part than I did. I've just had my life saved by the Klingon High Chancellor and her people. Klingons, Bones! Who deserves the credit? My old shipmates and my old enemies. I can't contribute anymore. I can't make a difference. Maybe I *should* be farmed out to pasture."

McCoy glowered. "Now that's poppycock and you know it, Jim."

"Although he may be surprised to hear me say it, I completely agree with the good doctor. You are a valuable resource and a magnificent teacher. Your students are extremely fortunate to have you as a presence in their lives."

"Spock's right," McCoy said. "I am surprised he agrees with me." He grinned. "And damn it, he's right about the other stuff, too. Do you have any idea, Jim, of the amazing vastness of your sphere of influence?"

"Well, maybe I can share what I've learned, but—"

"No buts. Let's take a brief look at just a couple of your students. Skalli managed to take her hyperactive emotions and put them to good use instead of falling apart in the midst of a crisis that would have challenged anybody, let alone a Huanni. She may be responsible one day for single-handedly uniting the two separate races. She learned that discipline from you. She wouldn't have even gone in to talk to Lissan if you hadn't put her up to it."

Kirk opened his mouth to object—Skalli had had that in her all along—but McCoy said "Ah, ah, I'm not done yet. Sulu goes in there and manages to wrangle the slipperiest characters in the galaxy into fighting alongside the Federation. Think that would have occurred to him if he hadn't spent years watching you pull stunts like that?"

"I wouldn't call them stunts," Kirk began, but again McCoy waved him to silence.

"And then there's the Vulcan and me and Uhura. You think we'd be hauling our tired old bones halfway across the galaxy if some idiot named Jim Kirk hadn't put that fire in our bellies years ago? Hell no. I wouldn't get out of *bed* for most people, Jim." He lifted his glass. "To Jim Kirk, who's a walking, talking inspiration." He narrowed his blue eyes and added, "And don't you *dare* say a word to contradict me."

Kirk glanced at Spock, but the Vulcan merely said, "As it is illogical to falsify and exaggerate one's virtues and importance, it is also illogical to deny them when all evidence supports their existence."

A slow smile spread across Kirk's face as, for the first time, he allowed himself to think that maybe, just maybe, Spock and Bones were right. Maybe he didn't have to save the day all the time. He couldn't deny the truth of what Spock had said. He *had* done a great deal in his life. He'd helped a lot of people, trained so many to "get out there and do some good."

Eventually, he knew, the day had to come when the baton would be passed. Kirk realized now how deeply he had dreaded it, how he feared in the deepest recesses of his soul that if he wasn't on the bridge of a starship, he might as well be dead for all the good he could contribute.

Maybe that line of thinking was, as Spock put it, "illogical." And damned selfish, too.

Perhaps simply by being himself, Kirk could continue to have a positive influence on those around him.

And whether or not it's true, he thought, *it sure as hell beats playing solitaire.*

He lifted his mug. "Gentlemen," he said, "far be it from me to contradict the sage words of two old friends. To the last roundup, and a warm bed at the end of a cold hard day."

As their mugs clinked, Kirk added, "Either of you ever try skydiving?"

Epilogue

Kirk was shrugging into the coat of his dress uniform when a message came. It was Standing Crane.

"Laura! Good to see you. What's going on? I'm just about ready to leave for—"

"I know, and I won't keep you." Her expression was somber. "I've got some bad news. Kal-Tor Lissan was found dead in his cell this morning."

"Oh, no." Kirk was genuinely sorry to hear that. He had hoped that Lissan would be one of the architects of the peace accord that might someday be hammered out between the Falorians and Huanni. He had respected the man. "What happened? An illness?"

"A murder," Standing Crane replied, chilling him.

"How did that possibly happen? He was in a Starfleet security cell!"

"We're investigating that right now, but it looks like

a hit." She took a deep breath and said, "It was pretty messy. His throat was slashed and someone had carved the number 858 into his chest."

"Damn it. He didn't deserve that. He was only trying to do what he thought was right for his people. Any idea what the number means?"

She shook her head. "No. We'll do everything we can to find the killer, but it looks like a professional job. I don't know that we will."

"Can you inform Skalli?" The young Huanni was on Falor right now. Huan was busily rebuilding its fallen buildings and mining the incredibly pure dilithium that the Falorians had revealed was there. It was Skalli who had suggested that part of the wealth be shared with the Falorians whose difficult physical labor had discovered it centuries ago, and who had been appointed head of a team to negotiate the exchange.

"She already knows. She cried buckets."

"Of course she did. I'm glad. Lissan deserved someone to weep for him."

"On a brighter note, your testimony really helped Julius Kirk," Standing Crane said. "A decision hasn't been reached, but it looks like his sentence is going to be reduced. He might even get out on time served with community service."

"That *is* good news," said Kirk. "He made some mistakes, some bad ones, but he's done what he could to atone."

"And that's going to be taken into account. Well, I won't keep you, Jim. I know you're looking forward to this afternoon."

Kirk rolled his eyes. She grinned, and then her image disappeared.

As he finished dressing, Kirk thought about the other colonists. Last he heard, Alex was in negotiations with the Vulcans about backing for a possible new venture. Now that would be a good match. He hadn't heard much from the others, but for some reason the words that Kate Gallagher had spoken before she left with Alex to hide in the cave system came to mind. He was suddenly curious: Why would she want to look at her thesis?

"Computer," he called. "Find information on Katherine J. Gallagher. Specifically, the title of her master's thesis."

"Gallagher, Katherine J. Known as Kate," the computer said in its crisp female voice. "Title of master's thesis is 'The Devil in the Dark: Starfleet's Blackest Moment Becomes Its Finest Hour.'"

"Display." Kirk began reading and then smiled to himself, touched. The rough, angry Kate had written her master's thesis on James Kirk's intervention on Janus VI to save the Horta. Apparently, it was this single incident that had captured the young Gallagher's imagination and set her feet on the path to protecting endangered species. No wonder she was so prickly around him when she thought him just another Starfleet bully. He made a mental note to drop her a line when he got back this evening.

Kirk put his medals on and examined himself in the mirror. Not bad for a retired legend. He was looking forward to seeing Scotty and Chekov again . . . and to walking the deck of a certain ship that he would always passionately love.

"Come on," he said to his reflection. "I hear Captain Harriman isn't a patient man. And besides, I hate to keep a lady waiting."

Look for STAR TREK fiction from Pocket Books

Star Trek®

Novelizations

Preserver
The Captain's Peril

Star Trek: Deep Space Nine®

Books set after the series

The Lives of Dax • Marco Palmieri, ed.

Millennium Omnibus • Judith and Garfield Reeves-Stevens

    #1 • *The Fall of Terok Nor*

    #2 • *The War of the Prophets*

    #3 • *Inferno*

A Stitch in Time • Andrew J. Robinson

Avatar, Books One and *Two* • S.D. Perry

Section 31: Abyss • David Weddle & Jeffrey Lang

Gateways #4: Demons of Air and Darkness • Keith R.A. DeCandido

Gateways #7: What Lay Beyond: "Horn and Ivory" • Keith R.A. DeCandido

Mission: Gamma

    #1 • *Twilight* • David R. George III

    #2 • *This Gray Spirit* • Heather Jarman

    #3 • *Cathedral* • Michael A. Martin & Andy Mangels

    #4 • *Lesser Evil* • Robert Simpson

Rising Son • S.D. Perry

Unity • S.D. Perry

The Left Hand of Destiny, Books One and *Two* • J.G. Hertzler & Jeffrey Lang

Star Trek: Voyager®

Mosaic • Jeri Taylor

Pathways • Jeri Taylor

Captain Proton: Defender of the Earth • D.W. "Prof" Smith

The Nanotech War • Steve Piziks

Novelizations

Caretaker • L.A. Graf

Flashback • Diane Carey

Day of Honor • Michael Jan Friedman

Equinox • Diane Carey

Endgame • Diane Carey & Christie Golden

#1 • *Caretaker* • L.A. Graf

#2 • *The Escape* • Dean Wesley Smith & Kristine Kathryn Rusch

#3 • *Ragnarok* • Nathan Archer

#4 • *Violations* • Susan Wright

#5 • *Incident at Arbuk* • John Gregory Betancourt

#6 • *The Murdered Sun* • Christie Golden

#7 • *Ghost of a Chance* • Mark A. Garland & Charles G. McGraw

#8 • *Cybersong* • S.N. Lewitt

Enterprise®

Star Trek®: New Frontier

Star Trek®: Stargazer

Star Trek®: Starfleet Corps of Engineers (eBooks)

Star Trek®: Section 31™

Rogue • Andy Mangels & Michael A. Martin
Shadow • Dean Wesley Smith & Kristine Kathryn Rusch
Cloak • S.D. Perry
Abyss • David Weddle & Jeffrey Lang

Star Trek®: Gateways

Star Trek® Omnibus Editions

Invasion! Omnibus • various
Day of Honor Omnibus • various
The Captain's Table Omnibus • various
Double Helix Omnibus • various
Star Trek: Odyssey • William Shatner with Judith and Garfield Reeves-Stevens
Millennium Omnibus • Judith and Garfield Reeves-Stevens
Starfleet: Year One • Michael Jan Friedman

Star Trek® Short Story Anthologies

Strange New Worlds, vol. I, II, III, IV, and V • Dean Wesley Smith, ed.
The Lives of Dax • Marco Palmieri, ed.
Enterprise Logs • Carol Greenburg, ed.
The Amazing Stories • various

Other Star Trek® Fiction

Legends of the Ferengi • Ira Steven Behr & Robert Hewitt Wolfe
Adventures in Time and Space • Mary P. Taylor, ed.
Captain Proton: Defender of the Earth • D.W. "Prof" Smith

STAR TREK

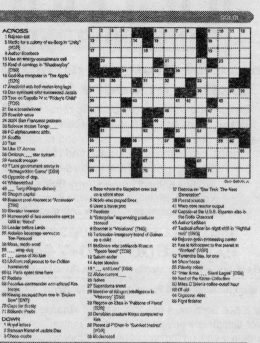

**50 ACROSS: Puzzles worked
on for amusement**

CROSSWORDS

by *New York Times*
crossword puzzle
editor John Samson

COMING SOON!

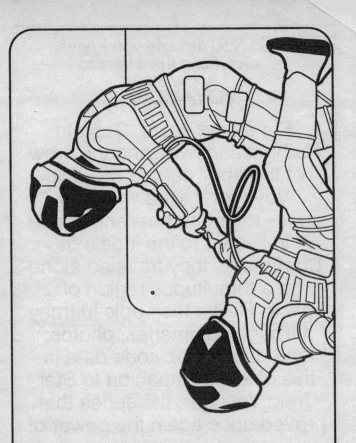

STAR TREK®
THE STARFLEET SURVIVAL GUIDE
AVAILABLE NOW... FOR THOSE WHO PLAN AHEAD.

STSG

When a Rake Falls

The Rake's Handbook
by Sally Orr

He's racing to win back his reputation

Having hired a balloon to get him to Paris in a daring race, Lord Boyce Parker is simultaneously exhilarated and unnerved by the wonders and dangers of flight, and most of all by the beautiful, stubborn, intelligent lady operating the balloon.

She's curious about the science of love

Eve Mountfloy is in the process of conducting weather experiments when she finds herself spirited away to France by a notorious rake. She's only slightly dismayed—the rake seems to respect her work—but she is frequently distracted by his windblown good looks and buoyant spirits.

What happens when they descend from the clouds?

As risky as aeronautics may be, once their feet touch the ground, Eve and Boyce learn the real danger of a very different type of falling…

For more Sally Orr, visit:

www.sourcebooks.com

Secrets of a Scandalous Heiress

by Theresa Romain

—— ❧ ——

One good proposition deserves another…

Heiress Augusta Meredith can't help herself—she stirs up gossip wherever she goes. A stranger to Bath society, she pretends to be a charming young widow, until sardonic, darkly handsome Joss Everett arrives from London and uncovers her charade.

Now they'll weave their way through the pitfalls of the polite world only if they're willing to be true to themselves…and to each other…

—— ❧ ——

Praise for Theresa Romain:

"Theresa Romain writes with a delightfully romantic flair that will set your heart on fire." —Julianne MacLean, *USA Today* bestselling author

"Theresa Romain writes witty, gorgeous, and deeply emotional historical romance."
—Vanessa Kelly, award-winning author

For more Theresa Romain, visit:

www.sourcebooks.com

Earls Just Want to Have Fun

Covent Garden Cubs
by Shana Galen

His heart may be the last
thing she ever steals...

Marlowe runs with the Covent Garden Cubs, a gang of thieves living in the slums of London's Seven Dials. It's a fierce life, but when she's alone, Marlowe allows herself to think of a time before—a dimly remembered life when she was called Elizabeth.

Maxwell, Lord Dane, is roped into teaching Marlowe how to navigate the social morass of the *ton*, but she will not escape her past so easily. Instead, Dane is drawn into her dangerous world, where the student becomes the teacher and love is the greatest risk of all.

Sapphires Are an Earl's Best Friend

by Shana Galen

She wants him…she wants him not…

Lily Dawson plays the role of the courtesan flawlessly while spying in the service of the Crown. Her mission now is to seduce a duke to test his true loyalties. She'll do it, even though she really wants Andrew Booth-Payne, Earl of Darlington—the duke's son.

Andrew finds himself rivaling his father for Lily's attention. And when he uncovers Lily's mission, he is faced with an impossible choice: to betray either his family, his country, or the longings of his own heart…

"This wild ride of a spy thriller sparkles with banter and radiates passion." —*RT Book Reviews* Top Pick of the Month, 4.5 Stars

"A fast-paced, sexy tale souped-up with plenty of espionage-flavored intrigue and dramatic adventure." —*Booklist*

For more Shana Galen, visit:

www.sourcebooks.com

Mischief by Moonlight

Regency Mischief
by Emily Greenwood

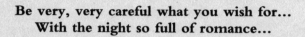

Be very, very careful what you wish for...
With the night so full of romance...

Colin Pearce, the Earl of Ivorwood, never dreamed he'd desire another man's fiancée, but when his best friend goes off to war and asks Colin to look after the bewitching Josie Cardworthy, he falls under her sparkling spell.

Who can resist mischief?

Josie can't wait for the return of her long-absent fiancé. If only her beloved sister might find someone, too... someone like the handsome, reserved Colin. A gypsy's love potion gives Josie the chance to matchmake, but the wild results reveal her own rowing passion for the earl. And though fate offers them a chance, a steely honor may force him to reject what her reckless heart is offering...

Praise for *A Little Night Mischief*:

"Love, love, loved this book! I was up till early-morning hours finishing it." —*Books Like Breathing*

For more Emily Greenwood, visit:

www.sourcebooks.com

Gentlemen Prefer Mischief

by Emily Greenwood

— ❧ —

When adversaries clash, mischief ignites passion...

If it hadn't been for the crazy rumors, Lily Teagarden would never have approached her neighbor, Hal, Viscount Roxham—the careless rogue who broke her fledgling heart. But strange noises and lights on his property are causing serious problems for her, and she needs his help.

Trouble is oh-so-diverting for Viscount Roxham, and what could be more amusing than investigating what's plaguing his prim, beautiful neighbor—haunted sheep, of all things. Every time he seems to make progress, though, she throws mischief in his path, and his attraction to her is becoming extremely distracting...too bad Lily's the only woman in England who doesn't think he's Lord Perfect.

— ❧ —

Praise for *A Little Night Mischief*:

"The hero is quite devastatingly gorgeous, and the writing is well-crafted." —*All About Romance*

"Lovely, lighthearted historical romance." —*Imagine a World*

For more Emily Greenwood, visit:

www.sourcebooks.com

Watch for the next in The Scandalous
Sisters series by Emily Greenwood

The Scandalous One

Coming March 2016
from Sourcebooks Casablanca

— ❧ —

Miss Elizabeth Tarryton was the toast of the London
Season the year she was seventeen and broke the heart of
her guardian's younger brother, Tommy Halifax. A careless
flirt who didn't know what she wanted, she was startled
into laughter by his public proposal of marriage. Furious
and heartbroken, Tommy promptly left home for a life of
adventure in India.

Seven years later, Eliza is widowed, wiser, and involved in
a humanitarian scheme that requires her to play a role she
no longer relishes. When Tommy returns to be knighted for
his service to the Crown, she finds herself drawn to win him
back. But Eliza has a lot to make up for…

For more Emily Greenwood, visit:

www.sourcebooks.com

About the Author

Emily Greenwood has a degree in French and worked for a number of years as a writer, crafting newsletters and fund-raising brochures, but she far prefers writing love stories set in Regency England, and she thinks romance novels are the chocolate of literature. A Golden Heart finalist, she lives in Maryland with her husband and two daughters.

Praise for the Regency Mischief series

"Tantalizing reading...the honest, natural fun and the playful then consuming love that emerges are best of all. Great entertainment!"

—Long and Short Reviews

"A devilish, charming ex-army captain, a righteous young woman, mysterious haunted woods, and a cast of delightful supporting characters make for a mix of delicious sensuality in Greenwood's nicely written and...emotional read."

—RT Book Reviews (on *Gentlemen Prefer Mischief*)

"Fun, lighthearted, engaging, and will grab you from the first page. A must-read!"

—My Book Addiction Reviews

"Intriguing, sexy historical romance."

—Romance Junkies

"Greenwood makes you fall in love with the secondary characters and keeps you wanting more."

—Historical Romance Lover

"A delightfully charming read, sprinkled with mischief...refreshing, fun, and entertaining."

—Lily Pond Reads

"Regency lovers have another author to add to their favorites list!"

—Once Upon a Romance

The
BEAUTIFUL
One

EMILY
GREENWOOD

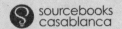

sourcebooks
casablanca

Published by Sourcebooks Casablanca, an imprint of
Sourcebooks, Inc.
P.O. Box 4410, Naperville, Illinois 60567-4410
(630) 961-3900
Fax: (630) 961-2168
www.sourcebooks.com

Printed and bound in Canada.
WC 10 9 8 7 6 5 4 3 2 1

Also by Emily Greenwood

A Little Night Mischief
Gentlemen Prefer Mischief
Mischief by Moonlight

For my agent, Jenny Bent,
with thanks for so many things.

And also for Molly,
who's always ready to pour a cup
of tea and talk characters.

One

Anna Black gave a silent cheer as the carriage she was riding in lurched and came to an abrupt stop at an angle that suggested they'd hit a deep ditch.

Perhaps, she thought hopefully from the edge of her seat, where she'd been tossed, they'd be stuck on the road for hours, which would delay their arrival at the estate of Viscount Grandville. She had reason to be worried about what might happen at Lord Grandville's estate, and she dreaded reaching it.

It was also possible she was being pursued.

Or not.

Perhaps nothing would happen at all. But the whole situation was nerve-wracking enough that she had more than once considered simply running off to live in the woods and survive on berries.

However, several considerations discouraged her from this course:

1. She had exactly three shillings to her name. Though admittedly money would be of no

use in the woods, she would at some point need more than berries.

2. She had agreed to escort her traveling companion, Miss Elizabeth Tarryton, to the home of Viscount Grandville, who was the girl's guardian.

3. If Anna abandoned her duty, along with being a wicked person, she wouldn't be able to return to the Rosewood School for Young Ladies of Quality, her employer.

Anna was nothing if not practical, and she was highly skeptical of the success of the life-in-the-woods plan, but the dramatic occurrences in her life of late were starting to lend it appeal.

"Hell!" said the lovely Miss Elizabeth Tarryton from her sprawled position on the opposite coach seat. Her apricot silk bonnet had fallen across her face during the coach-lurching, and she pushed it aside. "What's happened?"

"We're in a ditch, evidently," Anna replied. Their situation was obvious, but Miss Tarryton had not so far proven herself to be particularly sensible for her sixteen years. She was also apparently not averse to cursing.

Surrendering to the inevitable, Anna said, "I'll go see how things look."

She had to push upward to open the door to the tilted coach, and before stepping down, she paused to tug her faded blue bonnet over her black curls, a reflex of concealment that had become second nature in the last month. The rain that had followed them since they

left the school that morning had stopped, but the dark sky promised more.

The coachman was already seeing to the horses.

"Had to go off the road to avoid a vast puddle, and now we're in a ditch," he called. "'Tis fortunate that we're but half a mile from his lordship's estate."

So they would soon be at Stillwell, Viscount Grandville's estate. *Damn*, Anna thought, taking a page from Miss Tarryton's book. Would he be a threat to her?

After a month in a state of nearly constant anxiety, of waiting to be exposed, she sometimes felt mutinously that she didn't care anymore. She'd done nothing of which she ought to be ashamed—yet it would never appear that way. And so she felt like a victim, and hated feeling that way, and hated the accursed book that had given two wicked men such power over her.

She gathered up the limp skirts of her faded old blue frock and jumped off the last step, intending to see how badly they were stuck.

The coachman was seeing to the horses, and as she moved to inspect the back of the carriage, she became aware of hoofbeats and turned to see a rider cantering toward them. A farmer, she thought, taking in his dusty, floppy hat and dull coat and breeches. He drew even.

"You are trespassing," he said from atop his horse, his tone as blunt as his words. The sagging brim of his hat hid the upper part of his face, but from the hard set of his jaw, she could guess it did not bear a warm expression. His shadowed gaze passed over her, not lingering for more time than it might have taken to observe a pile of dirty breakfast dishes.

"We had no intention of doing so, I assure you," she began, wondering that the stranger hadn't even offered a greeting. "The road was impassible and our coachman tried to go around, but now we are stuck. Perhaps, though, if you might—"

"You cannot tarry here," he said, ignoring her attempt to ask for help. "A storm is coming. Your coach will be stranded if you don't make haste."

His speech was clipped, but it sounded surprisingly refined. *Ha.* That was surely the only refined thing about him. Aside from his lack of manners and the shabbiness of his clothes, there was an L-shaped rip in his breeches that gave a window onto pale skin and thigh muscles pressed taut, and underneath his coat, his shirt hung loose at the neck. She supposed it was his broad shoulders that made him seem especially imposing atop his dark horse.

A stormy surge of wind blew his hat brim off his face, and she realized that severe though his expression might be, he was very handsome. The lines of his cheekbones and hard jaw ran in perfect complement to each other. His well-formed brows arched in graceful if harsh angles over dark eyes surrounded by crowded black lashes.

But those eyes. They were as devoid of life as one of her father's near-death patients.

Several fat raindrops pelted her bonnet.

"We shall be away momentarily," she said briskly, turning away from him to consider the plight of the coach and assuming he would leave now that he'd delivered his warning.

The rain began to fall faster, soaking through the

thin fabric of her worn-out frock. She called out to the coachman, who was doing something with the harness straps. "Better take off the young lady's trunk before you try to advance."

"No. That's a waste of time," said the stranger from atop his horse behind her.

She turned around, deeply annoyed. "Your opinion is not wanted."

The ill-mannered man watched her, a muscle ticking in his stubbled jaw.

A cold rivulet trickled through her bonnet to her scalp and continued down her neck, and his empty gaze seemed to follow the little stream's journey to the collar of her dampening frock. His eyes flicked lower, and she thought they lingered at her breasts.

She crossed her arms in front of her and tipped her chin higher. Not for nothing had she sparred with her older brother all those years in a home that had been more than anything else a man's domain. Her father had been a doctor and had valued reason and scientific process and frowned on softness, and she'd been raised to speak her mind. Life as a servant at Rosewood School was already testing her ability to hold her tongue, but this man deserved no such consideration.

"Is not your presence required elsewhere?"

"Where are you going?" he demanded, ignoring her.

"I couldn't be more delighted that such things do not concern you."

The stranger's lips thinned. "Who comes to this neighborhood concerns me."

"If you would move along," she said exasperatedly,

blinking droplets from her lashes, "we might focus on freeing the coach."

His gaze flicked away from her. "Drive on," he called to the coachman.

John, apparently responding to the note of command in the stranger's voice, disregarded Anna's sound of outrage and addressed himself to the horses. With a creaking of harness straps, they struggled forward. The wheels squelched as they found purchase amid the mud, and the carriage miraculously righted itself.

She sucked her teeth in irritation.

"See that you do not linger here," the man said.

"We are on our way to Stillwell Hall," she replied, thinking to make him regret his poor conduct. He might even work for the viscount.

He looked down at her, his face shadowed so that his rain-beaded whiskers and hard mouth were all she could see. "That's not possible. No one is welcomed there."

From inside the carriage, Miss Tarryton called, "Can we not proceed, Miss Whatever?"

Anna ignored her. "It certainly is possible."

"The viscount might not be in residence."

His words would have given her pause, except that when Miss Brickle had sent Anna off with her charge and a note for the viscount, she'd said that he was certain to be at Stillwell, because according to gossip among the mothers of Rosewood's students, he'd been in residence there constantly over the last year.

Though why this man should be so set on discouraging them from seeing the viscount, she couldn't imagine.

"I have it on good authority that he is. Evidently, sir," she said, "you have been raised by wild animals

and so one must overlook your lack of interest in people, but I assure you Lord Grandville will wish to welcome us."

Something flickered in his eyes for the barest moment at her tart words, but his hard expression didn't change.

"No," he rasped. "He won't. Do not go there."

He turned his horse away and spurred it into a gallop across the field next to the road.

Anna found herself staring as the stranger rode off. And really, he *was* strange, because though he appeared to be a laborer, his speech was educated and his manner commandingly haughty. He might almost have been a gentleman, but he was too rough for that to be possible.

As the coachman climbed onto his perch, he gave a snort and called back to her, "'E's a friendly one."

"He probably keeps badgers as pets," she said, and mounted the coach steps amid the coachman's laughter.

Miss Elizabeth Tarryton, sitting composedly inside and looking as dry and untroubled as any princess accustomed to having things arranged for her, remarked, "Headmistress says ladies are above noticing the behavior of rough men. Not that *you* would know about proper behavior. Really, Miss Brickle ought never to have chosen a *seamstress* as a companion for the niece of a viscount. You—"

The girl hesitated, perhaps realizing how ridiculous additional comments would sound coming from someone who'd been discovered the night before kissing a lieutenant from the local militia in the school garden. When discovered by the headmistress, Miss Tarryton had almost proudly revealed that she'd

reached the garden by climbing out a second-floor window. Miss Brickle had wanted the girl gone as soon as possible, before her scandalous behavior could taint the reputation of Rosewood School.

As the only other person privy to this escapade— she'd been up late doing the mending, needing extra time for the work since she wasn't actually very good at sewing—Anna had been assigned to escort Miss Tarryton to her guardian.

"Yes?" Anna prompted, surprised to find herself being addressed at all. The elegant Miss Tarryton, who looked like angelic perfection with her red-gold curls and her gown of pale apricot silk, had spent their journey gazing mutely out the window on her side.

The girl closed her mouth and returned to looking out the window, where the rain was now coming down heavily as the late afternoon edged toward evening. Anna would have felt sorry for Miss Tarryton, since she'd been hustled away from Rosewood so ignominiously, except nothing in her demeanor suggested she was dismayed about leaving. If anything, she seemed impatient to arrive at their destination.

They set off at a careful pace on the muddy road. Anna dried herself as best she could with a clean serviette from the now sadly empty lunch hamper. She didn't dwell on why the stranger had said what he had about Stillwell. Even if it were true, it merely suggested that Lord Grandville was a hermit, which could only be good news.

She would simply deliver his ward and then be on her way back to the school. It had been a month since she'd had to leave home so abruptly, and now,

just when she'd been starting to relax her guard at Rosewood, she'd been sent on this unwanted journey.

A shudder rippled along her shoulders as a memory of curving pencil marks flashed through her mind, the lines of her own naked body caught in various positions on page after page of that appalling sketchbook. Images made without her knowledge. And three words written in garish red wax on the book's cover: *The Beautiful One.* Such an innocuous title for a thing that put her in danger of becoming the kind of woman no decent person could acknowledge.

She couldn't know for certain whether the Marquess of Henshaw was actually looking for her or how many people had seen that book.

A weak, vulnerable feeling threatened to overwhelm her, but she forced it down. She hated weakness. And she refused to let what those two men had done dominate her thoughts.

Sometime later the carriage slowed down and John called out to them. "That will be the manor, misses, on the left side."

At his words, Miss Tarryton surged toward the opposite window and looked out. Before she could catch herself, she uttered a startled sound.

She clamped her lips shut, sat back against the seat, and composed her features, as if the home of her guardian—and now herself—were just as she'd imagined. Anna leaned forward to peer out the window.

She almost gasped herself.

They had paused on a road that passed perhaps half a mile from the front of the manor, but the distance in no way diminished its enormity. The

rain had abated for the moment, leaving a clear view of Stillwell Hall in the gray early-evening light, and it was breathtaking, grander than anything she'd ever seen.

Set behind a large and tranquilly shining pond, the hall was a majestic arrangement of squares and rectangles that formed a large central building with two substantial wings, all of it on a scale that made her family home look like a hut. The hall's stone was a soft cream color, and the numerous chimneys on its gently angled roof gave it a cheery look.

She smiled a little, realizing that the stranger's words about Stillwell had caused her to imagine a vast, dark dungeon awaiting them. The manor was certainly vast, but it was also beautiful and balanced harmoniously among its endless grounds. Surely no one who made his home here could be as forbidding as the stranger had suggested.

She let the curtain fall back into place with a shaking hand. The viscount had a minor estate near her childhood home, a place called Littlebury Lodge, where his family sometimes summered. Though she'd never met the viscount, her father had, and he'd occasionally been called out to the lodge to treat members of the viscount's family. Over a weeks-long period, her father had treated the viscount's much-younger brother for a prolonged fever, and brought Anna along to cheer the youth. But that had been six years ago, and surely, if the viscount's brother were at Stillwell, he wouldn't recognize Anna.

Recent events had taught her that hope was very, very important for getting through the day. She stirred

it up now. But hopeful though Anna might strive to be, she was also unfailingly honest with herself. Viscount Grandville was important and powerful, and should it come to it, ruining her life would be as nothing to him.

"The estate is spectacular," Miss Tarryton said, her customary tone of boredom replaced with awe.

Anna forced herself to sound natural. "Yes, it is."

Miss Tarryton's brow lowered, so that she suddenly looked not like a spoiled, privileged young woman but a scared girl. Something occurred to Anna then.

"Have you ever met your uncle?"

"Yes. I used to see him sometimes when I was a girl because he was a close friend of my father's. But we moved to Malta when I was six."

"And have you seen him since you came to England from Malta?"

"No, but that's of no consequence."

Anna wasn't so certain. "Do you remember what he was like?"

"Only that he had dark hair and he was tall and kind. He's a very important man, so it's not surprising if he's been too busy for visiting."

The girl lifted her hand and nibbled at a fingernail for a moment before she realized what she was doing and dropped her hand. She might be impatient to arrive at the home of her uncle, but she was just as nervous as Anna, if for different reasons.

"Do you think Lord Grandville…" Miss Tarryton began, then closed her mouth. Her face smoothed into the look of angelic boredom she'd worn for much of the journey, and she turned a placid gaze on the floor.

The knuckles of her clasped fingers, though, soon turned even whiter than the rest of her pale, soft hands.

As close as they now were to the viscount's home, Anna knew she must finally face one of the possibilities that had concerned her during their journey: that Lord Grandville was acquainted with the Marquess of Henshaw.

That he might have seen *The Beautiful One*.

Two

WILL HALIFAX, FIFTH VISCOUNT GRANDVILLE, STALKED through the door to Stillwell Hall, pulling off his rain-sodden hat and coat and dropping them onto the outstretched arms of his butler, Dart. He sat down on an ornate bench, and Dart pulled off his master's extremely filthy boots.

"Your bath is ready, sir," Dart said as Will walked past and grunted, a response to which his staff had become accustomed. On a narrow hallway table sat a letter bearing his stepmother's handwriting that had been there for more than a week, and he walked past that too. Alone in his room, he stripped off his shirt and let his breeches fall to the faded rug.

He stepped into the waiting tub of steaming water. Crunching up his long body, he sank all the way down until the water covered his dark head and filled his ears, creating a new silence, one that allowed only the thud of his heart and chased away all thought.

If only he could stay under the water, away from thought. Thought was a wild boar that harried him, and escape was futile. No amount of liquor helped.

Nor had he been able to outrun grief—he'd tried running to the Continent after Ginger died, as if he could physically escape the pain of his wife's death. Nothing had helped.

There was only work now. Droning, punishing work, as physical as possible. For the time being, he had the cottages to labor over. He did not think beyond them.

Except now his mind was filling with an image that wouldn't leave of a certain bold, rain-drenched woman. He was aware for the first time in a year of sensations in his body, of its nakedness in the bath and the feel of the water against his skin when he shifted.

Reaching outside the tub, he grabbed the pitcher of cold water set out for him to drink and dumped it over his head.

He stepped out of the tub onto the old rug Dart had put down to replace the one sent to the attic along with all the other furnishings Ginger had bought. He couldn't bear them reminding him of her cheerful puttering and decision-making as she'd gone about freshening up the manor, putting her stamp on it.

As he rubbed his skin roughly with a towel, his mind again returned to the woman on the road, conjuring the image of her perched on the step of the tilted carriage. He'd been riding toward home and caught sight of the carriage just before it hit the ditch, and he'd paused. The coach door had swung upward and she'd emerged with a jaunty, boyish energy that had reminded him of a toy jack-in-the-box springing free.

Something about her had gotten to him and even now was annoying the hell out of him. It was that

damned pluckiness, he thought, grinding his teeth as he dashed the towel about his head. As if she would not be defeated by anything—not weather, not accident, not even a beast of a man in her path. She was pert and tough at the same time, an unholy combination.

As they'd stood arguing in the rain, he'd noticed far too much about her: That she was pretty in an unusual, sharp way. That her gown hung badly from a slim frame that suggested the supple bendability of a willow branch. That her breasts were small and he'd wanted to know more about them.

He shouldn't have looked at her that way. He didn't allow that part of himself to exist. It *wouldn't*.

He couldn't guess what business she thought she had with Stillwell, but he hoped she now thought better of coming there.

He jerked on clean breeches and a shirt, and made the simplest of functional knots in his cravat, then used his fingers to comb his dark brown hair without looking in the glass. His whiskers had grown into thick stubble from two days without shaving, but he didn't bother to call his valet.

He went over to his desk, on which lay a carriage clock with its back off, its springs and gears spilled around it. The night before, he'd taken it apart, drawn by an old impulse to see how it worked, but he'd lost interest. Now he halfheartedly took up two of the small gears to fit the pieces back into the clock and thought of how Ginger would have teased him about the mess he'd made.

"*What kind of gentleman will you be,*" she used to say with a smile, "*if you can't bear to be idle?*"

She'd known him as nobody else ever could.

She'd been the perfect partner, friend, and wife, the woman he'd respected above all others, the person with whom he'd planned to accomplish so much of value. They'd dreamed of making Stillwell a model estate for workers, a place where the needs of all were met, where the laboring man and his family had a life as meaningful and happy as the lives of those who lived in the manor.

Ginger had been a significant part of his moral compass, and now she was gone and he had no north. All his hope and purpose and goodness had died with her.

He tossed the gears back on the desk. The leaden weight in his gut, an old companion by now, was expanding as pain and anger and self-disgust fed it. Thinking always took him down a wretched road and threatened to turn him into nothing more than a lump of a person, useless for running an estate or dealing with anything practical, and he pushed the thoughts away.

His steward, Mr. Norris, would be along soon for the daily review of his affairs, and he welcomed the intense concentration their meeting would demand.

Will left his room and reached the top of the large central staircase just as he became aware that someone was knocking vigorously at the front door. He stepped into the shadow of the corridor, in little doubt as to who it was.

Dart opened the door.

"Good evening," said a female voice he'd heard barely three-quarters of an hour earlier. "I am Miss Anna Black, accompanied by Miss Elizabeth Tarryton,

Lord Grandville's ward. Please let his lordship know she has arrived."

What the hell? Elizabeth, here? Damnation! Why can't people leave me alone?

Dart said nothing for several seconds, then invited the two ladies into the drawing room and came in search of his master, who was already descending the stairs.

Will hesitated before the drawing room doors, knowing he must get rid of the two women. Elizabeth was Ginger's niece, but the last time he'd seen her, she'd been a child. He'd become her guardian a year earlier, not long after Ginger died, and by then he hadn't cared about anything at all. He'd paid her bills and made it clear she was to remain at the school. He'd done her a favor by ensuring she stayed in a place where she was already known and cared for.

So what was she doing here? One thing was certain: she couldn't stay at Stillwell.

The grand drawing room of Stillwell Hall was strangely bare in the dusk light, Anna thought, as if most of its decoration had been pared away.

The room held little beyond a piano, three unwelcoming wooden chairs in the vicinity of a small, square table, and one handsome if elderly upholstered chair. A large fireplace sat alone in a great expanse of wall, as if it might naturally have been flanked by a pair of comfortable armchairs. Two landscape paintings on the long wall adjacent to the hearth were unbalanced by a significant empty space, as if a now-missing painting had once been part of the set.

Was the viscount some kind of severely religious person who felt that ornamentation was sinful? Or perhaps some furnishings had been sold to pay debts? Yet the house was in fine condition. Its dusted surfaces and clean floors looked well cared for, and the mantel-piece held a collection of exquisite porcelain figures.

Anna's gown had dried somewhat, though it was thoroughly wrinkled. The ribbons of her bonnet had become knotted and tangled with her hair, and she pushed it off so that it hung from her neck, and worked quickly at the ribbons, wanting whatever concealment it might offer in the viscount's presence.

Miss Tarryton, standing by the hearth, was staring at a group of miniatures on the mantel, perhaps looking for a familiar face.

The drawing room doors opened abruptly, the butler announced their names, and Anna had to abandon the bonnet ribbons. She barely managed not to gasp as in strode a more formally dressed version of the surly laborer she'd just met.

Though he was still not clean shaven, he no longer looked so rough and unkempt. The dark blue coat that hung from his broad, rangy shoulders and the stone-colored trousers that skimmed well-formed legs were of fine cloth and well cut, and the waves of his dark brown hair, though they were not neatly arranged, shone cleanly.

But his features bore no warmer expression than they had on the road, and now she realized why his haughty air had come so naturally to him: he was a viscount.

"You," he said, pinning her with his dark eyes.

A number of tart replies suggested themselves to

her, but she was here on Miss Tarryton's behalf. At least she could put one fear to bed: From the moment they'd met, he'd shown no sign of ever having seen her before. Whether he'd seen *The Beautiful One* or not—and it seemed unlikely he'd been offered a view of the book of sketches, given his dislike of visitors—he didn't know her. And there was so far no sign of his brother, nor anyone else beyond the butler who'd received them.

Miss Brickle had said that if there were no female relatives present to see to Miss Tarryton, Anna might stay for a day or two if Lord Grandville required her to do so while he made arrangements, but Anna didn't envision this difficult man asking her for help. Which was just as well, because what she needed was to return to the anonymous security of Rosewood.

"My lord," she said, dipping her head. Even though he was the one who'd set the rude tone at their earlier meeting, Miss Tarryton would have to live with him, and she deserved a better beginning. Anna forced out words he didn't deserve. "Forgive me. I had not, of course, realized it was you with whom I was speaking on the road."

He made no reply, unless a further hardening of his jaw could be taken as a response. She wondered why he'd been dressed so roughly earlier, and why he hadn't said who he was.

Miss Tarryton came from behind Anna to stand next to her, and as the viscount's gaze finally took the girl in, he seemed, unaccountably, to flinch.

She curtsied and practically whispered, "My lord," then cleared her throat and said it more loudly. The

girl showed no awareness that her guardian was the ill-mannered stranger, but then, she'd been in the carriage the whole time and likely hadn't seen him. "It's a pleasure to see you again, Uncle, after all these years," she said.

The hard lines of his mouth seemed to slacken for a heartbeat as his head tipped slightly in acknowledgment of her words.

"Elizabeth. I did not expect to see you here."

She looked taken aback at the cool bluntness of his greeting, but she managed a smile. "I was so young when last I saw you that I couldn't remember very much about you. Do I look familiar to you?"

His mouth tightened, as if her harmless question was objectionable. Clearly he didn't want to reminisce.

Anna reached into her pocket for the note Miss Brickle had given her. "I've been sent by the Rosewood School to accompany your ward on her journey here. Miss Brickle thought it best she come to you."

She held out the note. "She has written to you." It was a brief, polite note, giving no particulars of the reason for the girl's departure; Miss Brickle had told Anna so when she explained that Anna was not to reveal what had happened. The midnight kissing in the garden had only been, apparently, the last straw as far as Miss Tarryton's behavior.

He ignored the proffered note, his lifeless eyes resting on her. Cold-as-the-grave blue eyes in a handsome, strong face. "I'm sure you can explain succinctly why my ward is here. Clearly there has been some problem."

Anna felt a spurt of pity for the beautiful, proud Miss

Tarryton. "Miss Brickle felt that Rosewood could no longer provide the right environment for her."

"Elizabeth," he said, "*why* have you been sent away?"

Miss Tarryton blinked at his abrupt question, then gave a tentative smile that acknowledged the awkwardness of the situation. "Oh, my lord, it was nothing serious." When his eyebrow slashed upward, she said, "Perhaps I had a few…disagreements with Miss Brickle."

"You must apologize to the headmistress then, and see that nothing like this happens again."

"I'm afraid," Anna said firmly, "that the school has made the decision it considers to be best and must now entrust Miss Tarryton's care to you." Miss Brickle had specified that under no circumstances could the girl return.

Some emotion traveled over the viscount's face—it almost looked like anguish, as though, strangely, his ward's arrival was a blow he could not absorb. He opened his mouth, closed it, pressed his lips into a hard line. Finally, he said, "Well, Elizabeth, if you can't return to Rosewood, you will have to go to some other school."

His words were clearly a surprise to his niece, who'd obviously been anticipating a warmer welcome from him, but she didn't crumple, and Anna liked her the better for it.

"Please, Uncle," Miss Tarryton said with a nakedly eager-to-please look that struck at Anna's heart. "I'd rather stay with you. I won't take up much room. You'll hardly know I'm here. And I can play the pianoforte when you want to hear it, and do

needlepoint, and…" Her voice trailed off as she saw that the viscount's commanding gaze had returned to Anna, the one who'd brought this problem into his drawing room.

He crossed his arms, and Anna's eyes were momentarily drawn to his hands. He had long, lean fingers that seemed perfect for an aristocrat used to holding nothing more than a quill or a brandy glass, but they were covered in nicks and scratches. He'd been dressed as a laborer on the road, and the tale his hands told was of hard use. Odd. And yet perhaps not, for someone who seemed so bitter. Perhaps he'd been boxing, as gentlemen loved to do. Though his battered hands made him look as if he'd been boxing with a tree.

"I'm afraid there is nothing at Stillwell for Miss Tarryton," he said.

"Of course you weren't expecting her to arrive," Anna said. "But perhaps there is some relative who might help? An aunt? A sister?"

"There is no one from the family here but me, and thus, she could not possibly be comfortable here. She must go to an inn and await a new situation. My butler will provide funds."

Anna saw something die in Miss Tarryton's eyes right then. How he could reject his niece so blithely, Anna couldn't comprehend. But then, he seemed to be a man whose heart had gone missing.

He turned to the girl, and Anna glimpsed again some hint of torment behind the hardness in his eyes, but it was quickly shuttered. "Miss Black will take you away," he said.

Anna's spine stiffened. *Oh no you don't!*

"Oh," Miss Tarryton said, blinking. Her lower lip trembled for a moment before she got control of it.

"Why, thank you," Anna interjected. "You're quite right that what she needs most now is a room in which to relax."

"That's not—" he began, but Anna cut him off.

"How very kind of my lord to wish for his niece's immediate comfort," she said, walking toward the rope hanging on the wall and praying he wouldn't stop her—she didn't want to consider how such a man might try. "Of course she will be too tired to do anything but rest now, after hours in a carriage."

She pulled the bell that would summon a servant and babbled on without meeting anyone's eyes in a desperate effort to drown out the tension in the room.

"Well, it was certainly a long journey," she said, forcing a cheerful tone and feeling like a ninny. "And such rain! Why, it's still raining now," she said, sweeping her eyes toward the windows, where sheets of water blurred the glass in the early evening gloom. The sight made her realize that no matter what happened, she and Miss Tarryton could not reasonably set out from Stillwell that night. She didn't, however, intend to leave with the viscount's ward at all.

It was perhaps not the most proper thing to leave a young woman alone with a gentleman, but he was her guardian after all, and her uncle, and he would clearly waste no time in finding some woman, whether a relative or a governess, to see to Miss Tarryton.

The butler arrived then, saving Anna from launching into an impromptu poetry recitation.

"Miss Tarryton will need a good fire," Anna

instructed the startled butler, "as we met with rain. And a tray ought to be sent up to her room so she can retire in peace."

The viscount grunted his acquiescence, and the servant led Miss Tarryton out and presumably to a chamber. Though how long she might stay in that chamber would depend on Anna.

What did this man have to be so bitter about anyway, with his massive grounds and his numerous servants? She stiffened her shoulders and turned around to face him.

She was met with dark eyebrows slashing over midnight-blue eyes that were not dead now, but alive with anger under their thick black lashes. With his height and his broad shoulders, Lord Grandville looked capable of anything. Dangerous.

In a heartbeat he had come closer on those long, muscular legs and stopped before her. She tipped her head up only slightly, knowing she couldn't afford to let him see the effect he was having on her. Besides, he wasn't the only one who was angry.

His hard eyes glittered down at her. "You have to take her away."

"This young woman is your niece, and you would send her from your home?"

"Stillwell is no place for her."

"And what is the best place for her?"

"You seem well suited to discover that. Find her another school and I will pay all the expenses of her travel and yours."

Another man making plans for her. After what had happened with the marquess—after enduring the

shock of seeing that book of drawings of herself and having to leave her home—well, the viscount was merely another bully, and she would not be pushed by him.

Outside the windows of the drawing room, a roll of thunder sounded, followed by a flash of lightning, and its energy steeled her spine.

"Even if I thought that were appropriate, which I do not, I cannot do that. I must return to Rosewood, and you must take up your responsibilities to your ward."

"Damnation!" he boomed, and her eyes widened as she realized that he wasn't so very dead inside after all. He certainly had an opinion about this situation. As a viscount, he must have been used to getting his own way, and he doubtless thundered to instant effect. Anna, however, was well versed in manly bluster, and if she'd learned anything from her father and brother, it was not to let emotion rule her and not to back down.

"I'm afraid that where Miss Tarryton stays is now your concern only, Lord Grandville." She thought of the girl's white knuckles and felt a pang, but then she reminded herself that not just any young lady would have been up to climbing out her window to meet a man in the dark.

"Impossible! I cannot see to the care of a young lady. No, Miss Tarryton needs firm, feminine guidance, and you appear to be a capable person to provide it. I believe you were ready to push that coach out of the ditch; my ward will be no trouble at all for you. You will take her to an inn tomorrow morning and wait with her until a new school can be found."

"I will not," she said, flushing hotly. "I am not in your employ for you to command as you wish."

"I *cannot* have her here."

His anger came off him, strong enough that she felt she might almost touch it, but she would not bow to it. Mingled with it was something desperate, like the pain of a wounded animal that lashed out at all around it. But he was not an animal; he was a gentleman, of whom civilized behavior must be expected.

"Can you not? You are her uncle by marriage and her guardian." She thought of Miss Tarryton's fidgeting in the coach as they drew near the manor and had an insight into the girl's anxiety. "You never even sent her a letter, did you?"

∽

A bolt of wildness shot through Will. His beloved Ginger was gone, and now her niece had come to Stillwell, hale and hearty and with that beautiful gold-red hair like Ginger's, to torment him, and he was supposed to welcome her? Never mind the absurd idea that he had anything to offer Elizabeth Tarryton beyond the funds that would take her someplace suitable.

"I bid you good evening," said the woman. "As it is late, I trust I may avail myself of whatever your man-servant can offer me in accommodation for tonight. I will depart in the morning."

He watched her dip what was surely an ironic curtsy, doubtless believing she'd resolved things to her satisfaction, and something shattered inside him, perhaps his last remaining tie to civilization. He was so sick of the pain and the anger, of the weight that was

always on him. Suddenly all he wanted was escape. This black-haired, sharp-tongued woman with her sapling body under that ugly, faded gown was making him want the one thing that might take him out of himself, even if only for a few minutes.

There was something about her, too—that boyish energy, those handsome black eyebrows arching over light brown eyes that glinted with some inner force. She was strong, alive, undamaged, and her vigor hinted at forgotten, lively things.

"Wait," he said, even before he knew he was going to speak. An idea was forming in his mind, an idea that should have appalled him, but there was so little left of the person he'd once been that he barely even heard the dying cries of his gentleman's heart. He crossed his arms. "I have a proposal for you."

Wariness crept into her eyes.

"Anna Black, isn't that your name?"

She hesitated before replying. "Yes."

He'd never done anything like this before. He shouldn't have had the words. "I will pay you to spend the night."

Her brows drew together in puzzlement. "There is no need. I am already obliged by the weather to remain tonight, and I'm sure your ward is well settled in her chamber, though I shall certainly check on her."

He stepped closer, so that only an arm's length separated them. Her cheekbones showed angularly under taut skin, suggesting hardship, and together with her shabby gown and bonnet, told of an existence at the edge of what was acceptable. And yet, if life had brought her troubles, she didn't seem mastered by

them. She hadn't let him bully her, and that emboldened him to speak now. That, and the attraction he'd felt since he'd traded words with her in the rain.

She was pretty, but in an unusual way that wasn't apparent at first glance. There was something about the way she moved, a lithe grace; it wasn't feminine exactly—not unfeminine either. It was the sort of athletic grace of a child who might clamber up a tree or take off running after a colt. Her face was smart, neat, interesting.

Actually, he imagined that with steady meals and a little grooming, she would be quite lovely. Doubtless she was unaware that she had an appealing look of dishabille with her bonnet hanging from its strings around her neck and her wild black curls floating in a blowsy halo about her head.

"Not for my ward," he said, wanting to stop himself from saying one more wicked word even as he gave in to the despair that told him nothing mattered anymore. "For me."

A pause as realization dawned and color flooded her face. "I cannot believe you would propose such a thing."

Her breathing had quickened, and a distant part of his mind was shouting that he was a devil and he'd shocked her horribly. But he was unmoored from that man now. He reached up and put his palm against her cheek. Dear God, the soft warmth of a woman's skin, the give of her smooth flesh.

He read mutiny in her eyes as she pushed his hand away. "How dare you!"

"I'm willing to make it worth your while. You

have the look of someone who would put a hundred pounds to good use."

His answer was a forceful slap that left his cheek burning, as alive to sensation now as the hand that had touched her.

Her eyes crackled furiously at him. "You, my lord, have behaved like a beast from the moment I met you. For the sake of your niece, I hope you will be able to find your humanity. It has clearly gone missing."

She turned and strode toward the door.

He'd already gone this far. He addressed the back of her head. "How do you know I won't do something dastardly to her? Or neglect her?"

She paused in front of the door, her spine as straight as a duchess's. "I'm willing to take that chance."

He laughed, a sound that disgusted him. She turned to face him.

"Where is your soul?" she said in a low voice, looking him straight in the eye as if she'd already seen the worst that life had to offer and what he'd just done didn't astonish her. Where did she get the damned spirit to stand before him, resilient?

"Why are you so calm? Have you perhaps drawn such a proposal before?"

She blinked at his words, as if he'd hit a nerve. "Must the volume of a woman's protest gauge her innocence?" she demanded in a husky voice.

"You are very sure of yourself."

"What else is there in this life?"

She walked through the doorway and was gone.

Three

ANNA PULLED THE LIBRARY DOOR CLOSED BEHIND HER with shaking hands. The viscount's manservant appeared out of the shadows, and she wondered if he'd heard any of what had just transpired. But he merely nodded when she said she would be staying for the night and led her upstairs to a bedchamber.

She entered the room, closed the door behind her, and leaned against it, sinking to the floor in the candlelit darkness. Her limbs quivered uncontrollably. Lord Grandville's behavior had been appalling. The man was a heartless pig, and not the first one she'd encountered in the last month. She was so furious and disgusted with men in general at that moment that if God had put the fate of all males in her hands, their future would have been in grave doubt.

As soon as she stopped shaking, she would go see Miss Tarryton. The girl must be crushed by the welcome she'd received. Anna could all too easily imagine how she was feeling: alone in the world, as good as abandoned by the man who should be responsible for her.

Although Anna's father had never been cruel, as the viscount had been to his ward, perhaps that would have been easier to bear. He—her only parent—had merely been uninterested in her. What drew Matthew Bristol, beyond the medical duties he fulfilled to the grateful satisfaction of his patients, was his obsession: birds.

A precise, composed man who never chatted and disdained emotions, Dr. Bristol had spent every free moment on his studies in medicine and nature. The fact that he had no attention to spare for his children hadn't mattered so much to Anna when her brother, Lawrence, was alive, but once he was gone, she couldn't avoid the conclusion that she was little more to her father than a dinner companion.

The only time he'd shown interest in her had been when he asked her to do the drawings for his two published studies of birds, *Anatomy of a Songbird* and *A Study of Owls*. She'd been happy to walk the woods and fields with him as they looked for meadow pipits and long-eared owls to sketch. But when the books were done, it seemed as though his interest in her was over as well.

There had been advantages to having an unconcerned parent. No one had scolded her if she was sometimes rather tan, or noticed that she didn't dress fashionably and that she was deficient in such feminine accomplishments as graceful tea pouring. She'd learned to ride and swim by copying her older brother, read every book in the house, including her father's medical texts (the ones having to do with the reproductive process holding particular interest), and studied drawing

and painting to her heart's content, becoming good enough to illustrate her father's bird books.

This last occupation gained her enough renown locally that she was engaged as a drawing tutor for the daughters of the local gentry, and she dreamed of one day using the money she earned to open a drawing school.

But being an unconcerned parent also meant that her father had never been *concerned*.

He certainly hadn't cared when she'd told him that his apprentice, who was often in their home, made her uncomfortable.

"I feel as though Mr. Rawlins watches me," she'd said.

"He's a decent apprentice," he'd said, not looking up from the prescription he was writing. "That's all that matters."

Mr. Rawlins had left a few weeks before her father sickened and died, and she forgot about him—until one day a month ago.

She'd been returning from giving a lesson that afternoon. Though she had inherited the cottage after her father's death, she'd discovered that he'd been funding a fellow naturalist who was to bring him specimens from South America, and there was hardly any money left, so she had to be very careful with her tutoring earnings. But she loved teaching, even though she knew that her pupils' families thought her unusual and not the sort of woman they'd want their sons to marry.

As she approached her house, she'd seen a carriage stopped there.

She knew from the crest that it belonged to the Marquess of Henshaw, who had an estate a few miles

away, but she couldn't imagine why his carriage was outside her home. The coach door had opened and the man himself had emerged, tall and grandly dressed, with a grand waistline to match.

His pink face had cracked in an enormous grin, and he'd said what a pleasure it was to see her again.

She'd politely pointed out that she'd never had the pleasure of making his acquaintance. Gleefully, he'd reached behind him into the coach and produced a big, black book of the kind Anna used for sketching. *The Beautiful One* was written on it in what appeared to be red sealing wax. Puzzled by a visit that was growing more bizarre by the moment, she'd looked down when he'd opened the book with a flourish, and felt as if she'd been kicked.

The first sheet of paper showed a scene she could not mistake: her own room. The artist was quite talented. There was her old wooden chair, the side of the bathtub, her window with the curtains drawn. The artist had caught her at the moment of pinning up her hair before stepping into the waiting water. With her arms raised to her head, her small breasts appeared prominent and the curve of her waist like a marker leading the eye downward toward the shadows between her legs, just as if she'd been a model posing for a study.

"There are more?" she'd managed to say, aware that the coachman could hear their conversation from his seat at the front of the coach. There were many sheets of paper underneath the first one, and more than anything, she didn't want to see what was on them.

"Of course." The marquess had sounded puzzled.

"You posed for Mr. Rawlins. He sold them to me."
He'd chuckled. "Or have you posed for so many artists
that you've forgotten what you've done for whom?"

"No!"

Rawlins had, she'd realized as a sick chill spread
through her body, obviously spied on her. She hadn't
even known he was an artist. And a talented one,
however unscrupulous.

A thought had come unbidden then, a shameful
thought, because the pictures were so wrong and she
was furious about them. But along with those strong
feelings had come this: Someone had found her beautiful? Her, Dr. Bristol's unfeminine daughter?

"I did not pose for these," she'd said forcefully.
"I've never seen this book before."

"Of course you haven't," he'd said, and winked.
"My dear girl, I've come to offer you a handsome fee
to pose for a large painting Rawlins is doing of me.
You are to be Aphrodite to my Ares. Nude, of course."

Anna had stood speechless before she'd gathered her
wits. "You have no right to those drawings. Rawlins
spied on me. I beg you to burn that book and never
speak of it again."

"Do spare me the injured maiden act. It's obvious
you posed for them. I've shown them to my friends,
and I intend to display them."

"You can't! I'll be ruined!"

He'd flicked a glance at the modest cottage where
she'd lived all her life. The whitewash on the front
door was peeling, and one of the windows was cracked.

"You are thinking much too small. Why, even now
you're quite hiding yourself with that ugly coiffure

and that pathetic gown. With what I will pay you for the painting, you can fix yourself up, become the toast of the art world. Your looks are unusual, and it's easy to imagine you draped across some moss, your legs bare, like a nymph…"

"Stop," she'd whispered.

"Though I do plan to keep your name secret, Miss Bristol, until after I unveil the painting, to safeguard the mystery behind *The Beautiful One*. And I will pay you fifty pounds to be my Aphrodite."

He'd left, telling her he would be back in a month, when Mr. Rawlins would have completed the Ares portion of the painting. Even before his carriage had rolled away, she'd known she'd have to leave home immediately.

She'd taken her tiny store of coins, packed quickly, and left her home, not knowing if or when she could ever come back. With no references, she'd been grateful to find the position as the Rosewood seamstress a few days later. She'd given her surname as Black, which had been her mother's maiden name and was her own middle name and would, she hoped, be easy for her to remember to use.

She had no way of knowing how many people had seen that book or whether the marquess had still not told anyone the name of the model. Doubtless she'd angered him by leaving, and he might retaliate in some way. And, of course, one other person knew her identity: the horrible Mr. Rawlins.

She was anxious to return to the school, where no one paid any attention to the lowly seamstress. Once she'd saved enough money there, she would be able

to go north to her Aunt May in Yorkshire, far away
from trouble.

She was, however, very concerned about Miss
Tarryton. Miss Brickle had charged Anna to see
the girl safely to her guardian and to assist him
if necessary. Could she really in good conscience
abandon Miss Tarryton to the care of the master of
Stillwell Hall?

⅌

He didn't want her there, Lizzie thought, fighting the
pressure of tears that wanted to come as she sat with
her head in her hands at the gold-finished vanity in the
room she'd been shown. With its soft blue carpet and
curtains in pale salmon, the well-appointed bedchamber looked like it belonged to a different house from
the oddly bare drawing room.

Being unwelcome at Stillwell had always been a
possibility, even if, when she'd dreamed of leaving
Rosewood, she'd discounted its likelihood. She hadn't
dwelled on Grandville's not writing to her because
she knew he must be busy and because her father had
chosen him as her guardian, so he would have to be a
good and responsible man.

What was more, Grandville had been her Aunt
Ginger's husband. Although Lizzie never saw her aunt
after moving to Malta, Aunt Ginger had written her,
always saying how much she looked forward to seeing
her again.

The dream that the man who was her uncle as well
as her father's closest friend would one day come and
take her to live with him had been what sustained

her over the last year. But the man she'd just met was nothing like the man she'd remembered hazily as a kind fellow with nice blue eyes. And now she knew why he hadn't come.

She'd hated Rosewood from the minute she'd arrived there from Malta eighteen months earlier. The other girls had snickered at her rough ways and her unfashionable clothes, and each day that passed had only increased her disgust for the stupid "finishing" instruction that didn't seem to be finishing her for anything but more time at Rosewood. How she'd hated her stepmother for sending her there.

The only good thing she'd discovered at Rosewood, during the times she'd slipped away unnoticed, was that gentlemen quite liked her. Men, she'd found, were *exciting*.

A knock sounded on the door. Probably that man-servant. Lizzie said nothing. She didn't trust her voice anyway—she had a huge lump in her throat.

"Miss Tarryton?" came a female voice. The seamstress. Doubtless she didn't care about Lizzie either, but considering what she'd seen of the woman so far, Lizzie trusted her at least to be forthright.

"What is it?"

"May I come in?"

"Please yourself."

The door opened and she entered. The woman really would be gorgeous, Lizzie observed out of reflex, if she would just do a bit of grooming. Her black hair had been pulled back with a careless firmness that left lumpy parts where the curls had not been tamed, and her ugly blue bonnet, its ribbons still tied

in a clump, was hanging from her neck carelessly, as if she'd just pushed it off her head.

Her sack-like bluish frock was plain awful. Not even Helen of Troy could have looked like anything but a dowdy matron in it. Never once during the whole carriage ride or after had the seamstress fussed at her hair, or tried to arrange her skirts so they wouldn't wrinkle, or engaged in any of the hundred little ways girls and women had of attending to their appearance. She simply seemed not to care about her looks, which Lizzie thought a foolish waste of the most important power a female had.

The seamstress also looked in need of a good meal or twenty—her cheeks were hollow, and Lizzie had noticed that she'd managed to eat all of her meat pie from the hamper they had in the coach even though they were terrible (Lizzie had discarded hers out the window), so she had to have been very hungry. Lizzie supposed from her speech and manner that she was a gentlewoman fallen on hard times.

The woman perched on the edge of the bed near where Lizzie sat at the vanity. She looked pale, and Lizzie wondered what had been said after she left the drawing room.

"What is your name again?" Lizzie asked.

"Anna Black." The seamstress cleared her throat. "Well, Miss Tarryton, do you feel comfortable here? Do you think you will be content with your guardian?"

"How the devil should I know, and what does it matter anyway? He is my guardian." Tears began to well in her eyes, and she hid them by looking at the wall and fought not to give in to them.

If Miss Black was taken aback at her rough words and tone, she didn't show it, and Lizzie wouldn't have cared if she had. She'd had enough of trying to be proper at Rosewood.

"If you don't mind my asking, how did Lord Grandville come to be your guardian?"

"He and my father met at university and became close, though now I don't see why. Then, when we were in Malta, Grandville became better acquainted with Aunt Ginger, who was a friend of his cousin, and eventually they married. So he is connected to me twice over."

Lizzie shrugged even as she felt her throat constricting. "A year ago, my father and stepmother and baby brother died of a fever," she said, pushing past the thickness in her voice. "They were in Malta. I was at Rosewood."

"I'm so sorry," the seamstress said quietly. Lizzie read the compassion in her companion's eyes, and if there had been any trace of pity there as well, she would have sent her away, but there wasn't. Lizzie crossed her arms.

"I hadn't realized Lord Grandville was married," Miss Black said.

"Not for much more than a year. Aunt Ginger died shortly before my family did."

"Oh. So much tragedy."

"I hadn't seen her since I was little. I was supposed to come to Stillwell for the summer, but she died and so I never came."

She'd had her own sorrows soon enough, when the letter telling of what happened in Malta had arrived.

With the generous allowance she began receiving

from her uncle, she'd buried her grief under mounds of pretty clothes, the kinds of things a poor church-man's daughter would never have owned. And she'd set herself to learning every bit of the reviled deport-ment. The girls at Rosewood didn't laugh at her anymore, but by then she hadn't wanted their shallow friendship. Gentlemen were better.

The seamstress's gaze rested on her. She had pretty eyes of a clear brown, like a glass of sherry with light shining through. Not that Anna Black probably cared what color they were. She seemed…functional. Lizzie looked away from the kindness on her face, knowing it would undo her.

"I want to go back to Malta. I shall ask Grandville to send me. Then he won't have to bother about me."

"Now might not be a good time to broach that idea." The woman's tone contained no surprise or judgment, but Lizzie wished she hadn't said anything about her beloved Malta, where life had been so much freer and better than it was in England.

"What will he do with me?"

"You must remain at Stillwell for the moment. Beyond that, all I know is that you can't go back to Rosewood."

"That is no loss."

A hint of a smile teased the edge of Miss Black's mouth. "I had gathered that. I rather suppose that you wanted to be sent away from there."

"All right, I did. I hated it."

Lizzie almost wished Miss Black were staying at Stillwell, because she seemed refreshingly unboth-ered by things that shocked other people. Lizzie

could feel her throat tightening up again and looked down at her feet in their apricot satin slippers, and took comfort in knowing that she was very likely the prettiest, best-dressed female within a fifty-mile radius. Grandville's property was huge, but she supposed there must be other people nearby. People, she thought, who would care that she was pretty and pleasing.

"I suppose I can understand that, Miss Tarryton."

Lizzie had a flash of understanding that Miss Black wouldn't have liked the deportment lessons either, if for different reasons.

"Oh, just call me Lizzie," she said impatiently. "'Miss Tarryton' reminds me of horrible Miss Brickle."

"Very well, Lizzie. And you must call me Anna."

&

Anna was not deceived by the stoic facade of the girl sitting before her. Lizzie was devastated by what had happened in the drawing room. She might not be a child, but she was still young enough for it to matter that she was an orphan. And her guardian had just made it clear that she was nothing to him but a duty he didn't want.

Lizzie was watching her with a wary look that reminded Anna of a young sparrow hawk she and Lawrence had once found. The bird's wings were not yet strong enough for flight, but as she'd discovered painfully, it was able to use its beak. Anna could imagine this girl using her own devices against Lord Grandville, and about as successfully as a fledgling hawk might challenge an adult. She sighed.

"Lizzie, I must be certain you'll be comfortable here before I can leave."

The girl lifted her chin. "I'm not afraid of my uncle, if that's what you're wondering. I can contend with whatever comes my way."

"Ah, yes, as you have already demonstrated." Anna's eyes flicked to the window. "I'm not certain that your solutions always serve you well."

"I'm accustomed to looking out for myself."

Right. Anna pressed her lips together, realizing she was about to make a foolish decision but not seeing how she could in good conscience do otherwise.

"I shall speak to Lord Grandville," she said. "Perhaps I might stay for a day or two, until you are settled. Miss Brickle said that I might, if there were need."

Lizzie looked up, clearly surprised. "You would do that?"

"Yes."

"That might be…helpful." Lizzie paused, her brow lowering. "You mustn't think that—in the garden last night with Lieutenant Scarsdale… It was never going to be more than a kiss."

"That may have been your plan," Anna said gently, "but you can't have known what his intentions might have been. Never mind what you were risking regarding your reputation."

A tinge of pink spread across the girl's cheeks. "No matter what, I'm better off here than at Rosewood."

Anna left the room thinking that Lizzie was, unfortunately, likely to find herself very much mistaken.

❧

Will sank into the chair behind his library desk in the dusky darkness, his long legs sliding straight under it, his head slumping forward into his hands. The belligerent lead ball in his stomach had exploded in the drawing room, blacking over the whole of his insides.

Dear God, what had he done? That young woman he'd propositioned might be someone who'd known hardship, but that should have secured his compassion, not given him leave to insult her. In his whole life, he'd never so offended a woman. Never even been tempted to do so.

Ginger used to call him her knight in shining armor, and it had always made his heart swell with pride.

The day before the accident that had killed her, they'd stood and looked at the place where the hamlet of cottages they'd planned would be built, and they'd been so happy.

"*You've done a marvelous job working with the architect,*" she'd said. "*The tenants will love these. And your father would have, too. No man is an island, right?*" It had been his father's favorite saying, and one Will had taken to heart from his earliest days of training to be a viscount.

But Will had had to become an island over the last year. After Ginger had died, he'd needed to be alone with his sorrow and anger, and after today, he saw how right he'd been to keep himself apart. If he couldn't control the darkness Ginger's death had brought, he must at least keep it from others.

Except now he didn't see how he could turn away this girl who was Ginger's niece and David's daughter.

God, the Tarrytons—there was nothing left of them now except her. David, the good-hearted knave,

who'd seen the light and gone off to save the souls of Malta, and his beloved Ginger—both gone.

Though Will had known Ginger because she was David's younger sister, he never would have come to court her after David left if she hadn't become friends with Will's cousin Ruby. Which now meant that seeing Ruby and her Halifax siblings reminded him painfully of what he'd lost, and so he avoided them along with everyone else.

He leaned forward and let his forehead fall against the top of the desk and pounded its ancient solidness with his fist. Damnation, where did Anna Black get the colossal nerve to tell him what to do? There was nothing here for his niece, and every time he looked at her he would be reminded that Ginger was gone.

Still, it was not the girl's fault that Will was her guardian. She deserved so much better than he could give her.

He flopped his arm across the desk and grabbed the brandy bottle and poured a large measure. He slung it all back at once so that it burned, but it helped not at all.

A tap on the library door indicated the arrival of his steward. Dragging himself upright, Will bid him enter and leaned forward to light the candles on his desk. He hoped Norris would bring some thorny estate problem to tangle his brain.

They had just finished discussing the expenses for the cottages, Norris tactfully refraining from commenting on the fact that his master was himself currently performing the work on the roofs, when Norris looked down and shuffled a few papers.

"And shall I make arrangements for Miss Tarryton to return to Rosewood for the summer, my lord?"

"No," Will said. "I wish you to find someplace else for her. Another school."

He wondered what exactly it was that his ward had done to make the headmistress send her away. It would have taken quite a bit of provocation for her to part with the ward of a viscount. Who was to say she wouldn't get into trouble again?

"Or perhaps she might live at another of my homes in the company of a governess. Look into it."

"Very good, sir," his steward said in the usual bland tone he used with his master.

Not a single person had gainsaid Will once since Ginger's death until Anna Black had done so today. His employees were unfailingly patient and kind toward him, and he knew much of this was due to loyalty, an earned indulgence he ought not to exploit. He frowned.

"Norris, did you never think other arrangements should be made for Miss Tarryton, so that she wouldn't always be at school?"

"My lord, it would not be my place—"

"I'm asking for your opinion."

Norris pressed his fingertips together, doubtless weighing his words. "She is, my lord, without family save your own. I had thought she might like to be invited to stay, or at least to visit for the holidays."

Will grunted and dismissed him.

It was unfortunate that he didn't have any female relatives who could take over the care of his ward.

There's Judith, a voice whispered before he could cut it off. *No*. Not his stepmother. Never in a million years.

It would take time to find a place for Elizabeth, probably at least a month, during which interval she would have to stay at Stillwell. He owed at least that much to David and Ginger. But he would need Anna Black here if he were going to do something about his niece.

She had refused his demands, but she was poor—that much was obvious from the scrawny, threadbare look of her. If he presented an offer in a better light—and it would hardly be difficult to improve on his first performance—he might be able to entice her. Although the woman was anything but manageable. Where did she come by her boldness? She ought to have felt how absurd she looked in Stillwell's drawing room in her shabby, hideous gown. Was it blue? Or gray? The color was so indistinct, he could not have said.

He would simply have to ensure that he spent as little time as possible in his ward's company, or that of Anna Black, if he could get her to stay. Stillwell Hall was vast, and he had the cottages to finish. At the end of the month, arrangements would be in place for his ward, and she would be gone.

Four

ANNA WALKED SLOWLY DOWN THE MASSIVE STAIRCASE in the growing evening darkness, astounded at what she'd just told Lizzie she would do. She was going to stay in the home of Viscount Grandville, the very man who'd just made an outrageous proposal to her. That was, if he would still have her, which she was fairly certain he would.

But what else could she do? Her conscience wouldn't let her leave Lizzie with a man who seemed dead to tenderness. He'd lost his wife, and perhaps that explained much about the way he was, but what must matter now was that Lizzie needed a family. And all she had was a dark gentleman who wanted to push the world away.

She heard the sound of footsteps. Lord Grandville appeared at the bottom of the stairs and stood in the light of a tabletop candelabrum, all shadow and hardness, and watched her descend. She was far from eager to see him again.

What on earth had made him make that offer to her? It was hardly as if she were dressed to entice or

had flirted with him—as if she even knew how. She'd been nothing but tart to him, yet since their meeting on the road, she'd felt something crackling between them, and there was no convincing herself she didn't find him incredibly handsome. But his character—ugh.

"A moment, please. I would speak with you," he said as she reached the foot of the stairs.

"Very well," she said. "I too have something to say."

"I wish to apologize for my behavior in the drawing room. I have never done such a thing before. You," he began, then stopped himself. "There is no excuse."

She blinked. Was humility possible in such a man? And yet she saw that his face, framed by that too-long dark hair, no longer looked angry but instead haunted, as though that hint of restrained torment she'd glimpsed in the drawing room had been unleashed. Perhaps he wasn't an entirely hard man after all.

"Very well. I accept your apology."

"And I would like you to stay until I can get things sorted out with regard to my ward."

"Ah," she said. "That was what I wanted to discuss. I was thinking it might be best if I stayed for a few days to help your ward get settled."

"A few days will not be sufficient. I will need you to stay for at least a month."

"A month! That's not possible."

"It will take me at least that long to find her a governess or a new school. I'll pay you two hundred pounds for your trouble."

Anna's heart skipped a beat. Two hundred pounds! What a huge sum. She wouldn't even need to go back

to Rosewood if she had that much money. She could
go directly to Yorkshire, to the home of her Aunt
May, her only relative. Aunt May, a serious, religious
woman, lived in a village that was far away from
anyone who might ever see *The Beautiful One*. Anna
could live there in peace.

But she couldn't arrive at her upright aunt's
home trailing an air of desperation, with no belongings or money of her own. Viscount Grandville
was offering more than enough to make such an
undertaking possible.

She might even open her drawing school in
Yorkshire with the kind of money he was offering.
The thought brought the first feeling of true hope
she'd felt in a month.

But how could she take his money when she
already disliked him so intensely? How could she trust
him after what he'd said to both her and Lizzie in the
drawing room?

And yet, he'd asked her pardon and appeared
wholly sincere.

"I might stay a bit longer than a few days, but I
don't require a salary. I would stay because I believe it
would be a help to your ward."

"If you stay, you will stay for the full month and
accept the salary." He regarded her with as arrogant an
eye as any falcon, every inch the aristocrat. "You would
act as a temporary governess and keep her occupied
with whatever it was you were teaching at Rosewood."

She narrowed her eyes and returned his haughtiness, not inclined to correct his impression of what
she'd been doing at Rosewood. There was only one

reasonable choice, and it seemed it would serve both her and Lizzie.

"Very well, I will stay for one month, with the understanding that by then you'll have made arrangements for Miss Tarryton—arrangements satisfactory to her and to me as well."

A dark eyebrow lifted sardonically. "You drive a bargain, do you? And what if, at the end of a month, I've chosen a gorgon as companion for my ward?"

"I suppose such a person *would* be to your taste. Tell me, my lord, are you always this jolly?"

He blinked, and the corner of his mouth trembled faintly, but he made no reply.

"You could at least *try* to behave as if you were part of humanity," she pressed, "now that you have a young lady in your care. She is homeless and alone, while you live a life of privilege."

His eyes met hers, smoldering, and a shiver ran down her spine.

"Do I, by God?" he said, and moved closer. Night had settled into the house early because of the rain, and the cool dampness of the air pressed against her heavily. Or maybe it was his presence.

"I'm sorry about your wife," she said. "Lizzie told me."

He flinched. "Don't," he said, just the single word.

"All right," she said quietly. She could understand not wanting to speak of something painful, of needing to allow a wound to develop a scab. Though she wondered, in his case, if the wound weren't festering.

His dark gaze rested on her. "Why aren't you afraid

of me? You should be, after what happened in the drawing room."

"Maybe I *am* afraid and hide it well."

"Pish," he said. "I don't believe you're afraid of anything you should be."

Oh, yes, she was. She was afraid of the marquess finding her. Afraid of how he might use that book of drawings. Afraid that he or Rawlins would decide to reveal her name and she'd be found out. An angry, brooding viscount simply paled in comparison to these threats.

"Perhaps it's simply that I've learned not to give in to bullies."

That struck something in him, and the light of remorse burned in those midnight eyes.

His gaze traveled toward her shoulder, where her hat hung from its ribbons, which were still tangled in a knot along with some of her hair. She hadn't had a minute to set it right, and in fact had forgotten all about it. She'd never paid much attention to hats; growing up without a mother (her own had died giving birth to her) she'd had only the housekeeper to remind her about protecting her skin, and she'd frequently ignored her.

"Why haven't you put your bonnet away yet? Or better, discarded it? And why should you wish, anyway, to wear such a thing?"

"It's my favorite bonnet for traveling."

"Then you have execrable taste." He sighed. "Do please take it off."

"I can't, actually. The ribbons are knotted and some of my hair is stuck as well. But if you will excuse me now, I'll go see to it."

He made no move to excuse her but instead squinted at the ribbons, then, to her astonishment, lifted his hands and took hold of the knot just below her ear.

"What on earth are you doing?"

"Untying the knot, obviously." He leaned closer, evidently to see the knot better, and she caught a nice soap smell and a hint of brandy, along with a note of something that smelled deep, like strength. She felt a soft tug as he began to work the knot, and the gentle, fiddling sensation sent a shiver of pleasure along her ear and down her neck.

She pushed down the desire for more shivers. "Really, my lord, I should like to find my room now. I have"—she cleared her throat emphatically—"rather an enormous amount of unpacking to do."

He ignored her and continued fiddling. More shivers. They felt too good.

"You're pulling my hair," she said untruthfully.

He paused for a moment and glanced at the side of her face, and she saw his skeptical look out of the corner of her eye.

"I doubt that. I am quite good with my hands."

Those hands. The long, lean fingers with the nicks that suggested hard use. There was certainly a double entendre to be found in his words if not his tone, but she concentrated instead on not melting into a puddle as the exquisite torture resumed just below her ear.

His fingers brushed her earlobe as he worked. The soft sounds of the old satin sliding against itself entered her ear and rippled along the tops of her shoulders

like something live. She clenched her teeth against the beguiling sensations.

"Hold still," he said.

She hadn't realized she'd moved.

"These ribbons are ridiculously knotted," he said some moments later, and underneath the terseness in his voice she detected a husky note that made the hairs on the back of her neck stand at attention. "What did you do, twirl them?"

She forced an even tone. "It was somewhat knotted to begin with."

"Somewhat? These ribbons have surely been the plaything of an army of cats."

She snuck a glance sideways, to where his dark head was bent over his task. He was being so gentle that, fool that she was, it felt like tenderness, and, startlingly, tears over the forgotten sensation pressed at the back of her eyes. She blinked them away. When had she last experienced human tenderness?

She couldn't account for it, but just the touch—the kind attention—of this troubled, bitter man was causing a terrible tightness within her to uncurl a little. She'd been on her own since her father died, though even when he was alive, she'd been in many ways alone. And she'd been in a state of desperation ever since she'd seen that book and been compelled to live as a menial in the basement of Rosewood School, a person of little interest to anyone. Now, here was this powerful, handsome man untying her knotted ribbons as a sort of apology.

With a last sliding, satiny tug, the ribbons came free. Holding the ends, he lifted the bonnet away from her.

"I insist you discard this."

His imperious tone helped her back to sanity, and she closed herself off to the feelings he'd stirred. With no way of knowing who or how many people had seen *The Beautiful One*, she needed that ugly bonnet as protection when she next went out in the world.

"My lord is too accustomed to ordering people about. I will have my bonnet back, please." She held out her hand.

He held on to the hat. "You would benefit from a new and pretty hat."

"Nonsense. You simply wish to assuage your conscience."

With a look that told her he was only acquiescing out of remorse for his earlier behavior, he laid the bonnet across her hands.

"You don't receive help easily, do you, Anna Black?"

"Well, I'm doubtless not as accustomed as some to receiving help. *I* do not have Dart and an entire staff of servants, my lord."

He gave a short, doubtless unwanted bark of mirth. "Heaven help us if you did. I can only imagine I'd find myself tossed out of my own house, with some far better plan for the use of Stillwell in place within the hour."

She looked up into that oh-so-handsome face and knew a creeping sense of disaster. She was very far removed at the moment from *The Beautiful One* and the troubles it could cause her, having arrived at a veritable fortress—and one with its very own dragon. But how was she ever going to stay in the same house with this man?

"Good evening, my lord," she said quietly, and escaped upstairs, guided by a maid. Anna stopped outside Lizzie's room on the way, but the girl must have been asleep already, because her knock brought no response. Tomorrow would be soon enough to let Lizzie know she had a home—for a month at least.

When Anna awoke the next morning to find herself lying in a grand four-poster bed on lovely fresh linens, she was briefly startled. In the darkness and exhaustion of the previous night, she'd taken little note of the room she'd been given, and now a throb of panic raced through her as she took in the distant ceiling with its stately wooden beams, the tall windows covered in fine lace curtains, and the thick red carpet on the floor.

How on earth had she come to leave the sanctuary of Rosewood for a month's stay at Stillwell Hall? Lord Grandville was very possibly acquainted with the Marquess of Henshaw, even if it seemed unlikely that the marquess—or anyone who'd seen *The Beautiful One*—might visit a man who so clearly wanted to be left alone.

Well, she told herself stoutly, if necessary, she would disappear, though escaping again with only a few coins to her name did not bear thinking about, now that she had the possibility of the money the viscount had offered.

But that was all in the hazy future. Today she had a task before her: she was going to find a way to help Lizzie worm her way into her guardian's heart, through whatever tiny chink might allow access.

Her stomach rumbled insistently. She'd been too tired to ask for a supper tray, and after the austerity of her servant's lot at Rosewood, going to bed on an empty stomach was so familiar that she'd hardly noted it. She supposed there would be some kind of breakfast, probably hard bread crusts and water, or whatever was customarily served in the households of stone-hearted viscounts.

She swung her legs out of bed and noticed that what she had assumed was a painting on the opposite wall, above a vanity, was, at second glance, a curious mural. A pretty scene had been begun, but the artist had only half-finished it, so that the sheep and half of the shepherd existed merely as vague pencil marks, while some of the hills had been painted in soft, rich colors.

It didn't match the manor's brooding master at all, but perhaps it was some decorating scheme of his late wife's.

As she stared at it, an idea came to her: Lizzie could finish the drawing and then the painting!

Drawing and painting lessons were part of the Rosewood curriculum, so surely she would have some skills in this area. If the painting were something his wife had wanted, might it not please him if her niece completed it?

It wasn't much, but it could be a start. And with any luck, Lizzie would have all sorts of talents. Perhaps she sang like a bird or played the piano like an angel.

They would practice drawing first so she could gauge Lizzie's skill, she thought as she walked over to gaze out the large window.

The vast grounds were misty with morning dew, the sun barely having risen, but she could see a dark figure striding out away from the manor. The regal stiffness of his posture left her in no doubt as to who he was. Why was the viscount alone here at Stillwell, roaming about dressed as a farmer, and not in town, charming the ladies? Handsome and wealthy as he was, if he made even the smallest effort at civility, he would doubtless cause every female he met to swoon.

A maid arrived with a warm smile and a tray, along with the news that Miss Tarryton was breakfasting in her chamber as well. The tray held a cup of rich, steaming cocoa, two boiled eggs, and nice bread, and Anna tucked into it with relish while reflecting that at least Lord Grandville's household knew the importance of a well-buttered roll, for which she was grateful.

After eating, she put on her brown gown, which was all she had besides yesterday's blue one, and ignored the observation that it was the color of a dead leaf.

She'd never bothered much about clothes, but once her father died, there hadn't been money to replace things, and she'd had to be careful to keep a gown or two in respectable shape for teaching. When she'd fled home, she'd taken her worst gowns with her, thinking they would make her so unremarkable she'd pass unnoticed, and she had—until last night. Lord Grandville must have been *very* lonely to have made that indecent proposal to her.

Before leaving her room, she penned a note for Miss Brickle, telling her that Lord Grandville required her services for Miss Tarryton and she would thus not

be returning to Rosewood, and gave it to a maid. Then she stopped by the schoolroom to see what supplies she might find.

When Anna knocked on Lizzie's door some minutes later, the girl opened it promptly, as if grateful for human contact. She wore a pristine white muslin gown embroidered with a dainty dot pattern, and her beautiful gold-red hair was dressed simply in a high knot with a few curled strands floating about her ears. Anna had merely scrabbled her own hair into its customary unruly knot, and she thought she saw Lizzie shudder as her eyes took in the sight.

"Well," Anna said. "I spoke with your guardian last night after you retired, and I am to be your companion here at Stillwell. For a month, that is."

"You are? For a whole month?" There was no mistaking the look of relief in Lizzie's angel-blue eyes.

"Yes. His lordship and I have agreed that you'll need a governess of sorts while he determines what will be best for your future." She paused, thinking Lizzie might wonder at a seamstress being promoted to governess. "I...have taught before."

But Lizzie apparently wasn't concerned about Anna's qualifications, and the edges of her mouth were already tightening. "He'll send me away after a month, won't he?"

"Let's not worry about the future just now." Anna smiled encouragingly. "I thought we might go outside and do some drawing."

"But Grandville—"

"Has gone out. The maid said he is generally from home during the day, seeing to some cottages being

built for his tenants. Now, I've had a maid bring some sketchbooks and pencils out to the terrace. Shall we?"

The sun was shining brightly as they seated themselves at the edge of the terrace, near some tall ornamental grasses. A soft breeze teased the hair at the edges of their bonnets and gently rustled the branches of a stately weeping willow that stood nearby.

After what seemed like only minutes of work, Lizzie sighed and dropped her pencil onto her paper and stretched her arms out behind her comfortably.

"I never was any good at drawing," she said, not sounding especially dismayed.

Anna slid over to look at Lizzie's work. There was little there. "But this line is very true," she said, pointing to one of the fronds of grass Lizzie had drawn. "Just try to really look, and follow the lines with your pencil."

"But grass is so dull. Who could want to look at it?" Lizzie glanced at Anna's sketch and gasped. "Lawks, you're really good!"

"*Lawks*? Lizzie, you must know that's coarse, and I've heard 'the devil' slip past your lips as well. Such words are not pleasing in a young lady."

Anna knew she was hardly the most appropriate person to be giving advice about deportment, but it wasn't as though she hadn't been taught by the occasional governess; she'd simply ignored their guidance when it suited her.

But as Lord Grandville's ward, Lizzie would be known to polite society, and she must acquit herself well. "Where did you hear such words?"

Lizzie made a knot in a blade of grass. "I suppose at the harbor in Malta. I used to watch the sailors."

"Your father didn't mind?" It seemed they had something in common.

"It never mattered until he married my stepmother." Lizzie reached forward and tugged hard on a long blade of grass, breaking it. "If only he hadn't married her, none of this would have happened," she said with a hint of bitterness. "How could he have let her send me away?"

"I don't know," Anna said gently. "People disappoint us at times."

After a minute, Lizzie said, "What did you used to teach? Drawing?"

Anna's heart skipped a beat, though it seemed impossible Lizzie could know that Anna Black was really Anna Bristol, drawing teacher. "Why do you say that?"

"Because you have loads of talent, of course," Lizzie said, abandoning the grass and looking up.

Anna relaxed and gave her a skeptical look. "If I draw well, it's because I've developed my skill. Actually, I had thought you might surprise and delight his lordship with some drawings."

"Oh." Lizzie looked dismayed. "Well, I want to do anything that he might like."

"Are you accomplished at the pianoforte?"

"Not *accomplished*…but I do sew quite nicely."

"Ah, very good," Anna said with a sinking feeling.

"I do think," Lizzie said with an earnest look, "that I might be more inspired to draw if I were sketching something pretty."

If only Lord Grandville could appreciate some of Lizzie's charms, for she certainly had them, and no ward could have wished to please him more. Anna shaded her eyes against the late-morning light and looked about. "I suppose there might be some lilies of the valley in the shade of those trees," she said, gesturing to a small wood perhaps a hundred paces off.

They took their things and went over to the trees, where they scanned the ground for the little white flowers. Lizzie soon uttered a cry.

"What can it be?" she said, bending to look at something on the ground.

A puff of white fluff rested not three inches from Lizzie's slipper-clad toes. Anna knelt next to it, peering closer, though she already knew by its heart-shaped face what it was.

"A baby barn owl," she said, not touching it. She'd once spent an entire month sketching an injured baby owl her father had found and brought to their home to heal. Lizzie knelt beside her and peered closer.

The owlet was young, perhaps five or six weeks old, and in addition to its fluff, feathers were starting to appear. It lay in the shade of the tree, not moving.

"Is it dead?" Lizzie breathed.

Anna looked around and saw telltale white droppings in profusion around a hollow in the tree directly over them. The hole was perhaps a dozen feet up, but there were several good branches below it.

"I hope not," she said, and gently slid her fingertips under the small, downy body. She felt the rapid beating of its heart and smiled, lifting it into her hands. "It's only pretending."

Lizzie gently stroked the creature with a fingertip. "It's darling. I've never seen an owlet before." She looked up at the tree. "Is that its nest?"

"Yes. It must have been trying to fly and fallen." She looked around. "Usually a parent will be nearby, but it may be away just now."

"Can't it fly back?"

"It's too young. And its parents won't feed it on the ground."

Lizzie looked stricken at this, and Anna discarded any lingering concerns she might have had about the character of Lizzie Tarryton. "But we can't leave it here to die or be eaten or stepped on! I could make a little home for it, in—in a hatbox. I should be happy to!"

"No," Anna said gently, "it must be returned to the nest. The parents will feed it there." She looked up at the branches above her. "If I climbed up onto that branch, could you hand the owlet up to me?"

"Is that a good idea? It sounds so unladylike."

Anna chuckled. "And this from the terror of Rosewood School."

"I'm sure *I* don't care," Lizzie said, "but what if Grandville sees you?"

"There's nobody about, and I'll be quick."

She carefully transferred the still-motionless owlet onto Lizzie's open palms and grasped a low branch, then swung a leg up and over it.

"Miss Brickle would be horrified," Lizzie pointed out cheerfully. "Your ankles are on full display."

Anna grinned and climbed onto the next highest branch, managing to get both feet on it. The nest was

right above her, issuing a potent smell of owl. She grabbed hold of the tree trunk and called to Lizzie, who was obscured now by the leaves, "Hand him up when I reach down."

Five

WILL WAS AT WORK ON THE ROOF OF THE LAST cottage, careless of the increasing warmth of the late-morning sun against his back. As he laid another S-shaped tile against the roof batten, he decided that after he whitewashed the interior of the cottage, he'd go back and do one more coat on the insides of all the other homes. And they needed fencing, he thought with a surge of relief. A stone wall would give him plenty to do.

He wasn't ready for the cottage work to be completed. It had been his only solace since he'd dismissed the builders months ago and taken up finishing the work himself.

From his position on the roof, he could see out across the estate's vast grounds, over the fields and the various blocks of homes where his tenants were now living. There would not, of course, be anywhere near enough of the new cottages to house them all, and he was sorry about that.

This first batch of cottages had been meant to be a trial run, a model that would be replicated over the

rest of Stillwell. He and Ginger had shared the hope
that the homes might serve as inspiration for other
estate owners, to encourage more action to better
the lives of workers. But now he couldn't get his
mind around all those plans and dreams. To start all
that again would be a tangle, requiring meetings with
architects, and commitments, and future thinking.

He leaned forward to reach a new stack of tiles
as the memory of his fingers working on a knotted
ribbon below a pretty, shell-like ear danced in his
mind. She'd shivered at his nearness.

"*You simply wish to assuage your conscience,*" she'd said
after he'd offered to buy her a new hat. But remorse
hadn't been the only thing that had drawn his fingers
to those tangled ribbons. He'd wanted to touch her in
the library when he'd made that contemptible offer,
and that desire hadn't gone away.

He thought of her pink saucepot's mouth and
how tart she'd been when his order had succeeded
in freeing their coach from the ditch. He'd deserved
everything she'd said to him.

The unaccustomed sound of his own chuckle
startled him, and the next moment he heard the crash
of the ladder as it fell away from the roof and onto a
stack of tiles below. He'd kicked it without realizing it.

Damn. An hour earlier he'd smashed his thumb
while hammering. What the devil was he doing,
thinking so much about Anna Black? Though his
body responded to her, his mind knew the wrongness
of wanting her. Even if she hadn't been a governess
and under his protection, it would be wrong. He
couldn't become entangled with a woman—any

woman. He would have nothing to give her, and he could want nothing from her but the satisfaction of his body's needs.

He would quit for the day before he did any more damage. There were accounts to review, and he'd been meaning to write to his brother, Tommy. He knew he should also write to his cousin Louie, who was like a brother to him, but he suspected that, after a year of hearing nothing from him, Louie would take a letter as an invitation to visit Stillwell. The last thing he needed was more guests.

He moved to the edge of the roof, dangled his long frame, and dropped the last six feet to the ground.

Rounding the edge of the wood at the back of Stillwell, he was startled to see his ward standing about. She was looking up at a tree in which, from the movement of its leaves and branches, some large creature seemed to be thrashing. A crow?

As he drew nearer to the oblivious Lizzie, he was almost certain he heard a woman's voice coming from among the leaves. Lizzie stepped closer to the tree and lifted her hands upward, and he saw that on a thick branch perhaps six feet off the ground were perched two feet in past-their-prime dark ankle boots, and above them, he was treated to a view he could not regret of trim calves. The surrounding leaves and branches mostly obscured the rest of his recently hired governess. In the instant before Lizzie became aware of Will, he saw that she held in her cupped hands a fluffy white ball.

Lizzie turned and saw him, her mouth forming into an O as a voice called from above, "Lizzie? I'm ready for the owlet."

"Er," said Lizzie, looking at him. In the clear sunlight, he noticed that her eyes were a different color blue than Ginger's had been. But the shape was Ginger's, as were the eyebrows. Not her fault, but he couldn't go the route of compassion. It would only muddy what had to be. He looked past her and lifted a hand to rub his eyes.

"Miss Black," he said, knowing he could not avoid asking, "what on earth are you doing?"

There was a pause as she absorbed his arrival and a shifting of the feet on the branch near his forehead as they drew together, perhaps in an attempt at modesty.

"Ah, my lord," she said from above him. "Good afternoon. Lizzie and I are engaged in returning a fallen owlet to its nest. It was her idea. She is very caring toward animals."

He could feel Lizzie's big blue eyes on him though his own were still covered by his hand. He had no doubt as to whose idea it had been to climb the tree. He hadn't truly expected Anna Black to be a typical sort of governess, had he?

"Come down at once."

"If you will wait just a moment, my lord," she said breezily, "I shall be down directly. Lizzie, the owlet."

Lizzie cleared her throat. "Here."

He tapped her on the shoulder before she could lift her arms farther. "Give me that creature, please."

She looked uncertain, but she clearly didn't want to displease him, and she handed over the motionless owl. He took it carefully from her and did not return her tentative smile. He could feel her eagerness for him to acknowledge her, but he let it flow past him.

The leaves and branches above them shook as Anna Black crouched down and extended her hand for the animal. Her bonnet, the same horrible blue one, had fallen on its strings around her neck again, and her hair, apparently loosened by her climb, curled crazily about her face as if she were some unkempt urchin, accentuating her pert nose and reminding him of her jack-in-the-box appearance from the coach.

Her pink lips pressed outward at the sight of him; doubtless she was annoyed by his arrival, but her expression didn't draw an answering wave of annoyance from him. Instead, her lips were making him wonder, unaccountably, what it might feel like to be kissed all over by pink butterflies.

"The owlet, please," she fairly ordered him.

"Don't be ridiculous. Get down this instant before you fall. I will return the owlet."

"I am already positioned to do so. If you will just give it to me, I can put it back and then receive your displeasure properly on the ground."

He grunted. Why did he keep finding himself in out-of-his-control conversations with this maddening woman?

In his palm the owlet's heart beat with a rapid, stressed flutter. He reached up his hand, and she gently took the animal and disappeared into the foliage.

From above came a few rustling noises, then the angry screech of what had to be an adult owl and a yelp. Fearing Miss Black would fall, he stepped forward to catch her, but at that same moment she jumped neatly down, so that she landed right in front of him.

He grabbed her arms, a reflex to steady her. She didn't need his help, but their eyes locked, and for a moment he read vulnerability there before it was replaced with the hard glint of independence. She smelled like sunshine and crushed leaves, and he felt the slim softness of her arms and his body's yearning to hug her close.

She stepped away from him. It had all happened in the space of a few moments.

But as he watched her brush some leaves from her skirts with her head down, that vulnerability he'd glimpsed tugged at him. Who was this woman? Where had she come from? She was clearly educated and intelligent, and though she was too forthright and she dressed terribly, she was not rough, merely unusual.

That life-on-the-edge-of-propriety quality he'd observed in her the night before had suggested that she'd known some hardship or that she had some burden she might trade for money. And yet today, in the company of his ward, she looked at ease, even if her eyes seemed to be hiding something.

Had a good night's sleep and a good breakfast solved her troubles? He was certain not. Something about her niggled him, but only trouble would come of interesting himself in her and whatever her story might be. He must leave her to her own obviously capable, if unorthodox, devices.

He cleared his throat meaningfully. She looked up briskly, as though little of note had occurred. "I didn't think the parent was in the nest," she said. "Though I might have paid more attention had I not been distracted."

There was a husky note mingled with the hint of irritation in her voice, and it satisfied a part of him he shouldn't be listening to, even as he was pierced by the thought that Ginger would have liked Anna Black.

"Anna," Lizzie said, staring at them quizzically, "what about the owlet?"

"He's safely reunited with his family."

Lizzie's eyes widened prettily, a look that Will supposed was meant to draw attention to her blue eyes and long lashes. Doubtless it generally had quite an effect on males.

It occurred to him then that his niece would likely be thinking of marriage soon. If only he had an appropriate female relative to help her. That person should have been his stepmother, Judith, but that would be wrong. He didn't trust Judith, nor did he respect her. Lizzie didn't deserve such a fate.

Though neither did he imagine how he would bring a young lady out in society. Definitely something he wasn't prepared to think about.

"It was fortunate that Grandville was here to save you, Anna, wasn't it?" Lizzie said. "You might have been badly hurt."

"Yes," Miss Black replied without much enthusiasm, turning slightly in his direction, as if just then recalling he was there. *Ha.* As if either of them could have forgotten what had just passed between them.

Lizzie looked surprised at her governess's tone and gave her a discreet, somewhat admonishing shake of her head. Miss Black turned fully toward him, the mutinous look just disappearing from her brow as she adopted a pleasant tone.

"Perhaps, my lord, after Lizzie and I have tidied up, you will join us for luncheon?"

Probably one of the most insincerely extended invitations he'd ever received, and he knew exactly why she was offering it when what she wanted was his head on a platter. Anna Black did her duty—or what she perceived it to be.

His ward smiled earnestly at him, trying far too hard to catch his eye. Will ignored her and settled his gaze on the base of the tree.

"I cannot, though I thank you," he said.

"Disappointing," Miss Black said. "Then we shall look forward to seeing you at dinner. And I should like to discuss some new supplies for the schoolroom. The atlas alone is from 1740."

"I'm sorry, but I shall be otherwise engaged for dinner. I do ask, though, that should you come upon any other homeless wildlife—a hapless porcupine, perhaps a wayward cobra—you will allow nature to fend for itself. Good day."

Lizzie turned to Anna, despair pinching her beautiful features. "He won't even look at me," she said in a husky voice. "He doesn't like me at all. He really doesn't."

"I think it's more the case that his lordship is accustomed to keeping to himself. Try not to take his behavior as a personal slight," Anna said, even as she willed her pulse to stop racing. Standing so near him had made her remember him undoing her bonnet ribbons. Considering how she'd felt about being made into the Beautiful One, she would have thought she'd

hate a man touching her or even being near. But that wasn't how she'd felt at all.

She told herself that she'd been the only one who'd found the ribbon-untangling a sensual experience, that he'd merely been performing a service out of remorse. But she knew that wasn't true. She'd seen attraction in his eyes from the first moments of their meeting on the road.

She thought of what she'd seen in his eyes the night before—the pain, the anger, the remorse. And the barest wisp of playfulness, though he gave it little indulgence. But it was there, and it hinted at something deep down that was decent. She felt certain now that under his hardness was a kinder man he didn't want to let out. Far better for her that he didn't.

"But everybody likes me," Lizzie burst out.

Anna arched an eyebrow at her, and Lizzie's eyes lofted upward in exasperation. "Well, I mean that gentlemen always do."

Lizzie knew her worth in the eyes of men, but that was hardly a recipe for happiness. "You know, my dear, it's not a good idea to have all your connections with people be based solely on your appearance."

Lizzie crossed her arms, her fair, elegant eyebrows crimping tensely. "I wish I could just go back to Malta. Can't you convince him to send me back? He doesn't want me here anyway."

"Malta won't be the same," Anna said gently. "You know that."

"But we had family friends there, and I know they would take me in." She frowned and tugged a loose strand of her Botticelli hair into her mouth. Anna gave her a governess-ish look and Lizzie pulled it out again.

"Grandville won't let me stay beyond the month, will he?" she said. There was no whine in her voice, as might have been expected of a thwarted, pampered young lady, but rather the awful calm of someone who'd already faced too many hard truths. "He's going to send me away at the end of the month."

"Lizzie, I know he hasn't been welcoming. But maybe if you just be yourself, he might come around in his own fashion."

"He's my only remaining connection to my father," she said in a voice tinged with huskiness, "and I'm certain he was once a good man." Her lips pressed together unhappily. "But I don't understand him."

"I think you will have to be the one who makes the effort to establish a connection," Anna said, though she wasn't confident it would make any difference, because he was only tolerating Lizzie out of duty and guilt.

"If it doesn't work, you have to convince him to send me to Malta, or…"—Lizzie's brow drew together fiercely—"or I'll make him want to send me a lot farther away than the next girls' school."

"Oh, Lizzie, don't be foolish." Anna caught her eyes and made certain she was really listening. "You do realize that you won't be able to make him do anything he doesn't want to do? You may be clever, but Lord Grandville isn't the kind of man to be manipulated."

The mutinous expression in the girl's eyes did nothing to reassure her. "Lizzie?" she prompted.

"I understand," she said in a dull voice. She bent down and gathered the sketchbook and pencil she'd put down when she'd found the owl.

Anna accompanied her as they made their way to

their rooms, wondering how wrong it would be to finish the painting on the wall of her bedchamber herself and tell the viscount that Lizzie had done it. But what difference would it make anyway, in how he felt about his ward? Her scheme, which had initially seemed sensible, now looked like the clutching-at-straws idea it had always been.

⁂

"The chit's flown. Miss Bristol's decamped I tell you, Rawlins," the Marquess of Henshaw said to the burly young man standing in his study, where the gloom of a rainy evening was being kept at bay by a substantial fire. "I gave her a month to make her decision, and when I came for her yesterday, the girl was gone. What a minx!"

Henshaw had been thwarted, Jasper Rawlins knew. But there was also an unmistakable note of glee in his voice, as if a gauntlet had been thrown down for him. Jasper would have laughed at the idea of Anna Bristol being a minx if this hadn't all been so important.

When he'd sold *The Beautiful One* to the marquess, he'd known his fortunes as an artist were finally on the rise. It had taken Jasper two months of moments stolen from his work as Dr. Bristol's apprentice to create the drawings. He'd known the pictures were special, had seen his talent coming to fruition as he'd captured her hidden beauty.

It was a beauty only he had had the vision to see—even her own father hardly noticed her. There was something different and fresh about her, and it started with those clear, sherry-brown eyes that would have

suited one of those rare birds she loved so much. And her body…

Her sharp wit had doubtless chased off any suitors who might have noticed the gem hidden beneath her careless clothes and coiffures. Just as well for him, or she wouldn't have been such a find.

"Yes, a minx," Jasper agreed. It didn't behoove him to disagree with his new patron, though he wondered if it had been such a good idea after all, telling Henshaw Anna's name. He was just on the verge of suggesting another model for the painting—he had a pretty farmer's daughter in mind—when the marquess cried out exuberantly.

"By Jove, but I love a hunt."

"A hunt, my lord?"

"Yes, man. She's run off, and now the chase is on." The marquess rubbed his hands with glee as Jasper swallowed heavily.

"You want to pursue Miss Bristol?"

"Of course! We can leave first thing tomorrow."

"But…my lord…"

The marquess's face turned dark at his guest's unenthusiastic tone. "You'll help me find her, of course," Henshaw said. "The painting's no good to me without her."

He cast a shrewd look at Jasper. Henshaw was a ruddy-faced man of perhaps thirty with pale blond hair and taller than Jasper, though Jasper was burly while the marquess was softly corpulent. "I won't pay for a half-finished painting."

"Of course not."

Damn.

"I've shown *The Beautiful One* to all my friends, and they're panting to know who she is. But no one's to know her name until I reveal it—and the painting—at my house party next month. I've already boasted about how lifelike she's going to look as Aphrodite. Good enough to eat, ha-ha!"

God, what an oaf, Jasper thought. He was an artist, but he couldn't afford to care if Henshaw had ignorant reasons for liking his work. He needed the money from the painting, and he needed the exposure Henshaw would provide, the entrée into a world of wealthy patrons.

"Right," Jasper muttered.

"I want that painting finished, and I won't be made a fool of—she has to be in it. We'll simply find her and pay her. Everyone has a price."

Jasper was fairly certain that Anna Bristol did not, in fact, have a price. From what he could tell, she didn't give a fig about things like jewels and fine furnishings.

He burned with familiar frustration. His father had pushed him into studying medicine, but what he wanted was to create art. First, though, apparently, he was going to have to hunt down Anna Bristol, the little fool.

Six

It was well before dawn, but Anna was awake. It was spring, after all, and at home, one of her chief pleasures in the springtime was to rise early and sit in the cottage garden as the sun rose and listen to the dawn chorus.

There was something special about those dark morning hours when no one else was about and she could hear the thrushes and blackbirds chirp energetically as they tried to attract a mate. She liked to stay until the sun was up and watch them.

She'd missed her spring bird-watching in the last month. At Rosewood, there had been too many people around to do such a thing, and for the seamstress to be found sitting idle in the garden would have attracted comment.

But now she dressed quietly and tiptoed through the still-sleeping house. There was a door to the terrace outside the ballroom, and she moved through that grand, silent room and out to the freshness of the morning. The beautiful cacophony of birdsong, which had been muted inside by the heavy stone walls of the manor, greeted her as she stepped outside.

It was chilly and still dark, and she pulled her shawl snugly around her shoulders and moved to stand near the edge of the terrace and listen. She picked out the bold notes of a wren and smiled. Wrens were small but mighty, and she'd always admired their pluck.

Long minutes of contentment passed, restoring something in her, so that when she became aware of the sound of footsteps announcing someone coming out to the terrace, she was disappointed. But she could see nothing in the dark beyond a smudgy shadow moving closer.

"Who's there?" she said.

"Grandville." He drew near. The whites of his eyes showed faintly, as did the flash of his teeth when he spoke, but she couldn't see his expression.

"What are you doing out here?" she said.

A brief silence met her ridiculous words.

"I meant," she corrected herself, "that I didn't expect anyone else would be about. It's quite early after all."

"I might say the same. What are *you* doing out here at this hour?"

She weighed her thoughts, a reflex developed over the last month, but didn't see any reason to hide her purpose. "I like to listen to the birds."

"You got out of a comfortable bed to *listen to birds*?"

"Yes. They're quite glorious this morning, the wrens especially. And I think I may have heard a tawny owl."

"Oh, well, if you've heard a tawny owl," he said dryly, and she smiled, glad they couldn't see each other. "But can't you hear tawny owls from your room with the window open?"

"It's not the same. There's something about being outside at a time when you know you will be alone."

A brief, rusty chuckle met her words, the first sound of mirth she'd heard from him. "And here I've spoiled your solitude. Do forgive me."

Was he teasing her? She couldn't tell from his tone. "Well, obviously it's your estate. I might ask your pardon for spoiling the solitude of *your* morning."

Another silence. He must have expected and wanted solitude at this early hour, with no one to want anything from a man responsible for so much. He was the viscount, thus the eldest living male in his family, and however much he might want to isolate himself, he would always have demands on his time.

"Perhaps I will allow it this once."

Was he teasing her again? The impossibility of either of them seeing the other's expression gave their meeting an unusual, outside-of-time quality.

"How did you come by this powerful love of birds?" he asked.

Her father had published those two books on birds, and he'd treated the viscount's family. But there was no reason he should connect Anna Black with Dr. Matthew Bristol, physician and naturalist.

"I had a…friend who was something of a naturalist. He loved to study birds."

"A suitor?"

She almost laughed, not just at the idea of her father being her suitor, but at the idea of her having a suitor at all. Suitors had simply never pursued Dr. Bristol's unfashionable daughter, with her too-sharp wits and her skin that was often tan from chasing after birds.

As she'd grown up, Anna had decided, despite the occasional pangs of loneliness, that she didn't care.

Why should she want a man, she'd reminded herself, who might tell her what to do and what to wear, and who would have power over her? She'd grown up as free and unchecked as the birds she loved, and if that meant she'd also grown up without having cultivated all the graces that attracted gentlemen, so be it. She'd had her students and her own art to pursue, and her dream of the drawing school to sustain her.

"No. An older gentleman, just an acquaintance." It wasn't even hard to say such a thing about her father—he'd so tenaciously kept to himself. And yet, she'd loved him, and she disliked speaking of him this way. She needed to change the subject.

"What do you do at those cottages all day?"

"They are unfinished and I prefer to be involved in the work."

"Perhaps Lizzie might come with you? I'm certain she would be very happy for you to show them to her, and delighted if she might be allowed to help in any way."

"I don't need any help." Any warmth had fled from his voice. "If you'll excuse me, I've things to see to. And I wouldn't wish to keep you from your morning's pleasure."

He wanted to go off by himself. She'd often been happy alone, but the solitude this man was seeking wasn't bringing him pleasure. It was a retreat from life.

"Wait. Please."

She could feel that he hadn't moved away yet. She'd had an idea, prompted by the way she'd felt when he'd fixed her ribbons the first night, how the

kindness in his gesture had loosened something in her that had felt so bound up.

Even his begrudging hospitality had kindness in it; it hadn't been the sort of cold, unwelcoming accommodations and sour treatment she would have expected from the unhappy servants of a hard, angry master. No, she'd been given a nice guest chamber with a good fire and delicious food.

And that painting in her room—there was a playfulness in it that hinted at some past mood of joy. Stillwell might have a spartan, underfurnished look, but it was cheerfully tidy, and the grounds appeared well kept. His staff had been nothing but kind toward her and Lizzie, and that told her something: they were well treated and they liked their master.

As the viscount, he was doubtless accustomed to being the one to see to others' needs. He was clearly getting no pleasure, however, from other people. She guessed that his wife's death had made him want to retreat inwardly.

But Lizzie needed him. Anna told herself that was the only reason behind the offer she was about to make.

"Can I…offer you an embrace?"

She could feel him absorbing her words. He moved closer, and she caught the sound of his breathing.

Will thought he must have misheard her. She couldn't possibly have said what he thought she had, but already his pulse had quickened. He stepped closer still, close enough to catch a whiff of interesting, pleasing scents. "I beg your pardon?"

"I know it's an odd thing to say," she said in that straightforward voice. There was nothing flirtatious about Miss Anna Black, though neither was she sharp. She was calm and smart and persistent, and she also clearly thought nothing of doing unusual things like climbing trees to achieve her purposes.

"But it's just that, after my father's funeral," she continued, "our vicar embraced me, and in that moment I knew, truly, a small release of sorrow from his kindness. And I've lately come to think there must be something healing in the touch of our fellow creatures."

She sounded like a doctor suggesting a prescription. *Take the waters for your health. Clear broth after a fever. An embrace when despairing.*

He couldn't imagine any other woman he knew making such an offer and not appearing as though it were some sort of seduction. But she seemed to operate without any concern for being either beguiling or deferential, as sufficient unto herself as the birds she liked so much. In fact, she reminded him of a bird on the wing, soaring in the sky for purposes no mortal could guess.

He couldn't understand why she was offering him an embrace, but he didn't think she had any motive other than what she'd stated. Here was the woman who'd returned an owlet to its nest; perhaps she simply saw him as another living creature in need of the appropriate attention.

He should say no. But he didn't want to listen to his better nature just then.

"Yes," he said, and pulled her into his arms.

She did not feel like a vicar.

Her frame was slender within the circle of his arms, her ribs and shoulders and everything about her on a smaller scale than his own, that woman-scale he'd forgotten about. She embraced him back firmly—she meant to be purposeful, with her arms wrapped across the sides of his chest and meeting snugly against his back.

Her hand rubbed his back twice with some vigor, consolingly. He almost groaned; her sweet, earnest embrace was achingly erotic. Her small breasts, crushed between them, made a fascinating cushion across his chest that he longed to explore. She smelled intoxicatingly of simple things: honeysuckle and pencil lead and warm skin. He closed his eyes as her scent filled him, and he brushed his cheek against her temple.

Dear God, she felt so good. He wanted to keep her there, in his arms. He wanted to explore her body as he'd yearned to do from the moment she'd said the first impudent word to him. He *liked* this woman. He admired her spirit, and he was drawn to her careless beauty.

His head dipped lower to move his cheek against hers, and longing rushed through him forcefully.

"Anna," he whispered. She was making him so hot, burning him with exquisite pain, like heat applied to a frost-nipped body.

He turned his head and his lips were just about to meet the softness of her neck when she gently released her arms and stepped back, as if that had been the right amount of embracing for the purposes of consoling. Or perhaps she'd sensed that she'd unleashed something in him.

He let his arms fall, aware that he was aroused as he hadn't been in a year.

She'd meant to do something of simple human kindness, to behave as though they were only people and not a man and a woman, as though their bodies merely needed a sort of physical communication. That kind of communication *had* passed between them. But it had brought other feelings too, and strong desires.

He couldn't allow them.

Her arrival at Stillwell had jolted him, and her presence in his home was distracting him. But none of that really mattered. All the burning aside, his heart was a frozen lump. He hadn't cared about anything or anyone for the past year because he was unable to do so. He didn't have anything to give anyone else. Nor, he was certain, had this woman been offering anything else.

"Um…" she breathed, and her unaccustomed hesitation told him their embrace had not left her unaffected either.

"Well," he said softly, "shall I say thank you?"

Dawn was beginning to lighten the dark, and he could just see her looking at him steadily. He felt like a wolf being watched from on high by a sparrow.

"Don't," she said. "Don't be sarcastic about this. The man I met the first day—that's not who you are."

He was weak. She brought out his weakness, and he must resist.

"Don't you believe it. Good day, Miss Black."

He made for the sanctuary of the cottages.

❦

Anna had been startled by the experience of being in Lord Grandville's arms. She saw now that it had

been naive of her to think she could embrace him as though he were a cousin or an uncle or some grieving man from her church congregation. Men were not interchangeable with each other. *This* man was not.

The thing was, aside from that one occasion with the vicar, she'd never embraced a man to whom she wasn't related, and even then, she'd hardly ever embraced her father, aloof as he was. It wasn't as though she didn't know men and women could have sparks between them.

But she'd never felt such sparks, not before those moments when Lord Grandville had been untying her ribbons that first night, and maybe in some unacknowledged part of her, she'd wanted to feel the sparks again, to see if they'd really been there. To find out if his nearness and his touch really were as intoxicating as her memory had told her they'd been.

They were. The sparks were there, and she'd felt them the minute she'd stepped closer to him. Just absorbing the warmth given off by his body had given her an excited thrill, and then he'd pulled her into his arms.

He was strong, and his chest was hard, and she'd loved the feel of it against her. She'd had to force herself to remain calm, to pat his back consolingly even though she'd longed to explore the breadth of his back and let her hands wander everywhere. He'd smelled very, very good, like fresh water and some kind of man's soap.

She'd discovered something else while standing in his arms: she liked this man. Despite what had happened the first night, she felt he was trustworthy. She

had a sense that he'd insisted Lizzie leave because he wanted to protect her from the effects of his bitterness.

She wondered if their embrace had had any good effect on him, whether it had relieved any of his grief, softened any of the hardness. For Lizzie's sake, she hoped so. She certainly couldn't do any such thing again.

Over the following days, Anna watched in dismay as Lizzie fruitlessly stalked Lord Grandville with the attentiveness of a hunting dog after a fox, listening for footsteps that never came and staring out the back windows.

Of course, Lizzie proposed more than once that she and Anna walk out to the cottages and surprise him with a visit, but Anna discouraged her firmly, telling her that would likely make him angry. Since Lizzie desperately didn't want to anger him, she instead tried quizzing the servants discreetly about his movements. But his servants were touchingly protective of him, and continually managed to avoid providing answers.

Lizzie had thus risen extremely early several days in a row, in the hopes of catching him somehow before he left. But as she moaned to Anna later, if he was actually still in residence at Stillwell, he must be possessed of a magical cloak of invisibility, because she hadn't seen him in the flesh since the owl incident.

Anna suggested that Lizzie was being a bit dramatic and that the viscount was simply busy and had access to some private staircase. Lizzie must be patient and not expect to see him frequently, Anna advised, while privately seething as she watched the light begin to fade from the girl's countenance. Anna knew he

spent most of his time at the cottages, and was in fact fairly certain that he was the dark-haired person she'd glimpsed working on the roof of one of them; she could see the tops of the cottages from her bedchamber window.

The viscount was, however, apparently not uncaring about his niece's presence on the estate. The day after the owl incident, Anna and Lizzie had entered the old schoolroom to find a handsome new atlas awaiting them, and with it a stack of new schoolbooks. And Dart had informed them that his lordship had arranged for a pony for Miss Tarryton, should she wish to ride.

Lizzie had been in raptures over Lord Grandville's thoughtfulness, eager as she was for any proof that he remembered she was there, any sign that buried under his gruff demeanor was the man her father had loved. She longed to thank him in person for what he'd provided, but of course that hadn't been possible.

By the afternoon of their fifth day at Stillwell, Anna found herself entirely distracted with impotent fury at Lord Grandville. She'd seen that he was capable of tenderness, and he did care about Lizzie—why couldn't he spend just a little time with her?

She understood that his spirits were depressed by his wife's death. But as the only person currently being clear-sighted about Lizzie's future, she couldn't allow him to remain detached.

Seven

FIVE DAYS DOWN, A LITTLE OVER THREE WEEKS TO GO, Will thought as he stood watching his overseer demonstrate drainage ditches in the west fields. Except for that early-morning encounter with Anna, he'd managed to avoid his guests. Anna had pressed him about Lizzie, but she couldn't understand that he had nothing to offer his niece, and their presence was driving him to find ever more ways to stay out of his house.

If only he could forget about Anna and her funny embraces and impertinent ways. He'd been struggling all day—struggling since the moment he'd met her on the road in the rain—not to think about her, but it was no use, and the thinking would progress to *savoring* and finally turn into *imagining*, and there was no end, damn it all, to the imagining.

His overseer was certainly pleased to see his master in the fields, though. For weeks Mr. Temple had been urging him to come see the progress on the ditches, which Temple believed might benefit many areas on the estate. Will trusted the man implicitly and didn't feel the need to check his work, but now that he was here he had

to admit that maybe he'd been shifting too many details of the estate's management onto Temple's shoulders.

All around, his tenants were at work in the soil, hoeing and weeding. Stillwell had fine tenants, whose families had worked the land with care for generations, and watching them now, he felt a sharp stab of regret that there wouldn't be enough cottages for them all. Maybe Norris could see to the construction of some others for those who wouldn't benefit from the ones Will was finishing.

Except the cottages had to be done just so, and he didn't see how he could cede the supervision of their construction to someone else. He certainly couldn't envision overseeing a new round of building himself.

His attention was drawn to two mothers who knelt nearby, chatting and laughing as they made a game of showing their young children how to pull weeds. The children's earnest, ineffective efforts stirred a deep pang in him. Shut away in his routine, he'd forgotten about children.

Ginger had wanted babies. Exuberant, optimistic Ginger, who'd always lived in the moment.

How could so much love and goodness have been destroyed? He'd never understood until the day she died how helpless he was against what life could throw at him, and he hated that.

He looked away from his tenants. Now he remembered why he didn't come out to the fields.

"So, what do you think, my lord?" Mr. Temple said as Will turned toward him.

"Fine, Temple. Do as you see fit." And with that, he made for his horse.

He spent the rest of the afternoon in a grim mood, sanding smooth one of the cottages' doors.

Early that evening, he let himself in the servants' entrance in the back of Stillwell. Dart, with his customary omniscience, was waiting in the hallway leading to the family apartments.

He bowed and handed Will a folded piece of paper with an apologetic look. Will was aware that his faithful servants felt he ought to be protected from troubling things like importunate relations, and he knew he ought not to let them shield him, but it was easier that way.

"Miss Black was most insistent, my lord," Dart said, "that this was of an urgent nature requiring your immediate attention."

Will cursed quietly under his breath and took the note.

Dear Lord Grandville,

As you may know, your ward, Miss Elizabeth Tarryton, or Lizzie, as she prefers to be called, is now in residence at Stillwell Hall. For your information, she can be found in the schoolroom in the morning, in the garden in the afternoon if the weather is fine, and in the evening in your dining room. As her uncle and her guardian, surely you will not wish to miss the opportunity to spend time in her company.

Yours,
The Governess

Saucepot! He was doing his best to ride out their presence here and determine some appropriate situation for his niece. But Anna Black clearly was not one to accept circumstances quietly, and considering all the bold things she'd done since arriving, he didn't trust her not to escalate her efforts.

He imagined her taking Lizzie around to meet all his neighbors, or sending out invitations to a dinner under his name, forcing his hand somehow. She was clearly accustomed to doing as she deemed necessary, and she was making a crusade out of his niece and her future.

It was almost as though there were something personal in Lizzie's situation that compelled her. He wondered what such a thing might be.

He crumpled the paper and addressed the waiting Dart.

"Bring Miss Black to the library at once."

Dart didn't blink an eye at the idea that his master was going to receive the governess in the dusty garments in which he'd been laboring all day.

"Very good, my lord."

Will was staring unseeingly at a bookshelf full of Greek philosophy when a knock sounded on the library door several minutes later. He told himself he was absolutely not looking forward to seeing her and to the release of arguing with her, but he knew that to be a lie.

"Come in," he said in his best lord-and-master voice. He turned around. "Ah, the governess," he said as she moved into the room. "And owl savior."

She lifted a single eyebrow at him, and he caught a smile starting to form on his lips and let it die away.

He took a seat behind the large old walnut desk that had been used by generations of viscounts. He was determined that the tree-climbing Anna Black would understand a few things about her position at Stillwell.

She was wearing the abysmal blue gown, which looked to have once been periwinkle but was now only faintly blue. And why did it have to hang off her so unattractively when he knew very well now how feminine was the slim body underneath?

"Yes, my lord?"

"Where is my ward?"

"I believe she is sewing. She did not require my company."

She folded her hands in front of her colorless skirts, doubtless unaware that the movement brought forward some of the loose fabric around her torso, delineating the graceful curve of her waist on one side. Her curly, glossy black hair was pulled into its usual messy knot on the back of her head; her customary look seemed to be that of someone who had little interest in her appearance.

And yet, she had those beautiful sherry eyes, and those black, assertive eyebrows, a pert nose, and that saucy pink mouth. She was invitingly lovely, like an exquisite wildflower growing at the edge of a rarely used path.

"And how do you plan to occupy your time together over the next month, Anna Black, barring any more calamities among the fauna of Stillwell?"

Did her lips twitch? "I thought we might study French and geography, and sketch in the garden when the weather is fine. Unless my lord wishes to propose some other course of study?"

He ignored her and took up the letter opener sitting on his desk and tapped it against the desktop. "What were you doing just now?"

She regarded him steadily as a few moments passed. "I wasn't aware that what I might be doing in my free time would be of any concern to you. My lord."

He abandoned the letter opener and took his time lighting two of the candles on his desk against the fading light. He sat back in his chair and crossed his arms. She continued to stand before him in ostensible meekness.

"Don't be impertinent, Anna. Though I am persuaded that is your customary mode of expression. You are living in my home and are in my employ, and your activities are certainly of interest to me."

"Miss Black, if you please, and I was reading."

"As I am paying you, and quite handsomely, I believe I shall feel free to call you Anna."

She opened her mouth, doubtless to argue with him, but then seemed to think better of it and said nothing. He was almost disappointed.

"And what were you reading, Anna? I suppose you helped yourself to a book from my library."

"I brought my own book."

"A novel of gothic horror, eh? The innocent young lady meets the beast of the manor?"

She tipped her head in answering mockery. And why had he said that, damnation? He was flirting with her.

"A book of natural history."

A singular choice for a young woman, but why should he be surprised, given her interest in birds? He frowned, realizing that probing her reading choices

was making him want to know more about her when he needed to keep this impersonal.

Her face looked less drawn now than it had when she arrived, and though the hospitality of Stillwell had clearly been putting roses in her cheeks and thus giving her greater energy for impudence, he felt pleased that she no longer had the look of a neglected kitten. His eyes wandered over her ugly gown. He supposed she could afford no better, and the thought made him feel guilty all over again for the way he'd treated her when she'd arrived.

"I shall provide you with several new gowns. The one you are wearing is unfit for the governess of my ward."

"No, thank you. The gown I am wearing is adequate."

"It looks like it was made from a slurry of dead flowers. The servants will all be wondering why Lizzie's governess is so poorly attired."

"As I shall only be here for three more weeks, it makes little difference." Her eyes flicked downward to his old brown waistcoat, still sprinkled with sawdust.

"And I wasn't aware that you were so very particular about attire, my lord. Your clothes are quite possibly shabbier than mine, and you can afford much better. One might ask why a viscount would choose to wear such things. But then, one might also ask why a viscount is working away on the roofs of cottages."

He crossed his arms and gave her a withering look, but she was unaffected. He, however, felt himself grow warm as his eyes sank into hers. They were so full of light.

He stood up and turned away to look out the

window behind his desk. The sun had almost set, and the smears of red and purple along the horizon reminded him of countless sunset rides he'd taken with Ginger, her elegant back straight and the ribbons on one of her fancy hats flying as she galloped laughingly from him. She'd wanted to ride Strider that last day. Strider, who was Will's horse and a more powerful mount than she was used to.

He cursed the turmoil his ward's arrival—and perhaps worse, Anna's—had brought and clasped his hands hard behind his back. He would have been ashamed for Ginger and David to know how poorly he'd welcomed Lizzie, but surely they would have seen how little he could offer her that was good?

"You made so bold as to send me a note about my ward."

"Perhaps a guest might be forgotten in a place as large as Stillwell."

If Ginger were still alive, doubtless they would have been close to their niece, but now it was impossible. Anna might be determined to push him to be the kind of guardian she thought Lizzie needed, but whoever that man might be, it was not he. He must keep Anna in her place, whether she wanted to accept what that was or not.

"In addition to Stillwell, Anna, I own other significant properties in England. I could, like a wizard, change your life in a moment by handing you more money than you would know what to do with, and it wouldn't impoverish me in the least."

"My lord is a most wealthy and powerful aristocrat," she said to his back in an unremarkable voice.

No one spoke to him the way she did! Where was

her subservience, the need she should have, as a vulnerable woman, to seek his favor? Except, from the moment he'd met her, the one thing he'd have said about her was that, while many women cultivated vulnerability, she scorned it. He turned around.

"You seem to have no very high opinion of viscounts and their kind," he said slowly as a thought dawned. "That leads me to believe that one of my peers has offended you in the past."

She flushed, and that told him something.

"Someone has!" he said, coming around to the front of the desk near where she stood. He leaned back against its edge, half-expecting her to back away now that he was close to her, but she didn't. He supposed she felt it a point of honor not to do so. He crossed his arms. "Who was he? I would know his name."

She made no reply.

"Well?"

She lifted her chin airily as if she were unbothered, though he was not fooled. Her color had gone higher. "Whatever may have happened to me before I arrived here is not your concern."

Had some aristocrat interfered with her? He was furious at the thought of some man taking advantage of this unusual woman, with her athletic grace and her messy black hair and steady brown eyes. Already he himself had insulted her. He couldn't bear to think that she'd been offered any other offenses.

He remembered how she'd been that first night, with that defiant look that told of hardship endured. "*Must the volume of a woman's protests gauge her innocence?*" she'd said.

"Anna, you are under my protection now. If some man has offended you, I would know his name." He paused. "Did one of my peers molest you in any way?"

"No," she said firmly. "And I don't need any protection."

Perhaps it had been something to do with a lover's spat of some kind. He found he didn't want to consider Anna with a suitor.

It didn't surprise him that she would insist she didn't need his protection, though whether or not she wanted it, should it ever be necessary, her wishes on that score would be irrelevant.

"You're something of a mystery, Anna. Indeed," he said, cocking his head, "I wonder very much who the devil you are."

❧

Anna forced herself not to betray in any way that she didn't want Lord Grandville probing her background. She couldn't afford to even think about the Marquess of Henshaw lest she grow tense or vulnerable.

"Why should you need to know anything about me, beyond the fact that I am your ward's governess?"

"What exactly were you employed in doing at Rosewood?"

"I was the seamstress."

"What? I thought you were a teacher."

His outraged expression made her want to laugh. She knew him a little now, perhaps more than a little, and she felt a sudden wish to know him as he might have been before his wife's tragedy. But that was a totally inappropriate wish. Even if there weren't a

scandalous book of naked pictures of her circulating among his peers, he was a viscount and she was the daughter of a country doctor.

But she was also a woman, and he was a very, very handsome man, albeit one with a generous smudge of something dark on his cheekbone and another one on the side of his neck. He'd obviously just come from his cottages; he was wearing a loose, frayed brown coat that had seen better decades, and his trousers had clearly been laundered so many times that their color could only be called darkish. But the soft, old clothes couldn't disguise the hardness of his muscles, and they hung with an appealing drape on his long limbs.

"I can't be responsible for what you have assumed."

"And so my niece is to have a seamstress as her companion?" His dark brows drew together in a scowl over stormy blue eyes. He was very good at bluster. She suspected it was an easy way to keep people distant.

"You didn't seem so particular about Miss Tarryton's companions before."

"And now I have engaged a hoyden for a governess." The note of exasperation in his voice made her want to smile. Was she insane, to be so enticed by this powerful, difficult man?

He watched her for a minute. "You said that your family was gone," he said finally in a softer tone. "Tell me about them, Anna. Where did you live?"

Oh, this wasn't good. She couldn't risk him knowing more about her because of the chance, however slim, that it might somehow help the marquess find her, but

she didn't have any confidence in her ability to create a believable fabric of lies. Nor did she like the idea of doing so. She must simply give him as little information as possible. "A village to the west."

"And your family?" he pressed. "Who were they?"

"They were not people of any particular importance."

"I doubt it felt that way to you."

He was waiting for her to say more, but how could she? It had been a year since her brilliant, complicated father had died, but thinking about him could still bring a lump to her throat, and the last thing she wanted was to stand before Viscount Grandville on the verge of tears.

"Tell me about them," he urged softly.

She forced a neutral tone. "My mother died when I was a baby, and I had one older brother, who was lost at sea some years ago. My father died last year."

"I'm sorry. You've had your share of troubles, haven't you, Anna?"

The kindness in his voice touched her and softened something in her that needed to be hard. She wished he would go back to blustering at her—it was safer.

"Was your father a gentleman?"

"He was an educated man."

"A scholar then?"

"Of sorts."

"And did he never remarry?"

"No."

"So you were raised by a man. This perhaps accounts for some of the less pliable aspects of your character. I think you must have been something of

a wild little thing, roaming about the countryside, climbing trees and making friends with animals."

He chuckled, and she was surprised by the way it changed his face and brought a little light to his usually haunted, dark blue eyes. *Oh...* She could see how this man might be completely irresistible.

"But why are you now forced to look for work?" he pressed. "What about your home?"

"It is...lost to me."

He frowned. "Was it because of debts? But surely you had friends who might have helped you? You are educated, the daughter of an educated man. Was there no one to be a friend to you, so that you were not forced out of your home and driven to do menial work? Were they even *feeding* you at that school?"

She laughed and didn't correct his assumption that money troubles were why she'd left home. He seemed touchingly outraged on her behalf. But she shouldn't be surprised; he was used to being responsible for other people. Though she felt that being a viscount was more than a role to him, that his sense of responsibility was innate to his character. He clearly had a strong sense of justice, or he wouldn't have felt so bad about the proposition he'd made the first night.

It was his sense of responsibility, she'd come to see, that made him believe he wasn't fit to care for Lizzie.

"You must see how you have me at a disadvantage," she said, "how, because of our positions, you might feel entitled to quiz me endlessly while offering no justifications for your own behavior or choices. Why, for instance, you appear to be building those cottages for your tenants yourself."

He arched one dark, well-shaped eyebrow haughtily, and it made something flip over inside her.

"That's because I'm the viscount and you're the servant. But you're not used to being a servant, are you, Anna?" He cocked his head thoughtfully. "What about after Lizzie's month is up here? I'm not sure I like the idea of you with a future in some menial position."

Oh, that she definitely didn't need—Lord Grandville feeling responsible for her future along with Lizzie's.

But he seemed to have reconsidered his words as well, because he sighed and waved his hand dismissively. "Go. You may go now."

She didn't move. They'd still made no progress toward what Lizzie needed from him. "Shall we expect you at dinner this evening, my lord?"

He inclined his head. "I cannot conceive, Anna, what has given you the notion that you might order me about."

"If you can't agree to make an effort to get to know Lizzie, then I'm afraid our bargain is voided and I will have to leave."

"You would forego your wages over this?"

Doing so would leave her desperate again, but she didn't know how else to get his attention for Lizzie. "If necessary. You may have supported your ward in lavish style since her family died, but money is no substitute for affection."

His eyes looked heavenward. "Do you appoint yourself my conscience?"

"I do care what happens to her. She is a bright, beautiful, and good young lady."

"She is apparently not so very good or she wouldn't

have been sent down from school. What was it she did, anyway?"

"She's only sixteen," she said, ignoring his question, "and has lost her family. It wouldn't cost you much effort to at least come to dinner and converse with her. If you would spend some time with her, I'm sure it would be to your mutual benefit."

He seemed to weigh her words.

"You're hurting her, you know, by avoiding her," she said. "Try to see it her way. She has no family to count on now but you."

"I know that. And I'm sorry about it. But I also think it will be harder to keep things separate if she becomes... attached." He hesitated. "I'm a single man. I keep to myself here. I'm not going to go to Town or throw balls. And, damn it, she reminds me too much..."

"Of the past?"

"Well, yes."

"But all we have is now," she said.

His mouth tightened, as though he didn't wish to be reminded that each of them had a life to be lived.

"Very well, I promise not to *avoid* her. I will come to dinner tonight. But, Anna," he said sternly, "remember, at the end of the month, she too will be leaving for a new situation. Another school will be found, or some other arrangement made. And it will be your job to see that she's ready to go."

"I understand," she said quietly.

"You will of course be at dinner tonight as well, Anna."

Oh, not that. This conversation, their embrace from earlier with its irresistible sparks, the attraction she felt for this man... She was more than a little fascinated

by him. She could feel herself wanting him to like her and weighing his words for flirtation, though she knew little of such things. She, who'd never drawn the attention of a man before the abominable Rawlins had shown up in her life. She, who needed to finish out this month at Stillwell and take her money and go north.

What she didn't need was extra time in the viscount's presence, and certainly not sitting at his table like some sort of guest or equal.

"Surely you would rather dine with Lizzie alone."

"No. And this way I can be certain the conversation won't lag, as you seem to have no trouble making speeches."

"As you wish," she finally said, because she could hardly refuse. "If my lord is finished with me?"

"It is customary, Anna, for the viscount to dismiss the servant," he said, but without any real spirit, and she turned to go.

She was almost to the door when a knock sounded on the other side and Dart appeared.

"My lord, the Dowager Lady Grandville has arrived."

Behind her Lord Grandville received the news with silence. And then a muttered curse.

Eight

"SHOW HER IN," LORD GRANDVILLE SAID, AND DART retreated to the corridor, closing the door just as Anna reached it. Apparently the viscount's mother was here. He didn't sound pleased to see her, though as this appeared to be his usual reaction to visitors, she wasn't surprised. She reached for the door handle.

"Where do you think you're going?" His voice sounded deeper than usual.

"Upstairs, of course, to prepare for dinner."

"I require your presence here."

"Oh, surely not," she said, turning around. He didn't look as though he were jesting. "You will want to receive your mother alone."

"Stepmother. And do not tell me what I want. You have an appalling habit of doing so."

"Very well," she said, coming back toward the desk. "If you're going to be overbearing, what can I do? I'm but a poor governess."

"What you're going to be in a moment is mincemeat."

The door opened again to reveal a woman who looked to be only a year or two older than the

viscount. She was several inches shorter than Anna, with beautiful butter-yellow hair shot through with soft strands of cream, which was pulled into a neatly wound braid high on her head. She wore a handsome dark blue frock that fit her gently rounded figure well, and carried a stuffed-looking reticule that had a rolled paper and some ribbons protruding from its top.

She seemed to draw herself up in the doorway before she entered the room.

"Grandville," she said warmly as she approached him. She let her reticule fall onto a side table as she passed by it and moved toward him, lifting her arms as if she would embrace him. But he stood unmoving, and she stopped and let her hands fall back to her sides.

"Judith," he replied in a bland voice, executing a barely perceptible bow. "I am surprised to see you here."

His stepmother's skin was fair, her cheeks perhaps a touch more hollow than they might have been in younger days, though the effect served only to make her more handsome. An apricot flush spread over them at her stepson's cold greeting. "I...came for a visit."

From behind Lady Grandville came a yawning sound, and a regal liver-and-white spaniel emerged to stand like a buffer between her and the viscount. Lord Grandville's eyes flicked downward to the dog, and he looked away, as if the sight of the animal pained him. What was going on?

"I suppose you would think it your duty," he said in that same mild tone which he might have used for a tradesman who'd shown up uninvited. Anna had glimpsed warmth and even a dark humor in him only

moments before, but that had clearly been locked away again.

Though Lady Grandville would be justified in being offended at his words, she seemed unsurprised by his treatment. But not unpained—the corners of her mouth trembled a little before she coerced them back to a smile, as if she were determined to be kind and patient no matter the provocation.

"Of course I didn't come just out of duty," she said. "I came out of affection."

"Then I thank you for the pleasure of your company today," he said, not sounding in the least grateful, "but I haven't time for visitors."

The dog at Lady Grandville's side tossed its head and pressed it against her skirts, as if to give her courage. She seemed to draw herself up.

"I won't be put off, Grandville. You've been locked up here alone for months. I know you're grieving, but…this isn't healthy. I'm concerned about you. With your father gone, I must act as I believe he'd want. And I'm certain he wouldn't have wanted you to shut yourself away."

His brows drew into slashes, and the thick fringe of lashes that hinted at boyishness couldn't soften the hard glint in his eyes. "Oh, for pity's sake. Can you never learn that your interference isn't wanted?"

And with that, he left the room.

Anna was still absorbing the full awkwardness of what had just happened as she glanced at Lady Grandville. The woman looked unhappy, but she didn't look surprised by his harshness.

The woman's eyes fell on Anna. "And you are…?"

"Miss Anna Black, ma'am." She curtsied. "I am Miss Tarryton's governess."

Lady Grandville's brow furrowed slightly, and Anna said, "My lord's ward has come to stay at Stillwell."

Lady Grandville absorbed this information. "Why, she must be David's daughter."

"Yes."

"I confess myself surprised that Grandville invited her here."

"Her arrival was unexpected. She had been at school, but the headmistress felt she would fare better in his lordship's care. I accompanied her here, and Lord Grandville engaged me as her governess. He is in the process of finding a new situation for her."

"Interesting," Lady Grandville said. "He's been alone here since his wife's death, as far as I know."

"I think…" Anna hesitated.

"Do feel you may speak plainly, Miss Black."

"Well, perhaps her arrival may do them both some good. It's very easy for a viscount to isolate himself from people."

"We're a warm family, aren't we? Though of course Grandville would prefer to believe that he and I have never been family at all."

"Maybe it would be best not to take his behavior personally," Anna said gently.

"Oh, I don't blame him for hating me," her companion replied. "I made mistakes. Let's just say he was very surprised when his father married me."

"I'm sure it's not as bad as all that," Anna said.

"It is, actually," the other woman said. "But I loved

Alistair Halifax, and I do care what happens to his sons." She sighed. "Perhaps I shall retire to my room."

As Lady Grandville was leaving, Anna saw her reticule.

"Don't forget this, ma'am," she said, picking it up. As she did so, she saw that the rolled paper protruding from it was a newspaper, and she glimpsed a headline: *Who is The Beautiful One?*

She couldn't quite swallow her gasp.

"Miss Black?" Lady Grandville said. "Is something amiss?"

"Oh—no," Anna said, walking toward her with the reticule.

Lady Grandville took it, her eyes falling on the paper. She pulled it out. "I suppose you haven't seen the latest news yet. Would you like this? I've finished with it."

"Yes, thank you," Anna said, certain guilt must be written all over her features. Her heart pounded furiously. How many people must now have seen and heard of that accursed book if it was in the newspaper?

At that moment the library door opened, and Lizzie herself entered with a book under her arm. She was dressed beautifully, as she had been every day. Her gown was a fresh green muslin that seemed to make her blue eyes brighter, and it looked to have been designed to flatter every feminine curve of her youthful form. Her red-gold hair was dressed prettily, with soft curls framing her face, a look she'd surely accomplished on her own, since the household had no lady's maid.

"I beg your pardon," Lizzie said. "I didn't know anyone was in here."

"That's all right, Lizzie," Anna said, and introduced them.

Lady Grandville smiled kindly. "I knew your father and your aunt, Miss Tarryton. Such lovely people."

"Will you be staying at Stillwell long, Lady Grandville?" Lizzie asked with a trace of eagerness Anna couldn't miss. Likely she was already hoping to charm Lady Grandville into advocating for her with her stepson, but that hope was unlikely to come to fruition.

"I'm not certain," Lady Grandville said. "But while I'm here I shall enjoy getting to know you, my dear. And you must call me Judith—after all, we are practically family. And now I'd better go and see where Dart has put my trunk, so I can change for dinner. Is Grandville setting a very fine table these days?"

"Oh, he doesn't come to dinner," Lizzie said, a trace of bitterness pinching her pretty mouth. It was a mouth that looked as though a discreet amount of lip rouge had been applied to it.

"Actually," Anna said, "the viscount plans to join us for dinner tonight."

"He's coming?" Lizzie's face instantly lit up. "But why didn't you say so right off? I must change, and there's hardly any time!" And with the quickest of curtsies, she was gone.

Lady Grandville shared a look with Anna. "I hope he won't disappoint her too badly."

"Yes," she agreed.

❧

Anna sought the privacy of her bedchamber, where she sat on her bed and took the newspaper out of her

pocket, already dreading reading it. It was dated two days before.

> *All the* ton *is abuzz with curiosity over a certain very naughty book—and the identity of the woman shown within, known as the Beautiful One. Is she an actress? The daughter of a country squire? A milkmaid? Rumors are flying!*
>
> *While some lucky gentlemen have seen the book, others are desperate for a glimpse of this paragon of beauty. Lord …shaw, the proud owner of this scandalous book of drawings, has promised a treat for all the guests at his annual house party this year: the unveiling of a painting of the Beautiful One—and of the identity of the woman herself!*
>
> *Invitations to this event are extremely sought-after this year, and a number of wicked gentlemen have pledged to discover her identity before then and have been placing bets at White's.*
>
> *Wherever you are, O Beautiful One, you shall not remain nameless for long!*

She gripped the paper with shaking hands. The marquess hadn't forgotten about her as she'd so fool-ishly hoped. And it was all much, much worse than she could have imagined.

He must surely be looking for her. With the whole *ton* expecting to see her in his painting, he would not want to disappoint.

More men had now seen the book and were making bets about her.

How she hated Rawlins and the marquess. Fury

took hold of her, and before she could think, she'd grabbed the small crockery vase on her nightstand and thrown it against the wall.

She blinked in shock at the mess. What was wrong with her?

Clearly, she must pull herself together.

She picked up the pieces and put them in the night-stand drawer. She was just nudging the last small bits of china under the bed with her toes when a knock sounded at her door.

It was Lizzie, in her dressing gown.

"Lizzie! Why aren't you dressed yet? You'll be late for dinner."

Lizzie closed the door and laughed. She'd dressed as far as her hair, which was arranged in a pretty, high, plaited knot. One hand was behind her back, as if she was hiding something.

"Gentlemen expect a lady to be a little late," she said. "It increases their suspense."

"I doubt your uncle is like that. And you want to make a good impression."

"Don't worry—I mean to. And anyway, I saw Lady Grandville's maid taking her gown downstairs to be ironed, so she'll be late, too. But you're coming to dinner as well, and here"—she brought her hand forward with a flourish—"I thought you might like something pretty to wear."

It was a pink gown. *Pink*. Anna had never worn pink in her life. She couldn't imagine its candy-sweet softness on her.

"Oh, Lizzie," she said kindly, "this is so thoughtful of you. But I'm your governess, and I could never

wear such a thing to dinner at his lordship's table. It wouldn't be appropriate."

Lizzie cast her eyes to the ceiling. "Who cares about appropriate?"

Anna reminded herself that when she was sixteen, she'd thought she knew better than any number of people as well. Lizzie would doubtless think quite differently of her badly dressed governess if she knew that Anna's naked image was currently making the rounds of the *ton*. Though if anyone would be inclined to overlook the scandal, it would be Lizzie, who would probably just encourage her to enjoy the attention.

Anna smiled. "As your governess, I do."

"But I'm dying to see you in something pretty. Your dresses are so drab." Lizzie laid the dress over the back of the chair in front of Anna's vanity. "I'll leave it here, in case you change your mind. I have another one that's similar, so I don't need it. No arguments!"

Anna didn't suppose it would do any good to say she'd never wear it. Instead she put her hands on Lizzie's shoulders and gently turned her around. "Very well. But *you* must finish dressing and not keep Lord Grandville waiting."

"I have some Pear's Liquid Bloom of Roses, too," Lizzie pressed, "if you should like to enhance your cheeks a bit."

"Face paint? Certainly not. Nor should you use such things. You're far too young, and you're already entirely lovely."

Lizzie's only reply as she left was a giggle.

So, Lizzie and Lady Grandville would both be late.

This meant that Anna might have a chance to talk to the viscount.

She fluttered her fingers over the pink gown. It was gossamer fine, fragile enough to be easily torn and smudged. Her eyes went to the looking glass on the vanity beyond.

Her thick, curly black hair was collected in its customary rough knot, the unruly strands pulling in bumpy sections across her head—she'd long ago abandoned trying to get it to lie smoothly. And her eyebrows were surely too strong—mannish, she'd always thought, and her face, too, with its angles and planes that seemed to her like a miniature version of her father's face. It was a sharp face, not soft and delicate, as women were supposed to be.

Flirtation and the artfulness of attraction were foreign to her. She'd grown up amid talk of the latest discoveries in medicine and her father's studies of birds. She could draw a sparrow hawk in intricate detail and knew the correct dose of willow bark to relieve a headache, but she didn't know about plucking eyebrows and piercing ears, and she'd never cared about fabrics or threads or all the other things she might have shared with a mother or sister.

She wasn't certain she missed those things exactly. But…Lord Grandville made her feel more aware of herself as a woman.

She changed into her brown gown and, smoothing the wrinkles out of it with a few rough swipes of her hands, went downstairs.

Nine

HE WAS IN THE LIBRARY, STANDING WITH HIS BACK TO her as she entered, and gazing at a small painting hanging on the wall by the night-dark window.

She liked the library, a room that was both grand and cozy. Its tall, handsome bookcases were filled with volumes new and old, and along the far wall behind the substantial desk, a set of French doors led onto the terrace and a view during the day of undulating fields and clusters of ash and oak trees. There were a few marble busts here and there, and a pair of chairs upholstered in a faded cornflower blue stood in welcome repose near the hearth, contributing to the room's feeling of cozy welcome, though they did make her wonder anew why some parts of Stillwell were spartanly furnished with threadbare furnishings.

He turned as she closed the door behind her, and the wary look in his eye told her he'd thought she might be his stepmother.

He'd changed into gentlemen's clothes. Of course he would come to dinner with his niece and stepmother well groomed. Still, she was hardly prepared

for the sight of him freshly shaved and with his wavy, dark brown hair trimmed into neatness, his broad shoulders encased in a bottle-green coat, and his long legs showing to advantage in a pair of black trousers.

It wasn't that he'd been unappealing in his work clothes, but now he looked darkly impeccable and exceedingly handsome, and very much the viscount. When he was wearing the old clothes, the distance in their rank was less noticeable to her. But it was always there, and now she was reminded.

She hadn't forgotten how it had felt to be in his arms, nor the wonderful way he smelled up close and the momentary bliss she'd known on that chilly, dark spring morning. She knew she wanted to be in his arms again, and that, of course, this couldn't happen.

"Ah, Anna. And where is my ward? She *is* coming to dinner, is she not? You have, after all, commanded that I be here."

"Yes." She moved to join him by the painting. "Lizzie and Lady Grandville will be down shortly."

At the mention of his stepmother, he pressed his lips together and returned to gazing at the painting. But she felt that she still had his attention.

"My lord, I wonder if you realize what a benefit your stepmother's arrival might be to Lizzie. How good it might be for Lizzie to spend time in her company and get to know her."

He turned around, and the hard expression on his face startled her. "You don't care for the wise course, do you, Anna? Or the path of least resistance? But this is one area where I will allow you no leeway whatsoever."

"But she might be a friend to Lizzie," she pressed,

"now, when she needs one so much. She could introduce her to society, perhaps take her to Town and give her a season."

"No." The masculine planes of his face seemed to have grown more pronounced. His dark blue eyes fastened on her with irritation from behind their inky lashes. "Has anyone ever told you that there's such a thing as too much persistence?"

"I don't believe I've ever heard that. Anyway, in Lizzie's case, I am prepared to be annoying."

"I can see that." He gave a heavy sigh. "I won't have Judith chaperoning her. She is not as wonderful as you think her to be. Shall I tell you about her? My parents were very happily married for all of my youth. The picture of contentment, a blessing to their friends and family. When I was eighteen, my mother became ill, and my father nursed her for a year with care and affection. He also began to seek comfort in a young mistress. That woman was Judith, and shortly after my mother died, he married her."

"Oh," she said quietly. "That seems...complicated."

"It wasn't that complicated. She was the daughter of a lawyer whom my father met on one of his visits to Town, a woman a mere three years older than I was. She saw her chance to be viscountess, and she cultivated him."

"I find it hard to believe she was that calculating."

"Believe it. When they married a few months after my mother died, Judith proceeded to do everything she could to erase our mother's presence. She had the paintings of Mother shifted to unused rooms and changed the way we did everything. I even overheard

her telling my father she thought Mother might have had a lover, which was ridiculous."

"Very well, I see it would be hard to trust her. And I can imagine it was awkward having a woman nearly your own age for a stepmother. But this all happened years ago. She was young. Perhaps she's changed."

He gave her a skeptical look, and she had to admit it did seem that his stepmother had given him much reason to doubt her. Though Lady Grandville had been so frank with her, admitting she'd made mistakes. Anna liked her.

"And what about your father's part in this? You're putting a lot on your stepmother, but he was capable of making his own choices."

"Enough of Judith," he said, waving his hand. "She will, God willing, be gone from Stillwell tomorrow morning."

Anna rather thought that Lady Grandville, who'd remained so steadfast in the face of her stepson's cool welcome, might not depart as quickly as he expected. But that was between the two of them.

"Come then, Governess, now that you are here, entertain me with your knowledge. Tell me something useful: The order of Spanish monarchs, how to draw a butterfly, your favorite part of speech."

He wanted distraction. She'd already guessed that arguing with her provided a respite from things he didn't want to think about. She sighed. "I am fond of the semicolon. And you, I suppose, prefer the period, which lets you say 'my will be done.'"

His bark of laughter gave her a little thrill, a sense of victory even. And, oh, how handsome he was with

the sides of his mouth curled up and a spark of mirth in his eyes.

"Not a flattering portrait in the least," he said, "though I don't suppose you would have such a thing to offer about me."

"Not true," she said. "I've heard these cottages you are making for your tenants are very fine. A generous thing for a master to provide."

His expression turned sober. "They were an idea that my late wife and I conceived of together."

"And you are building them yourself."

He shrugged. "Builders did most of the work. I'm merely doing the finishing. I like to keep my hands busy."

She was curious about something she'd noticed in the painting behind him, which he'd been looking at earlier. The picture was of a lake surrounded by cypresses. On the far bank, two figures sprawled lazily, and behind them people milled about, as if at a party. The whole feel of the painting—the colors, the light—was decidedly not English.

"Come, my lord, it's your turn to tell me something. Why is it that one of the people in that painting behind you looks familiar?"

His eyes settled on her. "I thought you were going to dress for dinner, but this is merely the other vile gown. Where do you get them? Is there perhaps a clutch of trolls somewhere sewing for you?"

She ignored him and peered closer at the painting. "It's you, isn't it, cavorting with the party people? I can see your viscountish nose, and isn't that a cloud of sour arrogance hovering about you?" She squinted at the

details. "No, oddly. You look decidedly carefree. In fact, rather like a young peasant. And is your shirt untied?"

He crossed his arms and leaned back against the wall to the side of the painting. "I was on holiday in Italy. Why don't you get a magnifying glass so you can see how I've arranged my hair?"

"Tell me about Italy. Did you love it?"

"Such an inquisitive governess."

He had a deep voice, and close as they stood to each other, it curled into her ears gratefully. She knew she would have been happy to trade questions with him all night just to hear it, which was not good at all, but she would allow herself this small indulgence. Somehow, talking with him soothed her wonderfully. She told herself this was merely because in his way, he treated her as an equal, something she'd missed over the last month, but it was far more than that. Talking with him—being with him—brought out new and magical feelings she'd never experienced before.

She wasn't so naive that she didn't realize these were the feelings of attraction—and a fairly strong attraction, it seemed—but she'd gone her whole life without knowing them, and she couldn't turn away from experiencing them now, if only a little bit. After she went north to her aunt's, she might very well have only them to savor for the rest of her life.

"I thirst for knowledge," she said.

His lips quirked. "I traveled there a few years ago with my younger brother, Tommy, just before my engagement."

Her heart gave a skip of fear at the mention of his brother, the one person in his family who might

recognize her. As casually as possible, she asked, "And where is your brother? Does he visit Stillwell often?"

"He's in Italy, along with our Halifax cousins. Apparently we had such a famous time there that he couldn't resist going back."

Relief flooded her. "Oh?" she said. "What did the two of you do there?"

"We traveled as merely a couple of gentlemen and thus dispensed with any courtesies or duties that might have been expected for a viscount. It was something of an adventure."

He turned back to the painting. "And no," he said, "I don't know the people dancing behind us—they were there for some kind of fete. Does that answer all of your questions, dear Governess, or will there be more?"

She hesitated. There was something she probably shouldn't ask about, but...she wanted to know more about him.

"I wonder, does this picture bother you?"

"Why should it bother me?"

"Because it's from a happier time, before your wife died. I suppose you must feel like a different person now, with all that's happened."

He lifted a hand to rub his eyes and the gesture drew her attention to the lines of fatigue at their corners, which seemed incised, as if he never slept well at night. He let his hand fall.

"Nothing is sacred to you, is it, Anna?"

"Doesn't it pain you never to speak of her?" she asked softly. "I get the sense *she* is rather sacred. Almost not human and fallible like the rest of us."

"Ginger had plenty of humanity!" he said with a vehemence that startled her. "She was a perfect person."

All his love for his wife and his pain at the loss of her was there, naked now in his dark blue eyes, and it pierced her to see it. Along with compassion, she felt a fierce stab of jealousy that his wife still held his heart. She wanted him to see *her*, but his mind's eye was turned ever toward his wife. Perhaps she was being selfish in speaking about her in this way, but there was also truth in what she had to say.

"Surely an oxymoron, since to be human is to be flawed. Perfect isn't real, and I'm sure, from all you've said about her, that she was real."

Will gave her a dark look meant to quell her. "I don't want to talk about this."

She said nothing, just regarded him with those steady eyes, and again he had the feeling he'd had the first night, that she'd seen too much of life. Only now that he knew her better, he thought it was more this: that nothing in human nature would surprise her. She was a very good observer. He thought of her love of birds, and how she must be accustomed to watching patiently.

His gaze slid away from her. There had been no one with whom to talk of Ginger, or the past, for so long, and he felt, suddenly, an overwhelming need to let his thoughts spill out.

"When my father married Judith, I left Stillwell and practically took up residence with my cousins. I saw hardly anything of my father for the next several years. And then he was gone."

"You felt he'd betrayed your mother. You're a man who takes vows and responsibilities very seriously."

"How can you of all people say that, after I insulted you so abominably the first night you were here?"

"And yet, here you are, finishing those tenants' cottages you and your wife dreamed up to benefit others. It seems there's some good in you after all."

He frowned, as if that were an unacceptable idea.

"You were a good son who loved his mother," Anna said. "The eldest son, responsible for a great deal. I'm willing to bet you were something of a moralist who believed in all the noble principles his parents had embodied for most of his life. Your disappointment is understandable."

He narrowed his eyes. "What could you possibly know about marriage, Anna? Surely, young as you are, you've never been married."

"No."

He arched an eyebrow. "Ever had a beau?"

Her gaze returned to the painting. "I've never been much interested in beaux."

Independent as she was, that didn't surprise him. He wondered anew about what had happened with that aristocrat, the one who'd made her flush when he'd questioned her about him.

"That man who imposed on you... Was he someone you cared for in any way?" He felt himself hanging in terrible suspense over her answer.

"No!" She seemed to shudder. "Absolutely not. He... wanted things from me. But he never touched me."

"Tell me his name. He must be made to answer for what he's done."

"No," she said firmly. "That would only give what happened more life. I've resolved the issue and put it behind me."

He didn't like this, but he would not undermine her wishes. "Very well, I won't pursue it."

But something in the region of his heart squeezed painfully. She was so lovely, and with no family, she would have been an easy victim for a powerful man bent on having her, a thought that made him furious. Yet she'd offered him that embrace in the garden, when she might easily have been skittish about men and the power they could wield over her. She was brave. Braver, perhaps, than he.

He wanted extremely to kiss her. From his own need, yes, but also to offer her something to counter this other man's actions.

Surely this was wrong of him? But she was looking at him so steadily and, he could almost swear, with the glow of wanting. He lifted a hand and gently brushed aside one of those wild, wavy black strands that always seemed to escape from the careless confines of her hasty coiffures.

Anna was undone by the look in Grandville's dark blue eyes. Kindness was there, and strength, but also a glitter that could only be desire. She knew what it was because she felt it too, like a thread that now connected them.

"I'm sorry for what happened to you," he said, then paused. "That man violated whatever connection was between you. But I wonder, Anna, have you ever known the sweetness that can be between a man and a woman?"

Oh, she was in deep waters now. He didn't know the whole truth—he couldn't; it was too awful and dangerous. But she *had* felt violated by what Rawlins had done,

and by the marquess's refusal to surrender the book. This awful thing had happened to her and changed her life, and she'd been unable to speak of it to anyone. Until he had asked. She hadn't been able to resist the simple human need to share her troubles a little.

Which was only making her feel more drawn to him.

Those deep, dark eyes...they compelled her with irresistible charm to speak honestly. "I... No, I haven't."

"Have you ever even been kissed?"

She lifted her chin and made sure to look away so she wouldn't be enchanted into saying more than she meant to. "This conversation is growing ridiculous." But her voice came out breathy, an invitation.

"It's not. I think, for a lovely woman of twenty-three, it's entirely appropriate. If you've never been kissed by an admiring man before now, surely it's an experience you ought to have. Tell me, Anna, would you like to be kissed?"

An admiring man.

She was a woman, and it wasn't as though she'd never sat in church admiring the handsome young men of the neighborhood. But their eyes had always skipped over her toward feminine, pretty ladies with sweet airs, and she'd early on told herself she didn't need that kind of attention from men.

She'd had proof that she'd never get it anyway at the few social events she'd attended, where the only men who'd noticed her had all been over fifty. The younger men had simply seemed not to see her, and she'd decided that if they needed her to put on flounced gowns and giggle at them to hold their attention, she wanted none of them.

But she'd yearned sometimes for the companionship and admiration of a man—and hated herself for
the weakness of that yearning.

She'd been a hypocrite, she thought now as she
looked into blue eyes fringed with crowded dark
lashes, because Grandville had a great deal of male
beauty, and it was attracting her as surely as the beauty
of the pretty ladies in her village had attracted the
young gentlemen.

Did he truly admire her? Their embrace on the terrace had suggested he did. Her heart thumped heavily
in her chest. "I…"

"Of course," he continued, and she was surprised
to hear an almost playful tone in his voice, "viscounts
shouldn't be kissing women in their employ. But let
us consider that it might be a useful experience for a
governess. How can you know about guiding young
ladies in their behavior with gentlemen if you've never
been kissed?"

His reasoning was ridiculous—and also not. A kiss
was an experience she suddenly felt in need of—but
not for Lizzie's benefit. *Of course* she'd never been
kissed, and now this handsome, charming, brooding
man wanted to kiss her. How could she say no?

"Yes, then."

His head moved closer and he lingered with his
mouth just in front of hers, as if absorbing the pleasure
of her nearness, and the thought made something in
her chest flip over.

He brushed his mouth against hers. It was wonderful.

Their lips moved against each other, pressed softly.
He kissed the corners of her mouth, the bow at the

middle. She lifted her hands to his broad shoulders, where her eyes had so often been drawn, and delighted in the hard, alive feel of his body under the exquisite fabric of his green tailcoat.

He grunted and pulled her firmly against his chest, and a little sigh of pleasure escaped her as she wrapped her arms around him. His rib cage was broad and sturdy beneath her arms, his back muscular under her spread fingers, and this time, she could explore it.

His lips teased hers, nibbling lightly, asking her to open to him, and she did. His tongue met hers gently, stroking beguilingly. All over inside, she was softening. She ran her hands deliriously up his back and over his shoulders as heat spread through her. His kiss was so sweet.

Slowly his lips traveled toward her jawline, placing precise kisses as he went, as though establishing a path.

"Lesson number two for the governess." His voice was a low rumble that curled all around her, wrapping her in a spell. "There are kisses for lips…"

He kissed a spot low on her neck, sending out shivers that danced along her shoulders. "And kisses for lovely necks…"

He brushed his lips against her ear. "And kisses for tender little ears," he whispered, and ran the tip of his tongue over her earlobe.

Her knees turned to jelly. She rubbed her cheek against his, feeling the light sandiness of his freshly shaved whiskers. His skin sent warmth rushing through her that felt like something she'd been waiting for all her life.

Where else would he kiss her? She yearned desperately to know.

She didn't get to find out.

His head moved to her shoulder, and he paused a moment, his forehead coming to rest against hers. His breathing had quickened, and he lingered there as if he were gathering himself.

When he lifted his head, his expression was unreadable. His previously neatened brown hair stuck up wildly about his head where her hands had explored. She wanted to reach out and smooth it, but the pleasure and the remaining lightheartedness were fading from his face.

"I suppose," he said in a husky voice, and cleared his throat. "I suppose that is enough of lessons for the governess."

He was pulling back from her, and she was ridiculously disappointed. Something in her had opened when he took her in his arms, but now she felt exposed and vulnerable, and her pride demanded that she not let him see this.

She blinked at him with pretend demureness. "Oh, kind master, to have been so enlightening to a lowly servant."

His eyes flashed a little, and she—foolishly—wished he'd kiss her again.

"Ever impudent." He sighed, the warmth nearly gone from his eyes. "Despite the evidence of my behavior since you've arrived, Anna, I would have you know I'm not in the habit of visiting my attentions on women in my employ. You needn't worry that there will be any more such lessons."

"I'm not worried," she said. "And your hair is mussed."

He frowned and ran a hand through his hair, then

moved to his desk and began picking up papers, shuffling them about. "Now, where is my ward? I value promptness highly."

She cleared her throat. "I shall go see. She does seem to be taking a rather long time."

She was still warm from his touch, but clearly he'd moved on from the moments they'd shared. Knowing him as she did, he was probably already deeply regretting his lapse in propriety. To him, she could only be a nobody, simply the odd young woman who'd arrived at his home along with his ward.

So he wanted to touch her—he'd been alone a long time, and he was a man, she told herself sternly. She mustn't read too much into his kiss. She mustn't allow herself to think anything could come of it. But…she'd loved it.

She was walking toward the door when a knock sounded.

"Come," he called from behind her.

The door opened and admitted Lizzie.

Anna sucked in a breath at the sight of her. She was wearing a creamy yellow gown decorated in crystalline beads and cut so low that the firm expanse of her young breasts was presented for view, the rounded shape easily discernible in the snug-fitting bodice. The gown might have suited a courtesan. Her face, touched deftly with color at the lips and cheeks, glowed with the almost too-perfect pinkness of rouge.

Anna snuck a glance at the viscount, who appeared to be swallowing heavily. She thought she noticed an air of penitential forbearance settling over him.

"Oh, la," Lizzie said in a high, precious-sounding voice, "you haven't been waiting for me, I hope?"

His eyebrows lowered, but he made no comment. Into the silence, Lady Grandville appeared and, behind her, Dart.

"Dinner is served, my lord."

Ten

LORD GRANDVILLE OFFERED LIZZIE HIS ARM, A SLIGHT to his stepmother, who gave Anna a rueful smile and linked arms with her companionably.

Lady Grandville looked subtly beautiful in a gown of shimmering olive satin, which contrasted richly with her butter-and-cream hair and picked up flecks of moss green and sunlight gold in her eyes. The gown had a square neckline that sat well on her gently rounded shoulders and fitted her handsome figure surely. She seemed like such a warm, good-hearted woman, and Anna really wanted to believe that she was different now from the person Lord Grandville had described.

They took their seats at the long, richly appointed table, the viscount indicating that Anna should sit next to him while Lizzie sat across from him and Lady Grandville across from Anna, as far away from himself as he could arrange, she guessed.

Servants entered to begin serving dinner and filled their wineglasses. Anna noticed Lizzie taking several large swigs of wine with the air of someone consuming medicine.

Next to Anna, Lord Grandville's arm rested on the table in its green superfine sleeve, and she felt a strong urge to touch it, as if they might be of comfort to each other in their trials. Which they couldn't be. That kiss, the closeness—they wouldn't change anything. They couldn't.

"And how do you find your room, Lizzie?" he asked, not including his stepmother in his hostly concern.

Lizzie winked at him. *Winked*. "With my two legs, Uncle." She batted her eyelashes at him as Anna stared. What had gotten into the girl?

"Ah," he said after a pause. "Very droll."

Several minutes of quiet eating ensued, and Anna allowed herself to hope that Lizzie would go no further in whatever ridiculous scheme she had embarked on. She was, though, dismayed to see the footman approaching the girl's glass with the wine. She tried to catch his eye and wave him off, but he merely gave her a puzzled look as he refilled it.

Lady Grandville cleared her throat. "Grandville, have you seen anything of the neighbors? Perhaps the Chittisters or the Tilbertons?"

"No," he replied. "Pass the salt please, Anna."

She did, and conversation died again. At least the food was delicious, she thought, savoring a mouthful of roast chicken that had been cooked to golden perfection. With luck, maybe it would distract the others from feeling a need to converse, because she didn't hold out hope that the tensions simmering beneath the silence would lead to anything good.

"Have you been to London recently, Uncle?" Lizzie asked some minutes later, giving her head a little toss

that made her pearl earbobs dance. It was becoming unfortunately apparent to Anna that Lizzie was envisioning a potential new role for Lord Grandville: suitor.

"No, I haven't," he replied. He took a sip of wine. "But perhaps you would like to visit there. Anna might take you."

She saw through that idea. Clearing her throat, she turned toward him. A curl of dark brown hair near his eye drew her attention, and she struggled not to be charmed by it. "I don't think that would be a good idea, my lord."

"I think it's a wonderful idea!" Lizzie enthused. "But wouldn't you come too, my lord?"

She leaned across the table, so that her crystal-encrusted bosom was prominently displayed for her guardian's viewing. He lifted his napkin and coughed into it.

"Actually," Lady Grandville said, "it would be a fine idea for Lizzie to be introduced to the society of your friends in Town, Grandville. And as your ward, she really ought to have a come-out."

"Thank you, Judith, for that bit of wisdom."

If he were thinking clearly, Anna thought, he'd have been leaping at the chance for Lizzie to go to Town, where she might find a husband who could take her off his hands. But he clearly had no intention of leaving his estate, and he seemed highly unlikely to ask Lady Grandville for such a favor.

"Lizzie has nothing to do with the past," his stepmother continued, looking at his profile since he seemed unwilling to return her gaze. "Don't punish her to spite me."

He made no reply, and silence returned to the table.

As the dessert custards were finally served, Anna reflected that she'd never sat through a longer meal. If only it could be over before Lizzie did something truly outrageous or the viscount gave vent to his feelings about his stepmother, she would count it a success.

Across the table, seemingly oblivious to the tensions present, or perhaps so occupied with her wineglass that she hadn't noticed, Lizzie said, "And how are your horses, my lord?"

He looked quizzical. "My horses? They are as usual."

Lizzie took another sip of wine, and Anna wished the table weren't so wide that it prevented her from delivering admonishing nudges with her foot.

"Lizzie, dear," Lady Grandville said, "that's a unique gown."

"Thank you. I'm glad somebody likes—" she started to say, before Anna broke in.

"Why don't you tell us about your childhood in Malta, Lizzie? I'm sure we'd all love to hear about it."

"Oh, I don't—" Lizzie began in a petulant tone, but then, as if a light had come on in her head, she said excitedly, "I did hear a very amusing story at school, about Lord Branwell's son."

"Are you certain this is a story we'd all enjoy?" Anna asked with a smile that she hoped conveyed the need for prudence.

"Yes, it's very funny," Lizzie insisted loudly, slurring her words a bit. "Lord Branwell's son was smitten with a young lady, so he climbed the trellis outside her window one night, hoping to enchant her with this manly feat. But when he reached what he thought was

her window and cried out for his beloved—ha!—it was her father's room, and he was there!"

"Thank you, my dear," Anna said, leery of what more the girl might say in her tipsy state, "you've regaled us very well."

"But this is the best part! The suitor yelped and dropped down onto his horse, which he'd tied below. But"—Lizzie giggled—"the horse threw him, and he was stuck lying there with a broken leg until the father rescued him."

Lizzie laughed, and hiccupped audibly. Anna stole a glance at Lord Grandville, who looked grim.

"You believe that someone falling from a horse and sustaining serious injury is amusing?"

Lizzie's brow crimped. "I only meant to entertain."

"Really? This is funny to you, Elizabeth, for someone to be hurt in the same manner in which your Aunt Ginger died?"

Anna barely managed to repress a gasp. So his wife had died in a riding accident.

Lizzie looked stricken. "I forgot. I'm sorry."

"My lord, I'm sure—" Anna began, but he shot her a quelling look.

"She meant no harm," Lady Grandville said quietly.

"Do not interfere, Judith."

Lady Grandville's face took on an uncomfortable look. "Actually, Grandville, I might as well tell you now the main reason I've come, partly because I see how much good it could also do Lizzie. I've arranged for a ball to be held at Stillwell."

Everyone simply stared at her.

And then, after a moment, he said, "No."

"Just for the neighbors," she continued, as if he

hadn't spoken, "to be held here in a little over a week. The invitations have already gone out."

Heavens, but Lady Grandville was bold.

"Oh, that's wonderful!" Lizzie said, the anxiety over her mistake melting away.

The viscount hadn't taken his eyes from his stepmother, and they were dark now with cold fury. "You always did have no sense of appropriateness."

"I've done this because your father would have wanted you to remarry and do your duty to the title. You won't find a wife if you're never in company with eligible ladies. Thus, the ball."

"You are mad."

"I won't stand by and do nothing," she said firmly, uncowed by his evident anger.

Anna, however, couldn't bear the tension. "A ball would be a wonderful opportunity to introduce Lizzie to society."

"It would! I should love nothing so much as a ball!" Lizzie exclaimed, but he ignored her.

"I will have no balls here."

She gave a cry of outrage. "Well…well… Bollocks to you, Grandville!" A ripple of horror went through Anna, but apparently Lizzie wasn't finished. "Do you want to know, *my lord*, why I was sent away from Rosewood? It was because I snuck out of my room at night to meet a man! How do you like that?"

Well then, Anna thought, hope wilting. She couldn't blame him if he wanted to keep himself apart from his niece now. That was, if he didn't just send her away immediately.

"Elizabeth!" he thundered.

"Oh, why don't you just send me to Malta?" she wailed miserably. "It's the only place I've ever been happy, and you'd never have to bother with me again." She dashed incipient tears roughly from the corner of her eyes. "Just what you wish."

"Malta is out of the question!"

She stood up, knocking her chair over, and fled from the room.

He stood as well and fixed his stepmother with a narrow-eyed look that would have doubtless made even a duke tremble. Lady Grandville tipped her chin up.

"You're here not more than four hours," he said, "and this is the result. Are you satisfied?"

"Of course I'm not happy that she's upset. But I doubt she would be if you'd expressed yourself more gently."

His lips twisted harshly. "I expect you to put a stop to what you've started."

Her soft mouth thinned, but her steady hazel gaze never wavered. "I know."

He strode from the room, his boots ringing on the old oak floors.

Anna looked across the table at her companion, who now sat with her eyes closed and her hands folded tightly on the table.

"I'm sorry," Anna said. "Are you all right?"

Lady Grandville exhaled, then inhaled again, deeply, her lush bosom rising and falling distinctly. Her eyes still closed, she said, "A trick I learned from a holy man during my trip to Egypt last year. A focusing on the breath."

She paused, then opened her eyes. Their hazel

lights looked bruised, but her lips took a small, rueful upturn. "Please call me Judith, dear girl. 'Lady Grandville' makes me feel far too serious."

She pressed her lips ruefully. "My announcement didn't go well, did it? But I did rather spring it on him, and I was prepared for his reaction. I'm sorry, though, that Lizzie got caught up in what's between the two of us. The last thing I want is for her to be hurt by what I've undertaken."

"I'm afraid she was already well on the way to ruining her chances of charming him tonight." Anna wondered what she was going to say to him to excuse Lizzie's behavior. "And if there is perhaps a silver lining in all this, it's that when you introduced the subject of the ball, it kept him from directing his full disapproval toward Lizzie."

"That is…something," the other woman said with the ghost of a smile.

"It's unfortunate that he won't allow the ball," Anna said. "I do think you're right, that it would have benefitted both of them."

"Well, I didn't actually agree to cancel the ball. Or to leave. I simply said that I knew that was what he wanted."

Anna stared at her companion. "Goodness," she said. "You are ready to go quite far with this."

"I am."

"Er…Judith…you do realize that he'll be furious tomorrow when he finds out."

"Yes, but with any luck, I shall have the auxiliary plan in place before he discovers his wishes are not being carried out."

"The auxiliary plan?"

"The pretty neighbor," Judith said with a twinkle in her eyes. "She will, I'm fairly certain, be very enthusiastic about her ball invitation."

Anna managed to laugh along with her, though the thought of the auxiliary plan made her miserable.

After they left the dining room, she stopped by Lizzie's room, but her knock received no answer.

Tomorrow would be soon enough to try to repair the damage of the evening, and with all the wine Lizzie had drunk, Anna supposed the poor girl was very likely already asleep.

⁂

Lizzie was not asleep.

In fact, she'd never felt so awake in her life as she made her way out the doors to the terrace, not quite clearing the frame as she passed through. More than awake, she felt wild. Heedless of the unaccustomed dullness in her arms and legs, she reached the edge of the terrace and tripped into a smallish stone vase, which fell over with a muffled clunk.

She felt free—*bloody free*—she thought rebelliously. Free to do whatever she wanted. Why shouldn't she? Nobody cared about her at all.

What right did Grandville have to be so cruel? Of course it was sad that Aunt Ginger had died, but Lizzie had lost her whole family and she didn't go around being mean to everyone. It wasn't as if she'd intended any disrespect to the memory of her aunt when she'd told that story.

She squeezed her eyes tightly shut and pushed away the memory of how she'd dressed so carefully that

night and tried so hard to make him want her. Not because she wanted him in that way—he was old, only a few years younger than her father, but certainly over thirty. Only because if he wanted her, he wouldn't send her away. She'd imagined that, if he came to care for her that way, maybe someday she would be able to feel that way about him, too.

And she'd been so encouraged that he'd come to dinner that night.

Foolish, despicable hope. He clearly hated her, no matter that she tried like anything to please him. Righteous fury swelled within her, and she wanted to lash out against him.

Opening her eyes, she waited for them to adjust to the moonlit darkness before walking toward the garden, looking for something she'd seen earlier in the day. Her eyes roved over the darkened area until she saw it: a pile of tools that had been left by the gardener next to a bench he was repairing.

She picked up a hammer from the pile and looked around for something suitable to damage. Her eyes passed over the bench, which, if wrecked, would only make more work for the gardener, and she searched farther, swaying as she stood. She was frustrated to find only bushes and pebble paths, none of which would be much affected by hammering.

Her eyes were just skipping past the pair of statues at the far end of the garden when she arrested their movement.

Apollo and Diana stood pristine in the moonlight, almost glowing in their white marble purity, with strands of dark ivy shining glossily at their feet.

Perfect.

She made her way over to the sculptures, stumbling at the edge of the path, and came to stand before them. They were about her height and important-looking with the weight of their classical heritage. Before she could lose her nerve, she raised the hammer to give Apollo a good crack in his muscled abdomen.

His stomach was not where her hammer landed. The blow fell instead against something near the vee of his legs. She gasped as Apollo's male parts fell away from his body in a chunk that landed in the ivy with a heavy rustle.

She gazed in horror at the jagged emptiness where once the stone had been carefully shaped. All her anger and frustration turned instantly into fear.

What have I done?

If Grandville might have overlooked her conduct at the dinner table, he would surely never forgive her after he'd seen what she'd done to his statue. It now looked obscene, and as though the site of the damage had been purposefully chosen.

Damn!

Her heart pounding, she looked around frantically for some means of fixing what she'd done. But the garden offered nothing but bushes, pebbles, and ivy. Had she expected a pot of glue to have magically appeared? She was doomed.

A wave of nausea washed over her and she sat down by Apollo's feet. Her head felt thick and achy, her tongue horribly sour. She hugged her knees to her chest and buried her head in her arms, unable to bear the sight of the statue.

Wait, she thought after a moment—the *sight* of it.

She couldn't undo the damage, but she could cover it up. And the perfect solution was right to hand: ivy. Ivy took over everything when neglected—it was already twining about the statue's ankles. All she needed to do was to coax the ivy up the statue and drape it so it hid the broken area. Who would notice? It was not as if Grandville strolled about the gardens all the time, and this part was at some distance from the manor.

She realized then that she'd have to cover both statues for it to look natural, but no matter. She set to work, tugging and draping the long strands of ivy and eventually going to the tool pile for a pair of pruning shears.

Finally she stood back and surveyed the effect. Apollo looked a bit like he was wearing a nappy, but that couldn't be helped. And some of the pieces she'd draped around Diana's waist looked precariously like they might fall away, but she was so tired now. This would have to do.

The shears and the hammer returned to the pile, she started for the manor, exhausted, terribly thirsty, and unhappy.

She crept quietly through the manor and dropped into bed with all her clothes on. But hardly had she closed her eyes when her queasy stomach sent her running for the chamber pot. Afterward, she climbed shakily back into bed.

Her hands felt raw, and she slipped them under her pillow and stifled a sob. She had no home anymore, and she missed her patient, kind father almost unbearably. Tears pooled in the corners of her eyes, and she slipped into a miserable sleep.

&

Bile pressed at the back of Jasper Rawlins's throat, and he cursed the heavy meal he'd had to eat that night. The Marquess of Henshaw had an iron stomach, and judging from its girth, it was used to rich food, but Jasper's was not, nor was it accustomed to so much riding.

Henshaw had been in a celebratory mood because they'd found a fellow that day who'd seen Anna Bristol: the driver of a coach that stopped at towns along the route leading out of Cheldney. Jasper had made a drawing of Anna to show around, and when they presented it to the coachman, he'd remembered her from weeks before because she'd seemed furtive, and he'd thought she was perhaps escaping an angry husband. She'd asked him if he knew of any young ladies' schools in the area.

"That's where she'll be," Jasper had said to the marquess as they left the driver. "At a school, likely teaching drawing."

They'd stopped at a school near the town where the coachman thought he'd left her, but had no luck. Still, now they had a plan: to visit all the young ladies' schools in the area.

The marquess's mood had only improved when they'd stopped for the night and he'd encountered one of his peers, a Mr. Thomas Halifax, at the inn. The handsome young Halifax, who was brother to Viscount Grandville, didn't seem to know the marquess well, though he'd been happy enough to run into him. But then, he'd already heard about the book.

Henshaw had delighted in talking to Halifax about *The Beautiful One* and its mysterious model, and hinted

heavily all night that he had the book with him and would bring it out. But not long after Henshaw had secured the gentleman's promise to attend his house party, the marquess had lied and said he didn't have the book with him. Halifax had left the dining room soon after, with the marquess's promise that he would see the book and the painting at the house party.

"Can't say when last I've had such fun!" Henshaw chortled now, and poured more punch for himself. "*The Beautiful One*'s the best two hundred pounds I've ever spent. Worth its weight in gold, it is!"

"I'm glad it pleases you," Jasper said.

But they still didn't have bloody Anna Bristol in their grasp so he could paint her. Every day they lost to the hunt made him more furious with her.

The marquess drained his glass and stood up, from all signs little affected by the night's excesses.

"We'd best retire, man, if we're to get an early start tomorrow. The innkeeper says there are three schools for young ladies between the next four villages—I'll be bound she's found work at one of 'em. "

Eleven

ANNA AWOKE EARLY THE NEXT MORNING, HER HEART pounding from a dream in which the Marquess of Henshaw had been hunting her with a pack of dogs.

She reminded herself that there was no reason he should look for her at Stillwell, unless he somehow traced her to Rosewood. It was not at all impossible that he might do so, if he persisted. The thought made her ill, and she knew she couldn't afford to entertain it. There was nothing she could do about him.

Besides, she had an important job this morning: making sure Lizzie apologized sincerely to her uncle.

He would likely soon be walking out to the cottages as he did every morning, and she got dressed and sat on the window seat to put on her shoes and watch for him.

Something fluttered inside her when his dark figure appeared, striding on long legs across the land that had been in his family for generations. From this distance he looked jaunty and vigorous, master of his world, and as she finished tying on her half boots, she watched him.

Indulging herself foolishly, she imagined the two of them dancing a waltz, together out in the world with no fear of scandal or judgment. How she yearned for him to kiss her again.

Her eyes were only half-focusing on his figure, and now they caught sight of something irregular just beyond where he was, in a formal garden where a pair of statues stood, looking decidedly different today. Her eyes widened as she saw that their heretofore whiteness was draped with something green, and in that second, it occurred to her that Lizzie might not have been sleeping in her room when she'd knocked after dinner.

Not bothering to twist up the long braid that had held her hair while she slept, she dashed out of her room and flew downstairs and out to the garden.

❧

Will's mind was determinedly focusing on the final work that needed to be done on the cottages and not on a certain black-haired woman when he passed beyond the arborvitae that framed the far garden. The sight that met him startled a laugh out of him.

The once-regal Diana and Apollo that reigned over their natural setting now looked silly and not a little lewd. Apollo's crotch was heavily draped in ivy that drew attention to the area, and Diana's top half had been covered in such a way that it looked like she was wearing a green shirt and nothing else, which only accentuated her lower nakedness. A particularly hairy tendril of ivy rested across one of her graceful nipples like a growth of fur.

He recognized the hand of a drunken young person and laughed a little, remembering how his cousin Louie had once inked a mustache on an ancient female ancestor depicted in a painting in the Stillwell gallery. He hadn't seen his Halifax cousins— Louie, Andrew, and Marcus and their sisters, Emerald and Ruby—since Ginger's funeral, and for the first time in a year, he thought that maybe it would be good to see them again.

The sound of quick footsteps drew his attention, and he turned just in time to see Anna emerge from the arborvitae at top speed. She looked even younger than usual, and he realized this was because her hair was not jammed into its customary knot but hanging down her back in a long, black braid, with wayward curls poking out here and there. It seemed as if she had just moments earlier jumped from her bed, and inevitably the thought continued along a lusty path.

She stopped abruptly when she saw him, but she was clearly not surprised by the appearance of the statues.

"Well, Anna? This is obviously Lizzie's handiwork. Or will you deny it?"

"No…" she said, though she sounded as though she'd like to. In the bright sunlight she looked pale, and there were dark smudges under her eyes, as if she hadn't slept well. Hell, he doubted anyone had slept after last night. Dinner had been a disaster, but even before then he'd felt stirred up by Anna.

What on earth had he been thinking, kissing her? And how could he have let himself get so carried away by desire for her? Because he'd wanted to do far, far more than they'd done. He'd spent an uncomfortable

night tossing in his bed, wracked with guilt that he could allow himself to be so tempted, as if his body had forgotten the wife he loved.

Anna had suggested that he'd made some kind of saint out of Ginger. He'd felt traitorous even listening to her.

Yet something in what she'd said had continued to tug at him amid the guilt, and he'd arisen from bed that morning tense and itching to put his hands to work.

He crossed his arms and gave her a viscount's distancing stare. "And what do you have to say for your charge now, especially after her behavior last night?"

"Er...it was only a prank."

"Done by a young woman who was by her own admission meeting men at night outside her school. Not good."

"Surely you see that she got herself sent away from Rosewood on purpose, exactly so she would be sent here. To you."

He muttered a curse.

She lifted an eyebrow. "Really, my lord, you ought to curb your coarser expressions, at least in Lizzie's presence. She is impressionable."

"Impressionable be dam—" He caught himself. He *was* beginning to sound like a sailor, but he didn't need her pointing that out to him. "She is obviously quite familiar with such terms. And I'm beginning to think that maybe she would do best in a school abroad, where she could start afresh. Perhaps there is one that can take her right away."

Although if Lizzie went, Anna would go too, and he didn't like that idea. It gave him a lonely, deserted feeling he didn't want to examine.

"Oh, no, you can't—" she started to say, and he gave her his haughtiest look. "I mean that if you would just be a little patient and forgiving with her, I know she'll settle down."

He smacked a hand to his head. "I know not where to begin. With the seductive clothes, the wine guzzling, the little-girl voice that I can only guess was meant to attract me?"

"At least she cares enough to want to gain your attention!"

"Or she has a diabolical plan to trap me into marriage."

She had the grace to look sheepish. "But you know that's not really what she wants. What she wants is simply a guiding male figure, like an older brother, or…" She looked at him out of the corner of her eye.

"A father," he finished for her. "Exactly what I cannot be. And I would like to point out that I'm only thirty-two." He sighed. "I like Lizzie. And I actually, fool that I am, like her spirit. But I cannot be her brother or her father or anything else she dreams up. You do see that, don't you?"

"Then ask Lady Grandville to take her."

She would ask this. "Absolutely not."

"I know you don't trust your stepmother, but I think if you gave her a chance, you'd see she's changed. I think she's sorry about the way she used to be and wants to make amends. Or will your pride not allow you to ask a favor of her?"

"I'm not fooled by Judith, as you obviously have been. But then, she always did have a talent for charming some people. She's not a fit companion for Lizzie."

He read the frustration in her sherry eyes. Such

pretty, light-filled eyes. He thought she would try to push him further, but instead she stepped forward and grabbed a handful of Apollo's ivy nappy and tugged it briskly off.

And gasped. Apollo's genitals had been hacked off.

"Well," he said, "I hope that's not a message for me."

"Oh dear. Was it a very valuable statue?"

"I didn't particularly like it, but Lizzie didn't know that."

Wondering if Diana had suffered similarly, he pulled off the ivy strands that had been twined about her torso. She appeared intact.

"Surely there is some way," Anna said anxiously, "that she might make reparation for this?"

He pulled the last of Diana's ivy free with a ferocious tug and dropped it on the pile at the statues' feet. "Has she a particular talent with a chisel? Or perhaps some powerful glue?"

She looked genuinely dismayed, but then, her fondest wish was for his ward to succeed in endearing herself to him.

"You're right," she admitted. "This can't be fixed any more than she can return to Rosewood. But I'm certain," she said, a steely glint coming into her eyes, "and in fact I will promise, that nothing like this will happen again."

He crossed his arms and treated her to a withering stare. He didn't care about the statues, but he couldn't let her know that. He couldn't let her see that, in another life, he would have been perfectly happy to have his niece stay with him, because Anna would definitely take a mile if she saw him budging an inch.

"See that it doesn't. I've said she may stay a month, but if she's bent on being outrageous, she may find her stay cut short." His eyes wandered over her form. "Are you wearing that repulsive brownish gown again?"

"Of course not. This gown is blue. Since it offends you so much, just stop looking at it."

He ignored her. "That gown is not blue; it is the color of boiled dust." He tipped his head. "You don't have anything else, do you, but those two offensive items that should be retired to the ragbag?"

He could practically see her spine stiffening. He'd managed to crack her sturdy outer shell, and over something about which he wouldn't have guessed she truly cared. But he didn't feel ungentlemanly in the least, partly because she was hiding herself, trying to cover her beauty, and that was wrong.

"I shall summon the dressmaker. You really need to order some gowns."

She bristled; he could almost see her black curls growing tighter, and it made a grin tease the edges of his mouth. "I will pay, of course," he added, before she could unleash her outrage.

"I don't need new clothes! Just because you're paying me a salary, you're not entitled to consider me a doll, to be dressed for your—"

She shut her mouth and blushed.

"Pleasure?" he supplied.

Black eyebrows lowered ferociously over her light brown eyes. He should have felt like a beast, but he didn't. She was a worthy opponent. He stepped closer to her.

"What is it with you, Anna?" he asked quietly, tell-ing himself he only pursued this conversation for her

benefit, even though he knew he was lying. "I know you were mistreated before you came here, but you have too much spirit to respond by hiding yourself, if that's what you're doing with these horrible gowns."

"Must you go on so about my clothes?"

"Yes. Because you are beautiful."

A blush swept over her face, but it looked like awkwardness, not pleasure in his words.

"Most women would dress to accentuate their prettiness," he continued. "But your clothes say 'I don't care what you think of me.'"

"What next? Messages from my shoes?"

Being so close to her was making him very warm, but he ignored the thought that he should move away. "Be serious, Anna. Are you perhaps *afraid* of attracting men? If so, your plan has failed. You have attracted me, for one."

Her lips thinned. "Stop talking nonsense."

He cocked his head to the side. "You can't accept a compliment, can you? Or have you never been complimented? Is it that no one has ever noticed your beauty under that carapace of clothes and careless hair? For those with eyes to see, their drabness only puts your beauty into relief."

She crossed her arms. "You seem inordinately interested in feminine attire—perhaps you have yearned to become a dressmaker? I might teach you a few stitches."

He laughed softly. "You are all prickles on this subject, aren't you?" But underneath her bravado, he saw her vulnerability. Perhaps, after all those years in a man's domain, she was afraid of her softer side. But

he wanted this for her: that she would understand her allure as a woman.

Her eyes regarded him with all the warmth of a falcon's beady glare.

He leaned closer. "You are very beautiful, Anna," he said softly. He wanted like anything to kiss her, though he knew he must not. "But your beauty is not showy. It's a glow that shines out of you."

"I…" She lifted a hand and placed it against his chest, where it burned through his shirt and made him want more of her.

Her eyes closed, and the air between them seemed to shimmer.

He placed his hand on top of hers where it lay against him. "I'm sorry if no one whose opinion you respected ever honored what is so lovely about you. Perhaps, growing up without a mother, you had no one to celebrate the feminine in you. Perhaps, in this, you were at a disadvantage compared to the other young ladies of your neighborhood."

Her eyes flew open and the moment of quiet connection was gone as her hand dropped from his chest. "On the contrary. I felt myself to be infinitely more fortunate. I had no deportment lessons to waste my time, no one asking me to sit all day inside with a needle while outside life was happening."

"You have many unusual talents for a young lady, and Lizzie is fortunate to have you for her governess. But did you never dream of a handsome gentleman to sweep you off your feet?"

Her pert chin lifted. "I've always preferred doing to dreaming."

He laughed. "Yes, I believe that. And perhaps no gorgon of a governess could have succeeded in hammering the feminine graces into you. Perhaps," he said, "I'm glad none did."

She had her own charms, and they were unique. She might have allowed herself to become brittle or bitter after whatever that man had done to her, but she hadn't. She was *noble*. And also playful in ways that continued to surprise him, and he was finding it impossible not to think of her all too frequently, each new occasion followed always by stabs of guilt. Because though his heart was ruined, his body was whole, and it ached for her.

He wanted more for her than life could offer a young woman on her own, forced into whatever work she could find. She deserved far, far better.

"And perhaps my words will fall on resistant ears as well," he said with a regretful smile, "since I know that my opinion may not be of much worth to you either."

Her eyes mocked him, which he knew was a way she had of refusing a deeper connection. "I don't need to be flattered to know my worth as a person."

He was not the man she needed, though he felt an inkling of how much she might bloom if she allowed love, affection, and trust to touch her heart. She knew how to give love—he could see that easily with all she was doing for Lizzie—but he rather thought she didn't know how to accept it.

She crossed her arms in front of her. "Lizzie is what's important here. With care, I know she'll improve. So I'm asking you not to send her away—no matter what. She's a little wild, yes. She

needs patience, but I know she would thrive here, if
you let her stay with you."

"I've told you it won't work."

"Because you want to live in the past?"

"You go too far, Anna." He sighed. "But I'll tell
you what. Since you are so concerned about her,
why don't you stay on permanently as her governess?
If you stayed, I wouldn't send her away. You could
both live here."

That caught her by surprise. And him. What the
devil had made him say that? He wanted her around,
yes, but how could he stand that much temptation if
she stayed beyond the month?

She stilled. "It's not possible."

"Why? Is something awaiting you? Or someone?"
he asked, knowing he cared far too much about her
answer. And why should he wish her to stay? Was he
not master of himself? The best thing was for her and
Lizzie to leave and his life to go back to the way it
had been. Except, already he knew that it would be
different when she left.

"My aunt is awaiting me in the north. Before I came
here, it was my plan that I would live with her and teach
drawing, as I was doing before I was at Rosewood."

"I see," he said, ignoring the stab of disappointment. "Well then, a month it must be."

"But will you promise not to send Lizzie away
before the month is out?" she pressed.

He inhaled deeply and exhaled. Really, if he were
wise, he'd send both Anna and Lizzie away today. But
he wasn't wise, it seemed.

"Very well. No matter what torment she visits

upon me, I won't send her away. And I'll even allow
you both to sit in on any interviews for her future
governess, should I decide to send her to my London
town house. Will that for once appease you?"

"Yes," she said, satisfaction lighting her eyes. "And
you must approach Lizzie with patience."

He arched an eyebrow.

"My lord—"

He put up a quelling hand. "I promise to be patient
with her, thereby doubtless opening myself up to all
sorts of outrages. But if it will please Anna Black, then
all is right in the world."

She smiled then with true pleasure, and it made him
feel so happy.

He propped his leg up against the base of the Apollo
statute. "I confess a profound curiosity about you,
Anna. I know so little. Tell me about your youthful
exploits. Did you spend all your time larking about
with that brother you mentioned?"

"Most of it."

"I wonder about that veritable man's world in
which you were raised. Considering how calmly you
handled the owl situation, I imagine you must have
come from some nature-mad family. And now I
discover you were a drawing teacher, which certainly
seems more in your line than seamstress work"—he
chuckled—"considering how little interest you have
in clothes."

He tipped his head. "You so intrigue me, Anna.
Tell me more."

Twelve

ANNA STARED, HER HEART BEATING FASTER EVERY moment as Viscount Grandville regarded her with a grin, clearly planning to tease all kinds of information out of her.

He'd shaved again that day, but although he was wearing work clothes similar to the ones he'd worn the day she'd first met him, he didn't look like the same man. He'd changed, or her idea of him had changed, and *this* man, *this* Grandville, did something to her.

A section of his dark brown hair had fallen carelessly across his forehead near one eyebrow, and the masculine planes of his face were tanned from work. In his rough, brown laborer's coat and trousers, he seemed far too approachable. Not a viscount, but a man. Strong, good with his hands. Physical. Breathtakingly handsome.

She felt so very tempted to tell him more about herself, and to admit that she'd given a false name, and why. To tell him about those men and *The Beautiful One.*

She so much wanted—no, she ached—to trust him: the man, whose broad shoulders might bear great

burdens, and the viscount, whose power could make problems disappear.

But why would he? She'd lied to him. And they barely knew each other, even if her foolish heart wanted to believe that on some deep, inexpressible level, they understood each other. Why should he trust her if she told him that a man had spied on her and made nude drawings of her? Why should he believe she hadn't posed for them? Even her own father hadn't believed Mr. Rawlins capable of any harm.

No. If there was one lesson she'd learned in life, it was that the only person she could trust was herself.

But he was looking at her so intently, as if she presented a mystery he couldn't resist, that she knew she must distract him.

"There's nothing else of interest to tell. What *is* interesting, though, are those cottages you're working on. May I see them?"

He blinked. "Do what?"

"See the cottages where you go every day. I confess a deep curiosity about them."

"Nonsense. You're only changing the subject."

"Or perhaps you don't wish anyone to see your work. After all, how good could a viscount be at building a cottage? Perhaps these cottages are horribly cobbled together and an embarrassment."

He arched a haughty eyebrow, and a gleam of challenge came into his eyes. "Come along then, Anna, and I'll show you. As you are not needed by your charge, who managed to get foxed under your very nose and is now doubtless lying abed with a painfully thick head, you can earn your keep with whitewashing."

And he turned and made for the direction in which the cottages lay. She congratulated herself on distracting him so effectively that now she was going to go stand and gawk at his cottages with him, and breathe in his marvelous scent and listen to his deep voice and feel his tall, deliciously broad-shouldered, magnificently handsome presence beside her.

Brilliant.

∽✧∾

She'd seen the roofs of the cottages from her bed-chamber window, but as she followed him through the border of trees and hedges that shielded them from view and emerged to take in the full effect, she caught her breath.

Before her stood a loose semicircle of ten stone cottages set against a pretty wood, with mature weeping willows reposing peacefully at either end. A landscape painter might have dreamed the cottages up, or even an artist illustrating a happy children's story, though they were neither sweet nor childish. They were simple but lovely, exactly perfect in their woodsy setting, similar in their style without any one of them exactly resembling another.

Some had thatched roofs and some had tiled, and their walls were made of handsome irregular stones that lent them a sturdy, timeless quality. The pretty window frames were all freshly whitewashed, and sunlight glittered off glass panes that would likely be a new experience for tenants used to only shutters or oiled paper for their windows.

"They're beautiful," she said quietly. A smile curled

the corners of his lips, and she detected a whiff of justifiable pride. "These are not just cottages. Someone has designed them with great care and thought."

"Yes. The architect John Nash did them as a favor. They're almost finished," he added, sounding oddly disappointed. Wasn't he eager to complete so remarkable an undertaking?

"But why are you doing the work yourself?"

He shrugged carelessly. "Keeps my hands busy."

He began striding over to one of the tiled-roof homes but turned to see her still standing where he'd left her. "There's whitewashing to be done inside. You can busy yourself with that while I finish with the roof."

She followed him, but she didn't go into the cottage. Instead, she stood watching as he approached a ladder propped against the cottage. He climbed easily up and swung himself onto the roof with an appealing, careless masculinity. Working on the roof, she thought, looked like fun.

Fun… She didn't think he allowed that for himself. *She'd* had none of it once that book of drawings had come to light. For that matter, though, it had really been so long since she'd felt the urge for spontaneous fun. Perhaps it had even been as long ago as before her brother's death. Daily life had narrowed her vision to a focus on needful things and small pleasures.

But here at Stillwell, she felt different. She supposed that having an entire vast estate and grounds to wander could give a person a feeling of lighthearted freedom, though she knew it was more than that. Being with this man made something joyful bubble up inside her.

She went over to the ladder. "I'm coming up," she announced as she ascended, not wanting to startle him.

"You're what? No—" she heard just as her head cleared the edge of the roof. He'd paused on his hands and knees near the end of a row of roof tiles, and he watched with a darkening brow as she swung her leg over the edge of the roof, which was surely far more difficult in skirts than trousers.

"This is absurd. Get down immediately. It's not safe."

"Clearly it's not so very unsafe, or you wouldn't have survived laying all these tiles," she said, inching along carefully and trying to keep her legs covered as she moved onto the still-untiled portion of the roof. Her heart was racing with the thrill of being there and, if she were honest, with the pleasure of teasing him.

"Besides," she continued, moving carefully to sit on the slanted wood and finally lifting her eyes, "I've always wanted to be up on a roof. And now here I am, and rewarded with an amazing view."

She thought she heard the sound of teeth gnashing behind her, which was followed by the resumption of his work. She didn't turn around to see. Instead, she looked out beyond her to a view of lush, rolling fields and trees bright with the new green of spring. In the weeping willow to the right of the cottage, a thrush was singing, and she'd never heard lovelier.

Long minutes passed as she sat near the edge and enjoyed the view while he worked steadily behind her. She reflected that if he'd been any other wealthy, handsome aristocrat, he would likely have been in Town, enjoying the adoration of numbers of ladies. But he was a man who obviously loved deeply, and

his heart was still captive, so none of that would appeal to him.

Love persisted beyond the grave—she knew that as well as anyone. But surely it wasn't meant to persist in bonds that limited the living, instead of wings that lifted them up?

"Judith's ball isn't a bad idea, you know," she said, not turning.

His only reply was a grunt.

"And I don't mean just for Lizzie, but for you as well. You're out of mourning now, though you don't seem inclined to seek the pleasures of Society…but surely you don't mean to shut yourself away alone here forever like some dragon in a dungeon?"

"A dragon in a dungeon, Anna?" he said in a tone that mocked the drama of her words.

She laughed a little, but she was imagining him at a ball full of his peers, dancing, charming the ladies as she was certain he could easily do. A ball like that would never be the place for the odd daughter of a country doctor. It wasn't a happy thought for her. But for him, surely the journey toward healing from his wife's death lay in abandoning the solitary haven he'd occupied for so long.

"I'll wager you had a life full of parties and balls not long ago. You can be charming when you wish. And you're not bad to look at."

The deep rumble of laughter behind her made her smile. "Lavish praise indeed. And what about you? When was the last time *you* went to a ball?"

"A few years ago."

She thought of the last assembly she'd been to, at

the rooms in Cheldney. She'd stood, a wallflower in an uncomfortably flounced dress she hated, and waited for a gentleman to pick her. She'd heard the sniggers about Dr. Bristol's daughter—*wild as a native!*—and heard the whispered comments that any man who danced with her risked getting his feet mashed. *Maybe Miss Bristol will want to lead,* tittered one of the local matrons, *since she behaves so much like a man.*

Anna knew now, with the wisdom of hindsight, that behind some of the talk had been the bitterness of the local women who'd resented that the eligible Dr. Bristol kept so much to himself. He never participated in gatherings where he might be a companion to one of the many unattached women, or sought the help of any of the local women in the raising of his daughter. They all thought him proud, and Anna by extension, and believing themselves scorned by this man they respected and needed, had offered no friendliness to his daughter.

Her father's failing hadn't really been pride, though; he simply hadn't needed other people. He was valued for his skills and respected in the scientific community for the discoveries he made, and that had always been enough for him. Society, fashion, fine manners—none of that had held any interest for him, and so these things had featured little in Anna's life as well.

"Tell me about David Tarryton," she said. "Lizzie said that you and her father were the best of friends."

"Changing the subject again, Anna?"

"It would help me be a better governess to Lizzie if I understood her family more."

He sighed. "We met at university. David was a few

years older than me, but we got on famously." He laughed a little, and she loved the sound of it. "He was, actually, the last man you'd expect to go off to a distant place to do worthy Christian things among strangers. He was rather a rascal."

"And you were the responsible friend, who kept you both from getting into trouble."

"Perhaps not *exactly* true, though I did keep him from climbing the spire of the chapel while drunk. But it was my idea to sneak into the clock tower later and change the time to an hour earlier. It caused an entertaining mild panic the next day when people got up extra early and earnestly set their watches to the wrong time."

She laughed. "And were you found out?"

"No, though my father did cast a stern eye my way when news of the prank circulated." He paused. "I'd forgotten about all that. Do you know, David once snuck into a vicar's garden and spelled out a bawdy phrase in pebbles on his lawn?"

"Devious and creative. I guess the apple didn't fall far from the tree as far as Lizzie is concerned."

He chuckled. "I hadn't thought about that, how like David she is."

"And Ginger…what was she like?"

A pause, and the sound of another tile being set in place. "You're determined to talk about her, aren't you?"

"She was part of your life. She still is, isn't she, in the way that anyone we've ever loved will always be? Tell me about her."

He was quiet for several moments, but she knew, from the lack of sound, that he'd paused in his work.

"Ginger always saw the best in people, she had a wonderful laugh, and her passion was doing good."

He laughed a little. "And she absolutely loved to embroider. The Christmas after we were married, she embroidered pretty little scenes for Tommy and all our Halifax cousins. Ruby and Emerald were delighted, and Marcus was only about three, so nobody was surprised when he used his as a cape, but her gifts rendered Louie, Tommy, and Andrew magnificently awkward as they tried to express their thanks. The scene brought *me* no end of private amusement though."

Anna smiled at the image. "She sounds like the kind of woman of which the world is in great need." And a perfect match for the responsible eldest son of a viscount. They'd been destined to be a couple who'd bring love and goodness to those around them, but it was as though all that possibility had been mangled for him when she'd died.

"She was," he said, fondness in his voice. "I felt like a king the day she agreed to marry me." He paused. "And I plunged to the depths of despair the day she fell off her horse. My only consolation was that she died instantly."

His love for his wife pierced her. Why had she brought this up? And yet, she felt certain it must be better for him to talk of his wife, that doing so might draw out some of the pain poisoning him.

"Ginger would have liked you," he said. "She would have admired your spirit."

She looked over her shoulder at him, but his gaze was directed at the roof. Beneath his words, though,

was the suggestion that *he* liked her, and they curled over her like a warm blanket.

She was falling a little more under his spell, even though she couldn't afford to care whether he liked her.

"You're not the shell of a man that you think you are," she said. "You've just been allowed, as a viscount, to wrap your sorrow around yourself like a cloak and cling to it. It's a tragedy that your wife had to die—that any beloved person has to die. But…you are here. And the question is, are you going to take up the reins of your life?"

When he didn't reply but just returned to working, she wondered if he regretted speaking as he had. The minutes passed, and she struggled against disappointment that he'd closed himself off to her again, even though she knew it was for the best.

He worked on, and she could feel him moving gradually closer to where she sat on the untiled portion, until finally he told her she'd have to get down so he could finish.

She descended the ladder and opened the door to the cottage, meaning to start on the whitewashing. But at the threshold she stopped and gazed around her at the cozy, light-filled room with its walls partially painted in fresh white, and was amazed anew at the truly fine thing he'd done.

He'd established these homes for his tenants, for men, women, and children accustomed to hard work who would expect nothing more than the functional, dark, and drafty cottages that people like them had inhabited all over England for generations. But he was doing something new here, something profoundly

good and not inexpensive. The cottages were modest, but they were designed with care and artistry, and anyone who lived in them would feel just as Anna had when she had walked in: happy.

The cottages did not represent the kind of charity that provided the occasional bowl of hot soup or medicines to a poor family, but a profound caring for the quality of one's neighbor's life. Her heart squeezed almost painfully with yearning for the goodness and strength in this man, and for the kind of life that she'd never even allowed herself to dream might be possible.

Behind her, he came into the house. She turned.

"Your tenants will love these. Having a home like this will change what their lives are like."

He just gave a brisk nod and frowned a little. "So, are you going to stand there, or are you going to work?"

"Work," she said with relief, and took up a brush and began applying whitewash to the walls.

They worked quietly for some time. It was companionable, with the soft sounds of their brushes going up and down and the sunlight streaming in the small window between them. They had the one bucket of whitewash to share, and they adopted a rhythm that allowed them to be dipping their brushes in the bucket at alternating times.

And then she became aware that her brush was the only one making painting sounds, that he had not dipped his for several minutes. She turned to find him staring at her, and her heart seemed to stop.

Thirteen

WILL KNEW HE NEVER SHOULD HAVE BROUGHT ANNA to the cottages, but their sparring had enticed him. And then she'd surprised him by climbing onto the roof. He'd been charmed by her spirit of adventure, and so distracted by her sitting there, bent knees tucked under her arms and the morning sun shining on the pretty, dark braid tumbling down her back, that he'd nearly hammered his thumb into mash. She'd been relaxed and contented as few women—and likely few men— would have been, sitting on a roof, and her presence had given him pleasure even while she'd probed him.

"Are you going to take up the reins of your life?"

Her question was fair, and he knew it said something about the way things had shifted since her arrival that he could acknowledge it to be so. His thoughts ranged over the last year, which was a blur, lost time in his own private island of sorrow and despair. Had he allowed himself to become a ruined man?

He'd almost wanted that, wanted the hopelessness and the anger and the bleakness to swallow him. It had felt right, an answer to what had happened to Ginger.

But now that a little space had been forced between him and that darkness…now he could see that beneath the anger was a sadness he could bear.

Anna's eyes regarded him frankly. Her cheeks were flushed, and she looked lovely and so appealingly real.

"You're thinking of your wife, aren't you?" she said.

"Yes," he said. "And no."

She lifted a questioning eyebrow.

He put his brush down across the top of the paint bucket, gathering his thoughts. "For a long time, I've been extremely angry about her death and about my own inability to stop it or change it."

A ghost of a smile hovered around her lips. "You're accustomed to being in charge. And perhaps anger is your natural response to injustice, even if it's unavoidable."

He frowned. "I've been thinking…well, that I can't go on as I have been, that perhaps you may be a little right."

His words seemed to surprise her. "Perhaps a very little," she said gently. "For what it's worth, I think it very fine that you loved your wife so much."

"I'll always love her. I'll always be so sorry that she's gone. And I never want to feel again like I did when she died. But"—he reached out and cupped her cheek—"I am alive."

"Yes," she said. And it felt like the most natural thing in the world to lean down and kiss her. She responded instantly and with a sweet urgency that only added fuel to the fire she'd already kindled in him.

"Anna," he murmured against her lips. "I can't tell you how much you've been in my thoughts."

He felt her smile against his mouth. "Who are you when you're not a viscount?"

"Will."

"Will," she whispered back.

She lifted a hand and found the gap below the ties of his shirt and slid her small hand inside to touch his chest. He groaned and pulled her against him, delighting in the soft give of her woman's body. It had been so long.

His hands shaped the curve of her neck and moved over her narrow, sturdy shoulders, luxuriating in the graceful shape of feminine muscles that had doubtless been made firm by climbing and lifting and running and *doing*.

He found the curve of her waist under her loose gown. Desire licked at him, leaving a burning trail along inner paths that had been a wasteland.

He threaded his hands through her hair, loosening heavy lengths of curls that seemed to want to be liberated, and the wisp of ribbon holding the ends together fell off.

"You are so lovely," he murmured, "that if you ever traded in these rags for something pretty, people would think a goddess had come to live among us."

He read a flicker of vulnerability in her eyes and remembered with a bolt of recrimination how she'd been mistreated by that man from her past, and he let his hands drop. He leaned his forehead against hers.

"Anna, forgive me. I got carried away. And you, who have been so imposed upon by a man. Already I allowed myself to kiss you yesterday—"

But he hadn't finished before she twisted her hands

in his shirt and pulled him closer, her wild black hair adding to the crackling energy in her sherry eyes.

"Do you think I want what happened with that odious man to shape my view of what men and women can be to each other?" she said fiercely. "Do you think I want to give him such power over me? My answer to what he did is to claim my own choice now and always. And right now, my choice is you, Will."

And she lifted up on her tiptoes and crushed her lips against his. He closed his eyes and hugged her hard to him, something loosening and flowing free in his chest.

But there was more than one reason he shouldn't have been standing there with her in his arms, and he forced himself to move his lips from hers. "You are in my employ. Touching you like this—it's taking advantage of you."

"You *can't* take advantage of me if I give freely," she said in a voice that was almost angry. "Kiss me, damn you."

He could resist his desire for her no longer. With a groan, he buried his face where her neck met her shoulder and kissed the bare skin lavishly. A soft whimper escaped her, making heat flare through him.

He traced the curves of her hips and waist with urgent desire as she explored his chest and moved lower, pulling his shirt loose from his trousers. Her smooth fingers skipped over his hips, her touch there a ticklish, erotic torture that made him shudder. He cupped her breasts greedily. She was heaven, and he had to have more.

With a grunt, he dragged her skirts upward to pile

over his arms and gorged himself on the feel of her gently rounded hips. He nearly exploded with lust as he found the curve of her small bottom and squeezed.

Dropping to his knees, he ran his hands up her slim, athletic legs, taking his time, exploring each hollow and curve. When he encountered the bits of frayed ribbon tying her saggy, plain white stockings underneath her knees, he growled.

"I'm buying you new ribbons and stockings."

"I like these," she said in a husky voice. "They're comfortable."

He kissed each of her knees until she wobbled, then steadied her with a firm hold on her thighs and kissed a little higher. She slumped back against the wall and her hand scrabbled in his hair.

"Come back up here so I can kiss you again," she said, sending a shaft of lust to his already-painful cock.

He stood up slowly, dragging his hand up her inner thighs as he did so, until he stood before her and his hand touched the secret heart of her. Her breath caught. She was wet, and she gave a little moan as he massaged her.

"Will," she whispered, passion glowing in her pink cheeks and her cloud of black hair a beautiful riot. "I didn't know…"

"That you could feel so good here?" Her sensual response was making him burn hotter every second, making him desperate to bury himself in her, but he couldn't do that. Besides, he wanted this to be for her.

A wordless murmur was her only reply. Her legs were shaking, and he slid a steadying arm around her as he stroked her. Her dark head fell against his chest in

a motion of surrender that tugged at his heart. With a soft gasp, she shuddered and hugged him as she found her release.

❧

Anna was barely capable of thought as she stood there in his arms. Her dress had fallen back into place, but her hands were still clutching his bare back. She was in *Will's* arms. She knew him differently now. Very differently. And the peace, the pleasure, the feeling of safety she'd found in his arms... How could she have known it would be like that?

Even as she knew that she didn't want to ever leave his arms, she felt a stirring of unease that she'd allowed herself to be so vulnerable.

"Anna," he said, his voice soft and husky as it drifted over her head. She wasn't ready to look at him yet. She didn't even want to speak and break the spell that had come over them, but she knew that was foolishness. "We can't go on like this."

"I suppose not."

"You *suppose*?" He sighed, a tortured sound. "Anna, this attraction between us...it's hot, unruly, powerful. But you *work* for me. I should never have allowed myself to touch you, no matter how much I wanted to do so."

Even though he was still holding her, his words told of regret, and they pushed away the lingering magic. She withdrew her hands, stepped away from him, and conjured all her inner resources to look him steadily in the eye.

"I'm not some blushing lady's maid you cornered

in the stairway, Will. You didn't force your attentions on me. We both know that. It's nobody's business but ours."

His mouth twisted. "But it's *my* business, Anna. I don't behave this way." He frowned, the blue of his eyes darkening to midnight. "Anna, I like you very much. I want you. And I want to take care of you. Let me set up a house for you."

Something inside her dropped like a stone falling in a dark, deep well.

"What, a little house somewhere on the estate?" she said, just managing to keep her voice even as she began to gather her hair roughly into a plait. "Governess for your ward by day, mistress to you by night?"

He pressed his lips together. "I can hire another governess for Lizzie. You would have your own life. In fact, there is a rather nice hunting cottage on the property. I could have it fixed up for you. Perhaps you would even like to draw there, or paint, if that's something you enjoy."

She wished he hadn't said anything, that he wasn't offering her the chance to be his mistress. Even the manner in which he was doing it was considerate, the way he was thinking about what it might be like for her.

She was so drawn to him, so very attracted to him, and she cared for him far more than she should. Being with him brought her such pleasure, as did the idea of a future with him. Measured against the future that awaited her with her aunt, even with her dream of the drawing school she wanted to establish… Well, his offer was horribly tempting.

But to be dependent on a man, even if it was this man, and to live her life as the pleasant diversion he reserved for himself was a role she'd never have dreamed of considering before her life had changed, and she didn't want it now. And never with this man, who was such a danger to her heart.

She bent down and picked up her ribbon that had fallen to the floor and, tying it back on, said, "No, thank you."

His mouth tensed in a stubborn line. "Anna, think. You would have a home of your own here. With me."

Oh, fool that she was, she was badly tempted by the idea of a home with Will, but that wasn't truly what he was offering, and it didn't take much imagining to conjure the pain she would feel when he did, one day, marry again to a woman of his own class. Because he would, now that he'd begun to truly put his wife's death behind him. It would be expected. He'd need a helpmate and an heir or two.

"No," she said again.

He crossed his arms, his viscount's air of command settling over him.

"I knew I was wrong to touch you, but from the first, you've been so lacking in subservience, so ready to do exactly as you wished, that I silenced my conscience by telling myself you made your own choices. But we both know that isn't how things work. And you've promised to stay and help Lizzie, but the desire between you and me is only going to get more powerful. What do you propose to do about the situation?"

"I *propose*," she began, though she had little notion what she was going to say, when the sound of a dog

barking outside the cottage door startled them. They just had time to move farther apart as Judith's spaniel, Tristan, trotted past the partially open cottage door with a triumphant woof. Women's voices sounded over his din, and Judith appeared in the doorway.

"Here you are, Grandville." Judith's eyebrows went up as she took in the scene. "And, Anna," she added, with a note of surprise, but she smiled. "I've brought a visitor."

She stepped inside, followed by one of the loveliest women Anna had ever seen. She was elegant and sleek, with golden blond hair fixed in a neat, braided knot high on her regal head. Her gown of palest yellow was an airy, gossamer confection that made her look like the princess of spring.

"Grandville," the woman said sweetly, smiling as she floated closer and held out her hands to him. "Here you are finally. I'd heard a rumor that the reason you have no time for your neighbors is that you've taken up roofing as a hobby, but I hadn't quite believed it. And yet here you are in surely the shabbiest clothes ever worn by any gentleman in the entire county."

He took her hands and bowed graciously over them. "Miss Miranda Chittister, you are looking well. I must beg you to excuse my attire, but I've been whitewashing."

There was a pause as the woman's eyes drifted toward Anna.

"May I present Anna Black, my ward's governess?" he said.

Anna dipped her head politely, though their visitor hardly noticed.

"You have a ward, Grandville?" she said, her

face lighting up. "How charming! How old is the dear thing?"

"Sixteen."

"A new young lady in the neighborhood! Already I long to meet her. Where is she?"

He laughed. "She had not yet arisen by the time I left, though perhaps by now she has at least breakfasted."

"I'm certain we shall be friends." Miss Chittister shook a playfully admonishing finger at him. "Really, you've been the most awful recluse, Grandville, not visiting with a single person in the neighborhood, and never at home to anyone. But all is forgiven now that you're holding a ball! We are all in raptures. Your stepmother has just been telling me how very festive it will be."

Anna saw his eyes flick in Judith's direction, and she could easily translate the spike of fury in them at the realization that he'd been outmaneuvered by her. But the face he turned on his neighbor was all that was gracious.

"Then," he said, "that must make me the happiest of hosts."

Well done, Judith, Anna thought, giving a silent cheer on behalf of Lizzie.

Miss Chittister looked around at the cottage. "So you've been *working*, Grandville. And you've apparently had help."

Miss Chittister's eyes came to rest on Anna. She felt their assessing weight on her hair and clothes and lifted her chin. Miss Chittister's gaze moved dismissively on, clearly having discarded the idea of Anna as any sort of competition. It wasn't an unfamiliar situation

for Anna, but for the first time, it made her cherish a secret smile.

Judith said, "The cottages look very, very fine, Grandville. They will surely put your tenants over the moon." Her hazel eyes sought his, and though he seemed to avoid her gaze, she was not deterred. "How happy and proud your father would have been to see them."

He was saved from the necessity of a reply by Miss Chittister. "*My* father is not pleased about the cottages," she said with a light laugh. "He says you'll give the tenants ideas above their station."

"Ah, well," he said evasively.

Anna was disappointed in him. Clearly he felt strongly that tenants deserved better treatment than they usually received, but he'd gotten used to withdrawing over the last year.

"I think," she said, "that his tenants will feel very much valued here at Stillwell and will return Lord Grandville's generosity with hard work."

Miss Chittister coughed delicately. "Well," she said, "Miss Black is certainly convinced of their merit. But come, Grandville, I'm here to carry you off for a visit to Trippleford Manor, and you must stay for dinner. Mama and Papa said I was not to take no for an answer, and indeed I shan't."

A pause. Anna supposed he wanted to decline and retreat to his manor, but the invitation offered him an escape from the three women there.

"How could I refuse such a gracious invitation?"

Miss Chittister clapped her hands with delight in a way that made Anna clench her teeth. "What a coup, the elusive Viscount Grandville to dine at our house!"

"Judith, Anna," he said, giving them a vague bow before he held out an arm politely for Miss Chittister.

Fourteen

Anna and Judith watched the viscount and his guest walk out across the fields toward the manor, where doubtless a coach would be waiting.

"Your auxiliary plan seems to have been successful," Anna said. She went over and put the cover on the whitewash bucket and used that moment of privacy to take a deep, gathering breath and remind herself that she was still just a servant at Stillwell Hall and nothing more.

When she turned around again, the older woman had a quizzical look on her face that made Anna's heart sink further.

"My dear," Judith said carefully, "is there something between you and Grandville?"

"No, of course not." That was true. There was nothing of substance between them. No promises had been made, nor could they be.

Judith allowed her eyes to rest on Anna, but Anna did not accept the invitation they offered to talk.

"I had wondered if perhaps there was some attachment between you two," Judith said. "And just now…"

"He had merely asked me to help, since Lizzie

was still sleeping and thus did not need me. Merely a matter of earning my keep."

"I see. Well, in any case, I'm glad not only for him but for Lizzie as well that he's accepted the ball. What I want most for my stepsons is that they each find a woman they love to marry."

Anna thought of what Will had said about his wife in the cottage. *"I'll always love her. I'll always be so sorry that she's gone. And I never want to feel again like I did when she died."*

Even now, the words broke her heart a little because she knew that, given the chance, she could easily fall in love with this man who didn't want to fall in love again. She supposed it would be just as well for him that, when he chose an appropriate woman to be his viscountess, aristocrats rarely married for love.

The two women left the cottage with Tristan trotting between them and started back toward the manor, whose cream-colored stonework could be seen in occasional glimpses beyond the trees and gardens. She'd come to find the enormous building ridiculously homey, and she must resist its pull. She must fight against anything in her that yearned for anything to do with Will.

They were walking through a section of the formal garden when Lizzie emerged from behind an enormous old rose bush a few feet ahead of them, obviously in a hurry.

She stopped abruptly when she saw them, her startled look telling Anna she was not glad to find others in the garden. Lizzie's white muslin gown was badly rumpled, as if it had been pulled on straight

from a resting place on the floor. Her face was pale, and her red-gold hair looked as if she had yanked it, unbrushed, into a twist. A thick strand hung loose on one side.

"Oh, hello," she said briskly, and made as if to continue past them, evidently anxious to undo her night's work. Anna caught her gently by the arm as she passed.

"I was out early this morning and saw Lord Grandville doing a bit of gardening. Removing some overgrown ivy."

Lizzie gasped and looked, if possible, paler. "Grandville?" she croaked. "The ivy? Truly?"

Judith coughed. "Certainly within his duties as lord of the manor to see to the garden," she said. Her eyes regarded Lizzie with a sympathetic expression that suggested she too must have seen the statues before they were cleared off.

"Oh no! He shouldn't have had to…er, clean up." Lizzie looked like she might be ill at the thought of her uncle discovering what had happened to Apollo.

Looking at her now, Anna thought it surprising that she'd ever considered Lizzie to be snobbish, when it was so obvious that her haughtiness had only been a screen for the hurt that was now laid bare on her young face.

Lizzie's troubled gaze dropped to the grass, and another piece of her hair slipped from its loose mooring, but she didn't seem to notice. "I expect he'll want to send me away as soon as possible."

Anna gave her arm an encouraging squeeze. "Actually, he and I had a chat. He's promised that

you'll stay a month, and he'll honor that. Though he does expect never to have to do any such tidying in the future."

"Oh!" Lizzie looked up, color flooding her cheeks. "That is so very kind of him! Of course nothing like this will happen again."

"I hope most ardently that you're sincere." Anna caught her eye. "You do see now that there must be no more schemes?"

"Yes, of course."

Judith said in a gentle voice, "You know, Lizzie, you would probably have been quite amused by Grandville if you'd known him when he was your age. He and his cousin Louie were known to pull the occasional prank. And of course, your father was the worst of the lot, a charming rascal."

"Sometimes it's hard to believe he and my uncle were friends, even if Grandville was different once. I wanted so much for the two of us to be like family, but I don't know if that will ever happen. Maybe I should just ask to go to another school," Lizzie said despondently.

"You mustn't give up hope," Anna said firmly. Especially not now that his spirits seemed to be lightening, she thought, though she could hardly explain *why* she thought they might be lightening.

"I agree," Judith said. "And I've known him for ages. Just give it a little more time."

"Very well," Lizzie said, a little cheered. She tipped her head. "How long have you known him, anyway?"

"Since he was nineteen. I married his father within a few months of Lady Grandville's death."

Lizzie looked shocked by this information. "Well,

he can't have missed his first wife so very much, then. My father didn't remarry for years."

"Lizzie, I'm not sure we should quiz Judith about such things," Anna said.

"No, it's all right. And Lizzie knows of what she speaks. I knew even at the time that Alistair was proposing to me out of a desire to distract himself from his grief. But I already loved him so much that I was sure it would be enough for both of us."

"Oh," Lizzie said. "That's not very romantic."

"No," Judith agreed. "Though I told myself it was, a sort of grand gesture for love that would make everything turn into happily ever after. I was very good at spinning fantasy into truth back then. I was going to make Alistair and his sons love me more than they'd loved the woman they'd lost."

"I guess it didn't work out that way?"

"No. And your uncle was old enough to see all the mistakes I made."

"I didn't want a stepmother either. Though you're so much kinder than my stepmother was."

"Thank you, my dear. But perhaps you might have come to care for her in time. It's not easy to join a family that already exists. I had never mothered anyone, and the three of them had suffered a tragedy. Trying to find my place in the Halifax family became the hardest thing I'd ever done."

Lizzie absorbed these words quietly. "I've never thought about it that way before, that it might be been hard for the stepmother."

Judith chuckled softly. "Being a stepmother has its advantages too. I've just now helped Grandville

to reconsider the ball, and he's decided that it must go on."

"He has?" Lizzie gave a whoop. "But that's wonderful!" she cried, enfolding a laughing Judith in a jubilant embrace.

"We'll have our work cut out for us though," Judith said. "There's so much to be done before the ball. For one thing, some of the rooms look ridiculously barren. I gather Grandville had a number of furnishings put away after Ginger died, the new carpets and paintings and such that she'd bought. So I hope to find them in the attics. Perhaps you two would like to join me?"

"I should like it of all things!" Lizzie enthused.

The ladies agreed to begin work that afternoon.

❧

Anna was glad to return to the peace of her bedchamber after all that had happened that morning. She felt storm-tossed and fidgety and couldn't settle down with her book.

A maid brought up a luncheon tray, and Anna put it on her vanity and stood nibbling halfheartedly at a piece of cold chicken. She caught sight of herself in the cheval glass and frowned. Her gown really did look like boiled dust.

And for the first time, she cared.

Putting down the chicken, she tilted her head. She tugged her hair out of its messy knot, letting her black curls fall in a glossy jumble to her waist, and tried to see what Will saw in her. He found her beautiful, and now she looked with new eyes at herself.

She'd always believed there was so much more to a person than his or her appearance, but, being attracted to Will, she also had to admit that physical beauty had a role in drawing people together, in making them take a closer look.

She looked approvingly now on her light brown eyes, her pink lips and cheeks, and her trim form. She'd always been happy enough with the way she was, but she'd never believed it likely that any man would find her special.

And so she'd dispensed with efforts to be alluring, telling herself that coiffures and jewelry and fancy shoes were for girls who wanted to simper and giggle. But perhaps she'd also abandoned caring about her appearance and cultivating gracious manners because she feared making a fool of herself if she tried—feared that everyone would have laughed at Dr. Bristol's hoyden of a daughter trying to pass for a lady.

With a shudder, she thought of the horrible Mr. Rawlins, who'd apparently seen beauty in her. He'd seen something in her and tried to make it his. But he wasn't the only one with vision, and now she wanted to own what was rightfully hers.

Lizzie's pink dress was still hanging in Anna's wardrobe, but such a sweet color would never suit her. Instead, she reached behind her waist and pinched the fabric of her dress so that it fit snugly under her breasts. Much, much better.

She unfastened her gown and stepped out of it. In her chemise, she sat on the bed and, taking her gown in hand, threw prudence to the wind. Drawing in a deep breath—this was after all one of only two gowns

she had, and she was not very talented with a needle—she snipped at the gown's high neckline. She folded it down and sewed it to make a pretty, scooped square. With a series of neat tucks, she took in the loose fabric under the bust and adjusted the side seams.

She put the gown back on and regarded herself again. The color was still a vague grayish blue, but it looked vastly better now that it traced the woman's body underneath. Humming, she went to work on the brown gown.

When Lizzie and Judith knocked on her door in the mid-afternoon, she opened it and they both stared at her.

"Gracious," Lizzie said, "but your gown looks marvelous."

Anna came out of her room, closing the door. "That is certainly a gross exaggeration, considering its color, but I do like it better now."

"You look quite lovely, Anna," Judith said as they walked along the hallway. "And you've changed your hair. It's softer and very becoming."

Anna blushed and smiled. "Thank you."

Fifteen

ANNA AND JUDITH WERE STANDING IN THE FOYER AT the foot of Stillwell's grand staircase the next morning and discussing with Dart the disposition of items from the attic when the viscount emerged from his library.

She hadn't seen him since the afternoon before, when he left with Miss Chittister, and she was surprised he wasn't now at the cottages. He had on a maroon waistcoat that looked very fine in contrast with his dark brown hair and hung perfectly on those broad shoulders that inspired the worst sort of weakness in her. Just the sight of him was giving her jelly legs. She looked away.

At least she would be leaving in a few weeks or, God forbid, sooner, if the effects of that book somehow reached her. For now she had Lizzie to focus on, and she would be grateful for any distraction the ball preparations would bring.

She could—she *would*—manage to live in the same house with him and behave as if nothing had happened.

"Judith," he said in the emotionless tone he used

with his stepmother, who nonetheless returned his greeting with serene warmth. He turned to Anna, and his eyes glittered at her with secret meaning. A rebellious heat warmed her lips in response. She pressed them together hard.

"A word with you, Anna."

At that moment, from outside Stillwell's double front doors came the sound of carriage wheels on gravel, and she supposed that he must be awaiting a visitor, perhaps Miss Chittister. Miss Chittister was an appropriate match for him, she told herself cruelly.

Judith, remarking to Anna that she would resume choosing furnishings from the attic, went upstairs.

"What are you doing with the furniture?" he asked Anna.

"Why not ask Judith? I'm sure she'd be happy to discuss her plans with you."

"I'm asking you."

She sighed. What was between him and his stepmother ran too deep for gentle prodding. "I'm helping her choose things from the attic to spruce up the manor so it will be festive for the ball. It does currently have rather the air of a monastery."

He frowned, looking off into space. "I had some things put away after Ginger died. She'd been in the midst of redecorating before…" He shrugged, looking back at her. "I didn't want the new things she'd bought around to remind me of her."

"Like the picture on my chamber wall?"

"What's that?"

"There's a half-finished pastoral scene on a wall in my chamber."

"That was Ginger's idea, putting murals in some of the rooms. She liked to support artists."

"I like her better and better," she admitted. "I was going to have Lizzie finish the painting."

"Really? Is she talented at painting and drawing?"

"As it turns out, those are not her best skills. She is, for one thing, extremely gifted in her studies. But *I* am quite fond of painting, and it rather undoes me to wake up every morning to a headless shepherd with no meadow for his sheep."

"Then finish it if you want to."

"Truly? You wouldn't mind?"

He sighed. "In truth, Ginger would have hated to see it left undone. To see the house so…"

"Barren? Monastic?"

He gave her a look. "Spartan. Disciplined."

"Nonsense. It looks odd. Even bachelors need a comfortable home."

"Maybe," he said halfheartedly, surprising her. "I'll have some paints ordered for you."

His eyes traveled over her body and she tingled under his gaze. Oh, these were going to be a hard few weeks.

"What have you done to your clothes? You look different."

"I had the urge to sew. I should think you'd be satisfied that all your browbeating has had a result."

"I am pleased," he said, though he sounded grouchy. "You look exceedingly fine."

"Thank you," she said, struggling not to feel too happy about his compliment. "I found something interesting in the attic this morning."

He raised his eyebrows questioningly.

"I think it might be for the cottages. A half-finished sign that reads 'Willow Glen Ha—'"

"Oh that. Yes, it was for the cottages," he said.

"It's funny that whoever started it never finished it." She had her suspicions about the sign's creator. It wasn't as if a craftsman would have presented partially completed work to the viscount. "Maybe that some-one would finish it and then it could be put out by the cottages. It would look very fine."

"Maybe."

At that moment, boots rang out on the stone steps outside the doors, as if someone were taking them vigor-ously and two at a time. And then, without so much as a knock, the tall doors opened and in strode an extremely handsome young gentleman of perhaps twenty years.

He had black hair that was wavy like Will's, but his had an insouciant streak of white near his forehead that gave him a striking air, as if he'd been touched by some goddess as a mark of favor. He was smartly attired in a dark blue superfine topcoat, crisp white cravat, and tan breeches that looked very well on his long, youthfully slim legs, and he came briskly into the foyer with a grin on his face.

"Hello, Brother," he said, and bowed playfully. "You are looking all the crack."

"Am I, Tommy?" the viscount returned with a wry smile as he stepped forward, and the two shared what looked to be a crushingly manly embrace.

He was clearly quite pleased at his brother's arrival. Anna, though, could not rejoice in the arrival of Mr. Thomas Halifax, and was wishing at that very minute

for a hole to open in the floor and swallow her. Especially when, the embrace over, their visitor's eyes finally settled on her. His brows drew together, and she knew she was in trouble.

"Why, Miss…Bristol, isn't it?" he said, cocking his head. He smiled. "What on earth are you doing here? Is your father here?"

"Oh. Er, no," she said.

"What's this, Tommy? How could you possibly know Anna? Or her father?"

Tommy looked surprised by this question. "Why shouldn't I know her? She's Dr. Bristol's daughter. He cured me of that terrible fever I had the summer I was fourteen, at Littlebury." He turned to Anna. "You *are* Dr. Bristol's daughter, aren't you?"

"Yes." The word came out like a croak. Out of the corner of her eye, she could see the storm clouds gathering in Viscount Grandville's face.

Tommy grinned. "I remember that you sometimes came when your father visited me, to act as his assistant. I'm very happy to see you again. And by Jove, but the years have been kind to you!"

They had been extremely kind to him as well, and she guessed that he did very well with the ladies. She returned his warm greeting, all the while feeling his brother's eyes on her.

She forced herself to face Will. His eyes had darkened to the color of a wintry midnight sky.

"I have met your father," he said. "Our families are acquainted."

"Yes," she said, managing not to croak this time. "And now, if you'll excuse me, I have work to do."

His eyes glinted at her, promising doom. "But I have not excused you, Anna. Why, I may develop some urgent medical problem on which I might consult with you. Or I may require some other service of my governess. Where is my ward?" His words were mocking, but the light in his eyes was far from playful. He was furious.

"Lizzie was overcome by sneezing from the attic dust, and so she's gone in search of Tristan to take a walk. Of course I will stay here if you wish, my lord, but I had promised to return to the attic."

Two servants were even then starting down the flight of stairs holding an enormous painting between them. Behind them came another servant carrying a small oval table.

"Go then," he said with a dismissive gesture that nonetheless said he was far from done with her. And with the quickest of curtsies, she took her leave before he could change his mind.

৵৹

"What doings are these, Will?" Tommy asked as he watched Anna ascend the stairs.

"Library." Will turned on his heel and his brother followed him into the room. They dropped into the striped chairs by the empty hearth.

"Well, and what has become of your male sanctum? Anna Bristol here, and Elizabeth Tarryton too, if I understand correctly. I didn't even know she was coming for a visit."

"Lizzie's arrival was unexpected," Will said. A satisfyingly righteous anger was growing within him,

and he was wishing he were in London and set for an appointment at Gentleman Jack's, because what he wanted more than anything at that moment was to pummel something. Or, rather, a certain someone.

"Anna is here as a temporary governess to Lizzie, though she may last for perhaps a shorter duration than foreseen, as I may strangle her before the day is out."

"A diverting image. So you didn't know she was Dr. Bristol's daughter?"

"No." Will ran a hand roughly through his hair and attempted to unclench his jaw. He supposed he knew why she'd given him a false name, but he didn't like it, not when they'd grown as close as they had.

"She's been going by the surname Black. But she did tell me that some damned peer had tried to take advantage of her in some way, and she was clearly in something of a bind when I first met her, so I can only think she may have adopted a false name to help put the incident behind her."

Tommy's face darkened. "Damnation! Who is this scoundrel? I'll wring his neck."

"Easy there. I'd have dealt with him myself, but she won't say. She insists no real harm was done and that she just wants to forget the whole thing. I don't like it, but I won't press her."

He thought a moment. "And I suppose you and I ought to keep this business about her name to ourselves. There's no need to create confusion at Stillwell by mentioning this to anyone else."

Tommy nodded, his lips pressed together.

"So," he said a few moments later, "if Lizzie is walking Tristan, then Judith is here as well?"

"Yes."

"Why," Tommy said, smiling, "I haven't seen Judith since I ran into her in London at least a year ago. How is she?"

Will felt a brief spark of gratitude that his younger brother enjoyed such untroubled contentment. He'd always been glad that Tommy, only seven when Judith arrived, never discovered that she'd been their father's mistress.

"She appears to be as usual."

"Wasn't she traveling in Egypt?"

"I know nothing of where she's been. But you may ask her yourself, now she's here."

"You have quite a houseful of guests, Brother," Tommy said, resting an ankle comfortably on his knee.

"Yes, damn it, and not one of them invited. What are you doing here, anyway? I thought you were in Italy with our cousins."

"They wanted to stay a bit longer, but I've been back in London a few days. And I've come to Stillwell for the ball, of course. I must say, your invitation was a surprise."

Will growled. "It was not *my* invitation."

"But if you didn't send the invitation, who did? Is there a prankster afoot?"

"Judith. She apparently wants to do her duty by Father and see me married. So she's taken it upon herself to arrange a ball here."

"Oh ho!" Tommy clasped his hands behind his head and flopped back against the chair, the very picture of relaxed enjoyment. "And now you are to have a ball. Excellent! But tell me, how did you

not recognize Anna? I must say I thought her a
very pretty nurse when she came with her father to
cure me."

"I never met her then."

"Ah, that's right. Judith and Father were away as
well, now that I remember. The servants were quite
worried about me. But Anna's tumbling black curls
rather caught my eye as I lay in my sickbed, and she
was charmingly serious about birds. Her father wrote
a few books on birds, come to think of it. Isn't there
one in the Stillwell library?"

Will leaned forward irritably and rested his
elbows on his knees. He could feel his brother's
measured gaze on the back of his head as he stared
at the empty hearth.

Bloody hell. He'd done wicked things to the daughter of a respected, if forgotten, family friend.

Damn it all!

"Things appear to be in a far different state than
they were at my visit a few months ago," Tommy said.
He peered at Will speculatively. "And you and Anna
seem to be on rather familiar terms."

Will ground his teeth together and shifted his
head to give Tommy a withering, older-brother
glare. "I know you are not even remotely suggesting
anything untoward."

"Certainly not," Tommy said, coloring. "How
the devil could you believe I would entertain such
thoughts about Dr. Bristol's daughter?"

Because I *do*, Will thought miserably. "Sorry."
He sat back in his seat again and crossed his arms,
feeling ferocious.

"What's going on in the attic, then? Are we selling off the furniture?"

"At present Anna and Judith are disgorging the contents of the attic into the rest of the house in preparation for the accursed ball."

"Doubtless not an adjective commonly associated with balls. But a festive event should jolly things up around here. Stillwell has had rather the air of a monastery for some time. Why, the entry hall alone, with only that single, plain table along the wall, makes us look like a family of severe people."

Will clenched his teeth. This was the second time someone had mentioned monasteries that hour. "Enough about the ball. How was Italy? And how are our cousins?"

"Italy was tremendous. The cousins are as usual, which means that Louie has charmed nearly every lady in the country, Andrew is climbing some mountain or other, Ruby is trying out all the Italian fashions, and Emerald has her nose buried in a book. Marcus is still at home, of course, stuck in the schoolroom."

"I look forward to seeing them on their return."

Tommy looked pleasantly surprised. "I'm certain they'd be delighted to see you. It's been rather a while, hasn't it?"

"Yes."

"Well," he continued, "London was *not* so diverting. It's all the same old parties and routs, and I'm glad to be away from it. In fact, there are a few people whom I won't miss seeing."

"Oh?"

"People keep trying to fix me up with their sisters and cousins and such. The young ladies are all very pleasing, et cetera, but not a thought in their heads. It's deuced awkward—you really can't have a conversation with a one of them. And it spoils the fun of the hunt, being fixed up with people."

"Your problems are truly monumental, Brother. But do consider that you might wish to marry before long."

Tommy shuddered, which amused his brother.

"Good grief," he groaned. "I'm only twenty—no need to even begin thinking about being leg-shackled. Why, Father didn't marry Mother until he was at least twenty-five, and look how marvelously their marriage worked out. I take them as my models—they had years of bliss. I'd be a fool to do differently."

Will only hesitated a moment before saying, "Indeed."

"And after your ball," Tommy continued, "I mean to stop over at Henshaw's estate for his 'Grand Party for Art' or whatever the devil he's calling the event. He's promised the unveiling of a magnificent new painting of this apparently stunning woman who's in a book of erotic drawings he's got. Have you heard about all this? She's called the Beautiful One."

"I saw something in the newspaper. Henshaw must be relishing being the center of attention. I suppose she's his latest mistress or something like."

"Doubtless," Tommy agreed, laughing. "But this Beautiful One thing really is the talk of the *ton* these days. Henshaw's obviously enjoying deciding who gets to see the book—*I* didn't make the list. But I've heard that she really is something to see."

He sighed ruefully. "It is a diverting mystery. Why

don't you come to the party? It would do you good to get out of Stillwell for a bit."

The last thing Will wanted to do was join a house party full of chattering hordes. But he appreciated his brother's concern. And he'd have to begin getting out in the world again at some point. "I'll think about it."

Sixteen

Anna had arrived near the library door just in time to hear Tommy mention *The Beautiful One* and Henshaw's ghastly party, and she'd stood there listening in helpless horror, holding a large vase she'd brought down from the attic.

A party was being planned at which her identity as the Beautiful One was going to be revealed. Dear God.

Will knew about the book.

He also knew she'd been using a false name.

She stood there shaking, her mind whirling.

She knew he was angry that she hadn't said she was Dr. Bristol's daughter, but he hadn't exposed her lie when Tommy mentioned her father, and she held out hope that she could somehow explain to him that the false name was just a detail.

Far more pressing, though, was the fact that his brother had apparently almost seen the book. What a disaster that would have been. He hadn't said whether it had been in London or somewhere else that he'd seen the marquess. Had it been somewhere close to Stillwell? It wasn't as if she could ask.

She lifted a shaking hand to rub her face. What she wanted at that moment was to sit down on the marble floor and bury her head in her knees and weep. Her father would certainly have pointed out that to feel fresh despair and rage over those drawings and the power they had to make her into an outcast was foolish. But something had changed. Now, she'd had a taste of what she might be losing.

She reminded herself harshly that she and Will could never have married. He was a viscount and she was a doctor's daughter. His sights must be set on women far above her. But what had grown between them since she'd come to Stillwell had touched her deeply, and she realized now how much she wanted to hold on to hope that something might happen, something that could change all the reasons he wasn't for her.

But that would be a fairy tale, and she knew better than to believe in such things. The book existed, and it was her ruin. She must stop hoping and dreaming.

She squeezed her eyelids together hard and took a deep breath. She *must not* allow herself to feel so deeply about Will. She would be leaving soon, and that was a good thing.

Behind her, she heard the sound of someone coming down the stairs, and she steadied herself and turned to see Judith, carrying a small oil painting.

"Was that Miss Chittister just arriving?" Judith asked when she got to the bottom of the stairs. "I thought I heard a coach."

"No, it was Lord Grandville's brother."

Judith's face lit up. "Tommy's here? The dear boy, how I've missed him!"

A bark of masculine laughter issued from behind the library doors.

"I was just going to get Grandville's opinion on putting this painting in the drawing room. And that vase might look nice there as well. Would you mind bringing it along, Anna, so I can welcome Tommy properly first?"

Anna would far rather not see Will and his brother again just now, but she almost had a sense Judith needed a little moral support. She seemed eager to see Tommy, but what if he were as unhappy to see her as Will had been? Anna nodded and followed Judith into the library.

"Tommy!" Judith said.

The young man jumped out of his chair as her greeting caught his attention and strode over to her with a grin.

"Judith!" He took the little painting out of her hands, putting it on a table, and pulled her into an enormous hug as Will stood with an impassive look and Anna lingered by the door.

"Why, you must set all the hearts of the young ladies and their matchmaking mamas to beating faster," Judith said, after he'd said how well she was looking.

He chuckled. "I cannot complain, though as merely the brother of Viscount Grandville, I don't merit anywhere near the attention I would if I were the man himself."

"Yes," Judith agreed, letting her eyes rest on the viscount. "I'm certain he is very much missed."

"You may put that vase down, Anna," Will said, and she could see that she was going to get the

haughty viscount treatment. She gave him a mutinous look but complied.

"Well," said Tommy, "he shall have to play the host in a very few days at the ball, and there will be no escaping the ladies then."

"Thank you, Tommy, that will do," Will said. His brother laughed.

"I've had such fun on my travels," Judith said, "to Egypt and here and there, and I do have my dear Tristan, but I miss family. It's so good to see you both."

"And where is Tristan?" Tommy asked, even as the dog trotted through the open door.

He crouched down to pet the dog. "He does remind me of Cadfael." He glanced up at Anna. "Cadfael was the sire, our father's favorite hound."

"Ah," she said, smiling. It was kind of him to include her, but then, he thought of her as the daughter of an old family friend.

He stood. "Doubtless Father would be glad to know part of dear old Cad is here with us."

Will cleared his throat. "Was there something you wanted, Judith?"

"Yes. I was wondering whether to put these things in the drawing room." Judith gestured to the vase and the painting. "It's quite bare in there, and guests will surely wander in during the ball. What do you think?"

He looked at her as though he barely knew her, and Anna thought how very good he was at using lordly haughtiness as a shield.

"I have no opinion whatsoever. But you may ask Anna. I am ceding all authority in the matter of the ball to her. In fact, she will be my hostess."

A prolonged moment of stunned silence greeted these words.

What? He couldn't. Hosting the ball was an honor due to his stepmother. And the last thing Anna wanted was to appear prominently at a public event.

He crossed his arms and tipped up his chin, and she saw that he meant to pay Judith out for forcing his hand over the ball.

"Of course," Judith said, "it will be as you prefer. But will Anna know what your wishes might be?"

"Is there some confusion, some problem with this direction?"

Judith folded her hands before her and made herself look into his hard blue eyes. "No, I understand you perfectly."

But Anna had a problem with his decree—a huge problem. How on earth could she be at this ball, let alone be its hostess, when men were looking for her?

She gave him a very dark look. "My lord," she said, "I'm sure you will wish Lady Grandville to have the honor of being your hostess."

"I believe I've made my wishes known, Anna. You are the daughter of an old and respected family friend who is doing me a service in caring for my niece, and I am repaying you by having you host my ball."

"But it's too great an honor," she persisted. "I don't wish—"

"You will handle all the arrangements," he said, cutting her off. "It's only a modest occasion for the neighbors."

The guests were to be the neighbors. Very likely no one in this country neighborhood would have seen the scandalous book—yet—especially since Henshaw

was apparently showing it only to selected people. She might very likely escape the ball with no harm done.

But what he was doing to Judith was nothing short of a public snub.

Tommy was looking at Judith with a concerned expression on his handsome features. "I say," he began.

The viscount raised one haughty eyebrow at his brother.

Judith turned to Anna. "Where shall we put these, my dear?"

❧

Will had to hand it to Judith; she did humble well.

Anna smiled at her and Tommy, pointedly excluding him, which did not surprise him but annoyed him mightily. They left with their furnishings.

Tommy crossed his arms and fixed Will with a grim look. His brother had grown into manhood when Will wasn't looking, and he made an imposing figure now. Tommy was twelve years younger, but increasingly now, that gap would mean less.

"That was badly done, Will. The honor should go to Judith, and well you know it. People will talk."

He shrugged. "It's only a small ball for the neighbors, and I am doubtless already considered eccentric."

"What the devil is it," Tommy demanded, "that's between you and Judith? You've always been so cool to her, despite her kindness to both of us. I would have thought that by now, whatever was between you might have fallen away."

"It's nothing. We have just never been friends. I was nineteen when she came. Maybe I simply did not

need another mother." He wouldn't for the world spoil Tommy's happy memories of their parents and the family life they'd shared with the knowledge of their father's betrayal of their mother.

A knock sounded at the door again, and Norris appeared with items needing attention.

"Well, I'll leave you to your papers," Tommy said with resignation. "But tell me, what about the cottages? Have you made any more progress since my last visit?"

"Yes. They're almost finished."

"I should be happy to help again," Tommy said as he strode toward the door, turning as he went. "I quite enjoyed swinging a hammer last time."

"Certainly. Perhaps after I finish with Norris. And, Tommy," Will said, smiling, "I *am* glad you've come. Stillwell has turned into a veritable henhouse."

Tommy's laughter rang out as he passed through the doors.

☙

In the drawing room, Judith rested the small painting against a wall while Anna put down the vase and thought how much easier things would be if she could just leave Stillwell now. Even though the ball would only be for the neighbors, playing a prominent role at the event was just the kind of risk she needed to avoid, never mind that if she left, surely Will would be forced to see that Judith was the right person to be his hostess.

But she couldn't leave. All was not yet resolved between Lizzie and him, and Anna couldn't abandon

her. And she needed the two hundred pounds he'd promised her.

She refused to pay attention to the tugging in her heart that said leaving the man she now knew as Will was going to be very, very hard.

Judith was looking at her quizzically. "I didn't know you were a friend of the family, Anna, before Grandville mentioned it just now. Why didn't you say?"

"Er...I didn't want to presume on such a small acquaintance. My father was a doctor who sometimes attended the family at Littlebury Lodge."

Judith squinted. "I'm afraid I don't remember any of the doctors, though Alistair and I were sometimes gone in the summer, and fortunately neither of us was prone to illness. Perhaps we were away when he came."

Anna nodded, then took a breath. "I'm not happy about what Lord Grandville has done, choosing me to be hostess. It's clear he's only doing it to hurt you."

Judith sighed. "It's all right. Truly. I came to Stillwell prepared for all kinds of resistance from him. And I forced his hand over the ball when I brought Miranda here. I'm not surprised he felt the need to retaliate."

"Well," Anna said, "since he'll never know what's decided between us, you must go on with the plans you have in mind for the ball, and I will assist you in whatever way you may require."

"Thank you." Judith smiled. "Lizzie is fortunate to have you as her governess." She traced a fingertip along the gilded top of the picture frame. "I do wish she could come stay with me at my house in Town, but he would never allow it."

"No," Anna agreed. He could be so frustratingly

hard-hearted and domineering. If she'd thought he was softening a little, today he had proved her wrong.

Judith cocked her head. "She would certainly benefit if there were some way you might stay longer. I don't suppose he's asked you to?"

"He did, actually, but I can't. Once my month here is over, I am to go to my aunt."

"Ah, well." Judith lifted the painting and held it up to a conspicuously vacant area. "Shall I have it hung here?"

When Anna got back to her room some time later, she felt dusty and exhausted and not a little gloomy. She rang for a bath, which the maid set up in her room. It felt like heaven, having someone make a nice hot bath for her, and she took what comfort she could in it.

When she emerged later, she found that the maid had laid two gowns out on her bed—two *new*, very pretty gowns—along with a pair of pert green leather slippers with blue satin ribbons. A note, folded and sealed, lay on one of the dresses.

In a strong male hand was written:

> *You'll need something to wear, as your other gowns seem to have disappeared. Truth be told, I think Vicar was looking for contributions for a charity sale.*

No! He hadn't!

She ran to the wardrobe, where she'd hung her blue gown next to the brown one before taking her bath, but the cabinet was empty.

He had.

Grimly, she went back to her bed and examined the new gowns. They were a pretty pair, both made of the finest muslin, one in a pale apple green and the other the clear blue of a May sky. They were not fussy or embellished—a governess could certainly wear them. But they were exquisitely made. These gowns would not let her pass unnoticed when she left Stillwell.

With a huff of frustration at his high-handedness, she took the green gown and slipped into it. Its fresh cloth fell softly against her skin, and the bodice fit remarkably well for something that had been made without her. She supposed he'd had a maid measure one of her gowns when she was out of her room. The soft shoes fit like a second skin after the sturdy leather of her old half boots, and he must have been very crafty about getting her size, because she only had the one pair.

She turned to look in the cheval glass. The vivid green fabric seemed to bring out the pink in her cheeks and set off the black of her hair. The gown's bodice revealed a tasteful amount of her bosom and expertly suggested the slim lines of her waist before falling in a pretty cascade to the tops of the darker green leather slippers. She'd taken care again that morning to put her hair up neatly, as she'd done the day before when she'd made over her gowns.

She looked quite fine. She *liked* the way she looked.

But she wished he hadn't done this. He'd taken away her disguises and made her feel instantly far less safe. She wanted to march downstairs and tell him just how angry she was.

But even a fight with him was time spent with him.

And what she needed was to engage with him as little as possible.

~∂∞~

Lizzie swept down Stillwell's grand front staircase, enjoying the way the white skin of her hand looked against the old dark wood of the banister. The tips of her cream calfskin boots peeked out saucily from under the draping hem of her ecru silk morning gown, a lustrous color that she knew complemented her red-gold hair and fair skin.

She only wished there were someone to admire her. She'd given up on Grandville doing so, though of course she hadn't really wanted him to admire her like that. Anyway, she was now feeling cautiously optimistic about her chances of staying at Stillwell. After all, he'd been really quite nice about the statues, and when she'd seen him in the hallway that morning, he'd actually been almost warm, and asked her how she was.

Tristan padded along next to her, his nails clicking on the marble stairs, and she reached out to pet his shining head.

"*You* want me to stay, don't you?" she said, smiling, and he gave a short bark as if in reply. She loved dogs.

As she reached the bottom of the stairs, she heard footsteps coming along the hallway, and then the surprising sound of someone whistling "Drunken Sailor," a tune she'd heard often by the docks in Malta. It was not the sort of song she expected to hear at Stillwell Hall, and she turned to correct whatever servant it must be.

Striding toward her was not a servant but a tall gentleman, well turned out in a beautiful dark blue coat and stone-colored trousers that fit his athletic build to perfection. He was a surprising figure for two reasons. One was the streak of white hair that fell in a careless blade across his forehead in contrast to the rest of his black locks. Two was that he was undoubtedly the most handsome man she'd ever seen.

"Hello," he said, grinning as they met at the foot of the stairs. "You must be the ward."

She blinked. Close up he was even more striking. His eyes were a sparkling green that suggested a lively playfulness, his face was beautifully formed, and the confident spring in his step made her think of dashing princes and naval heroes.

His mouth quirked upward as he waited for her to respond, and she realized that she'd been looking at him for too long. But she was a little overcome with the realization that she had, in a manner of speaking, met her match.

"Good afternoon," she said. "I am Lord Grandville's niece, Miss Elizabeth Tarryton. I'm afraid you have the advantage of me, sir." It was all properly said, but something about his jaunty air made Lizzie feel faintly ridiculous, like just the kind of stuffy twit she'd hated listening to at the Rosewood School. By her side, Tristan whined softly.

"Well, hello, Miss Elizabeth Tarryton," he said, sweeping her a bow. "And hello again, Tristan," he continued, crouching down to greet the dog as if she and the dog were of equal interest. He lingered for several moments, fluffing Tristan's ears playfully.

"I see you two are well acquainted," she said with creeping irritation to the top of his head.

He stood up and focused those clear green eyes on her with the trace of a knowing smile that told her he'd heard the stuffy note in her voice. "Tristan was sired by my father's favorite, Cadfael." He bowed elegantly. "Tommy Halifax, at your service. Grandville's brother."

Well, how wonderful! She forgot all about giving him a set-down and dipped him her best curtsy. She was pleased, on straightening, to see a glint of masculine interest in his eyes.

"And where are you off to, Miss Tarryton?"

"I was going to take Tristan for a walk." She allowed a brief lingering of her dark lashes against her cheek as she blinked, nothing so pronounced as batting her eyelashes, but an accentuation. Anna had been saying something earlier about Lizzie not connecting with people through her appearance, but as much as Lizzie liked Anna, the woman had no notion of the advantages of beauty and feminine charms.

"Might I join you?" he said. "I haven't strolled the grounds in what seems like ages."

"I should like that," she said, certain that his eyes had lingered at least twice on her lips. She quite liked Tommy Halifax. He would certainly be pleasant to have around, and he might even be useful.

He was from Town, she reminded herself as they passed through the doorway and Tristan bounded ahead of them. She must let him see she was sophisticated.

"So you have come very recently to Stillwell, Miss Tarryton," he said. "And what do you think of it?"

They stepped past a small hole in the ground and

she tightened her grip on his arm; men loved these kinds of little gestures that drew attention to their masculinity. "Oh lud, Halifax," she said. "I've never seen such grounds. And the manor!"

She sighed with extra pleasure to show that she appreciated the finer things in life. Out of the corner of her eye, she thought, strangely, that she saw him hide a smile, as though he found something about her funny, but she knew she must be imagining things.

"And you must call me Lizzie," she said, "for are we not practically family?"

"Are we?" he said, arching an eyebrow. "Then you must call me Tommy."

She chatted on, asking him about all the balls he'd been to and what was popular at the moment in Town in the realms of music and entertainments. His replies seemed strangely mild, as though he weren't particularly interested in such things, but she told herself she was being ridiculous. He was a fashionable gentleman, and these were the topics that fashionable men liked talking about, from what she'd heard. Well, and drinking and horseflesh, but she could hardly bring those up.

What did any of that matter, though, when she'd already caught his eyes lingering on her with the light of attraction? From her experience, men didn't care so much what a girl had to say if they admired her, and she felt certain this man did.

The only thing that troubled her, as he led her up the front steps to Stillwell, was that little secret smile she noticed again as he bowed to take his leave.

Back in her room, she sat on her bed, staring

out the window at the pale late-afternoon sky and daydreaming. She *liked* Tommy Halifax. None of the other young men she'd ever met had made her heart go pitter-pat in her chest the way it had the whole time she'd walked next to him.

Her bedchamber door, which was not all the way closed, opened slowly, and she heard a clicking sound as Tristan's shining red-brown head appeared.

"Hello, you," she said as he came to stand next to her bed. He looked at her with an expression both imploring and expectant, and she laughed softly and patted the bed. "I don't know if you're allowed on beds, but you can be on mine."

He hopped fluidly up, which suggested that Judith indulged him in this. He was all legs on the bed next to her for a moment before executing one tight circle and curling up next to her thigh.

She began to pet him, and something nagged at her, spoiling her pleasure in her reverie. *Had* there been something too amused in Tommy's manner toward her, as though she were entertaining him in some way she didn't understand? But no, she was being too sensitive.

Under her hand, Tristan's head stirred. She smiled. "I needn't pretend to you, at least," she said, leaning down and kissing the glossy fur on his head. "Tommy is smitten. He has to be. And for once, I'll have an admirer whose attentions I'll enjoy."

Tristan shifted under her and she sat up. He lifted his head, and his brown doggy eyes sought hers with a soulful look. He gave a funny shake of his head from side to side.

She cocked her head at him. "Silly. I'd almost say you looked skeptical." She was chuckling at the thought of a dog having such opinions when from Tristan's hindquarters came an unmistakable sound, followed by a small, ferocious cloud that knocked her back on the pillows, giggling.

"Exactly!" she said, laughing. "What does a dog know of the power of beauty? Tommy can be the very best sort of advocate for me with Grandville. And I needn't worry about what Anna said about scheming. Why, this isn't scheming at all; it's attraction!"

She lay back on the pillow and dreamed.

Seventeen

DINNER THAT NIGHT WAS THE KIND OF ROLLICKING good fun Anna suspected had not been had at Stillwell for some time. The viscount was out to dinner at the Chittisters', for which she was thankful, and so she escaped any discussion of his discovery that she was the daughter of Dr. Bristol.

But Tommy stayed home with the ladies, and since he gave no indication that he knew anything odd about her name, she could only think his brother hadn't let on. Tommy was as charming as Will was brooding, and already Lizzie seemed to have taken to him. She and Judith both remarked on how pretty Anna looked in her new green dress, and Tommy announced, with a roguish grin, that he couldn't imagine how his brother could forego the company of three such beautiful ladies, but that *he* was quite happy to be left alone in their charming company.

After dinner they all sat companionably in the drawing room while Lizzie read aloud from a light novel. Anna fetched her sketchbook and contentedly made a study of the scene.

As she was preparing to get undressed for bed that night, Dart knocked on her door. Apparently the master had returned. She could hardly pretend that his summons was unexpected, although the location was; he was on the terrace.

She passed through the quiet house and into the dark library, whose doors were open. She found him sitting on a backless stone bench near the weeping willow, facing away from her and out over the night-dark grounds. His arms were splayed out behind him so that he looked relaxed, but she was not fooled.

The moon was a fat crescent, and the sky was so dense with brilliant stars and so much vaster than Stillwell that for once the enormous manor seemed quaint. She drew closer to him, and he must have heard her footsteps because he said without turning, "Sit."

She sat down on the bench next to him but facing in the opposite direction, toward the manor, which seemed less intimate. She needed it to be.

"I do not wish," she said before he could speak, "to be used as part of your grudge against Judith. I like your stepmother very much, and I don't want to see her hurt. You do her a wrong, putting me before her as hostess."

"I didn't call you down here to talk about her."

She crossed her arms against the shivers that were starting in her just from his nearness. "And I am quite furious that you took my gowns. That was appallingly high-handed of you. They are my personal belongings—"

"Which were an embarrassment to my household," he interrupted. "And you deserved something far

better than what you had." He glanced over his shoulder at her. "From what little I can see of you, I'd say your new attire suits you. Now stop trying to distract me. I assume that you told me the truth when you said you've never been married."

"I told you the truth."

"Then why are you using a false name?"

"It's not false exactly; it was my mother's surname and is my own middle name."

"But why didn't you tell me that you were Dr. Bristol's daughter?"

"I had adopted using my middle name when I left home because of what happened with the man I told you about. Lizzie knew me by that name too, and I could hardly change it when I got here."

He grunted. "I guessed as much. I told Tommy some man had behaved badly toward you, and that you might have felt the need to change your name. He and I will continue to use Black."

She felt herself sag a little in relief. "Thank you."

"But, Anna, I'm not happy that you kept your identity from me. And I'm extremely unhappy that I've tampered with the daughter of a gentleman I respected. I feel like a scoundrel."

She crossed her arms. "You needn't. We both made our own choices freely. And no one else will know—unless, of course, you speak of it to someone."

"You dare," he said in a voice of leashed menace, "to suggest that I might babble about this?" He shifted, sitting up stiffly and crossing his arms.

"You're the one who's making a fuss."

"For pity's sake! By rights, I ought to marry you."

His words made her heart jump. *Married* to Will, who made her heart beat faster. Will, for whom she'd already come to care so much.

Stop it, she told herself sternly. He's only asking because he's a gentleman and he feels he compromised you. He was the responsible viscount, who'd already insisted that she ought to let him take care of her by becoming his mistress.

He had no idea that she was a woman on the verge of scandal. He'd said he admired her—words she cherished—and she couldn't bear the thought of him discovering that she was the woman he'd been discussing with his brother when they were talking about *The Beautiful One*.

But she had to know if he would say words that might make all the difference.

"Get married?" she said in as light a tone as she could muster. "Are you daft?"

"This is serious! We've become entangled. What if Judith and Miranda had arrived five minutes earlier when we were at the cottage?"

It was just as she thought. He was concerned with propriety, not love. But propriety, thanks to *The Beautiful One*, no longer meant anything to her, and she wouldn't have this good man marry her simply to do the honorable thing.

"They didn't," she said.

"But they *might* have, and considering what we did together, the appropriate thing for us to do is to marry."

She hated that he was proposing to her out of obligation. "I thank you, but I do not wish to marry."

She heard the sound of teeth grinding. "You are
the most contrary woman. You're telling me that you
don't want to marry me and become a viscountess?"

"I mean that I don't wish to marry anyone at all,"
she said, knowing in that moment that she doubtless
would never marry. What she'd tasted with him had
been something rare, and if she couldn't have that,
what need would she have of marriage? Even if she
could outrun the scandal of *The Beautiful One*, she
knew enough of the world to know that marriage
could be a prison, especially for women. "Let us
simply be friends, as we were before."

"Friends," he repeated in a dark voice. "*Friends?*"

But he said nothing more, and she supposed he
was relieved that she'd not accepted, a thought that
depressed her. She wished he hadn't proposed.

"I know I didn't behave in a way that invited
your trust at first, but since that time, things have
changed. You could have trusted me with the truth
about your name."

He meant that they'd grown closer.

"Perhaps," she said, but she knew she wouldn't
have. The more people who knew her name, the
more chances there were that Henshaw would
find her.

The sounds of night creatures filled the air,
crickets, and in the distance, the bark of a fox. He
uncrossed his arms and leaned back on them again,
and her own arms fell gently to her lap. She ought
to get up and go now—she had acknowledged what
she owed him.

But it felt so right, just sitting with him. She didn't

even have to look at him—just knowing he was there beside her felt so good. In the darkness, and with no one else around, they were just two people. His scent teased her nose, with its notes of strength and good soap and leather from his riding that day. She breathed it in deeply, but silently, so he wouldn't hear.

He leaned slightly backward then, so he could see her face, and darn him but his dark eyes shone softly on her, a sweet trueness flowing through them to her.

"It's best that I go," she said, realizing she was teetering at the edge of something dangerous. She moved to stand up, but he caught her arm.

"Wait. Stay a bit. I will behave. Maybe we'll even hear a...what was it you heard the other morning?"

She should leave.

But.

Whatever stolen moments she might have here with him were precious and unlikely to come again. No, she would have this time with him and save the memory of it for later, because she saw that though she would be leaving in a handful of days, she would never be able to leave behind the memories of him.

She sat back. "*Strix aluco*, a tawny owl."

"You seem to have a fondness for owls."

"I do, actually. They're my favorites among birds, which were a frequent subject in my childhood home. My father studied birds, and he wrote two books about them."

"Yes," he said dryly, "*Anatomy of a Songbird* and *A Study of Owls*. I found them in my library this afternoon. They are very fine. And the illustrations, done by one A. Bristol, were exquisite."

His praise made something warm bloom inside her. "Thank you."

He turned his body, swinging a leg over the bench so he straddled it and faced her. The darkness blurred the edges of his face. She told herself that the tender light in his eyes must be a trick of starlight.

"Tell me more about him," he said. "He was such a brilliant man. What happened to him?"

She could tell him a little. She so wanted to share herself with him. "He died last year after an illness."

"I'm sorry. You must have been very close to him."

She could not truthfully say that she had been. "His studies of nature required much of his time. I loved doing the drawings for his books."

"Ah." Something told her he'd noticed that she hadn't really answered his question. "He must have had quite a passion for birds. And he was a respected doctor as well. I wonder, then, if he had much time and attention for a young lady growing up with no mother."

He gave a light chuckle. "I can imagine you then, in a miniature dress of some indistinguishable hue, swinging from a tree branch."

She tipped her chin up and knew that long-familiar yet uncomfortable need to justify. She had so often justified her father's behavior to herself. "I had a very good upbringing."

"Did you? I rather suppose you raised yourself, and were allowed, through lack of guidance, to do all sorts of unsuitable things."

"Being left to roam with my brother had many advantages. I explored the countryside and the natural

world around me in ways that young ladies rarely can. I have no ill-treatment of which to complain."

"Perhaps not," he said in a more serious voice. "Merely, I imagine, neglect. Did it perhaps feel, with no mother, that you were almost an orphan?"

Something burned inside her, as if he'd touched a truth that dwelled there.

"He was a good man," she said, hating the husky note that had crept into her voice. "I think he needed his studies. People were harder for him to understand than birds."

She pressed her lips together, having said more than she'd meant to.

"You don't want him to be spoken against, do you? Which speaks to your own deep affection for him. Did it never make you angry, though, to feel of so little account?"

Anna crossed her arms. She didn't want to kindle the anger he was stirring. "Don't be absurd. How can you be angry at someone who's done nothing to hurt you? I loved my father."

"But you might at the same time have been angry over things he should have done that he didn't."

Well, she thought with an inward catch. He articulated so easily what she could not allow herself to think. "I... Maybe I was a little angry. Maybe I am still. There was a chipped china bowl in my room, and I'm sorry to say I threw it against the wall the other day. You ought to take it out of my pay."

He merely laughed. "It's nothing. I suppose men are allowed to get angry, while you women must always be yielding, the forgivers and the peacemakers.

But anyone with a working brain has to be frustrated and angry sometimes."

She felt as if he'd seen inside her, as if he knew her. In that moment, she had a fierce yearning to tell him her troubles. He would understand. He would believe that she hadn't posed for Rawlins. He was a viscount, a peer of the despicable Marquess of Henshaw. Will could help her.

No, he *would* help; she knew it. She allowed herself to imagine him tidying the whole thing up and making it go away.

No.

She was going to stop entertaining that fantasy right now. She couldn't allow herself to need his help like that.

To need him.

After yesterday, when she'd felt so open to him and then been crushed when she realized he saw her as someone else for whom he must be responsible, she knew that to accept his help would make her feel horribly vulnerable—groundless, even, like she might do anything. Like agreeing to a loveless marriage with him, or even simply asking to experience again what they'd shared the day before.

And what if she told him the truth, and he wanted to help her, and her scandal harmed him? Made him into a laughingstock if he tried to defend her honor, or even drew him into a duel on her behalf? He was too noble, and he'd feel the need to defend her. She could never allow that.

She must keep her troubles to herself. She was used to relying only on herself—her father had taught her

how to do that, if nothing else. She and Will were going to go their separate ways soon, and that must be the end of it.

She turned away from the appalling hollowness that had opened up inside her and said no more.

A fox barked again, somewhere on his vast grounds, and the sound hung in the silence that stretched on for several minutes. They had said so much to one another. Shared so deeply. And they had no future together.

"Well," he said finally. "You cannot stay. It is late." His voice was gentle. It was not a dismissal but a recognition of the way things were.

"Yes." It had been too late some time ago. She stood. His face was below hers and slightly tipped up, and she looked down into dark eyes that had touched her deeply.

Those eyes were not for her, she reminded herself. Those blue eyes, and everything else Will Halifax had to offer, were for someone else, someone of his own class.

Anna stepped away from the bench, and from the madness of sharing the starlight with him. He was Viscount Grandville, she reminded herself. She needed to stop thinking of him as Will.

"Good night," she whispered, and though he lifted a hand toward her, she turned and left.

❧

Will watched Anna disappear through the doors with a tug in the general area of his heart, an organ that he'd considered a ruined thing, incapable of anything good. It didn't feel that way tonight.

He made his way in through the library, closing
and locking the doors behind him, and entered the
corridor. A figure was standing at the bottom of the
stairs, in a rectangle of moonlight coming in one of
the large windows. Judith.

"A word with you, please, Grandville."

She had a candle, and the light played on features on
which he had focused so much disgust as a young man.

"Yes?"

She sighed. "I know I deserve your scorn. If I had it
to do over, I would have stayed away from your father
while your mother was still alive. But I loved him, and
I wasn't wise then."

"Do I really have to listen to this? Now? Here? And
from the woman who walked around the family wing
each morning in dishabille, letting everyone know that
she and the master were lovers?"

"I was foolish then. Young and foolish and afraid.
I thought your father might fall out of love with me."

"For pity's sake, you weren't here a month before
you were trying to get him to believe that Mother had
a lover!"

A pause. "I didn't realize you knew about that."

He gave a bark of mirthless laughter. "I heard you
talking in the breakfast room. 'Have some kippers,
dear Alistair. I think your first wife had a lover. I may
have found some proof.'"

He'd shocked her with this memory, and he was glad.
He'd spent countless hours in misery, doubting everything his family had ever been to him, until he realized
that Judith was only trying to besmirch his mother.

"You're right," she said. "I wanted to replace your

mother. Of course there was no proof of any such thing. I made so many mistakes. I'm sorry."

"It's easy to say that now."

She tipped up her chin with a pride he didn't think he'd ever seen in her before. She'd always been so needy, desperate for his father's attention and her stepsons' acceptance. She'd doted on his father, buttering his toast, watching from windows for his return whenever he was gone, draping herself on him when he was home, and the sight had always disgusted Will.

"I'm no longer a fragile young woman unsure of her worth."

"Good for you." He moved toward the stairs.

"I'm not done yet," she said. "I wish to address whatever is between you and Anna. I saw you on the terrace with her just now."

He turned around. "We had things to discuss, which is none of your concern."

"Really? You needed to meet with the governess late at night on a bench in the garden?" She crossed her arms and returned his haughtiness. "Anna doesn't deserve to be trifled with. She should be off limits to you."

Damn it, how the hell had he come to be discussing Anna with Judith of all people? "I see you have appointed yourself her champion."

"Anna is as fine a woman as they come, and I've seen the way you two are when you're together, each surreptitiously aware of the other. You need a viscountess. Would you choose her for your wife?"

She was right about what he owed Anna, but he'd be damned if he was going to listen to such

things from Judith. "Champion of virtue is a new role for you."

"I'm concerned that whatever you are up to with her is a way of avoiding a serious effort to find a wife for yourself, someone who would share your life." A hard glitter lit her eyes, as if from some inner fire, and he felt a surprising flash of admiration for her, but it was quickly replaced with the scorn she always stirred in him.

"You wish to claim a right to interfere, but what you have always failed to accept is that though you may be a stepmother, you are no true relation to me and Tommy. You are merely"—he shrugged—"a woman my father married. Though you *were* always fond of gestures. I can still recall the sight of the breakfast embrace to which Tommy and I were treated each morning."

"It takes two to embrace, Grandville. Your father and I did grow to love each other deeply."

He recoiled from her words. How dare she talk to him of love, she who had interfered in the love his parents shared? "Your marriage was wrong and ridiculous. He was vulnerable and you took advantage of him."

"Your father was desperate for companionship, or he wouldn't have taken up with me."

"No one recovers from the loss of a loved one so quickly. You preyed on him."

"You have always been so admirably loyal, Grandville, but there comes a time when loyalty, along with duty, must be weighed to see if it is merely something behind which one is hiding."

She sighed. "I do not press for your forgiveness. I seek to speak for your father, whom, whether you wish to accept it or not, we both loved. He wanted so much for Stillwell, and for his sons. He would have been proud of the way you've managed the lands, and of the cottages you're building for the tenants. But he wouldn't have wanted to see his oldest son turning into a man whose life was defined only by duty. Duty has such a capacity for harshness when it's not motivated by love."

"You take on too much in my father's name!"

"For his sake, I would see you married, and married well."

"Have I not agreed to attend your ball?" he said tightly.

"But that will be for naught if you don't see it as a step to finding a wife soon and returning to the land of the living. If that woman isn't going to be Anna, then you shouldn't allow yourself to be distracted by her."

"I hope you are not so far deluded that you think to choose a wife for me."

"Of course not. I am merely providing a push. The rest is up to you." She paused. "After the ball, I will consider my debt to your father paid."

"You will leave then, once I have fulfilled what you ask?"

She nodded.

"And I trust that I won't see you again."

"Very well," she said, "though I think it would disappoint your father. But if that is your wish…"

"It is."

He stepped past her and went up the stairs.

Once in his bedroom, he sat down on a chair and

lifted his leg to pull off his boot. It was a task that required contortions, but he was hardly inclined to rouse a servant at that late hour, and anyway the last thing he wanted then was the company of another person.

The words of his conversation with Judith still rang in his ears. Being in her presence was uncomfortable, a return to the same bind he'd felt when younger: awareness that his father had cared for her, and that he himself was disgusted by her. If his conscience niggled, whispering that she seemed different now, he knew better than to believe she didn't have an ulterior motive.

He threw the first boot to the floor and brought his other ankle across his knee and leaned over to grab the heel, a hideously uncomfortable position. Judith had spoken of loyalty and duty as if they were not the highest good. As if he'd been hiding behind his loyalty to his family and the duties of his title.

He pulled hard at the heel and the boot came off with a jerk and he dropped it to the floor. He slumped down in the chair, wishing he'd brought the brandy upstairs with him. But then he decided it was better he hadn't; he'd resorted to it too often over the last year, and that must end.

And while he was acknowledging home truths, Judith was right, damn it all, about what he owed to the title; he must marry soon.

Maybe Miranda, he thought unenthusiastically as he tugged his shirt over his head. Her face was not the one his mind supplied, though.

What if Anna had said yes tonight when he'd proposed the idea of marriage? He'd been relieved when

she'd refused, yet now he found himself wondering what it would be like to be married to her. He'd felt so close to her, out on the terrace, and he'd wanted nothing more than to enfold her in his arms.

But she hadn't said yes, and he knew it was just as well. She stirred unruly feelings in him when what he needed was to focus on carrying out his responsibilities in a steady, reasoned way.

He was far too restless to sleep, though, and he stayed up into the wee hours reading a report about crop yields, wishing fruitlessly that the words and numbers would chase away the image of shining black curls and the alluring memory of the scent of fresh pencil shavings.

Eighteen

WILL HAD SOMETHING ON HIS MIND THAT HE WANTED to discuss with his brother the next morning, and he found him in the stable.

As Will entered the building, Tommy was standing outside Strider's stall, petting the huge chestnut's head. Will hadn't touched the horse since the day he'd thrown Ginger, though he didn't blame the animal. Ginger had been riding Strider when he'd been spooked by a wild dog, and the powerful horse had pulled up suddenly in panic, throwing her off. She'd hit her head on a rock and been gone so quickly. He'd seen the whole thing and been powerless to stop it.

Will's grooms kept Strider in good shape, while he rode another of his horses if he required one.

Now, seeing Tommy with the animal, Will walked toward the stall, feeling the jumble of memories the sight of Strider brought, and he just…accepted them. They were part of him, but they weren't his future.

"Have you come for a ride?" Tommy said.

"No." Will's eyes drifted toward Strider's shining head. The horse's enormous dark eyes rested

on him, as noble and bottomless as ever. He lifted a hand and set it on Strider's muzzle and thought about what Anna had said about taking up the reins of his life.

"I was wondering how things are at Longmount," he said. He hadn't been to his other estate, or to Halifax House in London, since Ginger died. "You were there a few months ago, weren't you?"

"Yes," Tommy said, pulling a small piece of carrot from his pocket and offering it to Strider. "It fares pretty well, though the mill is in poor shape." He shot him a sidelong glance. "It could do with a visit from its master."

Will nodded. Perhaps it was time to consider paying a visit. Beside him, Strider finished his carrot and tossed his head gently against his shoulder. Will patted him.

"So," Tommy said, "what are you going to do about Lizzie? Will you take her to Town for the season and show her off?"

From the direction of the stable door at that moment came a small shuffling sound, but when Will glanced that way, he saw nothing.

Will shrugged. He *could* take Lizzie to Town for a few days, and a short visit would be an opportunity for him to return to society. The thought would have oppressed him a few weeks ago, but now he could imagine himself attending a small party or two, perhaps even hosting one.

Still, Lizzie only had a few more weeks here, and going to London would mean bringing Anna as well, and he found he didn't like the idea of bringing her

somewhere she would be in company with other men. It was disgracefully selfish of him, but she was so unique and lovely, and he knew he'd be jealous if she attracted the attention of other men. Anyway, he already had Judith's infernal ball; that ought to present Lizzie with enough society for the moment.

"London's not a good idea at the moment."

"So will you take her later, then?"

"No. She's only staying a few more weeks. There's really nothing here for her, you know. I've got Norris investigating some place that would take her. Perhaps she'd like to go to school in Switzerland."

"Why don't you just ask Anna to stay on?"

Will gazed off into the distance. "She won't." He flicked a glance at Tommy and raised an eyebrow. "Miranda Chittister was asking after you when I was at Trippleford for dinner. You really ought to have come."

Tommy shrugged. "Miranda's all right, but I knew I'd hear nothing but boring fashionable talk." He patted Strider's flank, then leaned casually back against a post by the stall and crossed his arms. "I say, but Anna is a fine woman."

Will gave him a look. "Enough, Tommy. What about Lucy Melbourne? I thought you had a tendre for her."

"Lucy's all right sometimes, when she's not blathering on about fabric and gossip and any number of stupid things. Young ladies are, unfortunately, so often like pretty candies, full of nothing but dry stuffing when you bite into them."

Will's eyebrows shot upward.

"Metaphorically speaking, obviously," Tommy said, grinning roguishly. "I mean they're not much

fun to be around. Anna's fun, though, and she must be almost my age."

"She is older than you."

Tommy seemed oblivious to the edge in his brother's voice. "She is really quite beautiful," he said, "and I'm certain *she* never says stupid things."

Will felt as though the top of his head would shortly blow off. "Anna is under my protection, and I'm certain that I will not have to be protecting her from my own brother's improper attentions." He ignored the voice of conscience calling him a hypocrite.

"Certainly not! She is too good—how could you even think such a thing?" Tommy crossed his arms. "How did she end up here as Lizzie's governess anyway?"

"She was working at the school where Lizzie was."

"Well, all the same, I wonder if Lizzie will want more learning. She's quite gorgeous, but there doesn't seem to be much else to her." Tommy tapped his head. "More hair than wit."

"Oh?" Will said. "I hadn't paid much attention." Or spent enough time around her to know much of anything about her, he thought guiltily. "I'll see what Anna thinks. Perhaps Lizzie would benefit from a school that focuses especially on social graces."

A sharp cry near the doorway drew their attention again, but a moment later the arrival of the stable cat provided an explanation.

Now that he thought about Lizzie, though, Will felt a pang of compassion; considering that she'd lost her family so young, she seemed remarkably resilient, and was it any wonder that she'd misbehaved

outrageously? He must be sure to have her to stay at Stillwell at least once or twice a year in future.

He shrugged. "Well, she's creative at any rate," he chuckled, shaking his head. "Do you know, she got angry at me and took a hammer to the Apollo statue's cock, then draped the gaping hole she made with rather wicked clothes made out of ivy?"

Tommy's eyes lit up. "Really? That's diabolically inventive."

"Yes," Will agreed dryly. "It wasn't by accident that she was discovered sneaking out of school and had to be sent down."

"You mean she got herself sent down on purpose?" Tommy's expression held growing admiration. "That's quite interesting. And unexpected. Perhaps she's not so lacking in wits after all."

Will groaned inwardly at his brother's interest in such inappropriate doings. And surely that wasn't the light of conquest in his eyes?

"You really ought to go visit the Chittisters," Will said. "People will talk about you being back, and they'll take it as a slight if you don't stop by."

"That's rich, coming from you," Tommy said, but cheerfully, and he called for a horse to be saddled.

At some distance from the stable door, Lizzie hid in anguish behind a large copse of juniper. She'd been approaching the stable with the intention of riding when she heard the men's voices. She heard Tommy say she was a ninny, heard Grandville agree and talk about the school where he'd send her. She hadn't

listened to the rest but had stepped away blindly, not noticing where she went until she stumbled into the cat.

Her heart throbbed louder each moment as the hurt grew. How could she have thought Grandville was softening toward her, that he might want her to stay after all? She'd been a fool. He didn't care about her, and he was still going to dump her at some school when her month was up.

And what pained her almost as much, she'd been entirely wrong about Tommy being attracted to her. He thought there was nothing to her but her appearance.

She ignored the jab of conscience pointing out that she'd *meant* for him to focus on her looks, because he was also supposed to see that behind her face and figure, she was special and different. She didn't blame him for admiring Anna, but listening to him sing her praises when he'd dismissed Lizzie herself had stung.

She watched bitterly as Tommy rode out across the grounds on a beautiful white horse. Grandville would still be in the stable, but she supposed he wouldn't stay there long, and the last thing she wanted was to see him ever again.

She peeked around the juniper bushes, and when she saw no one coming from the stable, she took off at a run for the manor. As she rushed inside and up the stairs, no one paid her any attention because everyone was busy preparing Stillwell for the ball. Tristan, though, appeared as she neared her bedchamber and followed her inside. He whimpered softly when he saw her take out her valise.

A familiar, hollow pain burned inside her. She'd

never really belonged anywhere, not since her father had remarried. That had been the end of all the good times. But at least she was no longer a helpless little girl, and she wasn't going to let herself be shuffled about at other people's whims anymore.

She put only a few things in the valise, because she was going to have to carry whatever she brought very far—all the way to Portsmouth. She'd dress in her coffee-colored silk, which would travel well, and play the part of a young lady whose maid had taken ill to explain why she was traveling alone. If she looked wealthy, she would be treated well.

She took out her pin money and rolled it up in a cloth that she tucked in the pocket hanging from the waist of her gown. It was enough to pay for passage to Malta, she was fairly certain, though she supposed she'd have nothing left when she arrived.

The voyage wouldn't be easy, but anything was better than staying where she wasn't wanted. She'd had enough of that to last a lifetime. She felt bad about leaving Anna, who'd been so good to her, but Anna couldn't help her. She'd send her a letter later and apologize for leaving as she had.

Everything would be better once she got to Malta. She'd go to the home of her old friend Cecelia Waltham, with whom she'd vowed eternal sisterhood on the Walthams' beach. If she could just get back to Malta, she knew they'd be like sisters again.

She pulled the top of her valise closed and tested its weight—heavy but manageable. It was perhaps five miles to the nearest town. Once there, she would catch the mail coach.

Tristan followed her to the window and stood by curiously as she opened it and looked out. The grounds below were deserted, and that sealed her choice. She threw her case to the ground and, hanging from the balcony grating, dropped onto the sturdy line of shrubs that grew below. From there, it was a quick sprint to the shelter of the trees that flanked the manor, and she was away.

✑

Stillwell Hall was like a hive that afternoon, bustling inside and out with footmen beating carpets in the warm sunshine and maids polishing woodwork and the housekeeper rushing about with lists, all in preparation for the ball.

Will had retreated to his library desk and was trying to add up costs for drainage ditches, but his mind kept skittering about every time he presented it with a column of figures. It wanted to dwell on other things, like where Anna had been all day. She hadn't been at breakfast or lunch, nor had he glimpsed her anywhere in the corridors. She was obviously, if subtly, avoiding him.

Of course he understood why. She was the daughter of a respected country doctor and learned author. She was not the sort of woman who should be doing the things they'd done at the cottage, and it was for the best if they stayed apart, considering the powerful attraction between them.

Unfortunately, his own good intentions about behaving properly toward her from here on out were being tested constantly by his imagination, which had

turned devilishly creative and kept supplying erotic scenarios involving the beautiful, unusual governess residing under his roof.

A sharp rap sounded on the library door, and Anna rushed into the room.

"It's customary to await a reply—" he began, ridiculously pleased to see her.

"Lizzie's gone!"

He blinked. "What?"

"She's run away, I'm sure of it. I haven't seen her these three hours. She was supposed to be working on a map of the world, and when I checked her room, she'd clearly packed a case and left. By the window."

The papers in his hands slid to the desk and he groaned. "I wish that part surprised me." He stood up and went over to where she stood by the door. "Do you have any idea where she might be going?"

She pressed her lips grimly. "Lizzie has such romantic ideas. My guess would be to the village, to catch the mail coach to Portsmouth."

"Why—" he began, but then they both said together, "Malta."

"An outrageous idea," he said, "for her to think of traveling there alone. And yet I believe her fully capable of doing so." He cursed softly.

"Yes," she said, her voice husky with worry. "So much could happen to her. She has far too much faith in the wisdom of her own way, and so little actual wisdom."

"I know," he said, feeling ill. This was his fault. "She may have reached the village already. Tomfool girl! Doesn't she know the danger she's running?"

There was no time to waste. He stepped to the door and bellowed for Dart, who arrived quickly.

"Send someone out to fetch my brother from Trippleford, where he's visiting, and tell him that Miss Tarryton has gone missing and he's needed to help search for her. Tell him to go east, toward Rillover." Dart nodded and left. Will turned to Anna. He didn't try to disguise the anxiety in his voice.

"Can you take a horse and ride along the road to the village?" he asked her.

"Yes."

"Good. I'll take the path through the countryside, in case she's trying to hide herself as she goes."

They left together and quickly reached the stable and chose mounts. As Anna climbed onto a roan mare that a stable boy had brought her, Will flew past her on Strider, Tristan at his heels.

Nineteen

ANNA FOUND NO SIGN OF LIZZIE IN THE VILLAGE, AND though this seemed like a hopeful indication that she hadn't taken the coach to Portsmouth, which hadn't yet come through, she didn't feel cheered. Lizzie might have been hiding and waiting for it, or she might even have found some farmer to give her a ride to the next town. They had no way of knowing. She only hoped that Will or one of the others had found her, because already dusk was falling and the shadows that might hide a traveler were pooling around bushes and hollows.

Galloping back toward Stillwell along the road where she and Lizzie had been stranded that first day, she caught sight of Will riding alone. As they neared each other, she saw how haggard he looked.

"Did you discover anything?" he asked breathlessly.

"No sign of her in town."

His face fell. "Damn. I've been all over, with no sign. Tommy just circled by to say he's seen nothing, but he'll continue looking. And Tristan's disappeared off into the woods, confound it, so no help there."

His enormous horse pranced restlessly under its master, as if in tune with his anxiety. "This is my fault. If anything's happened to her, I won't forgive myself." He shook his head. "If only I—" He looked away.

"Don't," she said gently. "I do wonder, though, why she did this now. I thought she had hope that she was going to charm you into letting her stay."

He looked miserable. "I know what happened. I was talking in the stable with Tommy, and we mentioned her. I did hear some noise by the stable door, but I thought it was the cat. She must have heard me speaking of my plans to send her away at the end of the month."

"Oh. That would have hurt."

"Yes, damn it." He was clearly furious with himself. "I've kept myself so detached from her—"

She raised an eyebrow.

"All right, from everyone. With the way I felt, it just seemed kinder." His mouth twisted. "She's so young."

"But she's also smart," Anna said firmly. "There's still hope that she's nearby. She was on foot. And we didn't quiz the stable boy very closely. He might know something."

Tristan appeared out of some bushes just then, barking when he caught sight of them. He bolted toward them excitedly, jumping as if to get their attention.

"What is it, boy? Have you found her?"

The dog continued barking and jumping, making as if to go back into the bushes. "Maybe's he's found her trail," Will said. "I'll follow him; you talk to the stable boy."

He was off before she could even agree.

❧

With Tristan leading the way, Will galloped through woods and across fields, never more grateful for the speed Strider could command. The dog raced onward for long minutes, finally stopping at a spot near the edge of the Stillwell property. When Will saw Lizzie sitting in the darkening evening shadows at the base of an old oak tree, he could have hugged the hound.

Her head was buried against her bent knees, and she looked up as they approached but immediately looked away when she saw who it was. Tristan raced over to bark excitedly and prance around her while Will dismounted and came to stand near.

She looked truly pathetic with her head buried in that defeated way even as Tristan tried to lick her. Her red-gold hair was piled up to reveal her fragile young neck, though several tangled, drooping strands suggested a long, hard day.

The skirts of her coffee-colored gown pooled around her bent legs, the once-pristine hem now frayed and dirty as it lay across a pair of equally dirty and impractical satin slippers. The sight of her clothing pierced him especially; it would have offered little protection from the elements and made her look like a rich prize ready for the taking.

Good God, what had she been thinking? She had no idea of her own vulnerability.

She didn't acknowledge him but pressed her cheek against Tristan's neck.

"Oh, Tris," she said in a husky voice that tugged Will's memory back to the time when he'd been

sixteen and frequently frustrated and angry. "You're the only one who cares."

"Not true," Will said, stepping closer. He waited for her to respond. Several long moments passed.

"Why did you bother?" she said finally, to his boots. "I made things easy for you. I would have been gone too," she said, her voice breaking, "if my feet hadn't hurt so much and slowed me down. Stupid slippers."

But he could only be glad she'd worn the useless things. He allowed himself now to hear the pain in her voice as he hadn't before, and it opened something inside him. He crouched down on his haunches next to her.

"I'm glad you're not gone," he said. And then felt at a loss for words. He didn't know how to talk to her. She was so unpredictable, and what did he know of sixteen-year-old girls? He suddenly felt ancient.

"Why?" She buried her face in Tristan's neck, and his fur muffled her voice. The evening air was growing cooler and he thought of offering her his coat, but he didn't think she'd take it. "You've made it no secret that you don't want me here. I know you're going to send me to some other awful school."

"You can't simply walk away from your responsibilities to family."

"I'm just another one of the viscount's responsibilities, aren't I?" She lifted her head to look at him with angry, teary eyes and sniffled. "You were supposed to care. My father thought you would care. But you're not the man he thought you were, or he'd never have made you my guardian."

"No, I'm not the same man," he said slowly, taking

in the determined set of her mouth and a firmness about her jaw that spoke of inner strength. God, how much of the world had she had to take on alone over the last year? "Life changes us, whether we want it to or not."

She looked startled by his frankness. Her mouth was drooping downward with emotion but she fought it. "That's all family is to you, isn't it? Responsibility."

"Sometimes that's all there is," he said, even as he realized he didn't really believe this anymore. He looked down at her young face with its lovely blue eyes dulled now by the pain of feeling unwanted, a pain to which he'd contributed.

He'd prided himself on doing his duty, but he'd turned duty into something hard and precise that could be discharged with a generous amount of funds. That was a mockery. All he'd done for her had been done out of a selfishness that had allowed him to shut out softer feelings he'd told himself he didn't need or deserve.

Like the way he felt about Anna.

It wasn't just that he owed his niece the kind of care her father would have provided, or that he owed something to humanity by virtue of being a viscount. If he didn't allow things like gratitude and hope to touch him, he wouldn't be able to return them to others.

He held out a hand. "Come back to Stillwell. Please."

"I don't wish to."

"Lizzie," he said with what he hoped was an encouraging look, "you don't have a choice. I'm your uncle, and I won't have you traipsing about the countryside—or the world—alone."

Will had no idea what he was going to do if she didn't capitulate. The idea of simply bundling her up onto Strider conjured scenes he didn't want to contemplate.

"Very well," she finally said in a dull voice.

Gently he helped her onto Strider and jumped up behind her, and they set off with Tristan following. She sat stiff and silent, even when he put his arms around her to steady her and provide some warmth against the dusk coolness. As they drew within sight of the manor, he saw servants who were part of the search milling about. Anna emerged on foot from the stables, the evening light burnishing her form with dark gold.

She caught sight of them and, waving excitedly, came running to meet them. He stopped and helped Lizzie down from Strider's back. She made for Anna without a backward glance, and Anna rushed toward her, catching her in a hearty embrace.

He let them have a few minutes alone as the servants dispersed, and watched as Anna spoke to Lizzie in a quiet voice. The breeze carried some of their words to him, and he heard Lizzie saying how sorry she was to have caused Anna worry.

Finally, he walked toward them, but Lizzie turned away as soon as she sensed him coming and made for the front steps of the manor.

Anna waited for him, the shadowy light falling softly on her willow-slim figure in the pretty blue gown he hadn't been able to appreciate earlier. Something in his chest squeezed at the sight of her.

"Thank God you found her," she said, the relief still visible on her face. "The stable boy knew nothing, and

I didn't want to think about all the awful possibilities of where she might have to spend the night."

"Yes," he said. "I know." He was extremely relieved that Lizzie was safe. And extremely grateful to Anna. It felt good to be grateful again, after so long.

"Thank you," he said quietly.

"For what?"

"For not giving up on Lizzie and me. You were right. She does belong here. I'm going to tell her she can stay always. That I want her to do so."

Light filled her features and sweetness chased away the last traces of anxiety on her face. "Oh," she whispered, "I'm so very glad to hear that. You must go directly and tell her."

He left her standing outside while he went to find Lizzie, who, not surprisingly, had retreated to her bedchamber.

She was sitting on the bed with Tristan curled up beside her and an untouched dinner tray on the bedside table, and when she saw him coming in, she didn't look the least bit happy. He drew closer and stood by the side of the bed.

"Lizzie," he began, crossing his arms. He uncrossed them. "I…want you to know you are welcome here at Stillwell."

Her brow lowered over stormy blue eyes. "What do you mean?"

"I mean that I hope you will stay here with me always. I'm sorry I haven't been welcoming, but I hope you'll give me a chance to make it up to you. I want you to know that I do care very much about you. We're rather like family, you and I, with our

memories of your father to share. You don't have to go away, ever. At least, not unless there's somewhere you want to—"

But he didn't get out the last few words because she whooped and rose up to kneel, nearly knocking him backward as she wrapped her arms around him. "Do you really mean it? I can stay with you?"

"Yes," he said as her young arms squeezed his ribs with a surprising strength that amused him. "Why should I say such a thing otherwise?"

"No, of course you wouldn't tease me."

"Well," he said with a chuckle, "I'm sorry to say that I am quite capable of teasing, contrary to what you may have observed thus far. But I'd never tease you about something like this."

She laughed and hugged him some more, and made him sit on the chair next to her bed and give her examples of silly things he'd done, because she said she hadn't had a chance so far to see him being anything but haughty.

After recounting a few choice escapades from his younger years, he said, "And there's a certain matter that must be resolved, to do with the ball. Will you, Miss Lizzie Tarryton, do me the honor of sharing the first dance with me?"

He was surprised to see trouble cloud her brow. "I'm glad there will be a ball, and I know I had been very excited about it. But now I don't know after all whether I should really like to attend."

What was this?

"But why not?" He gave her a look of mock haughtiness, hoping to tease her out of whatever it

was. "Are you concerned that a ball at Stillwell will not be up to your standards?"

Her clear, beautiful eyes looked back at him seriously, making him think of an angel with a tilted halo, and her mouth crimped soberly in an older-than-her-years expression.

"Oh, no, I'm certain it would be an absolute dream. It's just that, well"—she cleared her throat—"I don't think I should like the superficial way people behave toward one another at balls. And so much money is wasted on fripperies that might be spent on more improving things."

Will blinked. "Improving things?"

"Like maps, or books."

"Books?" What had books to do with balls? "Books about dancing, do you mean?"

"No, no. About important things, like…" Her brow furrowed. "Like botany, or *The Pilgrim's Progress*."

"You wish to read *The Pilgrim's Progress*?" He'd been forced to do so when younger and considered it akin to ingesting mattress ticking. "It is extremely dry, you know."

"Well, not that, then. But there are good books to read. We can ask Anna. She knows all sorts of good books."

"I'm sure she does," he said. "But can you not read and dance, if not at the same time?"

She made an impatient gesture. "People at balls are only interested in shallow things like beauty, when there is so much more of importance in the world."

"I see," he said slowly. This was interesting, coming from one of the most well-groomed young ladies he'd

ever encountered. "Well, it's true that people like to appear to their best advantage at balls. But if you'd like to come looking like you've just been mucking out the stables, I won't stop you."

She blinked and he hid a smile, guessing she was not quite so resigned to sackcloth as she had thought. After a thoughtful moment she said, "Well, I suppose I would consider attending. As long as there are no expectations."

"That is something to which I can certainly agree. No expectations," he said, at which they both smiled.

A knock sounded on the door, which was only partly closed.

"Yes?" Lizzie called, and Tommy entered with the windblown look of someone who'd been galloping about the countryside at high speed. He came to stand by the bed, so that Will thought they must look like a pack of doctors conferring at an invalid's bedside. They ought to get Anna in there too, to complete the entourage. Anna, though, he suspected, was some-where else, enjoying the thought of him in a *tête-à-tête* with his ward.

"Lizzie," Tommy said anxiously. "Thank God. Are you all right?"

Her chin seemed to poke higher in the air at Tommy's words. Interesting.

"Yes, I thank you, sir," she said in a formal tone, and then turned her attention back to Will.

Tommy spoke again. "Is there anything needed? Any service I might provide?" Will could not mistake the spark of attraction mingling with concern in his brother's eyes.

"None," she replied coolly. He remembered then that Tommy had said some rather unflattering things about her at the stable, and reflected that Tommy seemed to have miscalculated just how much more wit than hair Lizzie really had.

She turned her attention back to Will, drawing a brief look of surprise from Tommy, and Will hid a smile. Since the age of about fourteen, his brother had had a predictable effect on females. One thing to which he was not accustomed from them was a lack of interest.

"Oh, well then," Tommy said, sounding unwontedly unsure, "I'm glad to hear it." He bowed politely and took his leave.

Will and Lizzie spent a few more minutes talking, then he left her smiling and making a list of books she meant to read.

Anna was waiting for him at some distance down the corridor, leaning against a windowsill and looking out over the darkened grounds.

Hearing his approach, she turned, and he allowed his eyes to roam over her and take in all the feminine curves suggested by her sky-blue gown. It was remarkable how she dressed the color up even more with her beauty.

"How is she?" she said. "Did you tell her?"

"Yes, I told her she'll always have a home here. She seems quite happy now," he said, stopping next to her, "aside from a sudden aversion to pretty clothes." She smelled softly of honeysuckle, as if she'd brought spring inside with her, and it teased him mightily.

"Pardon?"

"I asked her if she'd save me the first dance at the

ball, and she told me she wasn't certain she'd like to go to something so frivolous as a ball. And that she wasn't interested in superficial things like beauty."

Her impudent black eyebrows drifted up. He loved her eyebrows. "Surprising."

"I imagine it's something to do with the experience of running off and being found," he said. "At any rate, I should think she'll perk up once she sees the gowns I ordered for the two of you to wear to the ball."

"You did what?"

"I chose garnet for you," he said, leaning closer so he could breathe in her honeysuckle scent more deeply. "You're going to look beautiful. It's quite a rich, reddish-brown color, tasteful but striking. I know you like to hide yourself, but it's time to put that behind you."

She gave him a look and leaned away, glancing about them at the quiet hallway. No one was there, he knew.

"I don't want a new gown. And what are you doing?" she whispered tensely.

"Breathing you in."

"Well, don't. That can't lead anywhere good."

"I beg to differ."

She crossed her arms. "I don't need another gown. I don't even need to be at the ball. I'm the *governess*."

"You're the daughter of a family friend doing me a favor by helping my ward, and you are to be my hostess. Thus, you need a gown for the ball."

"How can you ask me to participate in something that might hurt Judith?" Those sherry-brown eyes wanted him to feel just what a blackguard he was in

regards to his stepmother, but he let their little daggers float past him. He was in far too good a mood to care.

"This has nothing to do with Judith. I simply wish you to be my hostess. Indeed, Anna, I hope you will be far more."

She would make a fine viscountess, and he had no doubt they would make a successful union. Best of all, the thought of being paired with Anna seemed like such a good idea. He knew he wasn't ever again going to open himself to the kind of uncontrollable pain and grief that love could bring. With Anna, he'd have something better: companionship.

"The incident with Lizzie has made me see some things differently," he said.

"I'm glad."

He caught her gaze. "Anna, I need a viscountess. Lizzie needs a woman to guide her. And you and I understand each other. You refused to talk of marriage earlier, but now I'm asking you to reconsider. Marriage would have so many advantages for the two of us." He chuckled. "And you can't tell me you'd rather go live some spinsterish existence with your aunt."

He expected some smart retort, but he was willing to banter with her over this and press her—whatever it took to get her to be reasonable about her ridiculous idea of never marrying.

She crossed her arms. "We already discussed this. I don't need you taking responsibility for me."

"That's not what this proposal is about. It's about you, and what a fine viscountess you would make." He reminded himself that Anna made her own decisions, which was one of the things he liked best

about her. "I've come to think I couldn't find a better partner than you."

"You want us to be partners?"

"Yes! Exactly. Marriage should be a partnership, and ours would be an entirely congenial one. You and I have a strong attraction." He waggled his eyebrows. "And we understand each other."

He wished she looked more biddable. "You seem to have forgotten that I have no wish to marry at all."

"Confound it, Anna, that's ridiculous. Why the devil not?"

"I don't believe, actually," she said with the ghost of a smile, "that a woman is required to provide reasons when declining an offer of marriage."

He gave her a look that told her he wasn't going to accept the primness she was trying to use as a wedge between them. "Anna, we already know each other intimately."

She blushed. "Yes," she said quietly, "but that's over. And now that you've truly welcomed Lizzie, it's time I left."

She *would* be difficult. "Absolutely not."

He was going to have to push her to get his way. Marriage was the right thing for both of them—he *knew* she liked him, and she was completely dismissing all the advantages that marrying him would bring her—but apparently she was going to need convincing. Considering Anna, this would take craftiness. Already he was getting ideas, or perhaps the more accurate word was fantasies. He'd seen the passionate side of her, and he could see he was going to have to use it to his advantage.

He crossed his arms and gave her his most lordly look. "We had an agreement regarding your time here with Lizzie, and if you're not going to consent to marriage—"

"I'm not."

"Then I still need to find a companion for her. She doesn't deserve to be left with just me, a dull and busy old man. It can be echoingly empty around here."

She frowned. "But there's Judith. She would be a wonderful companion to Lizzie."

"You know that's not going to happen. As soon as the ball is over, Judith is leaving. She has already agreed to do so, and to stay permanently out of my life. So if you're getting ideas about her being a great friend to Lizzie, forget them. Lizzie needs a female companion, and for now, that person is you."

Anna didn't look happy, but he knew he could count on her sense of duty and her compassion for Lizzie. "Besides, you have to host the ball, and be there for Lizzie. If it helps ease your mind in regards to Judith, you can consider your hostess duties to be a way for me to acknowledge all you've done for my niece."

She gave him a glowering look that only made his blood heat up. When she got prim and governess-y, it entertained him no end. "Having me as your hostess is a ridiculous idea. *You* will look ridiculous."

"I don't see why this is so burdensome for you. You need merely put on a pretty gown and mingle with the guests."

"They'll think you are mocking them."

"No," he said softly. "They will be charmed by you."

He saw a flash of something tender in her eyes, but she was struggling not to let it show. She pressed her lips together. "Why are you doing this? You know we agreed to go on as if nothing happened between us. That was for the best."

"Actually, we agreed to be friends. I never said I would stop wanting you. And I haven't."

A blush rose in her cheeks. "I liked it better when you were brooding," she said, and walked away to his laughter.

❦

Anna hastened up the stairs toward her bedchamber, deeply bestirred.

She wished he hadn't spoken of marriage again. He didn't love her. What he wanted was a companion and helpmate. He seemed to think it would be fun for them to marry.

Fun!

For a moment, she'd been far too tempted to agree before reason overcame desire. But even if she could ignore the enormous problem of that book of drawings—which was a sword of Damocles hanging over her that would taint any chance they might have for a normal life—even if she could ignore that huge obstacle, her heart could not let her marry Will in lighthearted fun when she cared so deeply for him.

He did something powerful to her, touched her deep in a place that had nothing to do with practicality and reasonableness, and if she had said yes, it would have been a partnership forever unbalanced. She would have lost herself in it.

But none of that mattered anyway, because the book did exist, and if she married Viscount Grandville, it would find her.

She passed the grand staircase and stopped to ask a maid to bring her a dinner tray, then continued to her chamber, determined to forget his proposal. At least he hadn't seemed unhappy that she'd turned him down, though that wasn't exactly a thought to cheer her.

Twenty

THE BREAKFAST TABLE WAS FULL THE NEXT MORNING, with everyone there at the same time for once. The viscount, however, did not offer any conversation from his end of the table, where he sat mostly obscured from view behind his newspaper.

Anna had been surreptitiously searching the back of his paper for news of *The Beautiful One*, without success, and already planned to look at the rest of it as soon as she could. Not that she wanted to read a single word about that horrible book or the excitement it was causing. Stillwell felt almost like home, even if her stay there was bittersweet, and she wished so much that she didn't have to think about her troubles.

The room's tall windows were open to the bright June morning, letting in the gentle early sun and an occasional soft breeze that tugged the gold-stamped, white silk draperies in and out. Tommy, seated at the other end of the table from his brother, cheerfully speared his second portion of beefsteak and deposited it on his plate.

"I'm going to take a boat out on the river today and do a little punting," he said.

"A splendid day for it," remarked Judith, who looked very fine in a cocoa-colored gown trimmed with darker brown braiding. With her pale yellow-and-cream hair, Anna thought affectionately, she looked like a petite, rich cup of chocolate with cream.

Lizzie was wearing an extremely plain dun-colored gown. It was not exactly unattractive, but it was not a flattering color on her, and she usually had such exquisite taste. Anna wondered if the gown might have something to do with what Lizzie had said to Will about not being interested in frivolous things.

"Tea, my lord?" Anna said as she pressed the teapot's spout against his newspaper, allowing a tiny stream to stain it. He flipped the paper down and gave her a lordly scowl, which made her want to smile.

"No, thank you, Anna," he said. "I have had sufficient." He folded the newspaper and laid it by his plate. She would take it as soon as she could do so without attracting attention.

He looked around the table. "With the ball only three days away, might I ask how the preparations are coming? Anna? Judith?"

Judith looked surprised at being personally addressed by her stepson, and in so pleasant a manner.

"Quite well," Anna said. "Wouldn't you say, Judith?"

"Yes," Judith said. "Just the few last details to take care of today, flowers and such."

He nodded politely, though his eyes strayed to his folded newspaper.

Anna turned to Lizzie. "And what are your plans

for the day? We ought at least to do some French, perhaps in the afternoon."

Lizzie opened her mouth to reply, but Tommy spoke up first.

"Actually," he said, turning to Lizzie, "I was rather hoping you'd join me on the river. That is, of course, if you wish to, and if"—he chuckled—"your guardian will permit it."

Anna reflected that it was quite outrageous, how handsome the Halifax brothers were. What had the Fates been thinking, to give so much to two mortals? They were all dark, lean male beauty.

"Of course Lizzie may go if she wishes," Will said, reaching for the butter. "She hardly needs my permission for a boat ride." He smiled ruefully at Lizzie. "And I'm afraid I can't spare any time today."

"I don't wish to go, actually," Lizzie said, spreading a blob of jam on her toast very carefully, as if it required all her attention.

Anna sucked in a breath at Lizzie's rudeness and administered a small, sharp kick under the table.

"Eh!" yelped Lizzie, her vexed eyes meeting Anna's. "What I meant to say"—she half-turned toward Tommy—"was that I'm afraid I can't spare the time this morning. But I thank you for the offer."

His eyebrows drew together. "Perhaps you dislike boat rides? I had also thought of a walk up Little Rocktop."

"Thank you, but I really don't have time."

"Lizzie," Anna said firmly, "I'm sure that you're not so very busy that you need to decline Tommy's generous offer." She shot Lizzie a look intended to remind her that her uncle had promised her a home,

and the least she could do was be gracious toward the whole family.

"You young people ought to take advantage of such a glorious day," Judith said as she buttered a piece of bread.

Lizzie gazed rather woodenly at Tommy's plate. "Thank you, then. That would be pleasant."

"Splendid!" he said. "We'll go after breakfast."

⚮

Tristan followed Tommy and Lizzie to the river, and the only remarks Lizzie offered during the walk were addressed, affectionately, to the dog.

Tommy thought she didn't seem at all like the same girl he'd met the first day. For one thing, she hadn't uttered a single word about London or fashion or gossip, to his vast relief. And though he was sure, after what Will had told him about her assault on the statues and getting herself sent down from school, that she was a much more interesting girl than he'd first thought, every attempt he made at conversation simply died.

They approached a part of the path that was overhung with old apple trees, and he reached out and lifted a low branch that was in her way. She passed under without comment, apparently lost in thought, until Tristan began barking at some animal rustling in the bushes.

She laughed. "Is that perhaps a ferocious rabbit in there, Tristan?"

The dog bounded over to her and pressed his head against her skirts, and she crouched down to pet him,

tipping her head up and laughing as Tristan's face tickled her neck.

From where he stood above her, Tommy watched her and almost had to look away, so struck was he by her appeal. She was more plainly dressed than before, but she didn't need pretty things to set off her beauty. He was especially drawn to the little dimples that appeared when she smiled.

When they got to the river, they had to bring Tristan onto the skiff with them because he followed at Lizzie's heels and jumped into the boat right after her. He was a good-sized dog, and Tommy would not have laid money on his chances of extricating the animal from the boat if that was where he wanted to be. Tristan settled by her feet, Tommy pushed off, and they were away down the quiet river, riding somewhat lower in the water than he would have preferred.

The sun was not yet high in the sky, the air was fresh and calm, and the river flowed gently past tree-lined shores. It was just the sort of setting that young ladies adored, but none of it was having any discernible effect on Lizzie, who sat silently trailing her fingers in the water and watching the ripples she made.

Another man might have been discouraged, but Tommy, who generally found feminine attention no challenge at all to secure, was intrigued. Miss Elizabeth Tarryton was a very pretty apple dangling somewhat higher on its tree than he had at first thought. Of course, she was his brother's ward; it was not as if he had any wicked intentions toward her. He simply needed her to stop pretending that she didn't find him just as intriguing as he found her.

He pulled strongly on the oars, enjoying the skiff's increasing speed as his efforts combined with the river's current, and asked her about Rosewood School. Young ladies always liked to talk about their friends, and perhaps she might also feel moved to explain how she'd gotten expelled. Perhaps she'd snuck a sip of the headmistress's brandy, or been insolent. He shouldn't be curious, but she looked like an angel, and he was captivated by the idea of her being a bit naughty.

"I hated it," she said, still staring at the water. Behind her, Tristan adjusted himself and rested his head on the seat next to her. She began petting the animal's head. Why did she reserve all her attention for the damned dog?

"Tristan seems quite taken with you."

She continued petting and made no reply.

After a few moments of staring at the top of her straw hat, he made another attempt. "And what do you study with Anna?"

"French."

"My French is fairly awful," he said, "though I did pick up quite a bit of Italian when I was there. I stayed for a few months in Florence."

She made no comment. Irked, he pressed his lips together.

"Look here, if you're going to accept an invitation for a boat ride, you might at least participate in the conversation."

She turned to look at him then, her gold-red hair sleek and shining in the places where it peeked out from under her hat, her face so lovely it made his fingers itch to touch her smooth skin. Her bosom, which

he should not even be noticing, rose only slightly with each calm breath. All cool, unruffled beauty and annoying as hell.

"As you might have noticed at breakfast"—her pink lips formed each word precisely—"I did not, in fact, wish to go for a boat ride. I was urged into it."

She returned her gaze to the river, her hand again on the dog's head—Tommy felt sure Tristan was smirking at him—and he knew an intense desire to make her react, to break through that cool shell.

"So"—he pulled extra strongly on the oars—"what happened at Rosewood? Why did you leave so suddenly?"

She turned toward him, but her blue eyes were not flashing with anger; instead she looked oddly weary.

"I snuck out of my room at night to meet a gentleman."

He could not have been more astonished had she said she'd robbed a bank.

"You did *what*?" He bobbled the oars midstroke, so that he smacked the water at an angle and splashed them both. She turned and allowed her gaze to pass over him in mute reproach as she brushed droplets of water off her arms.

He dug in deeply with the oars and stroked, his jaw clenching tightly. "Who the devil were you meeting?" he ground out.

"That's of no concern to you."

"As you are my brother's ward, it damned well is," he said, knowing he was growing ridiculous but unable to stop himself.

She made no reply but turned her face away again and trailed her hand in that blastedly unruffled manner, and just watching her languid movements made his

temperature go up. She'd just uttered something totally outrageous, and she knew it. And she wanted him to think she was just as cool as could be. He didn't credit it; he wanted to see her eyes.

He shipped the oars abruptly and leaned forward and took hold of her hand, which was resting on Tristan, and tugged, determined to have an explanation, to crack her coolness.

But she resisted him. She was no soft wisp of fantasy but a flesh-and-bone girl, and she pulled her arm firmly back as he tugged it, making the boat rock so hard they took on a large plash of water. The skiff, already riding low, dropped closer to the waterline.

"Let *go*!" she cried, tugging harder, but now he held on because he was afraid they would overbalance if he let go.

"If you will stop lurching," he began through clenched teeth, but then Tristan jumped forward, knocking his arm away just as she gave an extra tug, and that was it. She fell against the side of the boat, pressing it toward the water, and it flipped over.

He was at the surface in a heartbeat and searching frantically for her. *Could she swim?* he thought in a panic, even as he knew it was preposterous. Young ladies did not swim, and she would have the huge weight of her wet gown pulling her down. He dove under the water, but it was too murky to see anything.

He came up, his heart racing with fear for her, and saw Tristan paddling toward the shore. But no sign of Lizzie. Had she surfaced while he was under, or was she even now drowning? He saw no sign of splashing anywhere and felt sick.

Dashing away the water streaming into his eyes, he began swimming methodically in circles, fighting the current that might have already pulled her away. Oh, please God that it hadn't!

And then, having paused only to drag in a breath, he saw her, a few feet from where Tristan was, near the shore. She had just broken the surface of the water; clearly she'd been swimming underwater the whole time he was panicking. And now, with a strong stroke and nary a backward glance for him, she was making for the shore.

❧

Lizzie reached the low riverbank and hauled herself out, chest heaving and wearing only her chemise, and flopped on the ground. Tristan hopped out and shook himself off and lay down beside her.

As soon as she'd fallen in the water, the weight of her wet gown had almost dragged her to the bottom until she'd ripped at the bodice strings and let it fall away. And then she'd taken a quick breath and swum all the way underwater, and it had felt *good*. She hadn't swum since Malta, since her stepmother had arrived and declared that young ladies did not swim. She'd forgotten how wonderfully free and natural it felt.

Above her as she lay on the grass, pure white clouds traveled briskly across a clear, cerulean sky. The sun was warming her wet skin, though the air was a little cool. But she didn't mind. She felt wonderfully alive.

From the direction of the river, she could hear the sounds of Tommy swimming toward the bank; she'd checked to make sure he wasn't drowning. She'd

surfaced and seen him diving under confidently and knew he was fine. She would get up momentarily, once she caught her breath.

She closed her eyes against the sun overhead, but a minute later a shadow darkened the brightness seeping through her eyelids. Tommy.

"I hope you are well," she said without opening her eyes. She crossed her arms over her wet chemise for the sake of modesty. Thank goodness she had taken to wearing drawers. Although they were stuck to her as well as the chemise, at least they were covering that part of her.

"I hope you are well," he mimicked nastily.

She opened her eyes and he stood dripping over her, his clothes plastered to him and water coursing all down him. He must have shaken his hair like Tristan had his fur because it flew wildly about his head, the slash of white in front sticking out and mixing in spikes with the black. In his dishevelment he looked dangerously handsome, and her heart gave a flutter.

She turned her head away and sat up, gathering her bent knees to her chest and looking down.

"You looked all right, and it seemed rather urgent to make for shore." She cleared her throat. "As you can see, I have lost my gown. You go back to the house and I will follow."

"Certainly not," he said, and she could see him out of the corner of her eye unfastening his clinging coat and struggling to remove it before finally succeeding. He dropped it at her feet. "Put that on," he said, turning away from her.

She picked it up. It was heavy with water, but

warm from his body, and when she put it on a wave of coziness washed over her, as if she would be protected by this coat. By his gesture.

Stupid. It was just a coat.

"Thank you," she said, standing up. "I would thank you for the boat ride as well, but I'm not sure I need offer thanks for being dunked."

He turned toward her and crossed his arms tightly, and she couldn't avoid noticing how his drenched shirt clung to the curves and planes of his chest. A muscle ticked in his hardened jaw.

"But you are welcome. I'd tip you in the river any time. You know, you might have called out to let me know you were all right."

"I saw that you could swim."

"Yes, I can swim, damn it, but I didn't know that *you* could. You might have some consideration for someone else. It isn't just you in the world."

"I'm sorry," she said in a thickening voice as she stood up. His words struck her and made her wonder at the costs of all those hard life lessons that had taught her to look out for herself, but she turned away from him and strode with urgent vigor toward Stillwell.

∽

Much to Anna's dismay, Judith had taken the newspaper with her as she left the breakfast table. Was there anything inside about the search for her? Though she needed to find out if there had been any developments, she very much didn't want to know. What she wanted was to enjoy the little time she had left at Stillwell, these stolen golden days at a place where she

felt, unaccountably, as if she belonged more than she ever had anywhere.

Her aunt's home was going to seem like a convent in comparison, though she supposed that if she could get the drawing school started, it would provide a wonderful distraction.

It's so beautiful here, she thought as she walked off the terrace in the late morning, past the weeping willow. Behind her the manor stood handsome and solid and large, its cream-colored stone glowing softly in the June sunshine. She was headed for some patches of daisies she'd glimpsed when she was up in the tree with the owlet.

With Lizzie and Tommy boating and Will gone about his business, Anna and Judith had gotten many of the last details set for the ball. They decided that wildflowers might look pretty mingled with the small quantities of pink roses they had, and Anna had volunteered to scout out wildflowers so that the servants could pick them on the day of the ball. She hoped the task would distract her from thinking about a certain gentleman, though she knew that was unlikely.

Passing the formal gardens, she wandered among the small woods and meadows, taking pleasure in strolling. She spotted several large patches of daisies and made note of them, then wandered farther. She was wearing the green muslin dress Will had given her, and though she wouldn't have given him the satisfaction of knowing how much she liked it, wearing it made her feel cheerful.

The sounds of someone approaching pulled her

out of her thoughts. It was a footman, come to deliver a note.

> *Lizzie's governess,*
>
> *Since you are not engaged with your charge this morning, I require your help at the cottages. You know which one. The trim on the windows needs a final coat of whitewash. I will not be there.*
>
> *The master of Stillwell*

What was he up to? Was he teasing her? Did have some plan to get her alone and press her about marriage again?

And yet, he wrote that he wouldn't be at the cottage, and she trusted him not to lie. Perhaps he was simply insisting she earn her keep, a return to the roles of viscount and governess, servant and master. Her foolish heart sagged at the thought, but she knew he was right.

She made her way to the cottages, which seemed farther away today than she remembered. Perhaps it was just that the day she'd been there with Will now seemed so distant.

All was quiet when she arrived at the little hamlet, save for a pair of geese picking their way among the grass and weeds. A foolish, weak part of her was disappointed he wasn't there.

She went into the cottage where they'd been before. A bucket of whitewash stood by one of the windows, with a few brushes lying next to it, along with a note in that same strong, slashing handwriting:

*The brushes should be washed in the pond when
you're done. It's in the woods behind the cottages.
Follow the path.*

Grr, she thought, irritation spiking at his blunt
commands.

She took up the brush and, because this was for
his tenants and not just him, carefully covered all the
trim work on the two windows in the room. The
task complete, she took the brushes and went around
to the back of the cottages and found the narrow,
overgrown path that led into the woods.

She walked for some minutes in grouchy silence,
wishing he hadn't asked her to do this small task that
another servant could have completed. It was as if he
purposefully wanted to remind her of that day in the
cottage and of all they'd shared together.

As the trees thinned, she saw the sparkle of sunlight
on water. A splashing sound arrested her footsteps.

Twenty-one

No. He wouldn't have...

Anna turned to go back down the path, but then she heard the honk of a goose and, rolling her eyes in exasperation at herself, continued into the clearing.

The pond was beautiful, like a hidden jewel, with only a few small ripples disturbing its crystalline surface. A little beach led into its sun-dappled waters, and a goose was high-stepping in the tall grass growing along the far edge. At the borders of the sunny clearing, the surrounding trees created a ring of soft shadow.

As she approached the pond with the brushes, a dark head broke the still surface perhaps fifteen feet in front of her. She caught her breath as Will's head and torso emerged.

He ran his hands over his face to clear the water streaming from his dark hair and opened his eyes and saw her. His grin flashed white in the sunlight, and he began walking toward her out of the pond, more of his body emerging with each step as he neared the beach where she stood. His white shirt

and dark trousers clung to him, water coursing down them.

"Fancy seeing you here, when I was just thinking of you," he said.

"You weren't supposed to be here. You tricked me," she accused.

"Actually, I wrote that I would not be *there*, at the cottage. And I wasn't."

She wanted to stamp her foot. Why was he toying with her, making all this harder? "It's the same thing. You directed me to come out here, where you would be."

He was moving closer with every step, his soaked white shirt clinging to his chest and outlining the muscular body beneath. She ought to turn around and leave. But she was weak. And fatally curious.

He chuckled. "Guilty." Now only his knees were still underwater "You look quite charming in this setting, like some fairy-tale character lost in the woods. Red Riding Hood, maybe. Or a bewitched princess."

His deep voice and teasing words sent little shivers along her spine as he drew nearer.

"You look like a fairy-tale character, too," she said. "The monster that lives in the well. Or the evil ogre."

"I'm far too small."

"Oh, for goodness' sake," she said, grabbing for her last shreds of sense as he stopped in front of her. His soaked clothes gave her a clear view of angular, sturdy shoulders and strong, capable arms, along with the outlines of hard ribs and flat abdomen and long, muscled thighs. He looked pretty much irresistible.

She swallowed. "I don't care why you lured me out

here, but I should like to get back to Stillwell. You can wash the brushes yourself."

He reached out and took them from her hand and tossed them aside. Then, before she could guess what he was up to, he grabbed her around the waist and pulled her against him.

"Hey! What are you doing?" she cried, struggling. He'd caught her with her hands at her sides, and now she was pinned. His wet chest met her bodice, and water, warm from his body, instantly soaked through to her skin.

"Let me go," she said, pushing down the glee rising up in her. "You're getting me wet in a way I won't be able to explain."

He laughed, and she felt it rumble through his chest. He lifted her off the ground.

"How about if you're wet all over?" he said, taking a step backward and lifting her higher, so that his chin was about the height of her breasts. "I can arrange that."

"No!" she gasped with a combination of horror and delight. His midnight velvet eyes were right below her face, looking up at her and sparkling with mischief.

"No?" He took another large step back, and the tips of her toes touched the water.

"Grandville, this is madness! I can't go back to the manor wet."

"Grandville?" he repeated. "What's with the formality, Anna? I think you must need something to refresh your memory as to my name." He stepped back again.

Cool wetness seeped into her stockings above her

ankles and trickled into her half boots. "Will!" she said, but that didn't make him behave. "This will ruin my shoes."

"I'll buy you a new pair."

"Someone might see us!"

"We're in the middle of nowhere and entirely concealed by the woods. I swim here all the time."

"Put me down," she said, trying not to laugh though she dearly wanted to.

His eyes lit with devilry. "Really?" he said eagerly, and his arms started to loosen.

"Not here!" His arms tightened around her again, and it felt so good. Now his wet head was just below her chin.

"Take me back to the beach, Will," she said, enjoying giving him an order.

"Give me a kiss first."

"Certainly not." The hands loosened again and she slid down farther.

"Wait," she cried, laughing. "All right. One kiss."

She leaned her head down toward him. It was so different and exciting being above him, and he tipped his head so she could press her lips to his. It was not a quick peck, but then, who was she fooling? Kissing Will was marvelous.

He groaned as their lips met, and tightened his hold on her with one arm so he could explore her breasts with his other hand, which was shiver-warm against her chilly, wet skin.

Oh, heaven help her but she loved him touching her. Sanity was fast slipping away.

She felt herself sliding downward and broke the

kiss just as, with a helpless grin, he fell all the way backward, taking her with him into the cool water.

She landed on her knees in the shallow area and stood immediately. Leaving him lying on his back, she began trudging out of the water, knowing she had to put some distance between them or she'd be lost to the wanting. But she was hampered by her soaked skirts, and he easily caught her about the waist from behind.

"Don't go," he said, burying his face against her neck. The vulnerable note in his voice and the way he was holding her against him made her knees weak.

"You were supposed to put me back on shore, you wretch."

He chuckled darkly below her ear and moved his whiskery cheek against her. "I have trouble playing fair where you're concerned."

His hands moved up to cup her breasts and she couldn't help pressing into him, straining toward his touch. At her back she felt the evidence of his arousal, and she knew he wanted her to feel it, to know how much he wanted her.

"Will," she said, her voice husky, her mind shouting that she was slipping fast and headed for danger, "I can't go back to the house like this."

"Why not? You look glorious. I think you should always wear wet clothes."

She made herself move toward the bank a few feet away. He held on to her, matching her steps with each leg right behind her own. "You must be pixie-led today," she scolded.

"Mmm, I agree." He came to her side and they

stepped out of the pond. "Come," he said, "we can dry our clothes on the rocks." He pointed to a group of large rocks near one part of the bank.

"And stand around in my chemise?"

She made herself step out of his arms. She had to break the contact, push down the flames licking at her inside, and get back to the manor, where she could hide safely in her room and make sure she avoided him, because only the frailest threads of sanity were keeping her from running back into his arms. "No."

"Why not?" he said, as though something as innocuous as tea had been proposed. The responsible Viscount Grandville was nowhere to be seen.

A hot blush spread over her.

"Besides," he continued, running his fingers through his wet hair, the movements causing the muscles of his arms and chest to flex fascinatingly under his clinging shirt, "what choice do you have? It's a warm day, and we'll wring it out well. Give it an hour or so and it will be presentable."

What choice did she have? She truly was soaked; the gown was positively heavy with water. Her bodice was wet, and from her thighs downward she might as well have been naked. She couldn't go back like this.

She told herself that she could resist him. She would allow her clothes to dry a bit and then she could go back. The sensible part of her pointed out that just the feel of his eyes on her was making her hot and that she'd never be able to resist him, but she ignored the little voice and unfastened her clinging gown.

He made no effort to look away while she pulled her dress off but crossed his arms with a grin as her

corset and chemise were revealed. And then she was standing outside in the sunshine in nothing but her undergarments. With Will, who made her heart pound and her blood rush crazily. What had happened to her?

It struck her that she was exposed before him now almost like she was in the book of drawings. Vulnerable before his eyes. But those blue eyes looked on her with respect and affection, along with desire. She was laying herself bare of her own free will.

He took one end of the wet gown and she took the other and they each twisted in opposite directions until no more water would come out, then laid the gown out on the rocks. And then he reached up and pulled off his shirt, and there was his strong back with its long, lean muscles and those shoulders that made her heart swoop, all displayed before her. He dropped to his haunches to arrange his shirt next to her dress and she told herself sternly not to get giddy.

"I don't think it's worth bothering to let my gown dry," she said grimly, assessing the dress's wrinkled state and forcing herself to keep her eyes anywhere but on Will's back flexing in the sunshine below her. "It's going to look appalling, wet or not."

He stood and turned, giving her a view of his chest, the taut muscles shining with water droplets. He cocked his head. "Come sit on the grass for a few minutes at least and give it a chance to warm up. It's not healthy to wear wet clothes, and anyway, I want to show you something."

"Oh, very well." She'd already thrown all sense away. What were a few more minutes in the company

of this devilish viscount? And if he'd just about stolen her heart, well, that was no one's business but hers.

They sat on the grass in the shadows made by the trees.

"What did you want to show me?" She leaned forward and began taking her hair down so that it too might dry. It was not as wet as his, since he'd fallen all the way in the water. He looked adorably tousled.

"Well," he said, and smiled crookedly. He reached out and ran a fingertip along the inside of her bare arm, and goose bumps followed where he touched. His head dipped down and he began to kiss the path his finger had just made.

Oh heavens, the feel of his lips on her skin, slowly going up her arm.

She was going to stop him in a moment, but she loved what he was doing, and it was only her arm after all. When he got to her elbow, she'd make him stop.

He reached the crease inside her elbow and paused to lick and kiss the sensitive skin there, making her breath catch.

She needed another minute, just a little longer. She'd let him finish there and then she'd stop him.

He tipped his head up at her and cocked an eyebrow. "Perhaps it's not exactly something to show you. More something I wanted to try."

"Something to try?" Her voice was little more than a husky whisper.

He lifted a hand and placed it at the neckline of her chemise. "Something slow."

She knew what he was saying. He wanted something sexual from her. She'd been wildly indulgent

in the cottage with him, and she was feeling more than a little out of control now, but she was not irresponsible by nature. "Will, I can't take a chance on getting with child."

"Yes," he said, "I know. But that only makes me feel more creative."

"Oh," she said. *Oh.* She ignored the inner voice saying this was a terrible idea, that it would only make it harder for her when she left. "Yes, then."

He grinned, a slow, very sensual grin. "Huzzah," he said softly.

He moved to kneel behind her, and she felt a methodical tugging on her corset laces. He took his time, as if he knew how tightly it hugged her and how she felt each lace slackening and yearned for each tug that made her body more available to him. When it was all the way loosened and her skin under the chemise felt the whisper of cooler air against it, he pulled the corset over her head.

"You look like a saucy Madonna with your hair tumbling around you," he whispered, threading his hands in her hair and running them up to her scalp. She closed her eyes and let herself sink back against him.

His warm, sure hands skimmed over the thin cloth at her waist and upward to settle possessively on her breasts, making her quiver with craving. He loosened the tie that held up her chemise, and he pushed the cloth wide and down her shoulders. It pooled at her wrists where they bent at the ground.

He spread his hands over her bare shoulders and moved them slowly downward over her chest, leaving

a hot trail. He took his time as his fingers crept onto the skin of her breasts and inched toward her nipples, and she almost begged him to hurry up and touch her there. A hot tingle pulsed between her legs.

He sat back on his heels and rested his slightly scratchy chin on her shoulder and they both watched his hands move downward. His breathing was ragged next to her ear as he neared the tips of her breasts.

"Lessons for the governess, part three," he said. "Friction."

Slowly—excruciatingly slowly—he slid his fingers over her nipples and rubbed. She'd never realized the appeal of friction. His palms dragged across her, those hands that were strong and deft enough to build a roof but tender and sure with her, and her toes curled in pleasure. He captured her nipples and pinched them, and she moaned.

He cupped her breasts roughly and buried his face in her neck. "Anna," he said hoarsely. "What you do to me."

What I *do to* him? she thought with her weakening mind. He was making her *melt*. She felt dampness in that secret, neglected place.

He spread his legs and pulled her so she nestled against his bare chest. His arousal pressed hard against her through his wet breeches, and he took hold of the bottom half of her chemise and drew it back.

"You…certainly know what you're doing," she whispered as the cloth bunched above her hips.

His mouth was just behind her ear. "I've been with a woman before, many times as you must guess. But none of that has to do with now, and us, and how we

are together. And I've certainly never sat by this pond with a nearly naked woman. I never had this fantasy, darling Anna, until I met you."

He hadn't? Her mind was hazy, but part of her claimed the power of having Will spinning fantasies about her. She pressed her backside against the hard ridge nestled behind her and wiggled.

"Minx." It came out half chuckle, half groan, and she smiled. She was a wanton, and she hadn't even known it until she'd met him.

His hands moved over her waist slowly while he kissed down her neck and along her shoulders, taking his time in a way that was exquisite torture. His fingers slid lower and nudged her legs apart to stroke her inner thighs. He circled lazily around, coming closer but not quite touching where she needed him, while his other hand teased her nipples. Yearning coiled through her, making her feel like a pool of warm honey.

But she needed more of him, and she pushed up to kneel in the soft grass and turned around. Her chemise slid all the way to the ground at her knees and she kicked it away. He came up to a kneeling position too, and their mouths met in a drugging kiss. She pushed her hands through his thick hair and clutched his shoulders.

"I like you like this," he said against her lips in a raspy voice. "Naked and mine to pleasure." His chest warmed her bare nipples and his soaked trousers dampened her belly, the hard ridge they restrained a pressure she wanted there.

He kissed a hot, moist trail down her neck.

"I don't think I've ever spent this much time in

your company, Anna," he said, moving, by a path of
kisses, toward the other nipple, "and not heard a peep
from you. Should it worry me? Maybe I should ask if
you like this." He captured her nipple, and the gentle
suction made her moan.

"Can't talk," she murmured. "Am melting."

"Don't melt just yet." He reached behind her to
squeeze her bottom and pulled her snugly against his
erection. "I still haven't touched you where I need
to," he murmured against her ear. "Open for me."

He nudged her legs apart and slid his fingers
between her folds.

Heaven.

She was beyond speech as he stroked her with
his fingers, a sensual drag that turned her insides to
pure flame.

"Anna."

She tipped her head back. His eyes were hazy, and
she saw that some of the moisture on his face was
perspiration and not pond water. He held her gaze as
he bent down and kissed her. And then he pushed a
finger into her. His stroking sent her over the edge,
into the purest, sweetest bliss.

He caught her as she slid against him, everything in
her loose and unlocked, and lowered them both to the
ground. He settled her on his lap and held her snugly,
her cheek pressed to his heart. And God help her, she
felt so happy.

ৎত

Will thought Anna's head felt extremely sweet settled
just where it was against his chest, and he supposed if

they sat very still like this for long enough, his raging arousal would subside on its own. He hadn't exactly had a plan for how things would work out when he'd seduced her—he'd just needed so much to touch her again, and to start making her see how good it would be if they married.

But now that things had progressed to a certain stage... Ah well, what did passionate but innocent governesses know about securing male release? Though he'd dearly love to know....

He let his hand fall away from her breast, and she stirred against his chest and sat forward. Her passion-drugged eyes and pink lips, plump with kissing, made his already rigid cock tighten painfully.

He caught a glint of mischief in her eyes as she lowered her lashes demurely and placed a small hand against the hard ridge in his trousers.

"Anna," he ground out in warning. She ignored him and rubbed slowly and with a sweet tentativeness that just about undid him. He whipped out a hand and covered her fingers.

"Best not," he grunted.

"I don't see why not," she said. "You had your chance to explore. Now it's my turn." She squirmed away from his hand and patted him with a curiosity that had him clenching his teeth.

"Now, as the daughter of a doctor, of course I've seen medical illustrations. But quite honestly, I don't *exactly* know how this works," she said, sounding like a young lady who'd just been handed a newfangled fan. Her petite, bare breasts teased him, creamy and sweetly rounded, and he wanted to bury his face in them and

nuzzle them endlessly, but after his year of monastic denial, he was dangerously close to exploding.

"We should get dressed," he said hoarsely.

"I think I'll start here," she said, and he felt every bit of friction as she worked on the buttons near his waist. He sprang free and she gasped.

"Oh. Um," she said.

He was panting and laughing at the same time, but when she took hold of him, he groaned.

"What do I do?" she asked in a tentative voice so unlike her usual confident tone. He couldn't see her face because her dark head was bent over him, giving her a charmingly studious air. Sections of her long curls fell across his lap, and her small, capable hand encircled him. He couldn't have imagined a more sweetly erotic sight.

"Stroke," he bit off.

She moved her hand up and down exploratorily, each inch she traveled making his head spin with pleasure.

"Am I doing this right?" she said in a half-teasing, half-curious tone. "Should I use both hands?"

Oh, sweet heaven.

"Please."

She might be innocent, but she wasn't afraid or shocked about what bodies could do. Dear God, she was *inventive*.

She took hold of him with one hand and stroked with the other, and he was almost thrashing, on fire with need.

"Can't stop," he rasped, meaning to contain himself. But she kept stroking and he lost control, everything within him shattering—fences, walls, limits

blowing apart, leaving nothing but a mind-altering chaos he hadn't expected.

He grabbed his shirttail and wrapped it around himself as his release poured out of him, flooding him with pleasure and a wordless unity, the sweetest feelings he'd known in so long.

He leaned backward, taking her with him, and they adjusted themselves so she was lying in his arms, next to him. They lay quietly in the grass as their breathing slowed. He'd forgotten how uncomplicated happiness could feel.

She was lying on top of his out-flung arm and gazing up at the cloudless blue sky. "You look ridiculously pleased with yourself," he said.

She laughed and rolled onto his chest and propped her chin up on her fist. Her eyes glittered mischievously at him. "That was...fascinating."

He brought a hand to his eyes and groaned. "I'm so glad you've been entertained. I'll have you know that kind of loss of control hasn't happened to me since I was a lad."

"Then I've made you feel young again. As you are already well past thirty, you should be grateful."

He laughed and swatted her perfect little naked bottom.

She rolled off him, much to his dismay, and, sitting up, began shaking out her rumpled chemise. She put it on and reached for her corset, which looked as though it was still damp.

"You're not getting dressed already?"

She glanced at him. "We can't stay here. I, for one, am supposed to be searching for daisies." She stood up and looked in the direction of her gown.

He stood and stepped close to her.

"What about a little lingering?" He gave her a rogue's grin that he hoped would do something to melt her anti-marriage resolve. "What about giving me a chance to say that I quite like you, Anna?"

Her feisty, luminous brown eyes gave nothing away. "I like you too, Will," she said lightly, "despite your many bad qualities."

He didn't think he'd ever met a woman with such a capacity to mask her true emotions, something he suspected she'd forced herself to learn growing up. She was very good at disciplining herself not to want what she didn't expect to get.

"Can you be serious?" he said.

Something flickered in her eyes, a slip of the shield.

"I am being serious. *Obviously* I like you," she said. "And you have…talents. But what just happened here was nothing more than a lapse."

"A *lapse*? I'd say it was more in the nature of an interlude. A fantasy made real." He arched an eyebrow at her devilishly. "I, for one, have a busy imagination. Who knows what we might do next time?"

She frowned. "We can't do this again. This afternoon was just a sort of whimsical accident."

Her gaze returned to her clothes, and he knew she was thinking of escape. She'd joked about him being some sort of evil fairy-tale creature. He *had* felt very much like a monster when he'd first met her weeks ago, but that had all changed. Anna had opened the door of his cage, even as she had her own places that she hid from light, and he suspected those places had something to do with her bizarre dislike of marriage.

Clearly, he would have to do more persuading.

But what if he couldn't convince her to marry him soon? They couldn't go on like this indefinitely, and considering all they'd already done, he would feel like a scoundrel if he failed.

No. He wasn't going to fail. She'd loved what they'd just done—of that he was certain. All he had to do was to get her to see that she needed him, and then all would be well.

"I wasn't thinking of repeating the pond," he said, lifting a finger to run it along her pink bottom lip. He loved her mouth, which was as often set in determination as it was pronouncing some saucy remark. Right now it was pushed slightly outward in leeriness. "I was thinking of how much I'd like to show you my folly."

"I'm sure I've already seen that on any number of occasions."

Her black curls were lying loose over her shoulders, giving her a young, artless look that was at odds with the way her eyes were crinkling with suspicion. She was adorable.

"Ha," he said. "In fact I was referring to a small, faux medieval tower that's been on the estate grounds for some time. It's quite charming by night. You might even say magical."

He could see she was tempted. He was counting on her not being able to resist.

"No," she said, but weakly.

"Come, Anna," he said, dropping a kiss on her forehead. "Let's just enjoy for a bit what is between us. I like sharing things with you, and"—he slid one corner of his mouth seductively upward—"I love to

pleasure you. We might play with no harm done as we did today, and enjoy each other's company while we may. Come with me tonight."

She pressed her lips together and looked away from him. He didn't allow himself to think about how much he needed her to agree.

When she spoke, she didn't turn toward him, but her voice was light. "Very well," she said, "let us play."

"Excellent. Meet me at midnight under the weeping willow on the terrace." He leaned in to brush her ear with his lips. "And you might want to fix your hair before you return to the manor," he said with a chuckle. "It looks as though you've been thoroughly tumbled."

"Scoundrel," she said, pushing him away. She gathered up her hair and twisted it firmly into a knot, making her way toward her gown as she did. He followed her and reached for his shirt, feeling more lighthearted than he had in so long.

⁓

"The Rosewood School is next, my lord," Jasper Rawlins said, barely keeping a check on his fury as they rode away from Saint Agatha's in the gathering dusk. It was the second school they'd visited that day, and there was still no sign of Anna Bristol.

"Very good, man," Henshaw said, sounding, predictably, not as disappointed as he should be with this giant waste of time. "As it's getting dark, Rawlins, we shall stop at Lord Minton's for the night before proceeding to the Rosewood place tomorrow. Or possibly the next day—he may wish to invite some friends over to see the book."

Though Jasper was ready to curse with frustration at how long this fruitless search was taking, Henshaw was evidently having the time of his life. Everywhere they went, gentlemen welcomed the marquess heartily, and it was obvious why. *The Beautiful One* and its mysterious model had given the man something he'd never had before, for all that he had a title and wealth: popularity.

Well, damn it all, Jasper had had just about enough. If they didn't find her soon, he was going to give the marquess the slip and make his way to London, where he'd sell Anna's name to the highest bidder.

Twenty-two

ANNA HAD INTENDED TO SPEND SOME TIME WORKING with Lizzie on her studies that afternoon, but when she knocked on Lizzie's bedchamber door, Lizzie asked to be excused. She seemed more serious than usual, and Anna asked if all was well, but Lizzie assured her that she was just a bit tired.

Considering all that had happened in the last few days, Anna supposed this was hardly remarkable.

Judith had apparently left with Tommy to visit some neighbors, and Will had gone back to the cottages. With a free afternoon, Anna decided to use the paints Will had ordered for her and work on the unfinished mural.

She tugged the vanity that stood below it aside and got up on a chair. First she sketched in the unfinished parts of the drawing. Then she spread a tatty old blanket on the floor and took up her paintbrush. She'd never worked on anything so large before, and it felt good to be applying color where it was so needed.

After she finished the shepherd's head, she moved on to add a soft glow to the sheep's eyes. She painted

varying shades of green in the field and dotted its grass with violets and cornflowers.

As so often happened when she was painting, the hours flew by, and she took only a short break to eat the meat pie and apple that Cook sent up. Around dusk the sounds of Judith and Tommy returning from their visit drifted up from downstairs, but no one seemed to need anything from her, and she continued working contentedly, lighting candles when darkness fell and turning her attention to smaller sections.

As she was putting the finishing touches on the robins she had added to the field, she realized that her arms had grown sore and that the manor was totally silent. She'd been painting for hours and hardly noticed the time passing.

She put her brushes in a cup and folded up the cloth and put away the paints. Then she flopped tiredly on her bed and stared at the painted wall.

In the golden candlelight, only parts of the picture appeared, like secret things emerging from their hiding places, as if the robins and the cornflowers were enchanted. It had been a strange feeling to fill in someone else's partially completed work, but the joint effort had produced something fresh and cheerful. She felt grateful that she'd been able to contribute to it—and that she'd be leaving something behind at Stillwell. She didn't want to think about why she'd felt so compelled to do so.

The grandfather clock on the floor below chimed ten in the quiet house, and she closed her eyes, thinking to rest for only a moment. It had been foolish to agree to meet Will at midnight but she hadn't been

able to make herself refuse his invitation. She was going to pay for all these indulgent moments with him… *Just not yet, please*, she thought as she curled her hands under her cheek and fell asleep.

A tinkling sound awoke her sometime later—pebbles against glass. She got out of bed and went to the window. In the midnight darkness below, she saw a glimpse of light cloth and the white flash of a grin.

"Come down, you," Will said in a loud whisper.

"Shh." She closed the window and pulled on her blue slippers, then crept quietly out of her room and through the silent manor. She eased out of the library doors onto the terrace but didn't see him, so she made for the large weeping willow.

As she neared the haven formed by the tree's drooping branches, she was abruptly pulled into a warm, strong embrace.

"You're late," he whispered near her ear.

"I fell asleep. It's not as if I'm accustomed to midnight meetings."

He took her hand and led her away, keeping to the shadows of the tall hedges and trees.

They walked for some time in companionable silence. The night air was pleasantly cool, and the shapes of the trees and hillocks looked new and different in their cloak of darkness.

As they were passing a small wood, a patient-sounding "woo" issued from within. Anna stopped, catching Will's arm.

"What is it?" he whispered.

"A long-eared owl, I believe."

"Oh," he said, starting forward again.

"Wait," she said, and tugged him toward a clump of overgrown forsythia bushes. She stopped behind the bush and crouched low, and he followed.

"What are we doing?" he whispered.

"Owl-watching."

A pause. "How long does this take, owl-watching?"

She smiled in the darkness. "Sometimes hours."

"Anna…"

She laughed softly. A few moments later a rustling sounded in the treetops, and she poked him and pointed upward. An owl flew out from the trees and across the path of the moon, which picked out its long ear tufts and orange eyes.

"*Asio otus*," she said, and experienced anew the wonder for the beauty of nature that she'd so often known when the patience of careful seeking and watching bore fruit. It was a wonder her father had nurtured in her, even if it had been done simply by mere proximity.

"Ah," he said with genuine appreciation. "Well worth the cramping of my legs." They watched its flight until it disappeared in the distance. "The next time we do that, we'll bring stools."

Oh, how she wished there could be a next time, and that she could have a lifetime of quiet moments like this with him, and sensual moments, and all the rest. What she'd come to feel for him went deep, and it scared her. If it was a small tragedy that when she finally did come to care deeply about a man, he was an out-of-reach viscount who'd vowed never to love again, she was also grateful, because knowing he couldn't truly care for her would make leaving easier.

The folly stood perhaps a half mile from the manor, beyond several rolling hills. Walking in companionable silence, they came over the last rise and stopped to look at the small tower below them. It stood solitary in the moonlight, petite yet noble with its walls made of neat stone blocks and its turret, as proudly defensible as any such structure fifty feet higher than its own twenty feet.

"I love it," she said. The little tower had a funny dignity, as if ready to defend itself against invaders who might crest the hill at any moment.

"Don't worry, I came this afternoon to tidy away all the cobwebs."

She was touched that he'd done so himself.

He produced a key and opened the door to a cozy, round room that constituted the entire ground floor. Moonlight from a small, arched window near the low ceiling bathed a table and two chairs in a silvery glow, and when he lit a candle on the table, it illuminated a narrow spiral staircase by the wall. Everything seemed to be sized smallish, and it felt wonderfully cozy.

"Up the stairs," he said, taking the candle and tugging her toward the step.

The top room had two arched windows, a bed with a table next to it, and a small desk with a chair. In one of the windows was the moon, perfectly framed, and she moved closer and looked out on the darkened valley below on which it shone.

"Your domain, my lady," he said, lighting the candle on the desk. He came to stand next to her.

"Thank you, Sir Will," she said. "Though I suppose it would be a step down for you, to be only a knight and not a viscount."

"Even the son of a viscount dreams of being a knight errant, free to wander with nothing to concern himself but the next adventure."

"I can see you as a boy, with a small wooden sword and a plan for slaying the dragon and saving the damsel."

He laughed. "It *was* a bit like that, especially when my cousin Louie was here, as he often was—he's only a bit younger than me, and of course Tommy wasn't born until I was twelve, and my other Halifax cousins are younger as well. But Louie and I were constantly embarking on missions to rescue people from things we imagined were about to threaten them. Wizards, wild boars, floods, that sort of thing."

She smiled. "I suppose you had more of a blissful childhood than most people, didn't you?" she said.

"I suppose I did."

"And then your mother died just as you were becoming a man, and Judith and your father married, and that must have been in a sense the end of an era."

"Yes."

She paused. "I know she was perhaps not the best stepmother, and really, considering that she was nearly your own age, it would have been hard for her to be any sort of mother to you. But can't you see how she's changed? How she looks out for Lizzie, getting you to hold the ball for her?"

"You've seen her for a few days. I lived in the same household with her for a year."

"She was so young. I think she was afraid she wouldn't measure up to your mother and that made her behave badly. But I also think you're

blaming her for things for which your father shares responsibility."

He was silent for a moment, gazing out the tiny window.

"I remember coming into the library one night, when Mother had been sick for perhaps six months. She was wasting away, keeping to her bed. I had to force myself to visit her, because I hated seeing her sunken cheeks and dull hair, the weakness in her limbs. I went to her as little as possible, this woman who'd been such a good mother to me. My father stayed with her for hours every day, despite the burdens of his responsibilities."

His cruel self-disgust stirred her compassion. "It's not so remarkable that a young man might be shocked to see his parent dying. Perhaps this was your first experience of death?"

"That's no excuse."

"One of the things my father used to say was that death and dying do strange things to the living. It's natural for us to cling to life, and it's understandable if you weren't ready to watch your mother die."

He shook his head, as if unwilling to allow that possibility. "I went into the library to get a book that night—the door was closed and I didn't realize my father was there. He was sitting at the desk, hunched over and sobbing. I had never in my life seen him shed so much as a tear. The sight of his shoulders shaking and the wracking sobs—I am ashamed to say that it disgusted me."

"To see him so vulnerable must have been startling."

He pulled his gaze from the window, his mouth

hard with judgment. "I turned to go, but he called me over to him. Though I didn't want to, I went to him. And he told me what a privilege it was to care for Mother, what an inspiration she was to him. How he loved her more each day. No one who listened to him could have doubted the depth of his love for her."

He paused. "My parents had a love match, but he was weak when she needed him most. He was vulnerable, and Judith took advantage."

"Will," she said, reading the emotion behind the tense set of his shoulders, "surely by now you see how a lonely, unhappy person might do things he never thought to do?"

Silence. She wanted to run her fingers over his stony jaw and smooth away his cares, but this was something he had to come to terms with on his own.

"What I did the night you came was not the same. I was motivated by pure lust."

"Were you? I doubt that's all it was."

He pressed his lips together. "My father was the most noble and considerate man I ever knew."

"And so you can't allow him to have made a mistake by taking Judith as a mistress when your mother was dying. You wanted to color yourself as a villain when I arrived at Stillwell, and you look on Judith that way too. Maybe putting most of the blame on her for what happened makes it easier than blaming a man you so admired. You're an idealist, Will Halifax, and personal failings make you angry."

"Isn't it right to strive to be the best we can?"

"Not if it allows you to believe that we are not, every one of us, capable of making terrible mistakes.

Not if it keeps you from appreciating what is good."
She touched his shoulder, then let her hand fall. "Find
the middle ground, Will. We're all human."

He crossed his arms, as though the idea were
unacceptable.

"Tommy doesn't have any idea, does he," she said,
"that Judith was your father's mistress?"

"No. And he needn't. He thinks our parents had
a marriage for the ages. What they had will be a
guide for him in choosing his own wife, and I won't
destroy that."

"You're so used to being the responsible one, the
person who has to ensure that everyone is looked
after. But should you really take on the responsibility
for maintaining a fiction about your parents? Do any
of us benefit from believing in a fairy-tale version
of life?"

He looked down his aristocrat's nose at her. "I don't
see any benefit to Tommy discovering his father's
worst weakness. We all have a right to privacy. I surely
wouldn't want my own sins to be made public."

"But your father's gone, and this trouble is lingering." She paused. "Have you never thought of
forgiving her, of letting the past just float away, no
longer tied to you?"

His only reply was the steady intensity of his midnight gaze. He reached out and pulled her to him. "I
didn't entice you out here to talk about Judith, Anna.
The night is slipping away."

"You like to change the subject when you don't
want to answer questions."

"So do you." But he'd allowed her to probe him

about things he didn't want to discuss, and that felt like some kind of victory.

He led her closer to the circle of light cast by the candle. Then he sat down on the chair, crossed his arms, and gave her his haughtiest look.

"Now, off with your clothes." The white of his teeth flashed as mischief curled his lips.

Oh good, she thought as something sizzled inside her, *the imperious viscount*. She clasped her hands in front of her and pressed her lips in the sort of prim line one might expect from a governess.

"Certainly not, my lord." She licked her lips slowly and forced herself not to smile. "The very idea."

He growled. "The top button of your gown. Now."

She lifted a hand tentatively to her throat. "Well, really, my lord." She didn't know how long she'd manage to keep from laughing, but she conjured a straight face and reached slowly and a bit awkwardly around behind her and undid the top button in back.

She brought her hands in front of her and clasped them.

"On consideration, I don't believe, actually, my lord, that this is within my duties."

"It is. Governesses are expected to undertake other duties as assigned. Kneel down so I can undo the others."

"Perhaps this would be easier if you spoke in French, my lord. I'm used to speaking French during lessons."

He lifted his chin and looked down his nose at her, which was ridiculously haughty since he was beneath her, sitting, and she repressed a grin. Sighing with put-upon resignation, she turned and knelt in front of him, and he undid each of the tiny buttons marching

down her back. She smiled as she heard a muttered comment about the miniscule size of the buttons, and then he was done.

She stood up and turned and pulled the neckline wide, letting the gown fall. At his quick intake of breath, a thrill ran through her.

"The corset."

Very slowly, she worked at the ties fastening her corset, then stilled her hands. "I'm feeling cold. I have a thick gray wrap in my room. Perhaps I should go get it."

"I will warm you up." His voice held a husky note that made little flames lick through her. She finished loosening the corset and it dropped to the floor, which left her wearing only her chemise.

"Come here," he said. Slowly, her eyes locked on his dark gaze and her mouth curled up with irrepressible mirth. She moved toward him. He uncrossed his arms.

"Sit."

She looked down at his bent legs, the thigh muscles long and hard under the soft fabric of his breeches. "I don't think there's room."

He caught her hand and pulled her forward so that she stood straddled over his legs, making her chemise ride up the outside of her legs. When he tugged her down, her naked bottom came against his thighs, and he groaned. Beneath her legs, he was warm and hard and incredible.

Will grabbed the hem of Anna's chemise and pulled it up over her body and tossed it away. He wanted her totally naked. The rise of her breasts was before him,

the soft, petite mounds irresistible, and he pressed his face against them, his cock aching. She had just about unmanned him with her governess act, and now he wanted nothing more than to bury himself in her.

He'd left a French letter on the bedside table when he'd come to tidy the place earlier. He was determined to marry her, and he desperately wanted to make love to her properly. But it would be her decision.

He rubbed his face against her breasts and kissed them lavishly, smiling when he heard her sounds of pleasure. Dragging his lips along her skin, he came to her nipple and closed his mouth over it.

"Oh, my lord!"

He smiled.

They were both breathing loudly in the quiet room, caught up in the growing passion between them. She tugged at the fastening to his breeches, and they opened to release him.

Her slim fingers gripped him, and he shuddered with need. He wanted to touch her everywhere, now. He pushed his hand between her legs and found her hot and wet. She moaned softly as he rubbed her.

"I want you like this. Open to me," he said.

She writhed as he slipped his fingers among her folds, and kissed her neck, her cheeks, and her soft mouth. He wanted to drink her in, all of her.

She pressed herself against his fingers, but he teased her, going everywhere but the sweet place where she wanted him, until he relented and rubbed the magic little spot. Her helpless sounds of pleasure only made him burn hotter.

And then she did something that was so

unexpected, so adventurous, he'd never even allowed himself to imagine it. She leaned back a little, bent downward, and kissed him. Opened her mouth and took him inside.

He nearly lost his mind. "Sweet heaven, Anna—"

He pushed his hand into her hair, clutching the silky black cascade as he groaned with almost unbearable pleasure. Tentatively, she swirled her soft tongue over him, and he nearly exploded.

She pressed her lips lightly against his length. "Perhaps the viscount has things to learn as well," she said. "What shall we call lesson number one?"

"Playing with fire," he ground out, gently pulling her up to kiss her. "We'll explore that more later."

He stood up with her in his arms and put her on the chair while he stepped out of his trousers and ripped off his shirt. Both of them were utterly naked, at last.

He picked her up and carried her to the bed, where he laid her. The moonlight shimmered in her eyes and draped her in silver and shadow, his beautiful, adventurous Anna.

"I want to be inside you," he said, sitting down next to her. "So badly. I'm burning for you."

"I…want that too," she said, and he could almost hear her blushing. "But I can't take the chance of creating a baby."

"What if we weren't taking that chance?" And then, while he slid his hands over her hips and traced the curve of her waist and kissed her nipples until she was shuddering, he told her about French letters.

"Yes," she gasped when he'd finished, and he was thrilled to hear the eagerness in her voice.

"Thank God," he said hoarsely. "But there's something else I need to do first."

"What could you possibly..." she started to say, sitting up, but he gently pushed her back down and positioned himself to kiss the insides of each pretty knee. He moved higher, nudging her legs wider, and she writhed, moaning incoherently, and clutched the top of his head.

"Wait," she murmured. "You can't—"

"Can and shall," he said, and took possession of her. As he used his tongue to push her to the edge, her sounds of pleasure made him nearly delirious with desire.

Anna was desperately close to finding her release when Will took his mouth away.

"Please," she whispered, needing him with an urgency that shocked her.

But he took his time, kissing across her belly until she was grinding her teeth and panting.

"Will," she ground out, and he laughed, but it was a very husky laugh. He reached for the table, and then he was putting on the French letter.

He climbed over her and settled between her legs, and she could feel him at her entrance. He looked into her eyes, and she thought he was going to linger there too, until she lost her mind.

"Please. Now."

"I don't want to hurt you."

"You won't," she said fiercely. "Do it quickly, and that part will be over."

A sweet, hot, possessive light burned in his eyes. "Anna," he said, his voice catching as though her

name did something to him. "You *would* refuse to be fragile."

And then he honored her wish and came into her in one quick thrust. It hurt for only a moment, making the pleasure that had been building flee, but then he began to move and the pleasure built again, and more.

He felt like absolute heaven—hot, real heaven. He stroked her until she burst into a shower of stars. Wonder washed over her, along with a feeling of timelessness.

Once, twice more he plunged into her, then he finally gave a strangled cry as he found his own release and collapsed on top of her.

They lay panting together as though having just returned from a run up a mountain. After a few minutes, he rolled off her and did something with the French letter.

He handed her a handkerchief and she tidied herself up, then he lay down behind her and pulled her to him.

Lying nestled in his arms, Anna had never felt so complete in her life. So utterly filled, so deeply joined. No use looking away from such a bone-deep truth anymore: she loved him.

She'd never felt more alive than she had since she'd come to know him. He'd opened her eyes to so much she hadn't known was missing: playfulness, pleasure, confidence in herself as a woman, a feeling of being valued for herself. She was so grateful to him.

But the love she felt for him was bittersweet, because she knew that for him this was just affectionate fun.

Yes, he'd offered her marriage, and she *could* say

she'd changed her mind and agree to be his wife. But their marriage would be a disaster. He'd been clear that it would only be a partnership; doubtless from his perspective, a very agreeable one, but she couldn't be playful with her heart. Just thinking about what it would be like to marry him when he didn't love her felt like falling toward the dark, hollow depths of a bottomless cavern.

And even if she'd wanted a future of heartache for herself, she still couldn't marry him—that book of drawings was in the process of thoroughly and publicly ruining her, and she could never allow him to be part of the disaster it would bring.

He stirred and pushed the hair away from the back of her neck. "I never knew how much fun a governess could be. We ought to come out here every night."

She smiled even as a lump formed in her throat, and allowed herself to savor the wonderful sensation of being in his arms. Tears blurred her vision as his breathing fell softly against her neck. She blinked away the wetness and forced her quivering mouth into a straight line.

"As the only sensible person here," she said as lightly as she could, "I must point out that it won't be night forever, and it's rather a walk back to our proper bedchambers."

"Spoilsport," he said, and kissed her neck again. But they did get up and dress. Their lovemaking seemed to have robbed them of words, or perhaps, Anna thought with a pang, it had already expressed everything that could be said.

They walked back to the manor almost silently.

Under the weeping willow by the terrace, she kissed him quickly and whispered good night.

Twenty-three

WILL SAT AT HIS DESK IN THE LIBRARY THE NEXT DAY going over accounts he should have saved for the evening so he could accomplish some work at the cottages while the sun was shining. But he didn't feel like going to the cottages, where there wasn't much left to finish. Although *someone* had brought the Willow Glen sign out to the hamlet and left it there.

He didn't feel like paying attention to the accounts in front of him either—instead, he was focused on the terrace outside the French doors, which had been opened to the noontime air of a gentle summer day. Anna and Lizzie and Judith had arranged themselves out there with plates of sandwiches and tea, which they were nibbling in between various pursuits.

He could hear snatches of their conversation, the soft tones coming to him like a random melody. Judith sat at one table with the tea and food and a pile of envelopes, while Anna and Lizzie sat at another. Anna's head was slightly bent as she listened to Lizzie reciting French verbs, and she was rhythmically petting Tristan, who had come to stand beside her. Lucky beast.

Last night at the folly had been incredible. Anna had been so open to him and to the pleasure they created together. One more interlude ought surely to be enough to change her mind about what fine partners they'd make in marriage. When he asked again, it would be a proper proposal she wouldn't be able to resist. He'd do it tonight.

He put down his quill and rested his chin in his hand and surrendered to watching the women.

After a bit Lizzie got up and went to Judith's table for some tea, and Judith smiled up at her in a way that was so familiar to Will from his youth. She'd tried so hard to win him over when he was younger, and he'd felt so justified in not respecting the woman who'd tempted his vulnerable father.

She didn't seem like such a villain anymore. She, like Anna, had pushed him to accept Lizzie. Judith was the one who'd forced his hand over the ball, and though her purpose had been to urge him toward matrimony, she'd also insisted on how important it could be for Lizzie, and she was right.

He thought about how harshly he'd judged Judith for what she and his father had done when his mother was dying. Their affair had been wrong, but human, and considering all he'd experienced in the last year, he realized he didn't feel comfortable judging them anymore.

He felt a little ashamed now as he acknowledged that, at nineteen, he couldn't allow himself to be angry at the only parent he had left, and so he'd hated Judith. She hadn't deserved having such a concentrated force of enmity directed at her.

He supposed in some ways that, having looked at

her through a poisoned lens all these years, he didn't really know her at all. And he probably never would. Tommy still didn't know she'd been their father's mistress. He still thought that their parents had had a perfect marriage, and Will didn't see why Tommy or Lizzie or anyone else should ever have to know otherwise. It was better that way.

He sighed and returned to the columns of figures before him.

⤜⤏

Anna was listening to Lizzie's verb recitation and trying not to look in the direction of the man seated at the desk inside the library.

"It's a regular *ir* verb, Lizzie," Anna said, waiting for Lizzie to come upon the correct form of the French verb "to finish." She sipped her tea.

Lizzie nibbled a piece of gingerbread and pondered. "*Tu finisses?*"

"*Oui,*" Anna said.

Tommy emerged then, coming from the direction of the stable, his windblown hair indicating that he'd been for a ride. Anna sensed Lizzie stiffening as he neared the terrace and wondered anew at the way the two of them had behaved at breakfast that morning. They'd obviously been avoiding speaking to each other, as if they'd had some sort of argument. But what could they have had to argue about?

Tommy took the steps by twos and offered a general greeting.

"Tea?" Judith asked, smiling up at him.

"Yes, thank you," he said, sitting down near her

and neatly avoiding looking toward where Lizzie and Anna sat. Judith poured his tea while he put away several small sandwiches and a jam tart.

"*Je finirai, tu finiras, il finira, nous finirons, vous finirez, ils finiront,*" Lizzie conjugated in a somewhat defiant tone.

"*Oui.*" They'd been proceeding entirely in French, but Anna felt she'd seem to be in collusion with Lizzie against Tommy if they continued, so she switched to English. "Now an irregular future. *Aller.*"

"Is there any gingerbread?" Tommy asked Judith.

"Yes," Judith said. "There are a few pieces on the plate near Lizzie."

He glanced in their direction.

"*J'irai, tu iras, il ira,*" Lizzie said, pointedly ignoring him.

"Never mind." He got up and went over to a stone bench, near where Tristan was sunning himself.

"Does Tristan know any tricks, Judith?" he asked as Tristan lifted his head for petting.

Judith chuckled. "I believe Tristan thinks it more than satisfactory of him to behave with decorum and that little else must be expected of so noble a being."

"Bah," Tommy said. "If he's allowed indoors, he ought to have some courtly manners. He's certainly intelligent enough to shake hands, at the very least."

"Courtly manners are nothing but a smooth surface that easily hides a shallow being," Lizzie said without looking up.

Tommy crossed his arms. "Good manners are a way of being respectful toward others," he said in a tone that seemed to carry some hidden meaning.

"Not when there's nothing genuine behind them," she parried.

Fortunately, before this testy exchange could progress further, Tommy turned his attention to the dog. He dropped to his haunches before the animal and said, "Shake, Tristan old boy," as he swept one of the dog's forelegs off the ground. He then repeated the command without the action. Tristan stared placidly at his instructor without moving.

"You might try encouraging him with cheese," Judith said.

"Nonsense. He'll come along."

Tristan, however, did not share Tommy's enthusiasm and shortly got up and made his way over to Lizzie, who looked up from her book with a triumphant expression when he appeared by her side.

She held out a corner of gingerbread. "Paw." He neatly lifted a foot to her hand and had his cake.

"People who try to get their way by cunning are destined to fail," Tommy said darkly.

Lizzie was drawing in an outraged breath as Anna searched for something innocuous to say when Judith, who was reading a letter, said, "Well!"

"What's that?" Anna asked, grateful for the disruption.

"It's that bizarre story about that scandalous book. You know, the one with the mysterious beautiful woman."

"Oh yes, I read about that in the paper," Lizzie said. "Did you hear about *The Beautiful One*, Anna?"

Anna, hoping desperately that she wasn't blushing, mumbled, "Yes."

"The Marquess of Henshaw has promised to reveal

the identity of the mystery woman at his house party, along with a new painting of her," Judith said. "But now there's a rumor that the model disappeared before the painting could be finished, leaving him on the canvas alone with a blank space for his Aphrodite."

Lizzie laughed. "*And* in danger of being made into a complete fool!"

"Yes," Judith agreed. "Now he's apparently gone chasing around the countryside after the model, like a hound after a hare. The poor girl. How awful for her."

Anna thought that all the blood must have drained from her face. She forced herself to lift her cup of tea and drink from it nonchalantly. She'd known Henshaw was looking for her, but to hear all the details and his plans to release her name, to have all this published in the paper—it nearly undid her.

"Ha!" Tommy said. "Wouldn't that be something, if he can't finish the painting? I ran into him on the way here, and he made such a production about that book. After getting everyone in the *ton* to promise to come to his party, he's going to have a fantastic audience for his folly if he can't find her."

Anna's stomach dropped.

Tommy had seen Henshaw somewhere on the way between London and Stillwell, only a few days before.

All this time since Tommy had arrived, she hadn't known that important detail. The marquess could be at the gates of the estate at that very moment, for all she knew.

"Have you seen the book, Tommy?" Judith asked.

"No, actually." He lifted an eyebrow roguishly. "Can't say I'm not interested, though."

Judith frowned. "It's utterly reprehensible of Henshaw to be chasing after the woman. If she's disappeared, it's likely because she doesn't want all this attention. Though I do wonder where the poor thing is. Probably in hiding."

"Maybe we don't need to feel sorry for her. Maybe she's having an adventure," Lizzie said.

Tommy crossed his arms and treated Lizzie to a withering glare. She crossed her arms and glared back at him. He let his eyes wander toward Anna.

"Why, Anna, the air of Stillwell must agree with you. It's put such roses in your cheeks."

"Yes, hasn't it?" Will said, emerging through the French doors, every inch the responsible viscount in his coat of dark green superfine.

Anna felt certain her face was far beyond rosy by that point. Every drop of blood in her body seemed to be rushing through her like a storm-swollen river, and yet she must not show it. She reminded herself that just because she'd heard news of Henshaw, it didn't necessarily mean he would arrive there any minute. That was superstitious. She was using a false name. And he likely hadn't been to Rosewood yet, or he might have found her already. He could be anywhere now.

But he might also be right on her trail.

Will allowed his lazy gaze to rest on her, as if he were merely a considerate gentleman and not the man who'd been with her at the folly last night. Oh, how well-named that building was in her case! It had been folly to meet him, to let herself fall more deeply in love with him. And it was a folly, she had just been reminded, that must not continue.

She couldn't stay at Stillwell much longer. All the thoughts she'd pushed away and the indulgences she'd allowed herself with Will must end. Reality was pressing in.

The reason for her being there to begin with—Lizzie's need for a home—had already been resolved. Anna had promised to stay the whole month, but Lizzie had Will and Judith now, who would care for her. Anna would have to leave sooner than she'd thought.

But she would stay for the ball the following night. It would be Lizzie's first introduction to society, and Anna wouldn't abandon her at that special moment. Her one relief was that apparently Henshaw was controlling who saw the book. She would take the chance that no one in the neighborhood had seen it, knowing that she would be leaving anyway—the morning after the ball.

"Doubtless I've merely taken too much sun," she said, and stood up. "Lizzie, I think that will do for today. It's getting quite warm, isn't it?"

"But you're not done here already, are you?" Will said, and he came close and pressed something against her hand. She felt it to be a paper folded very small.

"Yes. Lizzie and I really must go in." Which was true anyway, as she wanted to talk to Lizzie about whatever was going on between her and Tommy.

"We are certainly done here," Lizzie announced in the general direction of Tommy without actually looking at him.

As Anna went in through the library doors, she could hear Will asking Judith about Tristan's capacity to hunt, and realized it was the first time he'd tried to make friendly conversation with his stepmother.

As Anna followed Lizzie up the stairs, she surreptitiously glanced at the note.

Meet me in the wine cellar at midnight. W.

Her heart felt lower with each step upward. She knew what she was going to have to do that night, and she hated it.

In the corridor, Lizzie asked if Anna had finished the painting, and Anna invited her into her bedchamber to see it.

"Why, it's a marvel!" she said, beaming at Anna. "You really are so talented."

"Thank you. Though I merely filled it in, in places."

"Nonsense, you've added much to it. Robins and flowers and color—it's wonderful! Has Grandville seen it yet?"

"Oh, no…"

Lizzie grinned and marched over to the window, which was already open, and thrust her head out.

"Lizzie, really," Anna said ineffectually as Lizzie called hoydenishly out to the terrace.

"You must all come up and see Anna's artwork!"

She turned around. "They're coming up."

"Oh, for the decorum lost among the docks of Malta," Anna said, covering her eyes with her hand.

Lizzie moved closer and took her hand. "Now that I'm staying, I think that if I asked him, he would let you stay on as my companion. Would you like to do that? Because I truly can't bear the thought of you leaving in a few weeks." She looked down shyly. "You're like family to me."

Anna's heart squeezed. "Oh, my dear." She touched Lizzie's cheek, drawing her gaze. "That is so very, very kind of you, and I wish I could stay. In fact, he did ask me to stay. But I'm sorry to say that much as I would love to do so, I cannot. My aunt is expecting me," she said, hating that she had to lie.

Lizzie's face fell, but she gathered herself quickly and put on a sincere smile that pained Anna more than any fit of tears might have done. She was so proud of her.

"I understand," Lizzie said. "Really I do. But…" She gave Anna a long look. "I've seen the way Grandville looks at you when he thinks no one is watching. I'm almost certain he's smitten with you. Wouldn't it be wonderful if you and he…"

Anna shook her head. "No. Some things are better not spoken or even imagined."

"But if he cares for you, and you care for him," Lizzie said impatiently, "that's all that matters. I know it would be unusual, but it's not impossible."

How Anna wished that were true. "Dearest, I can see you've been dreaming on my behalf, but you mustn't. I'm a practical woman, and I know where my future leads."

"We all need to dream *sometimes*." Lizzie gave a sigh. "But I won't think about your leaving now because we still have almost two weeks left of your time here. I shall just enjoy that and be grateful for it."

"You are very good," Anna said, feeling low. Her abrupt departure after the ball would hurt Lizzie, but it couldn't be helped. She cleared her throat. "Now, tell

me, is there something the matter between you and Tommy? Did you have an argument of some sort?"

Lizzie flushed. "Just a little disagreement."

"Would you like to talk about it?"

"Oh, no. Thank you, but it's nothing."

Anna gave her a small, encouraging smile. "Very well. Just do please remember how important civility is for a happy household."

"I will."

Will appeared in the doorway then, followed by Judith and Tommy. They came into the room, Tommy lingering near the door perhaps to avoid Lizzie, and looked at the painting.

"Goodness," Judith exclaimed. "It's glorious!"

"Yes," Tommy agreed. "I didn't know you were an artist, Anna."

She wasn't used to having her work praised so openly—her father had been the only person to see it with any regularity, and he'd never been one for compliments—and she suddenly felt shy.

"*I* knew," Will said, crossing his arms and looking pleased with himself. "Her drawings have appeared in two books of natural history. I have them in the library, as it happens. *A Study of Owls* and *Anatomy of a Songbird*."

Judith blinked. "Why, Anna, your work is in books? You never said. I should love to see them."

A grin teased the corner of Will's mouth as he looked into Anna's eyes, but his words were serious.

"Stillwell's library is always open to the acquisition of significant works, of which those two books must number, both for their exquisite drawings and their

remarkable scholarship. I count myself lucky to have Anna's work on the walls here."

Her heart swelled with gratitude, pride, affection, sorrow, and too many other feelings to acknowledge. She'd never been such an emotional wreck until she met him, and everything would be so much easier if he weren't being so good to her.

"You're exaggerating terribly. Much of the work was already done."

"No, it wasn't," said Lizzie. "A partial sketch was there, and a few dabs of paint, but you brought it to life."

"There, you see?" he said, his eyes holding a secret meaning for Anna that spoke of all they'd shared. She realized how much, at Stillwell, she'd felt herself to be known, and needed, and part of something important. She sent up a fairy-tale wish that she wouldn't have to leave, that some magical means would make Stillwell her home, just as it was now to be home for Lizzie.

She thought of the note in her pocket and what must be done that night, and the hopeful glow of the fairy-tale wish disappeared like the vanished shimmer of a popped bubble.

Twenty-four

THE SHADOWS WERE GROWING LONG WHEN ANNA PUT down the book she'd been reading on her bed later that afternoon. She'd seen Lizzie go out to the shade of the garden an hour earlier with her own book and, feeling restless, she decided to see if Lizzie wanted to take a walk.

She approached the stairs distractedly only to find that Will and Judith were already standing on the steps talking. Their conversation was low but intent, and as she drew nearer the top of the stairs, they didn't notice her in the shadows cast by the balustrade. Will was speaking, and she caught a few of his words.

"…not a good idea for Lizzie to stay with you."

Anna reached the top of the stairs at this categorical statement, which made her lips press together. Judith, facing upward, saw her and looked away, but not before Anna saw the disappointment in her soft hazel eyes.

That did it. Anna moved down the steps briskly, and Will turned at the sound of her steps, a conflicted expression on his face.

"What on earth could be the harm, my lord, in Lizzie going to visit Judith?" she demanded. "You know very well this has nothing to do with concern for Lizzie. Why must you penalize Judith?"

"No, Anna," Judith said quickly, "he's not being cruel. It's best if I'm not close to the family. There's been too much water under the bridge."

Judith turned to go. Will looked strangely pained.

"Wait," he said.

Judith stilled.

"I'm done caring about the past," he said, "and all the things that caused trouble between us."

At these surprising words, Judith searched his face with a look of dawning hope. Whatever she was going to say, though, was arrested by sounds from the foot of the stairs. None of them had noticed the arrival of Tommy.

"What trouble?"

Will's eyes darted from his brother to Judith. "Nothing to concern you—" he began, but Tommy was already mounting the steps with a darkening brow.

"Yes it is, obviously." He stopped on the step below Judith and crossed his arms, and Anna recognized the stubborn set of his Halifax jaw. "I'll wager this has something to do with why you've never liked Judith, and I demand to know what it is."

Judith looked at Will, her eyes saying that she would leave the decision to him.

"It's merely some ancient history," he said, "that I assure you is better off left where it lies."

"I don't believe that for a minute."

"Tommy," Judith said quietly, "this isn't necessary. Not now."

But Tommy's handsome features were set. He turned to his brother. "Out with it."

Will inhaled deeply.

"No," Judith said, "I'll tell him."

She faced Tommy. "You were young when I married your father, too young to know something that he and I had managed to keep secret from everyone but your brother. You see, when your mother was dying, I became your father's mistress."

Tommy just stared at her. "*Father* had a mistress? *You* were his mistress?"

"Yes. I'm not proud that I took up with a married man, and one whose wife was dying. It was wrong. But he was so sad and lonely, and I had so admired him from afar."

Tommy's eyes had gone hard. "I can't believe this. Father and Mother were so happy together. Their marriage was everything a marriage should be!" he said vehemently.

"But they were human too," Will said quietly.

At this confirmation from his brother, Tommy's mouth twisted bitterly. "All this time I thought they had a great love story. Apparently, I was a fool."

Will put his hand on his brother's shoulder. "No, Tommy, don't. They did love each other, deeply. I saw it every day. Father was simply crushed by his care for her. He was vulnerable, and he made a mistake. They loved us, and they loved each other. Let's not let anything take away from that. We're all very capable of making mistakes."

Judith turned to Tommy, her soft mouth clearly at war between joy over Will's forgiveness and heartache

over Tommy's bleakness. "I'm sorry," she said quietly. "I know this is a shock."

But Tommy's only reply was to turn on his heel and leave.

Judith's face fell. Will made as if to follow Tommy, but Anna said, "Wait. Perhaps he needs some time alone."

❧

Lizzie was sitting in the grass at the foot of the Diana statue reviewing irregular French verb forms when she heard the sound of vigorous footfalls coming her way. She looked up and there was Tommy, striding unseeingly forward as if he didn't care where he was going. Probably trying not to notice her.

"You needn't pretend you don't see me," she called out as he strode past her without acknowledging her presence on the ground, "just so we won't have to have conversation. Surely we can be civil."

He looked startled, as if he'd been so consumed with his thoughts that he truly hadn't noticed her. And maybe that was possible, she thought, because there was a very troubled look in his eyes. She stood up.

"What's happened?" she asked.

"Nothing," he said dully, all vestige of the grinning, cocky young man she knew gone. "Please excuse me for not noticing you. It was not intentional." He turned to go, but his bleak look tugged at her heart.

"Wait," she said, reaching for his arm. Beneath her fingers, his muscles were hard with tension. "Something's happened."

When he shook his head, she persisted. "Look, I

spilled my scandal to you in the boat, how I snuck out and met a man in the middle of the night."

She gave a small, rueful smile. "I so wanted Stillwell to be my home that I contrived to be found with a man and thrown out of school. I didn't even like him! Although"—she laughed, hoping to crack Tommy's despair—"his presence did seal my fate at Rosewood quite effectively."

She looked into his face, hoping he would look triumphant or at least annoyed with her—anything to move him past the troubled place where he was now. But she saw nothing. And then, looking into the distance, he spoke.

"I've just been told the secret that's been between my brother and Judith. No one, apparently, saw fit all these years to tell me that Judith was my father's mistress before they married. I thought my parents had a love for the ages. And now I find it was all lies."

He pressed his lips together angrily. "I'm damned furious with my father! And with my brother too, for keeping this from me as though I were a child."

"Ah," she said quietly. "Very well, you win. That is quite startling." She tugged his arm to make him sit down, and distracted as he was, he didn't resist. They sat side by side in the grass against the base of the Diana statue.

"Why are they talking about it now?"

"Apparently my brother has decided to forgive her."

"I see. And do you think you might forgive her too?" she asked, knowing she was being horribly nosy, but she'd learned a thing or two about getting difficult topics out in the open.

"No! Yes! I don't know, damn it all." He let his head fall back against Diana's stone leg. "I don't know what to think, but I'm furious at having this information kept from me all this time."

"Well, it's not as though it would have benefitted you to know it. Look what it did to Grandville. He's been so mean to Judith. Are you sorry you haven't been mean to her all this time too? And rejected the nice things she did for you when you were young?"

He crossed his arms and growled a bit. "All right. I can hardly regret not being poisoned by anger for years. But what about my father—how can I respect him?"

"You loved him, didn't you?"

"Yes. But I thought he was the ideal of a man, and that their marriage was what we all ought to aspire to."

"Well, maybe it still is."

"How could that be? He was unfaithful to my mother when she was dying!"

"Well…maybe part of him was dying too. Maybe it felt like his world was turning upside down and he didn't know what was good or bad anymore."

Tommy gave her a skeptical look. "I think we can ask fidelity of those we love. And that was something I thought I learned from my parents."

"I'm not saying that what he and Judith did wasn't wrong. But…should the wrong things we do erase the good things?"

He didn't say anything but crossed his arms and leaned forward to rest his chin on his bent knees. He stared into the distance for some time. Finally he grumbled, "Very well."

"Very well what?"

"I guess I can decide this is ancient history. She's obviously sorry about it, and it's over and done. I suppose…I can choose to let it go."

She reached out impulsively and draped her arm across his back and gave him a squeeze. "I think that sounds like a good idea."

He shot her a sideways glance. "How did you get to be so wise, Lizzie Tarryton? It seems like only yesterday you were giving me lists of every dress pattern currently in fashion."

She gave him a little push. "A backhanded compliment if ever there was one."

His expression turned serious. "You might have let me go on my way, especially considering we were not exactly on friendly terms. So thank you."

She could feel herself blushing. "You're welcome."

He chuckled. "I'm afraid you've made me more frustrated and furious than any young lady I've ever met."

"That's not very flattering either."

He reached a finger under her chin and tipped it upward. "Actually, I'm afraid it's a sign that you do something to me, sweet girl."

She felt her lips curling up in a saucy grin.

When Lizzie and Tommy arrived back at the manor shortly thereafter, they found Will and Judith and Anna all standing about in the library looking grim. Tommy went up to Judith right away and embraced her, and that seemed to break all the remaining tension, because everyone started talking at once, a boisterous babble that put to rest any lingering worries about how the past might affect the future.

❧

Anna didn't have any trouble staying awake that night because she felt too bestirred to sleep. A little before midnight, she made her way downstairs by the light of a single candle. The door to the wine cellar was slightly ajar, and she opened it.

The underground room was aglow. As she descended the stairs, she saw that Will had lit scores of candles and placed them all about, some in sconces on the walls and some wedged among wine bottles lying in racks. He had turned what should have felt like a dungeon into an enchanted place of flickering light and welcome.

She drew close to where he stood quietly waiting next to a small group of barrels and a stand on which rested two partially filled glasses. There were two wooden chairs behind him.

"Welcome to the cellar," he said. "It's not the most hospitable place, but"—he waggled his eyebrows—"sometimes interesting things happen in such situations." He held out a glass to her. "Sherry?"

"No, thank you." She felt wretched. He'd put such thought into their meeting.

"No? Perhaps later." He put the glass down and stepped closer to put his arms around her. "I was thinking," he said, "of getting up a party to go strawberry picking a day or two after the ball. Perhaps some of the neighbors would come. Do you think Lizzie would join us? Or will she think it's too frivolous? I know Judith is fond of strawberries."

A deep pang pierced her. This time at Stillwell had been so magical, but like all magic, it would not stand the light of day, and it could not last.

"I think she'd love that," she said, letting her ear rest against his chest so she could imprint the solid thud of his heartbeat on her memory, because this must be their last time together.

"I hope you'll like it as well," he said, leaning away a bit and looking down at her with a crooked smile. "You've inspired me to see so many things I've been overlooking."

"Will," she said quietly, "I must go."

"Go?" He chuckled. "What else could be requiring your attention at midnight?"

She stepped backward, out of the circle of his arms. "I have to leave Stillwell. I mean to leave the day after the ball."

He stared at her, the candlelight flickering in his dark eyes, and she didn't allow herself to open to what was in them but pressed on. "I have to go, and I must ask you for half the money we'd agreed on as my salary. I have been here half the time."

It made her ill to speak of money with him now, when she'd grown so close to him. But she had to leave and make some kind of life for herself.

At the edges of her resolution, desperation cried out. If only he loved her, she could tell him her troubles. He would understand.

She forced down the yearning.

He doesn't love you.

And how could she even think to let her scandal touch him, and Lizzie and Tommy and Judith? That was the last thing she wanted.

He crossed his arms, his jaw hardening in that angular way that made him look as if no one would

ever win a point he didn't wish to concede. "How can you ask that now? How can you think of leaving? And what about Lizzie?"

"Lizzie will be fine now. She has you and Judith and Tommy—a whole family. It's time I was on my way."

"Damn it, Anna, why are you doing this? Why now? You're a penniless woman entirely on her own, except for this aunt in the north. Why not stay here where you are very much wanted? Where you'll have all you need?"

"Because I don't have all I need!" she burst out. "I can't go on like this. Meeting you secretly. Living here and seeing you daily."

"Then marry me!"

"I can't."

"But we're good together, and I want to take care of you."

Exactly what she didn't want to hear. He was so good at taking of care of things and people, and she couldn't bear to be another thing on that list.

"Will," she said as kindly as she could, "I don't want to get married."

Anger tightened his mouth. "*Why* won't you marry me?"

She could feel her traitorous eyes filling with tears and she blinked them away fiercely. She'd taken care of herself all her life. She'd never been a slave to emotion, and she wasn't going to crumble now.

"Please don't push me," she said, hating the huskiness in her voice. "I have my reasons."

"What are you keeping from me? What reasons?"

"I can't say."

"Is it something to do with that man who imposed on you? Do you worry that he's pursuing you?" A fierce, possessive light came into his eyes. "Because I can protect you. I would protect you from anything, Anna. And anyone."

"No," she said, forcing the lie. She had no choice, though her heart ached to accept what he was offering.

His expression darkened. "Is there another man you care for? Is that it?"

"No! There is no one but you."

"Then stay with me."

She folded her hands carefully in front of her skirts. "Will, you've come to mean so much to me. I've treasured our time together, but what more do we really have besides stolen moments?"

Will saw in Anna's eyes what she needed him to say, what her question really was.

Do you love me?

He'd loved the fun they'd had, the light and pleasure she'd brought into his life. And it wasn't just that. He wanted her around, needed her with him. She was *special*—though he hated the word as soon as he thought it, because it didn't even begin to do her justice. But how could he pin down the way she bedeviled him so deliciously and how she kept him on his toes? How she stirred him in about a million different ways and just plain made him so damned happy?

But he'd known the pain that love could bring, and he'd been careful not to let himself fall deeper.

For the first time, though, he allowed himself to think that he maybe he'd been wrong. That maybe he was coming to love her.

But he wasn't ready and he couldn't say the words yet. He needed time. And he wouldn't have that if she left.

"Of course we have more than just stolen moments." He reached for her hands and gently rubbed the backs of them, feeling the splay of her fine, delicate bones. She was so feisty that he could almost forget she might also be vulnerable.

He knew then that he'd been allowing himself to ignore what he should have realized: that she'd fallen in love with him. All the time they'd been playing and frolicking together, he'd been avoiding the very real possibility that she would come to care deeply for him.

He was disgusted with himself for choosing not to see.

But he'd offered her marriage. If she loved him, why wouldn't she accept and trust that the bond they shared would develop into something truly fine?

She looked away from him and said in a dull voice, "Even if I wanted to say yes, this is preposterous. I'm a doctor's daughter and you are a viscount. I know nothing of your world."

"I don't care."

"But you would, sooner or later. You've been shut away for so long that you've forgotten what it's like to be among your peers."

He brought his hand to her jaw and gently turned her face toward his. "Surely you've noticed that I'm not so very conventional a man. Despite my behavior over the past year, I am no hermit, and doubtless will not be always at Stillwell. But I'm my own man, and I care not one whit about how others think I should choose to live."

"Yes," she said in a husky voice that, coupled with the shine of incipient tears in her eyes, pierced his heart. "I believe that to be true. It's one of the things I love about you. But you see, that's the problem. I want love with you. And we cannot share that, can we?"

He wanted to speak the words she wanted to hear, but he couldn't. Those words were lodged somewhere deep inside where he'd locked them away. Though he was beginning to believe there might be a key to them after all.

"What if I told you I thought I could love you?" he said finally.

"I would think it was pity talking. And I would hate it."

"I just need more time," he said.

"I can't." She stepped away from him. "Please don't forget about the hundred pounds."

Twenty-five

THE DAY OF THE BALL DAWNED GRAY AND RAINY, AND despite the bustling of servants going about last-minute preparations, the manor held that air of heavy stillness often brought by dreary weather. Anna felt it entirely in concert with her mood.

She refused to even begin to worry about whether the marquess would appear, or if any of the guests at the ball might have seen *The Beautiful One*. It should be easy to slip away early the next morning since everyone would sleep late. She'd already written farewell notes to Lizzie and Judith, and she would pack up her small bag that afternoon.

In the late morning, partly as a way to keep Lizzie's excitement about the ball from overtiring her and partly to distract herself, Anna suggested they read a play together aloud. They sat by the fire in the schoolroom while the rain pattered outside. She chose a farce, hoping it would lighten her own spirits, and did her best to enter into its silliness with a very gay Lizzie, though her heart wasn't really in it.

Just as they were putting the book away preparatory

to eating the sandwiches Cook had sent up, Dart appeared to deliver a packet to Anna. She took it and knew by its thickness that it contained the hundred pounds. She slipped it into her pocket, where it lay with a leaden heaviness until they left the schoolroom in the afternoon to begin preparing for the ball.

Letting Lizzie go ahead of her off to her bath, Anna took the packet out and looked inside. The money was there, but she was disappointed that there was no note, even though she knew it was foolish of her to want one. They had nothing more to say to each other.

As she passed a high, round window near the top of the stairs, she stopped to look out toward the cottages, guessing, almost sensing, that he was there. Perhaps whitewashing, she thought, feeling tears burn at the back of her eyes as she remembered what they had shared in the cottage, and all the other things that had happened at Stillwell.

She took a deep breath and pressed together traitorous lips that wanted to quiver and turn down. She wouldn't torment herself with thoughts of what would never be.

৽৽

She was really going to leave.

Will plunked a flat rock on the wall and reached for another one to place next to it. Beside him, Tommy, in his shirtsleeves like Will, was selecting rocks and placing them close to hand. They'd been at work on a dry stone wall for one of the cottages since the rain had tapered to a drizzle before noon. Now, in the late afternoon, the sun was finally coming out.

How could Anna have rejected the security and

companionship he'd offered? He couldn't believe she wasn't going to give what was between them a chance.

What was between them.

He frowned and picked up a large, oblong stone.

"Easy," Tommy said as Will swung it into place with a clunk. "It's not as if we're going to finish this today."

Will reached for another rock.

"You're wretched company again," Tommy said cheerfully.

Will stopped and straightened, rubbing his battered hands. "Sorry," he said. "You're right."

"Has it ever occurred to you, Brother, that you use work to avoid other things?"

"Yes, damn it."

"You know," Tommy said, with a sidelong glance, "I can't help but to have noticed a certain *simmering* between you and Anna."

Another stone slammed into place. "A simmering."

"An attraction. Rather a lot of sizzle."

"All right, I get the idea." Will paused over the pile of stones, needing to choose another one but not really looking at them.

"Are you going to do anything about it?"

"I already proposed. More than once. And was rejected."

Tommy whistled. "I knew she was special."

Will gave him a look. "Nice words from a brother."

"What did you expect? You've been locked away here for a year, and I'm sorry to say it but you were getting to be terrible company. Brooding, morose… I sometimes thought you were punishing yourself for being the only one left of the pair of you."

Will grunted. "I suppose I was."

"I loved Ginger too. She was a great lady. But Anna's great too, in different ways. She has this fearless quality I admire. And I rather suppose she's needed to be…"

"With the beast of Stillwell Hall?"

Tommy laughed and tossed his work gloves by the stone pile. "Well, I for one am ready to quit now. It's getting late and we have a ball for which to dress."

"Go," Will said. "I'll be along shortly."

Tommy, who seemed inordinately excited about the ball for someone who'd arrived at Stillwell disgusted with such things, left with a spring in his step.

Will leaned his back against the wall and gazed at the cottages. They looked good. Ginger would have been pleased. She also would have told him to stop delaying and finish them up so the tenants could move in.

With a rueful sigh, he went over to the sign that Anna had had sent over and took up the tools he'd brought with him that morning.

An hour later, he surveyed his work with satisfaction. The *e* in "Hamlet" was a little messy, but it would do. He propped it against the outside of the wall and made a note to have Norris order a stand from the ironmonger.

Picking up his coat, he walked past the cottages, strolling until he reached the rise of a small hill not far to the east. He walked up and stood at the top and looked about him at the grounds of Stillwell, at wet meadows and woods sparkling in the sunlight. In the distance, dark specks that were farmers at work and white specks that were sheep showed against fields already hinting at the bounty summer would bring.

The pond where he and Anna had frolicked peeked out from its surrounding wood with a sunlit twinkle.

He realized how much contentment these sights now brought him. Even the manor was remarkably spruce and comfortable now that Judith and Anna had refurnished it. Happiness had crept back into his life when he hadn't been looking.

At first he'd thought of Anna as a respite from the anger and pain of his existence. But what had grown between them had gone far beyond that. He loved her pluck, though it frequently bedeviled him, and he loved the playfulness that lurked just beneath her calm surface. Never mind that just the thought of her made his mind spin fantasies.

He had her to thank for the way he and Lizzie had come to care for one another. And he never would have let Judith stay even one extra moment if Anna hadn't been there to… What was it she did? It was something intangible, something he could feel alive in him now, a goodness that he'd never thought he'd want to experience again.

Love.

He'd been playing a one-sided game with her, using passion to maneuver her into marriage for his own needs, not thinking of how she might be hurt. So badly done of him, but maybe underneath it all had been a depth of emotion he hadn't yet been able to admit.

She thought he'd offered marriage out of pity, but nothing could have been further from the truth: she was the strongest person he knew. Brave enough to let him know she loved him even though he'd done so many things wrong.

He respected her, and he loved her. And she was leaving tomorrow.

He set off for the manor, where all were gathering in readiness for a ball he had not wanted and now knew to be his last best chance.

～✦～

A beautiful garnet satin gown had been waiting for Anna when she returned to her room that afternoon, along with a pair of garnet-colored dancing slippers adorned with black embroidery. A simple jet necklace lay across the gown, the perfect finishing touch from a man who was very good at details.

Some would say she had no business wearing things clearly meant for a fine lady, but she swept them off the bed with a bittersweet smile and got dressed.

The hour of the ball was drawing near. She could hear an orchestra tuning below, and lively laughter, but she waited until the last minute before slipping downstairs to the grand black-and-white-marble foyer just as the first guests were arriving. Her bag was packed for the next day, but she wasn't going to think about leaving tonight. Tonight was for happiness.

As she reached the foyer, her eyes were instantly drawn to Will, a few paces away from the stairs. He was heart-stoppingly handsome in a black satin coat with a crisp white shirt and fancy evening cravat. His dark brown hair was, of course, devoid of any hint of the wood shavings and whitewash she'd sometimes seen there and was neatly brushed.

His midnight eyes fell on her, their expression unreadable, and his mouth had a serious slant. He

seemed about to speak to her, but an older couple just arriving claimed his attention, and all he could do was shoot Anna a dark look as she breezed past him and approached Judith.

Judith leaned close. "You look wonderful, Anna."

She blushed and thanked her.

"The garnet and black are a perfect accent for your raven hair," Judith continued. "You are glowing."

"Stop, stop," Anna laughed. "You'll make my head swell."

Judith was fingering a beautiful pearl on a ribbon around her neck. "Isn't this lovely?" she said. "Grandville gave it to me. It was his mother's."

Anna smiled, feeling her heart break a little more. "It's perfect on you. And you should always wear sage satin—it brings out the green in your eyes."

There ensued a great deal of greeting and welcoming, until the tide of guests finally began to abate and Will indicated they should enter the ballroom. Anna knew an inward sense of relief that none of the guests seemed to take any notice of her beyond polite interest; clearly, *The Beautiful One* hadn't made its way to this group of country folk.

The lemony scent of lilies of the valley met them at the door to the ballroom, along with the soft fragrance of the roses that had been mingled in large vases with the wildflowers the servants had gathered. Several polished, gleaming walnut tables that had been rescued from the attic held refreshments, while groupings of handsome gilt chairs upholstered in pale blue brocade stood to the sides of the dance floor. Three enormous landscape paintings

contributed to the grandeur the large room had been meant to have.

The grand crystal chandelier was lit, lively music was playing, and the happy guests looked ready to dance. All heads turned with pleasure as Will took Lizzie's hand and Tommy claimed Anna's and they all assumed their places in line. Judith was there too, led out by a handsome blond man Anna thought was the mayor. The music began, and Anna felt a surge of happiness to see them all dancing.

Will had asked her to join this family, and she wanted nothing more. But it was impossible. He'd said he might come to love her, but who knew if that would happen? Without love, they'd never have a chance of braving the disaster those drawings would bring. She needed to take her scandalous self far away from these people for whom she'd come to care so deeply.

But tonight, she'd savor the joy of knowing that Will, Lizzie, Tommy, and Judith had a very good chance of being just the kind of family each of them needed.

Hardly had the dance ended when she was approached by a Mr. Hartwell, who bowed and asked her to dance. As the music carried them through the steps, Anna realized that she hadn't danced since the last gathering she'd attended at the modest assembly rooms in Cheldney, and the last person she'd danced with then had been Mr. Rawlins. But he was not someone she wanted to think of on this magical night.

After Mr. Hartwell, another gentleman asked her to dance, and so it went, so that she sat out not a single dance. The neighbors all seemed to be very kind.

She saw Tommy dancing with Lizzie, and it was obvious that whatever had been causing friction between them the day before had been resolved.

She could not, unfortunately, keep her eyes from wandering toward Will. He danced with a succession of pretty ladies, including the exquisite Miss Chittister, who wore a gown of gleaming gold. She and the viscount looked very fine together, and Anna hated the sight. She forced herself to focus all her attention on her partner, who had many things to say on the subject of crops.

When that dance was over, Anna was ready to join Judith, who was sitting and happily looking about the room and tapping her toes. The opening bars of a waltz had been played, and Anna looked forward to watching the dancers glide about the room.

But before she could take a seat, she felt a hand on her arm and there was Viscount Grandville. Will.

He bowed elegantly, and her heart turned over as she remembered the playful way he'd ordered her around at the folly, and how warm and hard and good his body had felt against hers. Tonight, he was magnificent in his black satin clothes and silver-buckled dancing shoes, a smile of playful arrogance teasing his lips and something unreadable in his eyes.

"Well, Anna," he said, his deep voice sending a shiver along the top of her shoulders, "you have danced with nearly every man here tonight. Will you dance with me now?"

"Yes."

He led her out to the floor and they began the steps. He was a marvelous dancer, making her feel as if she

were floating and yet anchored by his sure lead. He bent low to whisper in her ear.

"You look beautiful, Anna."

"Thank you for the gown," she murmured. She looked up to see him gazing at her intently. "I love it."

His eyes held hers, as if they would impart some secret message. "The gown does become you. It sets you off admirably, just as a jewel shines best near a light. But even in your sackcloth you have always had the power to stir me."

It felt as if their hearts, so near in space just then, were beating together as one. And she knew that even if he asked her for another dance she must not accept, or she would blurt out something about her feelings, or weaken to the proposal she feared he might make again. And so she let the music enfold them in stolen moments and let herself love him silently, as though the night were a happy dream.

But all too soon, the music was ending. The set was over, and as the dancers stood clapping, he leaned close to her and whispered, "Come out to the terrace with me. We need to talk."

"No," she began to say, though everything within her wanted to agree. But just then his eyes shifted to a spot over her shoulder. She glanced behind her, thinking to see perhaps Tommy, and felt as if she had been struck when she saw who it was.

"Lord Grandville," the Marquess of Henshaw said, "my compliments, and may I have a word with your partner?"

Twenty-six

ANNA FELT THE BLOOD DRAIN FROM HER FACE. BEHIND Henshaw, she glimpsed Rawlins, and peeking out from the partially buttoned front of his waistcoat she could see the black edge of *the book*.

"Anna?" Will looked puzzled and not a little stunned by the arrival of the marquess and his abrupt request. "I didn't know you were acquainted with the Marquess of Henshaw. He was a patient of your father's, perhaps?"

The music was starting up again, but Anna could feel the dancers nearby lingering to see what was going on.

What could she say? She felt ill.

"Miss Bristol and I have been acquainted for some time," the marquess said with an air of bonhomie. He turned to Anna. "If you would come with me, we have things to discuss."

Will crossed his arms, his viscount's cloak of hauteur settling over his stiffening shoulders and the handsome planes of his face. "You can talk here."

"No!" Anna said.

Will's eyes darkened and he asked the marquess, "Did you receive an invitation from my stepmother? Of course you are welcome. But I wish to know about your connection to Anna, who is here under my protection."

"I would protect you from anything," he'd said.

But he'd had no idea he was speaking to a woman who was all but ruined.

Dear God, he mustn't guess that the marquess was the aristocrat who'd caused her to change her name, but how could he not wonder about a peer who had sought her out? Alarmingly, the light of suspicion glinted in Will's eyes.

The music petered out, as no one was now dancing. Everyone was watching the drama unfolding at the edge of the dance floor.

Henshaw gave a blithe smile. "Yes," he said vaguely. Will's brow slammed downward as the marquess offered nothing further.

"And you are, sir?" he said gruffly to the marquess's companion.

Rawlins bowed. "Jasper Rawlins, my lord, at your service."

"My associate," Henshaw said.

Anna's heart raced. She couldn't allow Will to see the book. She knew him—he'd champion her no matter what, even if he was disgusted with the drawings. But she couldn't bear for him to be disgusted by her, or for him to be hurt by her scandal. The awareness that all this could well end in a duel horrified her.

Emotion rose up, pressing her to bare everything

to the man who'd shown he cared about her, wanting him to help her, needing it deeply. Needing him to be with her as she faced this. Her breathing turned shallow with panic.

No.

She couldn't bear it, needing someone like this. She couldn't *need* him. He would feel sorry for her, and that would be the final straw. She couldn't have his love—she would certainly never accept his pity.

She forced her shoulders back, taking a little courage from the bold color of her handsome garnet gown. She knew who she was despite what appearances might show, and she would not merely surrender. "Let us go out to the terrace, Lord Henshaw."

"A wise idea," said Rawlins in that voice she'd heard for over a year in her own home and that now made her furious. His eyes slid over her with a cruel edge and lingered at her bosom, and she knew he wanted to remind her that he'd seen what was under her gown. Revulsion swept over her.

Will turned to her, and underneath his bristling she read deep concern, and it almost undid her. She summoned her voice. "Please excuse me for a few minutes, my lord. I should like to speak to these gentlemen in private."

"Let us go to the library then, for privacy. I will come with you."

"All right, the library," she said, staring firmly at his chin. If she looked in his eyes she would be lost. "But I'll go alone. Please."

He was not at all happy with her request, and he looked from the marquess to Rawlins. "Very well,"

he said finally. "But if you should require my assistance, Anna—"

"I won't, thank you," she said, turning away from him quickly, her mind struggling to adjust to the choices she must make.

She left the dance floor behind the marquess, who drew reverential bows from the guests looking on in silent curiosity. Rawlins followed them into the library and pulled the door closed behind him.

"There is little to discuss, Anna. It's just as Henshaw told you in Cheldney. Only you see, now, how unwise of you it was to refuse. You have nothing to lose—the pictures have already been shown to any number of people."

"It was evil of you to make those drawings," Anna said, and she knew some of the power that infused her voice had grown stronger in the weeks she'd spent at Stillwell. "You had no right to do it! And to show them to people."

Rawlins ignored her. She'd never liked his eyes, but now their snakelike coolness revolted her. "All you need do is come back with us to Henshaw's estate. I shall only require a few days of your time to complete the painting, and then you will have your fifty pounds."

"*And* be exposed utterly when the marquess reveals my name at his little art party."

Rawlins shrugged. "Just consider that you will have been the model for one of this century's most significant artists. You should be honored."

She gasped with outrage.

"Now see here, my girl," Henshaw said. "You

don't seem to realize with whom you are dealing. I can easily have my coachman simply carry you off. Or perhaps I shall share the drawings with Lord Grandville. I think he'd be very interested to see them."

Behind her, the door to the library, apparently not all the way shut, swung open.

"What the devil is this all about?" Will strode into the room and her heart plummeted. "I will not have Anna threatened."

Henshaw gave a blithe grin. "Just a joke, to help her think straight. The gel doesn't know what's good for her."

Will's eyes narrowed on Henshaw. "Anna, please explain," he said, still pinning the marquess with his eyes.

She was already going to be ruined in the eyes of the people here tonight, and everyone to whom Henshaw showed that book. But she had the money she'd earned, and she could still go to her aunt and begin her new life.

And she wouldn't have Will dragged into her scandal.

She looked him in the eye. "It's just some old business that doesn't matter anymore. But I need something from you: a promise that you won't get involved. This is not your concern, and I don't want your help." It hurt to say such hard words to him, but it was better if she offended him and made him wish to withdraw.

"You're not making any sense, Anna. Just tell me what's going on. I won't overstep. Trust me." His eyes pleaded with her, but she couldn't surrender.

"Promise me," she ground out, visions of him at a dawn appointment dancing in her mind.

"How can I when you won't tell me why?" he ground out, clearly frustrated with her.

"It's no use, Anna," Rawlins said with a repellent grin. "He's going to find out. All we need to do is show him the book."

"What's going on, Anna?" Will demanded. "What's this book he's talking about?"

The marquess stepped forward with a look of triumph. "Here, have a look."

Will glanced at Anna with a puzzled expression before he turned his attention to *The Beautiful One*. His eyes took in the weird wax words on the cover, and then he opened the book.

He gazed for several seconds at the first page. He turned the page. And the next one. He closed the book.

When he looked up, his jaw seemed so hard it might have been carved from stone, and Anna remembered the man she'd met on the road to Stillwell weeks before.

"What the devil's going on here, Henshaw?"

Henshaw crossed his meaty arms and tipped his chin up. "Miss Bristol modeled for these pictures, and now she is supposed to model for a painting. It's half-done, awaiting her posing, and she won't come."

"Anna?"

It was done. He'd seen the book, and he knew her secret.

But she could tell him the truth now. She must leave immediately, taking as much of her scandal with her as she could, but she could tell him the truth before she left.

"Rawlins spied on me when he was my father's

apprentice and made those drawings without my knowledge. He then sold the book to the marquess."

At her words, Will's expression turned furious and he muttered a curse, but she didn't stop.

"The marquess is showing that book around. And he wishes me to appear—nude—in a painting that he wants to display at his party. He means to reveal my identity."

Will opened his mouth to speak, but before he could, she turned to the two men who'd made her feel like a victim and drew herself up. They might do her harm, but she had power of her own that they could never take from her.

"Do it," she said. "Go on, show that book to everyone you know. Tell them my name, since it gives you so much pleasure to take advantage of a woman in this way. I refuse to care about the opinion of anyone who wants to think less of me because of that book."

The marquess was already scoffing. "Of course you posed for the pictures, girl. Stop this ridiculous lying."

But already she was walking out of the room, ignoring Will as he called to her. He needed her to leave—he just didn't realize it yet.

Once she reached the stairs, she went up as quickly as she could without attracting attention.

She rushed into her bedchamber and locked the door, lest Lizzie come looking for her. She couldn't have borne seeing her now. Or Judith, or even Tristan. A sob escaped her as she gathered the last of her things and began pushing them into her valise.

❧

In the library, Will clutched the strange book, the fire of his fury building more each moment.

Henshaw was clearly the aristocrat of whom Anna had spoken before, the one who'd caused her to use a false name. Of course: he had the power to ruin her life.

And this Rawlins creature—the man was a disgusting reprobate who'd stolen Anna's image and sold it. Both men were at fault for what they'd done to her.

His blood boiled more hotly as he considered that these cretins—and selected others, apparently—had seen her.

Anna—his daring, sweet, lovely, one-of-a-kind Anna—was the Beautiful One.

And she thought she was alone in this trouble.

Tommy appeared at the door at that moment, and Will pulled the bell for Dart and shoved the book at Tommy, saying, "Under no circumstances is anyone to open this or remove it from your possession. Stay with Henshaw and his man until I get back. Dart will assist you."

"Of course."

Tommy fixed the two men with a dark look and stepped inside the room, and Will left, closing the door after himself. A number of his guests were now milling about curiously in the foyer, and their presence there would ensure that the marquess and that Rawlins character could not simply grab the book and leave.

His heart pounding, Will took the stairs two at time and ran along the corridor until he came to Anna's bedchamber.

He knocked. She made no answer, but he heard small sounds coming from inside.

"Anna, open this door."

Nothing. He tried the knob, but the door was locked, and he sagged against it, letting his head knock against it in frustration.

"So this is all the explanation I am to have?" The silence stretched out, and he was afraid she wouldn't answer at all. "Nothing?"

"I... There is nothing to say," came the muffled reply. "I'm sorry."

He crossed his arms. "I don't care about that damned book."

Silence. His heart throbbed painfully in his chest. What if he couldn't get her to stay?

"I have to go," she said, her voice distant and uncharacteristically weak on the other side of the door. "It's for the best. Please just go away so I can leave quietly."

"Open the door, Anna. We need to talk."

"No. I have to leave. Now—tonight. Just let me go. It's for the best."

He pounded his fist against the door frame, so frustrated and furious with her for pushing him away when she so obviously needed help. He was pretty damned furious, too, that she hadn't told him about this book before now, because clearly this had been weighing on her. And now she meant to go.

He'd be damned if he'd let her.

Except, he thought as he blustered inside, the one thing of which he was certain was that he couldn't make Anna do anything she didn't truly want to do.

And right now she wanted to leave him. Leave his home. He had to believe that the book was the reason she had been so set against marriage, and he gambled on that.

"There you go again. You don't trust anyone, do you? You think it has to be you, alone, handling whatever comes your way."

"That's for the best." Was that a quiver in her voice? If only he could see her.

"It bloody well isn't. You might have been alone for most of your life for all intents and purposes, but you're not alone anymore. There's me. And Lizzie. And Judith. And Tommy."

A shuffling sound on the other side of the door, the sounds of her drawing closer. "I won't ever forget you," she said, her voice sounding thicker and louder. "Any of you."

"Open the blasted door, Anna. Let go of your mistrust and let me in so we can talk about this."

Silence again. He restrained the urge to pound his fist against the door.

"It's not a good idea," she finally said. "I can't."

"You can. I need to talk to you, and I can't do it through the door."

"Will, no."

Sending up a prayer that he hadn't left it too late and ruined his chances, he said, "Open it or I shall bash it in."

There was a pause, then the door opened a sliver. He stuck his foot in the opening and pushed it wider and took in the sight of her packed bag as he stood in the doorway.

He crossed his arms and gave her his best viscount's I-mean-business scowl. "You're not leaving."

❧

Anna was dismayed down to her toes. She had to get Will to go or she'd give in to whatever he wanted and lose all respect for herself.

"Your guests will miss you," she said, wishing her voice didn't sound so husky. "You shouldn't be here."

"Yes, I damned well should," he said. "I'm furious with you. Why didn't you tell me about this book and that despicable artist? Why didn't you tell me that Henshaw was the man who'd caused you to use a false name?"

She slumped against the door frame, the fight seeping out of her. She was so tired of fighting what she so dearly wanted. At least now that he'd seen the pictures, she didn't have to be afraid of him discovering them. "I was afraid of what you would think. That book makes me a ruined woman."

He looked hurt. "Exactly what in my recent behavior gave you the idea I wouldn't believe in you?"

"Nothing," she admitted miserably. "Though at first I could never have told you about the book and what happened, you've let me see what a good man you are. I wanted to tell you." She shrugged weakly.

"You darned well should have. Why did you run out of the library just now? Why were you in such a rush to leave?"

"Because I don't want the scandal of this book to touch you or any of the family," she said fiercely. "And if you'll just stop and think a moment, you'll realize I'm right and let me go."

He muttered a curse. "Your words to those scoundrels were brave, and they were also so true. Nothing to do with that book can really touch any of us if we choose not to let it." He paused. "Besides, I don't intend for those blackguards to leave with that book tonight."

Her eyes widened at the dark arrogance of his words. His blue eyes seemed to be tugging her soul to meet his, making her want to tell him everything.

"When Mr. Rawlins was working for my father, he made a hole in the wall of my room and used it to make those drawings without my knowledge," she said, needing him to know the details that had burdened her.

"That blackguard!" he growled. He looked furious, but he closed his eyes as if gathering himself. "I will deal with him later." He opened his eyes and reached out to rest his hand on her shoulder. "But now you and I must be fully truthful with one another."

What was he up to? "Will, don't try to charm me now. It's wrong of you."

He chuckled but the sound had a rueful, anxious note that she'd never heard in it before.

"Anna, more than anything I want you to trust me. I know it's hard for you to let yourself be vulnerable to others when life has taught you to rely so much on yourself. But I hope I've shown you that you can trust me."

In that moment, she realized that she did trust him. He listened to her, he cared what she thought, and he took care of those he loved. He'd earned her trust. She had only been unwilling to give it to him because doing so laid her open to being hurt. But she

didn't feel hurt right now, with him looking at her with a deepness in his eyes that he seemed to want her to feel.

"I do trust you." Speaking these words felt like stepping out into a void, but surprisingly, she didn't feel afraid.

"Good." He lifted his hands to frame her face. His eyes looked so different tonight, and she realized that there was an open quality to them she'd not seen before. Her heart, so long refused a voice, whispered to her that maybe something had changed.

"I love you," he said. "With all my heart. You stirred me from the moment I met you on that road, and awakened things in me that I didn't know I needed. What I felt then has only grown each day, into something that I didn't want to allow but that now I welcome. I want you, and I want love and everything that promises."

Could it really be? Even though she didn't doubt his sincerity, she also knew that she had to ask. "You said before that you only wanted a partnership. That you couldn't allow yourself to love again."

"I said many things that I've come to see were wrong, or at least not the whole truth because I didn't know what the whole truth was. I thought I would never want to love again, but I've come to see that refusing love kills something infinitely important within us. You've helped me to see that, Anna, and I'm grateful."

"So it's gratitude you feel." She didn't even try to keep the dull note from her voice. They were being fully honest with each other.

He closed his eyes and kissed her forehead, and the spark of hope flared again.

"Yes, gratitude, but that's only a corner of what you inspire in me. Lust, definitely, and deep pleasure in your company. But underpinning it all is love. I love you, Anna, with all my heart."

She saw the truth of it in his eyes, heard it in his voice, and let it wash over her. A smile was growing on her lips as if it would never stop, and she laughed, the wonderful, light laughter of release. Will's brows drew together darkly.

"Don't torment me, sweet. Laughter isn't what I want from you just now. Do you love me?"

"Yes," she said, rising up on her toes to kiss his dear face, "a thousand times yes. I love you."

He hugged her to him hard. "Then it's settled," he said, pressing his mouth against her hair. "We'll be married as soon as possible. I'll get a special license."

She smiled against his cheek, her heart overflowing. "Did you propose again, my lord? Because I didn't hear anything."

"Anna..." he said with a note of warning that only made her laugh again.

"Yes," she said exuberantly. "Of course I'll marry you."

They embraced, both so happy that it was like their happiness was one.

"But what about *The Beautiful One*?" she said as they moved apart. Will kept his arm around her. "So many people have seen it, seen *me*."

"You know, I don't think there will be any trouble. I'm quite certain the marquess is going to want to arrange all this to our satisfaction."

"But—"

"Come along, Anna," he said, taking her arm and looking into her eyes with love shining from his. "Your presence is required in the ballroom."

She let him lead her downstairs, still a little amazed at all that had changed.

Judith and Lizzie were waiting for them at the bottom of the stairs, looking anxious. Beyond them, it appeared as though most of the curious guests had returned to the ballroom.

"Anna," Judith asked in a low voice, reaching out to take her hand, "is anything the matter? Are you well?"

"Yes, quite."

"But what's going on? Why is the Marquess of Henshaw in the library?" Lizzie whispered urgently.

"There were some misunderstandings," Will said. "But if you two would accompany Anna back into the ballroom, Tommy and I shall sort them out and join you momentarily."

"Will, you're not going to do anything outrageous," Anna began, but he just put a hand on her back and gave her a gentle push toward the ballroom.

"Do please see Anna back to the ball, Judith. There's just a small matter to be resolved, and then I shall rejoin you all."

Judith lifted an eyebrow at Anna as he made for the library. "All will be well, dear girl," she said, leading her toward the ballroom, where the dancing had resumed, doubtless aided by the lack of any of the more dramatic entertainment of earlier.

"Yes," Lizzie agreed. "He's the most capable of men, and I'm sure that whatever it is, he'll sort it out

perfectly." She smiled cheerfully. "Let's get you a glass of lemonade."

≈≈

Will pushed open the library door to find a red-faced Henshaw looking daggers at Tommy. The weasel of an artist was standing by an open window and examining the bloom of a rose bush that was just outside the windowsill as though he'd had nothing to do with the night's events. Dart stood guard by the door, and Will directed him to step outside and keep anyone from coming in.

"Lord Grandville," the marquess growled once the door was closed, "I demand you return my book this instant and stop behaving as if I am a prisoner here!"

Will ignored him and strode over to Rawlins. "You are a foul and despicable scoundrel," he said fiercely. "Only the lowest of the low could spy on a woman and make pictures of her."

Tommy sucked in a shocked gasp. "*Anna* is the Beautiful One?"

The artist shrugged carelessly, though he was looking somewhat paler. "Miss Bristol should be grateful I chose to celebrate her. She was a little mouse that nobody even noticed before I made that book. Now half the lords in London want her for a mistress."

"The devil!" cried Tommy, thrusting the book under his arm and striding forward. Before he could get any closer, though, Will drew his fist back and sent it crashing into Rawlins's jaw, knocking him back against the sill of the open window. The artist gave a sharp cry.

"You will never speak of this book, or Miss Bristol, again," Will ground out, "or I will see that you never sell another painting, never mind what I will do to your person."

Rawlins grimaced and panted, apparently unable to reply.

"I say!" Henshaw interjected angrily, striding forward with Tommy on his heels. Will sent his fist into Rawlins's jaw again, and the momentum carried the man backward. There was an anguished cry as he fell out the window and landed with a heavy thump amid the rose bushes. A moment later, it sounded strangely as though he were casting up his accounts.

"Well done, Will!" Tommy cried.

Will turned around to find the marquess spluttering.

"What the devil have you done to my protégé?" Henshaw demanded.

Tommy's voice was drenched in scorn as he said, "No more than he deserves for what he did. The man is a snake."

Henshaw rolled his eyes dismissively. "That gel tried to peddle her lies to me as well, as if she were a victim. Of an artist, for God's sake. Don't tell me she's got you believing it."

"Entirely," Will said.

"Well, that's your problem. I'll have my book back now."

"You will not."

Henshaw's thick face turned red. "I damned well *will* have it. I paid hundreds of pounds for it."

"Then you may consider that a small price to have paid to begin to atone for all you've done to an innocent

woman. My God, man, even if you believed she'd posed for Rawlins, why the devil would you chase her down when she told you she wouldn't be in your painting?"

"She made me look bad. Everyone knew she was to be in the painting." Henshaw smirked. "Everyone has already seen her in the drawings."

"'Everyone' has not seen those drawings. And anyone who has will be easily convinced they are mistaken if they imagine any connection to her."

"Why the devil are you going to all this trouble for this chit?"

"Will," Tommy said, furious, "you are being far too indulgent."

"I wish to be certain that Henshaw understands he will never mention Anna in relation to those drawings," Will said in a dangerously calm voice. "She has consented to be my wife."

He felt Tommy start in surprise, but all his attention was on the cretin standing before him.

"Your *wife*?" the marquess said, careless of Will's tone and words, and chuckled lasciviously. Will sent his fist forcefully into the man's nose.

Henshaw fell heavily against the table behind him. He stood up with a growl, a hand flying to his face, where blood was already streaming from his nose, which was now twisted at a sickening angle.

"You blackguard!" Henshaw balled up his fist and drew his arm back, but Will was quicker, and he knocked him to the floor with a mighty punch.

"I'm struggling against the urge to kick him," Tommy said through clenched teeth as he stood over the prone man.

"Get out of my house," Will growled at the marquess. "I'm certain neither my brother nor I will ever hear another word about any of this, lest we find the need to come after you. And make no mistake: We *will* come after you if necessary. And we won't be so civilized next time."

The subdued Henshaw was escorted from the room and marched discreetly out the back door by Dart.

Will took the book and locked it in his desk. Then he and Tommy straightened their clothes and made for the ballroom.

"I say," Tommy said as they drew near the doors, "that was a shocking business. Is Anna all right?"

"Yes," Will said as they entered the room and he saw her, her face shining at him across the room, regal as a queen in her garnet gown. "She is quite fine now. Simply marvelous."

"And to be your wife." Tommy shook his head, a huge smile breaking over his face. "You lucky devil. Congratulations."

Will felt a tremendously pleased smirk coming over him, because he did feel like one hell of a lucky devil. "Thank you."

"Tell me, though," Tommy said seriously, "what will you do with the book?"

Will sighed. The book had caused so much trouble, and he wanted nothing more than to destroy it that very moment. He felt fairly confident that the men who'd already seen the drawings would never dream of associating Viscount Grandville's new wife with them, and without a book or a painting to reinforce memories of her, no one would give it much more

thought. The identity of the Beautiful One would simply be a delicious mystery that would fade away.

"I think Anna should decide. But tonight is not for such things," he continued, as he moved toward where she was standing with Lizzie and Judith. "Tonight is for celebrating."

Anna was watching Will, her eyes asking him questions as he approached.

All is well, he told her with his eyes. *You are mine and I am yours.*

And then Anna was in his arms and all was right in the world.

Twenty-seven

THE GRAND CELEBRATION OF THE MARRIAGE OF Viscount Grandville to Miss Anna Black Bristol was held on an afternoon in late June, two weeks after their wedding ceremony.

It was a joint party meant also to celebrate the completion of the estate's new tenants' cottages. A profusion of hollyhocks and pansies had been planted under the windows of all the homes, and the white-washed shutters and doors were open to let in the gentle, warm breezes. Just in front of the entrance to the hamlet, a small child chased a dog around a handsome iron pole from which hung a wooden sign carved with the words "Willow Glen Hamlet."

The whole neighborhood had come for the festivities. Long tables piled with food and drinks had been set up next to an old apple tree, games had been organized, and a wooden platform had been erected for dancing, with a small band arranged nearby.

The dozen families who were to move into the homes were happily occupied in giving enthusiastic tours to all the guests. Lord Grandville had promised

that construction would soon start on the next hamlet of cottages, so that all his tenants would eventually have new homes.

Anna, with the help of Lizzie, was engaged in forming lines of children for a sack race, and a cheerful crowd of parents and neighbors stood around talking and waiting to watch the hoppers. Across the meadow, Anna's new husband was standing in front of one of the cottages gesticulating to Mr. Pilchard, the local vicar, in a way that suggested he was discussing roof construction.

Will felt his wife's eyes on him and looked her way, and the two shared a knowing smile that told so much the other wanted to know.

"Anna," Lizzie said, recalling her attention to the matter at hand, "I really think we must start or the lines will collapse." Already the small hands of three-year-old Maggie Lennox had begun tugging imploringly at Anna's skirts. Laughing, Anna turned her attention to the row of young racers.

"All right, then. On your mark, get set, go!"

The children took off amid cheers and clapping from the spectators. Lizzie laughed as little Maggie, with barely more than her head showing above the top of her sack, fell over on the course and began rolling around, laughing and creating an obstacle for the other racers. At the other end, a beaming Judith stood ready to welcome the winner.

The musicians began to warm up near the dancing platform, and hardly had the opening notes of a dance sounded when Tommy appeared at Lizzie's side. He'd come from the archery butts, where he'd won the

prize of a book of verse, which he now presented to Lizzie with an elegant bow.

"Well, Lizzie," he said as he straightened, "I have only two days left before I must go to do my brother's bidding at Longmount. As you and Judith are going to Town next week and I won't see you for a while, I mean to get in some dances while I can. And you must promise not to be snapped up by some London fellow."

Anna and Will had decided that Lizzie should have a London holiday, but that she wasn't quite ready to have her come-out that year.

Lizzie laughed and tossed her head and took his arm. "I promise nothing, Tommy Halifax."

Anna began to make her way toward the lemonade table, but she was intercepted by her husband, who draped a proprietary arm around her waist and drew her to him. He smiled down at her, and she looked up at him, and felt so very grateful and amazed at all that life had brought her.

"Do you think, Lady Grandville," he said with a mischievous look as he glanced around at their guests, "that Miranda Chittister will be able to tolerate talking to the baker's wife for much longer?"

They looked together across the meadow where, among the other merrymakers, the baker's wife stood speaking animatedly to Miss Chittister, about whom hung a long-suffering air.

"It's good for her," Anna said.

"Mr. Pilchard is very much in support of our plan to build a village school."

"Wonderful." She smiled at him, feeling silly with happiness. "The cottages are beautiful, and the families

are so very pleased. I can't wait for work to begin on the next batch, and the school."

Their eyes were drawn, though only briefly, to the top of the pretty hillock where, a week before, Anna had kindled a little fire that consumed *The Beautiful One* most satisfactorily. The ashes had been carried off with the wind, along with the shadows of the past.

"You know, my sweet," her husband said in a low, delightfully wicked voice, "there are things I cannot wait for as well."

She knew that tone, and it made her toes curl. "Is that so? But you must study patience, my lord. We have guests."

"Hmm," he said, looking about them again. "Everyone seems to be happily engaged. I don't think we'd be missed if we took a walk. I want to show you something."

"Well," she said, pretending to consider carefully, "perhaps a short walk."

He led her over the little hill, toward the folly. As they crested the hill, she saw that a neat wooden sign had been hung over the little tower's door.

Birdseye Tower had been neatly carved onto it in letters that looked identical to those on the Willow Glen sign.

"You made a sign for the tower?" she said as he pulled her closer. "Goodness, it's quite nice—really, you're becoming accomplished. Surely you are the only viscount in England who makes such nice signs, never mind your talents at laying roof tiles."

He chuckled at her puzzled praise. "Come inside."

The first floor had been newly furnished with two

pretty, comfortable-looking upholstered chairs. "In case you want guests," he said cryptically, but they didn't stop as he steered her toward the circular staircase.

When her head emerged above the second floor, she gasped in wonder.

"It's for you," he said.

"Oh," she breathed, stepping up into the room. "I don't know what to say."

The round, stone room had been transformed.

Beautiful pale blue-and-white patterned wallpaper now covered the walls, adding to the airy feel of the space. She hadn't been to the folly since the night they'd made love there, and now she could see that it really did have wonderful lighting. In the center of the room stood an easel, a stool, and a shelf full of paints and brushes of all sizes, plus a neat stack of canvases and another of sketchbooks. The bed was still there as well, covered in a fresh, pretty quilt, and a pitcher with cups stood on the table beside it.

"A place of my own for painting and drawing," she said in awed tones.

"And you can welcome pupils here too, if you like. Though I hope your first little students will have the name Halifax, if we are lucky."

She smiled, her eyes already beginning to grow moist. "I hope so too. It's wonderful, Will. I don't know how to thank you."

"We'll think of something," he said, and pulled her into his arms for a kiss.

Then he looked into her eyes, and the love flowed back and forth between them, free and boundless. "It's you for me," he said.

"And me for you," she said back. "And it always will be."

Tears of happiness pooled at the corners of her eyes.

"Oh, not again," he said, gently wiping the wetness with his thumbs. "How can a man bear it if his wife is going to be crying with joy all the time? Is there really so much happiness that it must overflow this way?"

"Yes," she said laughing, "there really is."